THE GATE AT THE END
OF THE WORLD

Philip Glazebrook was born in 1937. His books include *Journey to Kars*, which describes a lonely journey taking him through the Serbian and Greek provinces of the old Ottoman Empire, and through the ruined classical cities of Asia Minor as far as Turkey's frontier with Russia and the fortress of Kars. These travels in the Levant furnished the picturesque background for *Captain Vinegar's Commission*, the idea for which had grown out of his fascination for nineteenth-century accounts of adventurous Eastern journeys, and for the heroic character of the men who undertook them. His fifth novel, *The Gate at the End of the World*, is the sequel to
Captain Vinegar's Commission.

Philip Glazebrook's novel *The Walled Garden* (originally published under the title *The Burr Wood*) is
also published in Flamingo. The author lives with his family in Dorset.

THE GATE AT THE END OF THE WORLD

Philip Glazebrook

FLAMINGO
Published by Fontana Paperbacks

First published by Collins Harvill 1989
This Flamingo edition first published
in 1990 by Fontana Paperbacks
8 Grafton Street, London W1X 3LA

Flamingo is an imprint of
Fontana Paperbacks, part of
the Collins Publishing Group

© Philip Glazebrook 1989

Printed and bound in Great Britain by
William Collins Sons & Co. Ltd, Glasgow

CONTENTS

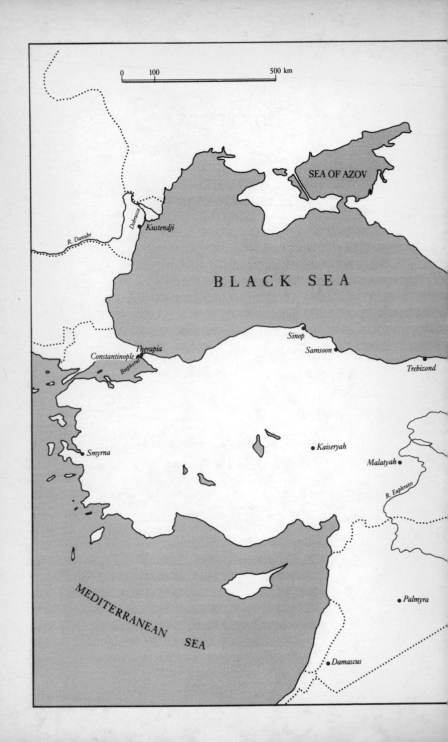

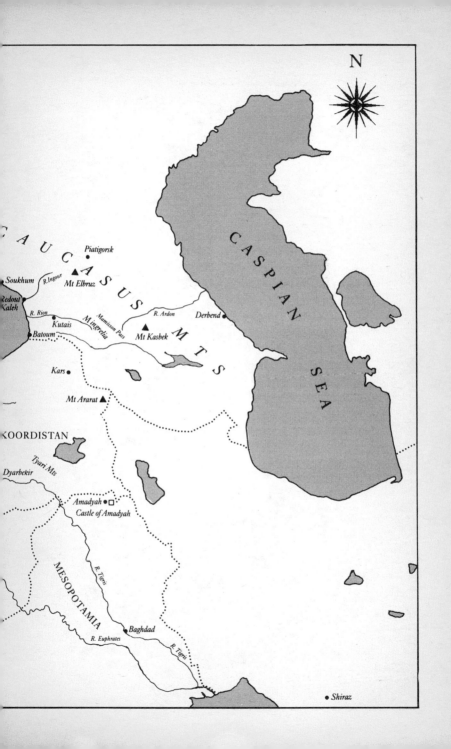

I

London

IT WAS AN EARLY SUMMER'S DAY of sudden heat, such as may scorch London as thoroughly as though it were Rome or Baghdad. Dust rose above the chaos of wheeled traffic rattling and glinting down Piccadilly, dust hung in the sunlight, dust powdered down again everywhere, dulling silk hats and the varnish of carriages, peppering parasols, whitening the respectable black clothes of the crowd, and giving every tongue a gritty taste. Heat wavered and throbbed in the air.

The ghost of martial music, too, throbbed in the air. The thumped drum – the tramp of a march – receded eastwards toward the Haymarket. The passage down Piccadilly of a body of troops from their review before the Queen at Buckingham Palace, to their embarkation for Constantinople at the Waterloo station, had held up crowd and traffic which now pressed in again at urgent cross-purposes, as the current divided by a steamer presses in upon its wake. The London crowd, rich or poor, was pretty well used to the spectacle of a marching regiment destined for the East, and very many of all ranks in life by now had a friend or a relative caught up in the conflict, for England, allied with France and Turkey, had been at war with Russia in the Crimea since March 1854, and it was now the May of 1855. Why England was at war few in the crowd could have told; however, they watched the troops go by with fair enthusiasm, and put up with dust and dislocation, for the pleasure of hearing a military band, at least.

Dust had thoroughly dulled the varnish of a dark blue carriage which now stopped against the shaded southern pavement of Piccadilly. In a rapid manner there stepped out of it into the road a sturdy, elderly man with an old-fashioned white hat on his head. By mischance or inadvertence he had got out of his carriage on the wrong side, and now

[9]

stood amid the traffic. He stood square, indifferent to his danger, settling his white hat with a thorough good thump to its crown which gave off such an air of resolution as silenced even the abuse of the cab-drivers. Rescue was at hand. From the other door of the carriage a neat, light, sharp little man had sprung out, and now darted round the horses to protect his master from danger.

Nothing was said between the two. The servant handed his master gloves and a stick, which the elderly man stared at as though they were altogether unfamiliar and unwelcome objects. He took them nonetheless, and allowed himself to be guided round his carriage to the pavement, the servant's hand just under his elbow, the servant's quick eye keeping him clear of collisions. There was a kindliness about the discreet firm manner with which the servant handled his master's irritable response to this ministry, which showed the affection between the two.

"105 Piccadilly, eh Wicker, is that it – is this their shop?" the master now asked, peering up at the façade above him. "Buckle and Stourpaine we want."

"Next along, Sir Daniel, first floor." Evidently it was blindness, or extreme short-sightedness, which had caused Sir Daniel to alight from the wrong side of his carriage, for 'Buckle & Stourpaine, Publishers, First Floor' was written up very plain beside the entrance to the next house. "Will I come up, Sir Daniel?" enquired Wicker at the doorway.

"No – Lord no – I can walk up a flight of steps I suppose. Oh, better come, better come. Miss Enid will be down on you else." He resigned his arm to Wicker, and allowed himself to be led up in the cool sudden dark of the stairwell. His figure was stocky, and his face clean-shaven and strong featured, in the rather coarse way which shows power of will rather than breadth of intellect.

"Not so blessed hot here sir," said Wicker as they ascended.

"Hot? Upon my soul, wait till we are at Constantinople, Wicker. Then you will learn what heat may be!" There was a sort of triumph in his tone, as though knowing of the heat ahead of them made up for his dependence on Wicker's arm and Wicker's eyes. "You won't like it, I'll be bound."

"I daresay I shall do well enough," retorted Wicker. They had reached the first floor, and a door stood open into an anteroom. "Now then," he said, raising his voice to address the backside of a clerk lounging out of the window, "you there, look alive!"

The lad turned. He had been whistling the military air which echoed the fife of the marching regiment, and he regarded his two visitors contemptuously, as though the Queen's Shilling immunised him from civilian orders. "What's wanted?" he asked in surly style.

"Your master, that's what's wanted," said Wicker, looking fierce at the boy, "Sir Daniel Farr to see him."

"Just stepped out, Mr Stourpaine has, nor he won't be back before tomorrer."

Sir Daniel now rapped his stick twice on the floor. "It is Mr Buckle I am come to consult with, boy, by appointment," he said in a voice which had a grate of the North Country in the vowels when he raised it.

The office boy responded by fairly scampering down the passage. Sir Daniel used the interval to take from his waistcoat pocket a pair of gold-rimmed eye-glasses whose wires he fitted clumsily over his large ears. Whether he saw more of the world through them or not, they had the effect of making him appear less blind, and better equipped to interview a publisher. In a moment the boy returned and asked Sir Daniel to "step this way". Leaving Wicker, Sir Daniel walked independently down the passage and was shown into a room at its further end.

It was a fine, high, sepia-coloured room, lined with bookcases, and lit by two tall sash windows which were open, admitting the dust and rumble of traffic from Piccadilly below. From his chair behind a wide old writing table rose a cheerful stout man, no taller than his visitor, who stepped out and shook Sir Daniel's hand in both his own.

"Kind to spare me your time, sir – a busy man I know – most obliged," he said, his rosy face fairly glowing with heat and benevolence as he set a chair for Sir Daniel across the writing table from his own.

"I have time and to spare in the West End, Mr Buckle," said Sir Daniel as he sat down with his hat on his knee. But he did not give the impression of a man with time to spare, ever, for what was not to the point. He peered towards Mr Buckle, who was mopping his face with his bandanna. "Besides," he went on, "any communication from Captain Vinegar affects me. Affects my interest. You said you had news for me from Vinegar. You wrote in your note."

"I should be interested in your opinion of Captain Vinegar, sir," said Buckle obliquely, hunting among the papers on his table.

"I believe Vinegar to be a scoundrel," replied Sir Daniel very flatly. "There's my opinion since you ask it. But I told your partner Stourpaine the very same two years back when he did me the honour to ask me, and he took no account of it, but brought out Vinegar's book just the same."

"Nothing of the scoundrel in Vinegar's intention now, I assure you. There's money owing, I understand?"

"Aye. Money he owes me."

"Just so. Money he had of you before the journey with Mr Pitcher and your son, which ended in so tragical a manner?"

"Aye."

"He wants it repaid, sir, every penny of it, out of the royalties we hold to his account here on his *Land-March*."

"The devil he does!" Sir Daniel was taken aback. "Well, that's handsome, I own, for I had written it off."

"And you will think him a scoundrel no longer?"

"As to that, why, no, he shan't buy off my suspicions, no he shan't," retorted Sir Daniel, shading his eyes against the light as he looked across the table at the other, whose back was to the window.

"What are your suspicions, Sir Daniel?"

"That I was made a monkey of by your Captain Vinegar, Mr Buckle. I knew at the first go off there was summat amiss with Vinegar. If I didn't quite twig where it was he was lame, I knew well enough he didn't go flat all round."

"But you trusted your son to him, sir – and your money."

Sir Daniel looked down unhappily at his short-fingered hands laid on the table's edge, and bowed his head over them in thought, or contrition, for a moment. "Lord, how Vinegar has made me suffer!" he suddenly flashed out, looking up with a strength of feeling which seemed to surprise even himself, for he modified it at once, adding "Well – he has made us all suffer, at home."

"Of course." Buckle bowed his head now. "I know it. I feel it."

"You cannot know! You cannot feel it!" Again the irascible outburst; again the milder qualification: "Happily, you cannot know, Mr Buckle. Though it is near four years since my son's death at

[12]

Damascus – four years come another autumn – the bitterness of it don't go off."

"The loss of a son never is repaired, I suppose."

"Oh, aye, there's that, there's the loss, of course there is," said Sir Daniel. "But a man may be reconciled to a loss, in time. A man may be reconciled to a death, Mr Buckle, when he ain't reconciled to an injury."

"An injury . . ." Buckle took a moment to consider this. "You blame Vinegar for . . .?"

"I should never have trusted him. Never have trusted Roland to him. But I thought the boy would profit by it, do you see. Independence. Hardship even. But he went to his death. However," finished Sir Daniel, taking up his hat again with the air of a man turning to pleasanter subjects, "the money: Vinegar is flush now, is he?"

"A tidy sum has accumulated in his account since last we heard of him – oh, a year or more ago, at Baghdad. Now he has turned up at Constantinople, as legate to the Allies of some panjandrum amongst the Circassians, so he says, and wishes his money sent there – when his debt to your good self has been deducted, that is."

"The Circassians!" Sir Daniel tossed up his head as if he would believe it when he saw it. "What has been the creature's life, pray, since he left my boy at Damascus?"

"I suppose you read in his book of travels how he lived among the Koords, and led the Tyari against Bedr Khan?"

"I read his book, sir, yes I did, and it seemed about as pretty a tarradiddle of nonsense as anything in Scheherezade. But there! Folk will believe any gammon about the East just now, with the war. And where has he hid himself since his travels brought him to Baghdad and the book's end?"

"It seems he stopped a good many months at Baghdad, whilst we wrote back and forth about the *Land-March*. Mr Pitcher had employment in the Assyrian diggings, opening the mound at Susa, I believe, with Mr Loftus, which kept them to Baghdad a longish spell."

"Pitcher! So Vinegar has not severed himself from Tresham Pitcher, eh?"

"I think not. Indeed I know he ain't, for it is Pitcher who is at Constantinople now."

"And how do the Circassians enter into the picture? I am a good deal interested in Circassia and the Caucasus just now."

"It is all in here." Mr Buckle tapped a sheaf of manuscript on his table with the satisfaction of a man tapping a well-filled purse. "He has sent me some account of his adventures to date, so that we may agree terms, you know, terms for a new book. They was at Baghdad when the war came, and of course Vinegar was keen as knife to be in it, so he resolved to make himself a useful man to the Allies – this is his own account of it – by reconnoitering along the line of the Turk's frontier with the Russian there where it runs through the Caucasus. So off the pair of them rode from Baghdad to Kars, and we heard no word of them more till there came a letter from Constantinople, bidding us pay your debt, sir, and send out the cash to himself."

"So Vinegar is at Constantinople now, is he?"

"Unless he has darted off on some fresh adventure," said his publisher hopefully. "Pitcher is there at all events. We are to reply to Vinegar under cover to Pitcher, at Misseri's hotel."

"Misseri's!" Sir Daniel's chair creaked as he flung back his weight, stirred to his soul by the familiar name. Even his dim eyes gleamed. He said eagerly, "I am off too, do you see. Yes. My daughter Enid and I leave for Constantinople next week I hope. I hope we shall not be prevented. I have known the place all my life nearly, of course."

"Indeed. And you are concerned in the war?" Buckle was now beginning to look sideways at papers on his desk, and to draw letters towards him, from press of business or a lack of further curiosity in his visitor.

"I have interests much affected by the war, yes I do." The egotism of an uneducated mind, assisted now by blindness, concentrated Sir Daniel's thoughts on his own affairs. "Railroads are my business, as I daresay you know, and I was a party in the constructing of the line across the Dobrusca there, which the row was about in Parliament tother week, when it was found out the Allies had mined the line to keep Paskievich from making use of it. But I can hear nothing here. I must go out if I'm to learn what's to do." He mused, tapping his white hat, then recollected himself: "Aye, I must learn how they are destroying my works amongst them all, with their confounded war. I shall have lost quite £100,000 by it, I don't doubt. Quite that. Then there's the

Caucasus, where Vinegar and Pitcher have been amusing themselves, you say. The Caucasus interests me most particular just now."

"Oh," said Buckle, surreptitiously reading his correspondence, "how so?"

"I project a railroad through the mountains, sir. An iron road for trade from the Black Sea to the Caspian and Persia that shall have none of the uncertainties and blackguardly ransoms of the Arabian route. It is possible. I'm sure it is possible, with the Allies to pacify the tribes of the Caucasus for us. The war makes the opportunity. Now, sir," he said, looking across towards Buckle, "there's a grand scheme for a book, eh? – a grand enterprise!"

"I fear you overestimate the reading public, Sir Daniel. It is this they want" – he tapped Vinegar's manuscript – "tales of adventure, in any quantity. See here, sir," he added, a way having occurred to him of putting his visitor out of his room, "should you care to read Vinegar's narrative? You might look over it in my outer office whilst my clerk is away at the bank fetching the money the Captain owes you. Ah, but I forget. Your eyes. You perhaps cannot read comfortably?"

Sir Daniel raised himself to his feet. "My man Wicker shall read it to me," he said. Then he took up his hat and put it on his grizzled head. "Wicker shall read it to me. It will make a change from Milton, and that's a fact."

So it was arranged. Along the passage Wicker and the clerk shared the ante-room uneasily, like a lion and a lion-tamer in a cage together. The boy jumped at the chance of an outing to the firm's bankers, and took his hat from the peg, and ran off. Whilst Wicker sat at the table with the Captain's manuscript before him, Sir Daniel took a chair with his back to the window, where he sat with his hands on the knob of his stick, his white hat on his head, listening to the tale which Wicker now began.

from ADVENTURES IN THE CAUCASUS,
AT THE TIME OF THE CRIMEAN WAR,
by O. Q. Vinegar (Capt.)

About three months after quitting Baghdad, during which interval I had inspected the lamentable state of the defensive works at Kars, and had seen a good deal of the border country between Russia and Turkey, I had the misfortune to fall ill in the wild lands – and they *are* wild lands – about the headwaters of the river Rion (anciently the Phasis, of Golden Fleece fame) where they tumble down from the heights of the Caucasus between Satchkerri and Khidiskhari. Now, for the solitary adventure-seeker to fall ill, is among the worst of mishaps. It was my old enemy, the intermittent fever which had well-nigh killed me at Constantinople in '50, and I knew that I was in for a sharp dose.

I had been riding through vast oakwoods mantling the slopes; incessant mist and rain had trailed through these forests for days, thoroughly chilling me as well as confusing my feverish brain into a conviction that I was doomed to ride forever in circles among the accursed misty trees. Thickets of rhododendron, with the rain dripping loudly onto their gloomy leaves, seemed exactly those same doleful thickets I had passed an hour earlier. My faculties were trapped in the downward vortex of nightmare or fever.

When, therefore, chance led me to a rude cabin in a ravine, I picketed my horse, and threw myself on the cabin floor, too grateful for dry ground under me, and a roof above, to enquire if guests were taken in at the establishment or not. I remember the roar of the torrent in the defile raging through my head as if it were a cataract of blood pounding and shaking through me as the mill-race shudders the mill. Then I lost consciousness.

I have the clear recollection, next, of finding myself supported in a saddle (not my own, but one of the wooden-tree'd saddles of the country, with a felt girth over it) whilst the pony under me picked its way across an open scree in blinding sunlight, and the familiar scent of the yellow azalea perfumed the air. Then again I recall nothing until I came to myself in a Stygian hovel, sufficiently raised off the earth for there to be pigs bivouacked under its floor, as I could hear (and smell) from my straw pallet on the boards. It seemed to be night-time. There I lay, rejoiced that the bout of fever had spent itself, but uncertain as to how much else I had to celebrate. My money and arms had gone. I was not bound, but my boots had been taken from me, and the fellow at the doorway had very much the physiognomy of a gaoler – the harsh, indifferent, slow-witted phiz of a man who will look on at the grossest torture without taking his pipe from his mouth.

It was then that a most surprising event occurred. The guard rose, and there rustled past him into my cell a Scotch nurse-maid. Of course I did not know at that instant that she was a nursemaid, but she evidently belonged to the class of genteel servant and, when she spoke, it was in the accents of the Lowland Scot:

"Are ye English as they say ye are?" she asked me, looking down keenly into my face by the rushlight which my guard had brought.

"I am an Englishman," I agreed, "though I don't know how these fellows have discovered it, for I have nothing English in my possession, I think."

"Ye had this," said she, holding out the little calf Milton which I had taken from poor F—'s death-bed at Damascus, and had kept by me ever since. "Ye had *Paradise Lost*, and ye spoke in English the whiles ye were sick, so they say." She stooped, and put down the book beside me. Then she stood up very straight again and folded her hands in front of her grey dress and looked down upon me. "Aye," she said, "you're an Englishman." She was about fifty, her face much seamed and lined, the grey hair scraped severely back from it to be secured under a cap. She appeared to be deliberating what was to be done with me; and I, meanwhile, with the incuriosity and indifference of utter weakness, fell asleep.

I awoke to find sunlight filtering through the cracks in the rude cabin's timbers, and myself restored to health. It is very wonderful how the situation which seems to extend no hope to a fever-patient, may offer at least novelty and the chance of adventure to the sportsman who takes himself off the sick-list. I have found, too, that a man's treatment among a half savage people depends very much on how he goes to work, and I determined to have the upper hand with my captors. Calling out, therefore, for breakfast, and for my arms and boots to be restored to me – I spoke of course in Turkish – I awaited results, and said "Good Morning" to piggy rootling for tidbits under my bedroom floor.

If my sword, rifle and pistols were not returned to me, my horse and saddlebags at least were, so that I rode away from the *dukan* "under my own steam", though attended by three mountaineers. My mount was the little grey Arab, scarcely fourteen hands high, which had carried me nobly since Kars, at which town I had rid myself of the bright bay Turcoman, a rangy, plain scouring sort of beast on which I had started out from Baghdad. Each of my three companions wore the long, close-fitting *choga* with cartridge-loops on the breast (made of silver if he have any claim to birth or wealth), and had on his head the wadded sheepskin *calpac*, whilst behind his saddle was tied his felt cloak, or *bookha*, a useful appendage which can at a pinch be converted with a couple of others into a wigwam. For arms, each carried a carbine with a straight stock and no trigger-guard thrust into a felt *ghilaf* to preserve it from knocks; a falchion sword without a cross-piece; the long two-edged *khingal* dagger which these ruffians use to such deadly effect, and sundry long pistols stuck about his person where space afforded them a hold. Altogether the three of them clattered like tinkers as we set out at a gallop through the forest on that fine May morning.

The chestnut woods were just in leaf, rains had sweetened the air and freshened the brooks, in glade after glade we came upon a mass of the yellow azalea, or the purple rhododendron, whilst everywhere the cuckoo's double call echoed among the mountains: what more, save his liberty, could a man desire upon a morning's ride? Already, before my bout of fever, that early spring season in the Caucasus, the unlocking of the earth after the thralldom of winter, had touched me with its beauty. My upbringing had been a harsh one, in which "poesy", and the soft influences of the feminine mind, had held scant place. Now, when I refreshed myself at a sparkling brook and came face to face with the shy innocence of a celandine shining amongst its mosses, I could have shed tears for old days and missed chances – for old England and the vanished past. But – *revenons à nos moutons*. As I rode with my three guards I considered, as what Englishman would not, making a bid for freedom. I was unarmed, and unacquainted with the terrain. I guessed, too, that my companions would prove bad fellows to run from, and would offer no quarter to an escaping prisoner. I decided to bide my time. Though they understood my Turkish, we talked but little as we rattled down through the steep forest.

After an hour or so we emerged from the trees into a wide grazing country of rolling slopes still blanched of verdure by the winter's frosts, the pastures cut here and there by wooded ravines which defiled to plains half obscured by mist far below. An outcrop of rock, crowned with a species of stone tower, could be seen at some distance standing guard over one of these ravines, and it became clear that this gloomy tower, above whose battlements circled several ravens, was our destination. As we clattered across the wooden bridge flung over the moat, and I glimpsed the precipice on which the tower was built, plunging its sheer rock into pines and mist a hundred fathoms below, I confess to a shiver of apprehension, and a regret that I had not made a run for it, neck or nothing, over the grass.

But it was too late. Into the fortress we rode, and I was ordered down from my horse. A lame fellow dragged himself out of a doorway, followed by a little three-legged white dog trotting along yapping to itself. I was transferred into this lame gaoler's charge, and my escort rode out of the castle and away. You will think that I had easy work to overpower the cripple and recover my mount, but he kept a pistol trained steadily upon me, its barrel resting on his forearm, whilst he led my horse into a covered corner of the courtyard where another pony was already tied by its head. It was then that I heard, very considerably to my surprise, a clear voice ringing down from the tower:

"Who is it that's come, Bulat, eh? Is it herself, is it?"

Recovering from my surprise I sang out, "Vinegar here, Captain Vinegar, late of the —th Dragoons!"

"Vinegar?" questioned the voice, which was surely that of an Irishman, "is it you was travelling on a boat a few years back from Kustendji with that ass V—?"

I could make no reply to this, for the gaoler had driven me across the yard by now with his pistol at my back, and had pushed me through a door which he kicked shut and bolted behind me. In the darkness I had time to reflect.

Certainly I remembered the voyage from Kustendji to Constantinople. I had ridden over the Dobrusca from the Danube to look into Sir D— F—'s railway works upon that isthmus, and had joined the Constantinople steamer, and Lord V— at Kustendji. I seemed to have the recollection of a noisy Irishman aboard, who had attacked his Lordship for mismanaging his Irish estates, whilst pretending sympathy for the poor Wallachians. I had rather liked his spirit, until the vodky had overcome him. If by chance this Irishman shut up in the tower was that same Irishman – Hoolaghan was his name, I recollected – I should at least have a fellow of pluck at my back.

What had he meant, though, by expecting "herself" when he had heard my arrival? I could not help recalling tales of the imperious queens of old, who captured travellers to indulge their unhallowed pleasures, and then invariably hurled them directly from the voluptuous cushions of the royal chamber into some smoking ravine. The hoarse roar of the river a good many hundred feet below the barred window of my cell came up rather uncomfortably to my ears. However, when I discovered that this aperture in the stone wall allowed me a view of the pasture land sweeping down from crags and forest towards the castle, I established myself at my "window on the world", and tried to compose my thoughts to patience, whilst I listened to the river.

How the sound of water, of rivers and falls and runnels and rains, had marked my journey among these mountains! Never far off, the roar of water had been the *leitmotif* of my travels, the very heart-throb of the Caucasus. I did not know that that heart-beat, multiplied to the nth degree, was to accompany the climax of my adventures in the chapter now beginning.

It was towards evening, when the low light of the sun threw wrinkles of shadow across the slopes, that I saw a hunted creature break from the forest and bound over those slopes above the castle. It was a stag at full stretch. But, fast as it flew through the blood-red light, its pace was not good enough. Gaining upon its fleet form came three grey shadows fleeter yet. Wolves, or dogs? Now, breaking from the rim of forest, appeared a horseman, then another, and a third. Hard they rode, cheering on the hunt, their little mounts' legs flickering over the ground like drum-sticks. A captured creature myself, I could not but feel my heart and hopes racing with the quarry. Alas, not a bowshot from my window, the dogs closed on the swerving stag. Up went his head, and down went he in a sprawl of limbs as the dogs plunged in their jaws and broke him up. Now the hunters, who had ridden up apace, flung themselves off their smoking cattle and dashed into the mêlée. Now the victim's antlered head was held up again, severed this time from his body; and now I made out the fact that the hunter who held up the trophy was no hunter but a huntress, no Nimrod but a Diana!

It was not long after this that I heard the horses of these fierce sportswomen clatter into the yard at my cell door. An interval of an hour more had passed before my door at last opened into the dusk, and the limping gaoler beckoned me to follow him. Once in the yard I shouted up at the tower "Hoolaghan?", but no voice replied save the echo of my own. The tower was by now in the shadow of the mountains, and the chill of evening had brought wraiths of mist out of the ravine. Up a worn spiral stair I climbed ahead of the cripple's pistol. At a new-made timber door in a stone arch I stopped. My guard opened it. Before me, down a couple of steps, lay as comfort-ably furnished a room as might be found in a Highland castle, the stone walls softened with hangings and the stone floor with rugs, whilst well-stuffed sofas and a bright fire completed the domestic scene.

I must have looked astonished, for my entry brought a good-natured laugh from a tall, merry-looking man who stood with his back to the fire like the squire in his 'snug'. He strode forward with hand outreached. I judged his age at about thirty-five.

"Well then," said he, "and it is the Vinegar I remember, indeed and it is. Hoolaghan is myself, Quin Hoolaghan. And I'm a colonel," he added, leaning his face towards mine with mock ferocity, "that's to say, I had a colonel's command in the last battle that ever I fought, for every blessed *yuzbashi* and *bimbashi* was killed but me. There now, though, we won't stand upon rank, captain, we won't indeed. Come in to the fire with you. Her Highness will be here directly."

"Her Highness?" My fears returned.

"Sh!" He indicated the door behind me, and I saw him bow.

I turned. First three dogs of the lurcher variety bounded in, rapping the furniture with their tails and sniffing at Hoolaghan and myself. Then a young woman entered the room with a rustle of her dress, her hands clasped before her and a *de-haut-en-bas* sort of smile on her pale face. There followed the Scotchwoman whom I had already met. I too bowed, intending the stiff inclination of my neck for politeness to the sex rather than subservience to my captress. It was the Scotchwoman who spoke:

"I do not know your name," she said, "else I would present ye to the Princess Mazi."

When I had supplied my name, and the old woman had gone through the form of presenting me, I said "I think I saw your pack kill their stag a little earlier, Princess."

"Pack?" she said in a pretty foreign accent, "Stag?" She looked at Hoolaghan as if bewildered. Her accent I took to be French, and I was about to repeat my observation in that language, when she laughed, and said, "Oh, my little dogs! You see them catch one hare just then, when we were riding? So good they are, so quick." She patted the narrow heads of her lurchers.

Now, that I had seen hounds twice these dogs' size pull down a stag, I was certain. But, if it be a firm rule that a guest should not start work by contradicting his hostess, how much less wise for a captive to do so. Had the scene of venery which I had witnessed perhaps been magnified by low light or mist into something it was not, these lap-dogs enlarged into hounds, the hare into a stag – a ladies' afternoon excursion into a maenad's headlong hunt?

Princess Mazi had engaged herself in conversation with Hoolaghan, leaning on one side of the mantleshelf whilst he leaned on the other, the firelight animating their faces. They spoke low, but I was sure the language was English. Left with the nursemaid upon my hands I said,

"It is quite a surprise to come upon a Scotchwoman in these parts."

"Lord love ye," said she, "I am not a Scotswoman!"

"Come," said I, for I seemed surrounded by riddles and illusions, "is it not time that these conundrums were explained to me?"

"Well," she replied, "my own story is soon told. Ye may as well have it. I was born a Circassian, but sold for a slave by my papa when I was but a scrap of a bairn. In the Bazaar at Nishkaya I'm told I was put up for sale, and the merchant-man who took a fancy to me carried me away down to Soujuk where his ship would be, I suppose, and there I was chanced upon by Mr Abercrombie."

I waited, but it seemed that she thought her whole history explained by the pious pronouncement of this name. Seeing that I looked blank, she said, "Gracious heaven, do ye not know of Mr Abercrombie of Karass?"

"I have been buried at Baghdad, madam," I excused myself.

"Whisht!" She clapped her hands at my ignorance. However, she was not averse to the chance of instructing me. Karass, it seems, is a colony of Scotch missionaries to the north of the Caucasus – a clean little town, by her account of it, with a green, and streets of neat wooden dwellings, and clear rivulets – and to Karass she had been brought by Mr Abercrombie from the Soujuk slaver, and there she had lived with the industrious, but quarrelsome, Scotch missionaries until she was fifteen, when a post as nursemaid to the children of a

French doctor at Piatigorsk, a few *versts* away, had been found for her. Part of this tale she told me at once, and part when we had gone in to supper, a meal eaten quite in the French style, servants handing the dishes, in a dining room fitted up next door. . .

"Stop a bit!" called out Sir Daniel to Wicker. "Where the devil is this clerk got to with my money? Is Buckle here? Ask him how long he means to wait before calling a policeman."

The rattlings and bangings of Sir Daniel's stick on table and floor had brought Mr Buckle to the waiting-room door, where he said, "I don't know how much experience of English clerks nowadays you have, Sir Daniel?"

"As little as possible, sir, for I fill up my clerking places with Jews and Armenians if I can find 'em."

"Just so. Well, I may tell you that Atkins here ain't been long gone, not in the way an English clerk reckons time."

"So we must be patient I suppose. Go on, Wicker, you may read on," he directed with a wave of his stick towards Vinegar's manuscript.

It was a strange party (continued Wicker), that first dinner at the Princess's tower, and I learned much that was curious. Rather than recount the facts piecemeal, as I acquired them, I will here set down the circumstances in which I found myself involved as shortly as I can.

The Princess Mazi into whose hands I had fallen was the sole surviving child of Prince Rachinskiy, hereditary ruler of a territory above the Rion river which consisted of high pastures, and forests, and snow peaks, with here and there some orchards surrounding a small wooden town, or *aul*. Now, the strength of this poor kingdom lay in the fact that it ran up into a high pass of the Caucasus, the Mamisson, giving access to the Ardon river on the mountains' further slope. For this reason Rachinskiy had ever found himself courted by Turk and Russian alike, and so had begun to nurse ambitions of independence from either power. His intention, and his daughter's intention, was to secure if they could a treaty with the Allies, the English and French, which would protect them equally from Russian or Turkish subjugation, in return for which they would offer access to the Mamisson Pass through the Caucasus to Derbend and the Caspian trade with Persia and India. This much was plain; what was less clear, was whether Hoolaghan and myself were intended as a means of communication with the Allies (who were then, in the spring of '54, daily expected to land in force on the Mingrelian coast) or whether our value was as hostages, obliging cooperation on the British.

That the Princess Mazi had herself grown up a hostage of the Russians made the keeping of prisoners in isolated towers as natural to her, as was the keeping of birds in cages to an English miss. Her story, as I later learned it in some of our intimate rambles on horseback together, was this. In the Russo-Turkish War of '28 her father had first attempted to play the game of independence from either side, but his ambitions had been pretty well extinguished in '29 when the Russian general, Paskievich, returning from his capture of Kars, had burnt Rachinskiy's stronghold at Alatstchinsk, and had demanded hostages for Rachinskiy's good behaviour in the future. Well, Paskievich was satisfied with Princess Mazi, then aged five, whom he sent away to Piatigorsk. Rachinskiy too was well pleased, for he then had seven sons besides his daughter, and hardly considered his hands tied at all by the bargain.

So began the Princess Mazi's exile at "the Russian Cheltenham". She was brought up in the family of a French doctor – the same practitioner, a Monsieur Lemarteau, who had engaged a few years previously, as nurse to his own infants, the Circassian slave freed by Mr Abercrombie, who now sat beside me at supper. At Piatigorsk the princess continued, learning the manners and habits of a European, until 1845.

In that year Vorontsoff mounted his campaign against Shamyl in Daghestan. Once again the Caucasus tribes were convulsed in the wildest disorder. Amongst innumerable acts of brigandage, Rachinskiy managed to secure the person of an

ADC to Vorontsoff himself, a disgraced Russian nobleman, Count K— by name, and to carry him off to this very tower where we sat over supper (which had been decorated in its present style at the Moscow dandy's whim). This hostage Rachinskiy offered to Vorontsoff in exchange for his daughter Mazi. All his seven sons had by this date fallen victims to duels or *chappaws* or ambuscades, and the disregarded daughter stood sole heiress to his kingdom.

The offer was accepted. The Princess Mazi, and the nurse who was by now too much attached to be parted from her – and who was, after all, a tribeswoman like her mistress – rode up with a strong escort of Cossacks to make the exchange for Count K— in a snow-blown pass. What a watershed in her life was that scene, I could not help reflecting to myself as she described it to me on one of our subsequent rides together! Why, the very Cossacks must have seemed to her civilised beings compared to her father's wild envoys flourishing their *tskhounkés* above their heads! And the life she came down to on this side of the Caucasus range – ! In circumstances which cannot be divulged without harming a lady's reputation, I came to hear, from her own lips, how near to despair and suicide she had been in those first weeks of homecoming. Her father's intention was to wed her to a minor Mizurskiy chieftain across the Mamisson, and so to secure that back door into his kingdom, but this fate she contrived to put off by demanding of him the traditional 'ordeals' of a Mingrelian bridegroom, such as the fetching to her of the cock which is believed to roost on the summit of Mount Kasbek, the slaying of sleepless serpents, etc, etc. She had acquired, moreover, so she told me – laughing as she did so – the reputation of a witch, with an armoury of potions and spells (in reality a few of Monsieur Lemarteau's medicines) which no doubt did a good deal to dissuade young Mizurskiy from pressing his suit. Now had come another war, and with it the rumour of an imminent landing by an Anglo-French force – an Allied fleet had appeared off the coast a year earlier – which the Rachinskiys determined to turn to their advantage. So Hoolaghan and myself had been laid hold of as counters in the game, and brought to the tower where we now found ourselves detained.

*　　　*　　　*

Some little of all this I learned that first evening from old Hannah, the nursemaid, and I had time enough to reflect upon it in subsequent days, when Hoolaghan and I were kept, without arms or horses, at that isolated tower in the princess's absence. If we were her guests, as Hoolaghan asserted, we might as well have been her prisoners. She had said that we would be "escorted" to her father's palace within a day or so, when she had informed him of our existence, and had resolved with him, I suppose, some stratagem for our use; but, just as I was haunted by the appeal of her face and figure, so was I perplexed by numerous discrepancies between what she appeared to be, and what her conversation had revealed of her understanding and her ideas.

How might it be, for instance, that a young woman with the appearance of a beautiful and educated Frenchwoman, should seem to believe that "England" and "France" were two small tribal territories very much like the Caucasian principalities, so subjugated to the Sultan of Turkey that they were obliged to fight for him as mercenaries in his war against Russia? Yet these fairy-tale notions appeared to govern her "foreign policy", and probably governed her father's too.

And what was the truth of the stag-hunt which I had witnessed? The kill I had seen – the stag's severed head raised in triumph by a woman's arm – would recur to my mind's eye. Who were the wild attendants? And with whom had she ridden away the morning after our meeting? Hoolaghan maintained that they were tribesmen escorting her to her father's head-quarters; but Hoolaghan evidently cared little for puzzling over inferences or implications of our situation, or for what the morrow might hold in store for us, so long as he was in a comfortable billet today. I was perfectly sure that the princess's attendants clattering out of the gate were young women like

[27]

herself, and that they were bent upon some hunting excursion; but whether to increase the store of venison in the castle larder, or to supplement the store of "guests" in the "bachelor wing", I could not guess.

"Young," did I say? When I reckoned up the dates in her history (she had been five in 1829) I computed her age at thirty years. Now, what tribeswoman – what female wheresoever – looks as *she* looked, at thirty? For her cheek was as smooth and fair as alabaster, with the black hair sleek and lustrous as though painted in Indian ink upon it, and the eyes so brilliantly dark under the heavy lids, and the red tint of her mouth such a touch of lively colour. I could not remember having seen a girl half so handsome, at least since quitting Europe. Perhaps her reputation for practising the black arts was a right one, and she guarded in this wild kingdom, amongst her fierce huntresses, the secret of eternal youth.

I wondered, too, in what relation Hoolaghan stood to this bewitching princess. Of course he was blessed with the easy manner of the Irishman, which assumes an intimacy where an Englishman would see an acquaintance – he had come within an ace of chucking old Hannah under the chin – but there was a good deal that was unexplained in the talk that I had overheard between the two of them. Since he had been upon the ground before me, I could scarcely claim to be ill-used by what I detected of intimate intercourse between Hoolaghan and our hostess, nor yet by his choosing to withhold explanations from me. But I could not succeed in wholly banishing from my mind the savage queen in the fable, who tosses down her lovers from the nuptial couch into the chasm below her castle, and I comforted myself in my jealousy with the reflexion that Hoolaghan would at any rate precede me into the gulf.

Here Wicker broke off reading, for Buckle's clerk had come clattering into the outer office from his mission to the bank, and had dropped down a chinking satchel upon the table. Sir Daniel could not prevent himself from putting out his hand to lay claim to the cash.

"Not so quick," said the clerk, taking up the satchel again, "we don't want none of that to go missing."

Then Mr Buckle was brought in, who counted out the gold into Sir Daniel's hand. Business done, Sir Daniel said (as Buckle showed him to the stairway), "It's maybe of consequence, what Vinegar's found up there in Mingrelia – if it's true, mind. Something might be done with Rachinskiy's little kingdom, I fancy. Aye, I shall look into it when I'm at Constantinople. Lord Stratford at the Embassy listens to me, whoever else don't, for he knows the value of trade, does Stratford. But tell me, sir," he said, pausing a moment and peering into Buckle's face, "is it Vinegar who is come down to Constantinople, or Mr Pitcher? For there is no mention of Pitcher in what Wicker has read to me."

"There ain't? Nor there is," Buckle agreed, puzzled. "Yet it's Pitcher I'm to send the money to, at Misseri's hotel. Queer."

"It is deuced queer, Mr Buckle."

"Do you think – ?"

"I don't know what to think, Mr Buckle. Suspicion ain't a nice thing. Anyways," he added, holding up to view the bank satchel as he descended the stairs on Wicker's arm, "I have my money, and that's a fact."

II

-•-•-•-•-•-•-•-

Constantinople

1

"WHO THE DEUCE is this fellow Pitcher keeps sending us up messages?" squeaked out little Frank Smallwood as he stirred the spoon round in his breakfast coffee. He was seated at a table in the window of the attachés' room at the English Palace, at Therapia on the Bosphorus. Into the room had just entered Mr Broadbent, another of Lord Stratford's attachés, who had peremptorily sent away for fresh coffee the Turkish servant bringing in a visitor's card.

Broadbent didn't reply. He examined the rolls, and the butter, and Smallwood, with a contemptuous eye. Then he sat down heavily at the breakfast table. He was the elder of the two, a fleshy young man of twenty six or seven. Smallwood watched him anxiously, eager to talk but uncertain of pleasing. Only when the servant had returned with the coffee pot, and had again placed before Broadbent a card with some words scribbled beside the name "Tresham Pitcher", did Broadbent speak.

"Upon my soul!" he ejaculated, "if the war don't throw up some queer fish upon the beach! Any of these stray mongrels with nothing to do may call at Embassies and send us up messages nowadays it seems. Tresham Pitcher, indeed!"

"Ain't he tied in with the fellow who wrote the travels? Vinegar – Captain Vinegar? And Farr, of Trinity, who died at Damascus?"

Broadbent looked at him. "Wake yourself up, Smallwood. We all know who Pitcher is, it's what he's at now I don't fathom, turning up here like a bad penny." He tapped the pasteboard against his teeth and looked judicious. "Farr's papa is here, too, in Constantinople. Old Sir Dan."

"Is he by Jove! He's a dreadfully savage old party I've heard. What brings him out here, do you think?"

"He's suffered in his pocket by this war I suppose, and he's come out to see what may be done. These commercial johnnies," went on Broadbent expansively, leaning back with his coffee, "whose fortunes are founded in the Levant, these sort of fellows – "

He heard the door behind him open quietly. He saw Smallwood bob to his feet. He rose himself, and turned.

In the doorway stood Lord Stratford. Grey eyes scoured the two young men's faces coldly. "Has Mr Pitcher called, or sent word? Come – has he, or not?"

"Ah – yes – ah – he may have done," stammered Broadbent, "I'll send to enquire."

"Send? Go, damn your eyes!" shouted Lord Stratford. "Heavens and earth! Go!" The blue veins stood out on his high pale brow, and his whole handsome face fairly glowed with passion under the snowy hair. Smallwood was out of the door in a flash, as if blown through it by His Excellency's rage. After a glance round the room which might have shrivelled up every object in it, and Broadbent and his breakfast too, the Ambassador stalked out and slammed shut the door.

Into the silence presently came heavy steps on the stairs, and the clatter of steel against balusters. Broadbent, pretending ease, had dropped back into his chair and taken up his coffee cup when his visitor entered.

"Mr Pitcher?" He turned, and rose reluctantly.

A large, commanding figure had stamped through the door with a clash of his heavy sword. It was a small room, and this visitor seemed to darken and oppress it with sensations of wilderness and camp brought indoors to threaten the fragility of diplomatic porcelain and lace.

"I am Tresham Pitcher."

He announced his name as though it was a spell of the "open sesame" variety, and stood awaiting doors to fly back without more ado. He was tall, and might once have been heavy, though lean enough now, his restless, light-coloured eyes having a look of unhappiness in a gaunt face. His hair was cropped close to his skull, and it could be seen that turban and beard had protected most of his face from suns which had burned dark his cheekbones and nose. He wore the loose, collarless tunic of the Caucasus, with its silver cartridge-loops stitched on each breast, and baggy trousers thrust into his boots. He had unbuckled the English cavalry sword which had clattered against the balusters, and he now held out the old-fashioned weapon for Broadbent to take.

"Your sword ain't a bit of use to me, sir," said the attaché with disdain.

"I supposed you would want to keep it whilst I went in to your chief," growled Pitcher.

"Lord, we ain't like your viziers and what-have-yous, you know, expecting you to run us through the moment you're let indoors. But leave the thing with Smallwood here if you like it better, and I'll put you into His Excellency's room directly."

Smallwood took the sword, having edged into the room behind their warlike visitor. He was standing fingering the weapon at the window, rather dreamily watching the shipping on the Bosphorus below, when Broadbent returned.

"I'll tell you what it is, Broadbent," he said with determination, "if H.E. don't take me with him to the Crimea when he goes up next month, I shall throw up my place here and go to the war on my own hook, hanged if I won't, and see if Omer Pasha won't take me on in his force."

"What, and become no better than Pitcher here, and all the rest of the ragamuffins looking for employment?"

"I thought Pitcher looked a grand fellow."

"Did you now! Listen a bit, I have his letter to H.E. here," said Broadbent, throwing himself into an easy chair and cocking up his boots on the table, "listen: '. . . well acquainted with the shores of the Black Sea . . . in a position to offer an alliance with Prince Rachinskiy and his forces in Mingrelia . . . attack would sever Mouravieff from his depôt' – and so on and so forth. Well now, what's the real case? I'll tell you: Rachinskiy no doubt is some dirty little freebooter hid in a cave in the Caucasus somewhere, who sees his slave-trading ventures going smoother for him if he has the Turks instead of the Russians for master, and our friend Pitcher somehow or other sees advantage to himself in the thing. This war," he pronounced with feeling, "this confounded war, it serves for offal to a pack of blowflies, the way it's drawn every half-bred ruffian in the Levant out of his hiding-place and brought him down upon our heads. Oh, ain't they just sure that all their murder and treachery and beastliness will pay off at last, and put them into an officer's uniform so that they may go swaggering back to Europe at the end of it just as if they was heroes. See here where Pitcher says Captain Vinegar is left behind him at Rachinskiy's 'court' in Mingrelia. Vinegar and Pitcher! – a pretty pair for the British Empire to depend upon, by Heaven!"

But Smallwood stuck doggedly looking down through the window at the transports lumbering up the Bosphorus, and fingered Pitcher's sword, and said without turning round: "Only think, though, what fun such fellows get for their money."

2

"What!" said Sir Daniel Farr to his daughter, pausing in their walk to give emphasis to his vehemence, "What? – did you suppose I would treat with Vinegar? No, no – it is Pitcher I speak of. It is Pitcher who is at Constantinople."

"Oh, I see, papa. I supposed they were both come down from the mountains together. I supposed that they were – inseparable, you know."

Enid's arm was clasped through her father's, but she turned her face away so that the wide round brim of her hat hid the mischief which had lighted her eye as she said this. She need not have troubled: not only was her father too blind to see her expression, there was also in her face so pensive and sad an air, that the keenest-sighted observer would not have noticed the fleeting light of mischief in those curiously slanting dark eyes. They walked beside the Sweet Waters, as the stream feeding the Golden Horn is called. The meadow there was the resort of the people of Constantinople, to which Sir Daniel and his daughter had ridden on ponies one July afternoon. Under a willow by the water where they had left their mounts, Wicker was making preparations for their picnic. "We will walk along to the Sultan's kiosque," her father had said.

He knew it all so well, she thought. He needed less guidance from her hand on his arm here, than he needed amongst the new-built steps and terraces at Ravenrig, their castle-home in Wales; but it was through a vanished Eastern past he walked here by the Sweet Waters, and it was old scenes his dim eyes saw. What would he make of the present, if he could have seen it clearly? – the Crimea officers cantering about the valley, groups of Europeans everywhere smoking and staring, the Turks themselves unhappily hybridised into frock-coats and umbrellas? She steered Papa down to the stone lip of the pool which reflected a ricketty little palace on the further shore.

He leaned on his stick. He had on the same white hat he had worn in London, or another like it, and a blue coat with square tails. "Old Mahmoud, the old Sultan, I've seen come out of that kiosque many a time. Many a time. It was archery he came for. He'd fire off an arrow on the *ocmeidan* there, and a fellow would run after it – oh, ever such a way. Far beyond the arrow. The Sultan stood under his red umbrella, stood waiting. Then the fellow would hold up an arrow some immense way off, and there would be cheers all round. The black fellows would cheer, and the ladies from their waggon. The distance would be quite beyond belief. But they'd put up a marble pillar at the spot, with the date and distance upon it, all as solemn as church. For a Sultan, you know, will believe anything of himself, any humbug you like. I suppose he becomes so well used to hearing the great claims made for him by the fellows toadying him, that he will credit any feat of himself at last."

Enid did not suggest, though it occurred to her mind, that many a man, even her father, runs the risk of supposing himself capable of miracles, once success has isolated him from his critics. As they strolled on, and he told her of gold-encrusted bullock-waggons laden with the beauties of the harem which had once creaked over this sour turf, and of the paradisiacal greenness and freshness of willows and water in those days, she could not help reflecting that she had come too late to this dusty, dirty, cockneyfied Turkey which surrounded them. Indeed, she had come into the world too late.

Two purposes had been before Enid's mind in agreeing to go with her father to the East. First, there was papa's promise that they would make an excursion to Damascus, where her twin brother Roland had died of the plague in 1850. Second, she would avoid going to London with her mother for another Season.

She hated London; or, rather, she had come to hate herself in London, to hate her inability to enjoy the gardenia-scented ease of that London life through which her mother swam so gracefully, and to such applause. Why could she not be allowed to stay at Ravenrig, near to Roly's grave by the sea-shore – to remain within the landscape commanded by the mighty obelisk which Sir Daniel had erected to Roly's memory on the mountains – and so to keep faith with his spirit? But Lady Fanny had sent for her to the tower which she occupied at Ravenrig, where she sat on a sofa with her little white dog among the open portmanteaux and heaped dresses and rustling excitement which heralded her departure for Berkeley Square. "What is this, Enid, pray, about you not wishing to come up to Town?" Outside were the yellow daffodils and the spring air, but little of that light penetrated the armorial glass, the lancet windows, of this gloomy tower. Moving among the shadows and carved pillars, Enid had mentioned Turkey, and Damascus. "Roland would not have been content with moping about here," Lady Fanny told her sharply, seeing into her heart. "You make Roland the excuse of all your foolishness, you do indeed."

If Roly had been by, to ride with her in the Park, to lead her into London drawing-rooms, how gladly she would have gone! But she had stood out for Turkey, and the promise of Damascus when papa's Constantinople concerns allowed him leisure to travel south. Sir Daniel too had come in for Lady Fanny's mockery, a blind old man setting out for the war, but Enid had fancied that she saw, in his contempt for her ridicule, the echo of his disillusion with the aristocratic conduct of the Government and the war. In Sir Daniel's disgust at the war's misman-agement, his deference for Rank had foundered. So he and his daughter had set out. Enid's only outward concern about a long absence – the health and safety of her Cochin fowl – irritated her mother more than any other aspect of the plan.

Papa had taken a little house, a painted wooden affair in the style of the fretwork scenery of the opera, on the waterfront at Bebec, and there Enid idled away her days on a window-seat watching warships and transports move up and down the Bosphorus, or watching the ferries bustling in to the quay below her window, or the *kaiks* fluttering over the water to Asia.

Often she had sent her imagination to follow a party of veiled women carried in their *kaik* across the strait to Asia; and one morning, with Calliope her Greek maid, she had herself hired a boatman to row them over to that mysterious shore. Behind the Asian housefronts, which resembled very much those at Bebec, she had found stately trees, and lawns, and fountains, which had delighted her, and had encouraged her to venture further inland. Before they knew it, she and Calliope had found themselves in a deep valley enclosed by woods. Suddenly a sense of loneliness, and peril, had come upon her. The valley apparently was deserted: only the hum of bees disturbed its silence. She did not dare turn her head for fear, or look into the wood-shadow. And then, exposed like a sacrifice on a stone in the sun, they had seen a bunch of grapes partly eaten, laid down only moments before, the juice darkening the stone. Something savage was offered her in these grapes, half dreadful, half tempting. Her instinct was to scream, and run: her desire was to stay.

And now papa had told her that Tresham Pitcher was at Constantinople. Another tremor ran through her nerves. "Shall we walk back now, papa, to our picnic?" she suggested. Of course she wouldn't see Mr Pitcher, for she saw no one out there at Bebec, her father having quarrelled with the military over his plan for procuring timber to hut the Crimea army, and not wishing to take her into the native society he frequented himself in Stamboul. "I'm sure Wicker will have boiled up his Magic Kitchen by now," she said.

"We will go back if you like it," her father replied. "Enid, you are not too dull, eh, at Bebec there?"

"Not a bit dull, papa – not more dull than I am anywhere, at least."

"I try to tell you what I am at, but it ain't very clear always, and you see none of the fine folk I'm afraid."

"I don't care a pin for fine folk," she said, squeezing his arm, "and we are going to Damascus in a little, aren't we?"

"We are, my dear. If there ain't some progress made soon in sending up Omer Pasha's force to clear a way through the Caucasus I shan't stop on here, I shan't indeed."

"But you would build a railroad over the Caucasus, would you papa? I mean if Omer Pasha did go, and if Mr Pitcher's mountaineer friends did clear a path over the pass?"

"I don't know about building myself any more. I should like it. I should like to be at the work exceedingly. But perhaps . . . your mother would say I am too old. Too blind at all events. But I shall make sure a railroad's built right enough – aye, and I'll make double sure it don't fall into Herr Novis's hands, too, like the Trebizond route's done, and the Aleppo road, and about every other road east. I believe there ain't a bale of cloth goes from Europe to Persia but it pays duty somewhere along the route into Novis's pocket. Not a bale. But with the Caucasus route open we should give him a run, by heaven!"

Vigour had come into Sir Daniel's stride as he spoke of his plans, and of his adversary. All his energy was combative. Unable to admit to a mistake, if his affairs went amiss he would look about for an enemy to blame, crediting such a one with the powers and the malignity of Satan. His enmity with Herr Novis was of old date; in the '20s he had worked for that Vienna banker, managing coal-mines for him on the Black Sea, laying meanwhile the foundation of his own trading and railway-building fortune. Then, suddenly, the Sultan had turned him out of his Empire (perhaps at Novis's suggestion) and Dan Farr had been left to scramble back to England with what he could carry, leaving Novis to manage his Eastern interests. Novis had not kept faith, or had not been lucky in his stewardship. Whether there were issues between the two men besides money and commerce – moral issues which might justify Sir Daniel casting Novis in the Adversary's rôle – Enid did not know. There was in her father's sanctum at Ravenrig a certain antique statue ('My Phidias', her father called it) which had a significance apparently above even monetary value in his eyes. The statue was headless, and represented Dionysus. Its history he had told no one; unless he had told it to Captain Vinegar when commissioning him for the disastrous journey of 1850 which had ended in Roland's death. After that tragedy, seeking as usual someone to blame, Sir Daniel had made Vinegar his scapegoat. Now Tresham Pitcher, Vinegar's inseparable companion, was to be brought forward as the saviour of papa's interests in the Caucasus. Her father's thinking confused Enid's brain, which had never been forced out of true by the necessities of the moment, as his had very often been.

"So, Mr Pitcher is to be your commander-in-chief in the Caucasus, is he?" she asked as they walked along, responding to a tendency of her mind which desired to bring Mr Pitcher's name back into the conversation.

"If he will join up his forces with Omer Pasha, yes."

"Oh – Mr Pitcher has 'forces' nowadays, does he! He was a clerk at the Waterways Board when first he came to us at home."

"Aye, Enid, maybe so," rejoined Sir Daniel, "and I was wheeling a barrow about Whitechapel afore I shipped East aboard a Smyrna currant brig. Mind that. The East may make a man, where the West would keep him in a clerk's place all his days. Now then, see here, Mr Pitcher has got himself into cahoots with some of these native chiefs of the Mingrelians, what holds the great pass through the Caucasus there, and he offers an alliance which would cut off the Russian army at Kars from its depôt, and achieve no end of advantages, if only the Allied command down here weren't too stupid to see it. Likely their objection to Pitcher is what yours is – that he began on life as a Waterways clerk."

"I don't object a bit to Mr Pitcher," said Enid hotly. "At least, I had no objection to him when he came to Ravenrig," she added, lest her ardour should be misunderstood. She felt sure she ought to hate Mr Pitcher. "Have you seen him yourself? I suppose you have."

"Not just spoken with him myself, no. I thought – better not. But I've requested of Lord Stratford to speak with him, and to have in some of the military blockheads to listen. It should succeed. It should. But there is no limit upon the stupidity of what's done here."

"Meanwhile Captain Vinegar sits up in Mingrelia, does he, with the native chieftain?" asked Enid, testing the ground cautiously.

"I don't give a button where Vinegar sits. He may go to the Devil for what I care."

Despite this robust assertion, papa must know (thought Enid) that any alliance would be as much with Vinegar as with Pitcher. He could not abuse the one, and take the other into partnership – could he? Not if he was honest. But perhaps business partnerships, and military alliances, were not required to be honest, in a private gentleman's sense of the term. He had once said to her, in speaking of his desire for revenge against Vinegar, "What, did you suppose I would be content with putting up an obelisk to Roland's memory, and then calling the score square? No no: I shall destroy Vinegar, mark if I don't." Yet by proposing this alliance with Pitcher, and therefore with Captain Vinegar who stood behind Pitcher, it seemed just as though papa *was* prepared to call the score square, after all.

Enid, as so often, came back from these reflexions to her sad conclusion: that she alone continued truly to mourn her dead brother; that she alone possessed his spirit; that she only had truly understood him in life. Sad, but comforting. Thinking of this with her usual satisfaction, and guiding her father towards the spot which Wicker would now have made comfortable for them under the willows, she became aware of a horrid red-faced Englishman grinning at her.

"Oh papa," she whispered, "here is that dreadful Mr Crabtree who was at Misseri's hotel with us. I'm sure he'll come up and – oh!"

"What's up?" Aware of the tremor in her arm, her father stared about blindly for its cause.

"Only – only – "

She bent her head so that her hat brim hid her face, into which the blood had rushed. Beside vulgar, squat Mr Crabtree rose a tall companion. It was Mr Pitcher – Mr Pitcher coming up to her, Mr Pitcher being introduced! She stretched out her hand automatically as Crabtree uttered his name.

"We are already acquainted," said Mr Pitcher, bowing stiffly without taking her hand. Looking up for a moment she had the impression of a loose tunic, a sword, a rough fur hat. Crabtree spoke to her father. Mr Pitcher leaned forward, quick, to whisper to her "I am sorry for this, which I didn't contrive, pray believe me. I will take myself off – if you wish it."

"No no," she stammered, the blood still heating her face. Here he was, whom she had thought of so much, Roland's friend. "That is, don't go away on account of me."

His pale eyes looked into hers keenly for a moment. He must have made a decision based on the confusion he saw in her heart, for he broke into Crabtree's chatter to present himself in a clear voice to Sir Daniel: "I am Tresham Pitcher, sir, who came to you once at Ravenrig, and was with Roland at Damascus."

At this speech, Enid's feelings were allowed to swell into admiration. And Roly came back to her so clear, as if he had walked up on his friend's arm, the pair of them sprung out of the mountains of Circassia like heroes of old. Now they were all walking together towards the place under the trees where Wicker had laid out saddles and rugs to make a bower for their picnic. Confused, her eyes downcast, she noticed how Mr Pitcher's long soft boots stole along beside her like a leopard's pads.

Wicker was found imperturbably brewing tea on his knees in front of one of the little spirit stoves known as Soyer's Magic Kitchens, which the great chef had invented especially for the Crimea troops and which were soon sold out to the onlookers flocking to the seat of the war. The admirable order of Wicker's picnic arrangements surrounded him, and beyond that a circle had been cleared of Turks and others by his sharp English tongue. Through the crowd of beggars and tinkers and gypsy musicians which watched Wicker's preparations from a distance, Pitcher cleared a way for Enid with a few words in Turkish.

"So," said Sir Daniel, peering towards Pitcher to see him as plainly as he could, "you've picked up a little Turkish in your wanderings, have you?"

"Hobson's choice, sir. I should have got along very ill, I suppose, by speaking in English to the Koords of the Tyari mountains when I lived two years amongst them."

"Ah, I daresay."

They seated themselves against the saddles in the shade, Crabtree plumping himself down beside Enid, Pitcher settling cross-legged near Sir Daniel, whilst Wicker stepped amongst their legs in his billycock hat distributing tea-cups to all.

"And what was your business among the Tyari, Mr Pitcher?" asked Sir Daniel.

"Oh," (Enid heard him reply carelessly) "trying if I could have myself killed. I looked after some of the Nestorian Christians about Amadiah, whom I found were being very thoroughly abused by the Koords."

Enid heard no more, for Crabtree's loud flat voice in her ear drowned Mr Pitcher's. She did not listen to Crabtree. She fancied that in saying that he had "tried to have himself killed" Mr Pitcher had offered to her an expiation for his part in Roland's death. It seemed so to her sensitivity. But oh! (she thought) you are so anchored at a picnic, and cannot face your chair about to dodge a bore as you may in a drawing-room. Such a bore as Mr Crabtree was, too, with his explanations a mile

[40]

long attached to every circumstance of his life. Behind her Mr Pitcher and papa were discussing Baghdad . . . she looked into the little watery eyes fixed upon her and prayed for release. The shadow-pattern of willow leaves quivered on her dress like a figure of her impatience, as Mr Crabtree explained why he was not a major, and how he might have been a baronet, and why he could not stomach oysters. When Wicker came by with the sandwiches, one gloved hand correctly behind his back as he stooped over her, she seized the chance to say loudly.

"I don't know how you contrive it, Wicker, I don't a bit. You have given us the very picnic we should have had on a Welsh moor – hasn't he, papa? Mr Pitcher, a sandwich?"

Mr Pitcher broke off his talk with Sir Daniel and stared hard at the plate. "Sandwiches, by Jove!" he exclaimed. "I don't know how many years it may be since I saw a sandwich."

Wicker, profoundly shocked, hastened to present his handiwork to the warlike figure reclining on the grass.

"Wicker doesn't believe the world would go round at all without sandwiches, do you Wicker?" said Enid, anxious to hold Mr Pitcher's attention as he took the morsel in his large hand.

"Ain't so foolish as that, miss – but there's few says no to sandwiches."

When sandwiches had been further discussed, Enid would not go back to her tête-à-tête with Mr Crabtree. She attended to her father, who asked Mr Pitcher, "How did you choose to go up to the Caucasus when the war came?"

"All of us at Baghdad saw the thing as an Eastern war. Russia against Turkey, and Russia with her eyes upon our road to India. An Asiatic war. So we looked to Russia's frontier with Turkey in the East. Kars. The Caucasus. I thought I would take a ride along the frontier there. I thought I would see what intelligence might be picked up which would be of service to the Allies when they came to land on the Black Sea coast there – which I thought they would be sure to do straight off." He laughed. "That was 18 months ago, and they haven't landed yet."

Lying there on his elbow plucking grass in the dappled willow-shade, and speaking of these adventures, he looked to Enid like a hero. Crabtree said, "It has disgusted you, hasn't it old fellow? – the way you and I have been ignored?"

"Constantinople would pretty well disgust any man just now, I suppose," said Pitcher coldly.

"It wouldn't disgust you I daresay," said Sir Daniel, "if the powers-that-be was to adopt your ideas and invade the Caucasus for you."

"In that event I shouldn't have been here above five minutes," Pitcher replied, "and I shouldn't have seen Englishmen misbehaving themselves in the streets in a way that's disgusting. Doubtless, yes, I would have gone back to Mingrelia believing great things of Europe. I daresay the benefits of civilisation always do appear larger at a distance. I certainly find it a good deal easier to believe in the superiority of the English when I am not amongst them."

This rather crushed Enid. She had somehow hoped that the tea and the sandwiches would have suggested the delights of English domesticity to this wanderer. She looked away from his face into the dreary world. Her father said, "Never fear, Omer Pasha will be sent to the Caucasus at last. You are right, Mr Pitcher, it is an Eastern war, and even the French and the English will be made to see that in the end. Williams will lose Kars for us else, and we shall waken up some of these mornings to discover the Russians straddled across our path to India. Aberdeen might have stood for it, but Palmerston won't. By heavens, Pam won't."

"I hope you may be right. I despair of it, I must own, waiting upon the diplomatists and the military men here."

"Don't despair, Mr Pitcher. Try what reinforcements may be gained from hope."

Pitcher looked at Sir Daniel, surprised. "You read Milton."

"Every blind man should read Milton."

"You must give Edmond credit, papa," put in Enid, hoping that the conversation would become general, and familiar.

"Aye, true. I never had read Milton, till one day my son Edmond – you will remember him I daresay Mr Pitcher, from the time you came to us at Ravenrig – one day Edmond told me that Milton was blind, and seemed to do well enough upon it. I suppose I had complained of losing my sight. So I sent for a Milton out of the library. A wonderful work. Wicker reads it to me."

"And I do too, papa."

"You do, Enid, but you can't care for it as Wicker and I do. No no.

You mayn't grasp *Paradise Lost* – mayn't take in the tragedy of it – till you have lived enough for the poem to reflect a great part of what you have learned of life for yourself. The humanity of Satan – the young mayn't understand that, and be ready to half-forgive him. And then, 'tis a book for a man that wants but one book, to be turning over and over again. You, Enid – you and Edmond – you suffer by your education, and must have a dozen books open at a time. That don't allow old Milton to have the silence of your mind."

Enid looked to see if Mr Pitcher would offer a view on this, having recognised Milton's line in her father's mouth. But he sat cross-legged again on the grass and silent, turning his fur *calpac* in his hands, musing. Mr Crabtree was watching the gypsies. The sun was declining. Soon (she thought desperately) the picnic would be over and Mr Pitcher would vanish. The promise of intimacy in his whisper, "I will take myself off, if *you* wish it," was unfulfilled. She heard her father say,

"And Captain Vinegar, Mr Pitcher: you have left him up in Mingrelia, have you, with this Rachinskiy and his daughter, I forget her name?"

"The Princess Mazi."

"Just so. You may tell Captain Vinegar, by the by, that his publisher, Mr Stourpaine, came to me a few years back – it was just when the manuscript of *Land-March* had come in from Baghdad – and asked me did I believe Vinegar to be a real personage."

"Did he now. And what did you reply, sir?"

"I didn't quite know what to reply, Mr Pitcher."

"Ah, well, there it is," said Pitcher, concentrating his attention on pulling grass; "I daresay he hasn't enquired as to the reality of Captain Vinegar since the profits came in. The doubts of a man of business may be pretty well quieted by a good set of figures, I suppose."

Sir Daniel smiled, if grimly. "I own it, Mr Pitcher," he said, "they may that. And if all was to go according to plan in the Caucasus, and trade through to the Caspian should be set going by means of this Rachinskiy that you and Vinegar have found out between you – why, I daresay the world would look very rosy on the pair of you. I daresay I should. It's human nature, to forgive and forget when reparation's made. A long memory for injuries is left to Satan, you'll remember. 'The study of revenge, immortal hate.' Satan's words. No, you travel back to Mingrelia, Mr Pitcher, and bring us out this Golden Fleece of a safe pass through to the Caspian for us, and you shall have claim to a hero's reward when you come back to England. Ain't it so, Enid?"

"I suppose it will be so, papa, if you promise it."

3

Tresham Pitcher leaned on the paddle-box rail of the Sinop ferry, and watched the Bosphorus villages slip past, and rejoiced. At last he was outward bound. At last, after weeks of idling on that shore, and watching the traffic of war pass between these cypress slopes, he was a participant in the game again, his face turned towards the open sea and a distant Eastern landfall. Three weeks more of knocking upon doors and waiting in anterooms had passed since the Sweet Waters' picnic.

Once only in that period had he seen Enid Farr. In despair at the evasiveness and inactivity of the military and diplomatic gentry he sought to meet, he had found out Sir Daniel's residence at Bebec and gone to visit him there. Sir Daniel was out; but a Greek servant-girl had shown him into an upper room, and there at the window sat Enid amid a dazzle of evening light reflected off the water. Found alone she had the timidity of a startled wild creature, her head held up aslant to listen, a doe snuffing her hunter on the breeze. But he induced her to seat herself again at the window, and sat down himself near to her. He would not let her go even to the door to send for candles. The dusk was soft at the open window, and watery sounds came up to them, the slop of waves against the quay, the creak of an oar: they might have been in a boat together, rowing across a darkening lake. Almost before he knew it, as if to show himself to be as susceptible to hurt as herself, he found himself telling – confessing – how it was that he had left her brother dying of the plague at Damascus, whilst he had ridden on to Palmyra. His sorrow and grief he showed her like wounds that had never healed. "It was not you," she said, "it was Captain Vinegar"; the words were as gentle as a blessing. "Only you can forgive me," he said to the ghostly presence at the window. She sat still as death. "Why me only?" "Because you were most injured." Now she moved, and put out her hand to him. He found that it was wet with tears, and put it to his lips, the softness, the salt juice

of her heart. "He was mine," she sobbed, "they have all forgotten."
They sat in the dusk in silence, each heart full of gratitude towards the
other, hearing as if with one shared consciousness the wailing cry of a
kaikji afloat on the dark strait. Long ago on a snowy road across the
moors above Ravenrig, driving in a pony-chaise, she had said to him
"You speak as if one summer was all we might have"; and it had always
seemed to him in memory that her words promised summers to come.
This moment was such a summer. He moved closer to her, and she
allowed it.

Now, on the Sinop ferry, passing a twinkle of lights which showed
along the Bebec waterfront, he looked back on that evening, and
wondered if Enid's *mashrabyah* showed one of those fitful gleams from
the shore which his ferry passed with the thud of its engines, the
feathery flutter of its paddles, outward bound. He had not waited for
her father's return that night. At the door she had said, looking out after
him into the cobbled crooked lane, "Remember the promise". Already
his mind had run ahead, for she had told him that she and her father
were leaving in the next days for Damascus, so that he must look
elsewhere for support in his Caucasus plan. What promise had she
meant? Seeing his doubt, she had said, "Papa's promise, that you
should be welcome at Ravenrig." "Ah, welcome so long as I bring him
the Golden Fleece." "You will. Come. You will see my Cochins if you
come." And she had closed the door in the fretted, painted, pasteboard-looking housefront, like the heroine of a play who goes
"indoors" through stage scenery at the end of the Act, whilst the hero
strides offstage to pursue his adventures.

Promises! Sir Daniel, having lifted not a finger to help him, was now
to leave Constantinople without informing him. So much for promises.
Lord Stratford had made himself inaccessible behind his exquisite
attachés; from the military, who appeared to live entirely upon hearsay
and rumour, nothing certain could be learned of Omer Pasha's
projected expedition to the Caucasus. Meeting Mr Broadbent by
chance on the Therapia ferry, and enquiring for news, Tresham was
told: "Omer Pasha? Going nowhere, depend upon it. You have the
Ministry at home determined he should go to Kars by way of Trebizond,
and His Excellency here just as determined he shall go by the Caucasus,
and the finish will be, he'll stop in his tent and go nowhere."

[45]

Smarting under the sensation that he had been let down by those who might have helped him, Tresham had resolved to act upon the suggestion of an acquaintance made at Misseri's table d'hôte (a Polish soldier of fortune), that he should contrive to meet a certain Ismail Bey, who had 'interests' among the Circassian tribes, and who was described to him by the Pole as "the last chance for a fellow who don't give a hang for the rights and wrongs of a case, but wants to see some fun". A messenger sent to seek this Bey had brought him back an appointment at a khan behind the Spice Market at Stamboul.

He had presented himself at iron gates in a decayed wall, and been admitted into passages echoing to the whispers and slippers of black servants. Put into a long, low, shadowy chamber, he waited. It had the silence of a vault underground, though he had descended no steps into it. Here and there the dim gloom was patched with brilliance where lamplight gleamed upon enriched and encrusted objects of Byzantine taste, such as gold-chased armour, and silver plate, and gilt ikons. A treasure-chamber? A prison?

He explored cautiously. The entombed silence had put him in mind of the Palmyra tower, and the presence of death. Tapestries he came upon, and chain-mail; silk, swords, a bronze casque whose eye-cavities watched him like the very eyes of ancient time. There had been the smell of dry earth and corruption in the Palmyra tower, and the touch of cold dead lips in the basket. To shake off a tremor of horror he took a quicker step and looked into revealed archways of the vault. There! A head!

For an instant shock transfixed him. Then he saw that the head was marble, beautiful and savage under clustering curls and the tendrils of vine. It was the head of Dionysus, the head missing from Sir Daniel's Phidias. Tresham knew it beyond doubt, as the round perfection of the full moon is recognised without need of a calendar. He was amazed by its beauty, how it glowed in the dimness. Aloof, savage, silent: the indwelling fierce light of its spirit spilled out from the curve of lip and nostril. No question but that it was the head possessed by Herr Novis, and sought by Sir Daniel. Who then – the corollary leaped like fear into Tresham's mind – who then was Ismail Bey?

At this moment he had realised that he was not alone in the vault. Did a sound like scuttering leaves, a memory, make him turn? His host may have been at hand all along, certainly was, for now he only stirred in a stone chair in the shadows, as a tortoise stirs under leaves and so reveals his presence where no reptile had seemed to exist a moment earlier. Tortoise-like Ismail Bey was, too – if this was Ismail Bey who now came to life in his stone chair – for he was encased in a quilted shell-like surtout, and his movements were testudineously slow, and his face darkish, a map of wrinkles, with a glittering eye. He spoke in Turkish, careful of words. Pitcher, and Pitcher's past, were evidently not unknown to him. Coffee was served by blacks, and a narghileh apiece, but the furnishing of hospitality by no means dispersed the chill of the vault, or warmed the blood of the scaly oriental. Words trickled from him like an oracle's predictions; where Pitcher would go, what he would do, how events would fall out. The interview terminated merely by the words ceasing to drop from his lips. A black appeared at Tresham's elbow, and he was returned to the alley outside the iron gates – the silent and dirty alley which led down to the waters of the Golden Horn – returned, commissioned, to the upper world.

It was Ismail Bey's commission which had put Pitcher on board the Sinop ferry. Ismail Bey, whoever he was, had set him free of the trammels of Pera and the European hierarchy. He cared not a button now for the condescension of Lord Stratford's attachés, or for the difficulty of meeting with this Colonel or that. To be free of Crabtree, too, was a wonderful thing. At Misseri's hotel it was impossible to escape intimacy with other idle men kicking their heels awaiting employment, or hoping for it, and with intimacy came a degrading sense of self-association with men like Crabtree, whom he despised. The table d'hôte, the gossip about the war, the eternal lounge in the hotel doorway: day by day he had felt the singularity and independence of his spirit diminish, melting away in the torpor of ennui like a snowman in the sun. Thank heaven than Buckle's royalties, as well as repaying his debt to Sir Daniel, had spared him the necessity of borrowing off Crabtree at famine rates, as many had done. Crabtree procured cash off the *serrafs*, the native money-lenders (so the story went) and let it out again to Englishmen at extortion interest, against security at home which the *serrafs* wouldn't accept.

Under him the paddles shuddered in the paddle-box. Vibration thrilled through planking, rattled hatch-covers. The paddles drove harder, clapping like mill-wheels, whitening the dark water. Pitcher's heart lifted and tightened as he looked ahead, between the castle-crowned capes of Europe and Asia, to the low dark wastes of the sea. Still on the ship's port side evening light flooded the upland pastures and gilded the woods of Europe. To be quit of Crabtree and mediocrity was it necessary to quit Europe and go to the ends of the world? So it seemed. Such evening light as this put into his mind (as many another Eastern sunset had done in the years since he had left England) the painting over the fire in his step-uncle's library at Rainshaw Park, in which a sea shore, and columned temples and blue distances, were flushed *couleur-de-rose* by a sinking, classic sun. In the foreground armoured figures standing on their long shadows enacted rôles in a legend never quite to be made clear, or understood . . . he thought of them now, thought of Rainshaw wondered if he would ever look into that painting again. He could not quite separate in his mind the landscape in the picture from the real landscape at Rainshaw's windows, of turf and lake and wide oaks. The same peace and repose lay upon each in his memory like the blessed evening light . . . "the cloud-capped towers, the gorgeous palaces, the solemn temples": all dissolved as he turned away from the gilded scene and looked ahead.

The capes of Europe and Asia seemed to make a needle's eye of the passage between them into the Black Sea. Close on the port quarter the surf seethed over the Cyanean Rocks. Through the narrows shot the steamer; then the land fell away on either side, her bow lifted and crashed on ocean waves, and she was at sea.

III

The Black Sea

TWO DAYS LATER Tresham Pitcher sat against the wall of the Sinop café to which Ismail Bey had directed him, and felt himself sucked down into an Eastern scene whose dirt and squalor even a few weeks among Europeans in Pera had caused him to forget. The café was kept by a Circassian, and stood close inside the walls of Sinop, which had been pretty well shelled into ruins by the Russian bombardment of '53. Besides sinking a Turkish squadron in the bay, and knocking down the town walls – and cutting into two halves a maidservant of the British consul – the Russian shells had lopped to pieces the plane trees sheltering the café. Their maimed state seemed to speak to Pitcher of the cruel indifference of Turkey, which ignored such damage save for pulling down what firewood a Turk could reach without stretching himself.

It disquieted Pitcher to find that the casual cruelty of the Turks had begun to make him uncomfortable, as it had never done before. What was the susceptibility creeping into his mind which made him uneasy at seeing animals ill-used or children beaten? In his apprehension of the East, a sense of its languor predominated, something tempting and voluptuous which cold steel guarded. An image of this mésalliance had lodged in his head: a harem under guard in a stone kiosk above rippled water. Upon the Tigris at Baghdad? The Bosphorus? No matter; somewhere in his Eastern travels, glimpsed in some stone kiosk above that rippling water, the image had struck him, the white-robed flutter of feminine doves under guard of an Arnaut spearman glittering with steel. The cold steel of his eyes had the swagger and insolence of the armed ruffian in Eastern lands, who doesn't care a rap for gentility and the settled order. Set as a guard over women, he signified all that was barbarous between the sexes. It was an image of the East which caused Pitcher a tremor of dismay, like the premonition of danger. Was it a warning that he did not still possess that strong nerve required of the man who would pursue a life of independence in the East? If he did not, he must fall back upon the ironclad Captain Vinegar to supply nerve enough for two, until this adventure was done, and he might return to safe Europe. Vinegar would certainly not be unstrung by a few maimed plane trees.

He had left the Trebizond steamer at Sinop in order to meet with a merchant designated by Ismail Bey who was to supply sufficient cloth (*bez*, *aludja* and *chivit*) to make up a respectable deck-cargo for the final leg of Pitcher's voyage, which would take him from Trebizond to the Caucasian coast. This merchant, a fat flushed Turk very fond of raki, had met him in the café yesterday and had talked mighty loud of his determination to run the cargo along the coast himself, and to add to it at Trebizond the arms and ammunition which were to be the real purpose of the passage to the Caucasus. He had walked Pitcher up to the ridge of the isthmus on which Sinop is built, and had showed him the tub-shaped cutter lying in the lee of the promontory in which he proposed making the long and dangerous voyage. It looked to Pitcher like certain death. However, the Circassian café-owner told him that the cloth merchant, who always talked big of fighting the Russians after a few glasses of raki, had never yet left Sinop by boat. Relieved, and yet irritated, Pitcher was obliged now to see that the cotton stuff was loaded aboard the Trebizond steamer, and that he received what he had paid for with Ismail Bey's gold, for of course no one concerned could be trusted. He sat against the café wall and viewed each wearisome stage of the work ahead with profound disgust. It was disgust with the East. It seemed to him that he had spent a thousand years kicking Asiatics into performing their promises, and he was sick to death of it.

The truth was, Constantinople had upset him. Before going there, he had forgotten Europe. Now, even what had seemed at the time most tawdry about Pera's Europeanisation – the table d'hôte at Misseri's, say, or the crowd of half-bred Indian officers giving themselves such airs of swagger at the Sweet Waters – even those memories now affected him with nostalgia. As for those damned dandyish attachés breakfasting at Therapia, they seemed now, from a dirty native raki-shop at Sinop, to be blessed above the angels in Paradise by merely living like gentlemen. In the café – in the whole province – there wasn't a soul he could joke with, even such a poor kind of joke as might be poked at things with Crabtree. If Crabtree should walk in at the door now, he said to himself, I would fall upon his neck. But there was no Crabtree, no fun, only a set of shabby Turks smoking upon cushions with their pompous air of do-nothing, and a skinny child running amongst them with hot coals for their narghilehs, and a crust of dirt upon everything, and fleas hopping into your shirt, and a stench you might cut into slices with your knife. All the while Rachinskiy, and the princess, and all those other people and concerns in Mingrelia, lay as formidably across the future as the Caucasian Gates lay across Sir Daniel's proposed route to Persia. He rather wished that he had never come down from Mingrelia to Constantinople; or, if he had, that he might have stayed down and gone away to the West.

But he had not, and to survive what now lay ahead he must rapidly recover the temper and mettle of Captain Vinegar, or he must expect to go under. Vinegar was indomitable. Vinegar might have sailed that cutter to Trebizond, or he might have counted the bales aboard the ferry, but he would have made out of either task, for his *Journal*, a work of high significance demanding heroic qualities. So too he would have sat smoking his narghileh in this café, reflecting on the drama of his position with much complaisancy . . .

To find oneself at last clear of "the dismal habitations of mankind" – of that portion of mankind, at least, which passes its days in a high collar and cravat paying calls upon secretaries of embassy and other useless ornaments of the Othman capital – to be clear of such occupations, I repeat, has a wonderfully tonic effect upon a man's spirits. I looked about me, and, in contrast to my feelings of being a wolf-among-the-lambs at a Pera Ball, I felt myself blood-brother to the most villainous of these loungers in a Sinop divan. Rascals, no doubt, and idle rascals too, quite as much so as the secretaries of embassy aforesaid – and men capable of treachery as deep as any Periote, yet do they not have about their impassivity, and dignity, and be-hanged-to-you air, as they lounge smoking

[51]

upon their bolsters – do they not have the appeal of a truer, and older, aristocracy than any concocted of the mere baubles and coronets of Europe? Mayhap, thought I, old Jason had something of the same feeling as myself, when he found himself clear of the drawing-rooms of Iolchos, and the stratagems of King Pelias, with those same Symplegades behind him which I had navigated two days since, and a world of adventures before the Argo's keel.

Vinegar and his *Journal* were wonderful armour to put on. They had saved Pitcher from himself at many a low ebb of his Eastern wandering, most notably at Dyarbekir, in the autumn of 1850, where he had fetched up after sending home Roland Farr's body from Damascus.

He had left Damascus himself hardly caring what became of him. It had been his plan, on leaving England with Roland Farr, to have marched overland to India, where the post of ADC to a relative of his mother's had been offered him. Now, in his grief and guilt, it had seemed to him that he might as well follow the Indian road from Damascus as any other. So he had struck out north-east by way of Urfa's plains into Mesopotamia, eating up the grassy distances day after day with no purpose but to put distance between himself and the past. Then at Dyarbekir he had stopped, volition gone. He had lodged in a stone khan where it seemed to him that all roads ended. He was absolutely alone.

One who stands outside the black walls of Dyarbekir may watch from an eminence the Tigris flow through its valley to the East. It had seemed to Pitcher that to cross that river would be an irrevocable step. Over there began the Indian life for which he had no eagerness. In a letter he had received at Damascus, his step-uncle Marcus, of Rainshaw Park, had seemed to hold out the promise of making Pitcher his heir – so long as he did not "cross the Rubicon" of his Indian journey. That had been before Farr's death, when the idea of returning home as his step-uncle's probationer "to lie under the Rainshaw plum-tree with his mouth open" had not appealed to him one bit. And how could he now return alive and well to England, whilst Roland Farr's body went home to Ravenrig pickled in a barrel of spirits? Still, the Tigris had seemed that Rubicon of which Uncle Marcus had written, and he was unwilling to cross it. The stained current of the Euphrates he had crossed at Bir: it suited his inanition, and dejection, to stay suspended in the black-walled city between the two rivers, and to do nothing. Sometimes he walked out of the southern gate, meeting donkeys laden with green and yellow melons being driven in from the countryside, and sat on a knoll to gaze at the Tigris. It was that fine autumn weather whose clarity reveals the far-off wintry snows upon the mountains. But he did not go on. A dervish from Jullundur, who lodged in the next stone chamber of the khan to his, attached himself to Pitcher, and taught him Turkish day by day. Pitcher submitted to the lessons as to all else.

For a book he had only the little calf-bound edition of *Paradise Lost*, printed at Edinburgh in 1767, which he had taken from amongst Roland Farr's possessions in the convent at Damascus – he had never known until then what book it was that Farr used to draw from his pocket and sit reading at odd moments – and this greasy volume he conned over word by word at Dyarbekir. It seemed to him strange that Farr should have cared for Milton. Perhaps Farr had been less simple than he had supposed.

Himself satiated with Milton – for he had studied every page of the volume, from the Editor's preface through the *Life of Milton* and all twelve books of the poem, to the advertisement on the final leaf for Mr Pope's *Iliad*, which he wished most profoundly might have been procurable at Dyarbekir – satiated and weary of Milton at last, he one day took Captain Vinegar's *Journal* out of his saddlebag and began to leaf through it. He had not looked at it since he had written the last entry.*

First his attention was caught, then held: soon he was captivated by this fire-eating version of his own and Roland's journey from England to Damascus. Here was a companion to dispel gloom and loneliness. For the character of the narrator as it emerged from the *Journal's* pages cheered him and heartened him, even made him laugh aloud to himself in the echoing khan, to the surprise of the dervish from Jullundur. Vinegar was indomitable. Here was a man armed at all points, so it

* The author of Vinegar's *Journal* was Tresham Pitcher. Captain Vinegar had never existed. Pitcher and Farr had invented this hard-bitten Eastern traveller as a means of extracting an advance of money from a publisher for his account of the journey they intended making, and as a mentor whose credentials would quiet the anxieties of Farr's mother. Only Enid Farr knew of the deception. If Sir Daniel had guessed it, he had not said so.

seemed by his own account of events, a man whom no adversity could daunt – a hero.

He finished reading the *Journal*'s final entry, made the night before Vinegar had left Damascus for Palmyra – "Having performed for young Farr every duty of friendship, I now throw my mind forward to tomorrow's adventure" – seated on the sunny slope above the Tigris. The tinkling of a flock's bells came to his ear from a fold of the grassy hillside out of sight, the wavering voice of a woman or a child singing rose and fell from its source in orchard or garden near the black walls; he was aware of the vividness of existence, as he had not been before reading the *Journal*. Vinegar had revived his creator to life with a transfusion of the heroic ink which flowed in his veins, so that Pitcher re-awoke among the real scenes and sounds of this world. Lying there on his elbow on the grass in the remains of his European clothes, burnt by the sun as he was and infested with the khan's lice, his imagination began to suggest to him a continuation of Vinegar's *Journal*, an account of the ride to Palmyra which would rewrite his own failure as Vinegar's success. For Vinegar had caught up with him once more. There, cropping the grass nearby, was the little horse ready to carry him anywhere in Vinegar's spirited company . . .

He might ride north through the mountains to Malatyah, and investigate the Jullundur dervish's tale of colossal stone heads on a windy plateau up there; or he might go to Kaiseryah, under Mount Argaeus, and look into the rumour of painted churches hollowed out of pinnacles of tufa; or he might ride with this caravan to Trebizond, or with that one to Shiraz, or offer his sword to the pasha of Mosul to fight the Koords – or to the Koords to fight the pasha, if the Koords seemed a jolly set. In the wide East "between Roum and Cathay", lay objectives without number for an adventurous journey such as the author of Captain Vinegar's *Journal* might make from "black-walled Amadir".

Squatting on the floor of the Sinop café Pitcher remembered that mood of buoyancy at Dyarbekir. He remembered the clear autumn weather, and the little fleecy clouds drifting in from the plains of Mesopotamia, and himself riding over the wind-bent grass as brimful of Vinegar's urge to live, as a planet shines brimful of the sun's reflected light. The spirit which had carried him onward then into Koordistan, should drive him onward now to run the cargo of cotton and guns to Mingrelia for Ismail Bey.

He rose to his feet, threw down some paras for his pipe and coffee, and stamped out into the wretched street. Of course the Turk merchant would not show himself, but must be dragged by the ear from his harem, and cursed, and bullied, and paid baksheesh, merely to perform his promise, and produce the cotton in time to have it carried aboard the Trebizond steamer. Ah, for two pins he would give away "Captain Vinegar", money and all, so that he might go home unencumbered to Europe and to Enid Farr. The alley downhill to the port was a drain between rotting hovels which oozed out a green effluent over his feet. He passed under the shell-shaken gate arch and found himself on the shore of the wide bay. It was stilly calm, sky and sea a colourless wash, long ripples gleaming as they rolled in to collapse amongst the rubbish and rinds and carcases littering the beach. Out of the shallow water protruded the wrecks of the Turkish squadron sunk by the Russians, gaunt as the black bog-oak that sticks out of a Scottish loch. Scotland! Among the Koordish mountains he had often thought of the summer long ago when his mother had taken himself and his two step-sisters from their Clapham house to stay with her own father in his parish in Wester Ross, and he thought now of that sea coast, and of the hills and lochs in mist behind it, as he stood on the Turkish shore and watched a slack-sailed English sloop-of-war manoeuvre in the roadstead. Would he ever again see those scenes of childhood, and those faces? His mother? With that past, and with his own painful sudden nostalgia for it, Captain Vinegar had no connexion. It was Vinegar's strength, to have sprung up from the furrow full grown, fully armed, unhampered by a childhood.

The glint of the sloop's gun-ports as she turned in the bay reminded him that she would be a vessel to avoid when sailing to Mingrelia with his cargo of arms. He had not cared to enquire into the right and wrong of running guns to the mountaineers. To assist Omer Pasha's Allied invasion, certain tribes must be armed: to pacify the Mamisson Pass over the Caucasus for Sir Daniel's trade-route, certain tribes should be armed: but just which tribes it was that Ismail Bey intended arming, whether pro-Ally or pro-Russian – or pro-anarchy – was a question he had not asked himself. But he hoped he would not have to explain his cargo to the captain of a British sloop, once he had sailed from Trebizond for the coast of Circassia.

As he stood among the slimy débris of Turkey on the shore, and watched the British sloop as though she carried an enemy flag, childhood and Scotland vanished away like a mirage, and left Pitcher as unencumbered by a past as Captain Vinegar.

IV

* * * * * * * * * * *

Adventures in the Caucasus, at the time of the Crimean War

by O. Q. VINEGAR (Capt.)

1

IT WOULD BE but a poor specimen of the English race whose bosom would not expand were he to find himself, as I had the good luck to find myself on the evening of October 6th, 1855, aboard a piratical little vessel standing out from Trebizond for the distant snow peaks of the Caucasus. Add to this enviable situation, firstly, that the vessel's hold be crammed with arms to enable the wild Highlanders of the Caucasus to throw off the Russian yoke, and, second, that amongst those far-off mountains a beautiful princess waits to greet the traveller, and I think it will be voted *nem. con.* that all the elements of a romantic adventure are to hand.

The sky was without a cloud, and the west wind blew strongly out of heaven's empty vault. The desperado-looking crew were hauling up the anchor to a ragged chant. As the sail clapped and filled overhead, the very planking of the craft seemed to come alive underfoot like a barb touching turf. She leaned on the swell and sped chuckling away from the castled steep of Trebizond.

Some seventy feet in length, the vessel was a lateen-rigged *tchek-dermeh*, such as is favoured by the smugglers and pirates of the Euxine for low lines and speed. Under my feet, hidden below bolts of cotton in the holds, were concealed the cases of Enfields and ammunition which had been carried that day down to the beach by Turkish *nizam* from the arsenal which was supposed to supply the army at Kars. Ismail Bey's name had produced vessel, cargo and captain within a day of my reaching Trebizond from Sinop.

As to this captain, I had rather wished that Ismail Bey's name might have procured someone a little steadier. The creature now at the tiller had already confided to me that he had been obliged to sell wife and children at Constantinople, to settle his debts, and was on his way back to Circassia to pick up another family. The crewmen, too, were of the type who might go to the bottom of the Black Sea without being missed: altogether it was very certain that no one in the world would rescue us, should we meet with misfortune; and such isolation added mightily to the satisfaction of the adventure which I had in prospect.

Nothing more untoward than a fight amongst the crew, and a very bad dinner, befell us during our passage, and the next evening found us hove-to in a steep sea off the mouth of the Ingour at Redout Kaleh. Omer Pasha, I knew, had left Trebizond on October 3rd to take command of his troops on this shore; it was now the 7th, and we had been running along the coast from Soukhum, where we had observed troops and supplies being landed in quantities from the transports. It did not quite suit us to come ashore under the public gaze, and so we had gone about, and had beat down again to Redout Kaleh. Here, too, alongside the miserable low town which seemed hardly to rise above the water, we could make out the white tents of an encampment. The weather was gloriously clear, and, above the level wooded plains which threw up a miasma of mist, there rose into heaven the snow-capped line of the Caucasus, Mount Elbruz itself peering from behind a nearer range. On my ride north from Baghdad the previous autumn I had passed close to Mount Ararat, and I do not know which is the more splendid, that solitary perfect mountain above the Araxes, or the giant of the Caucasus amongst his mighty companions. Whilst I debated the point, the skipper let his craft a point off the wind, having hoisted sail, and again we beat south-westward along the coast. I learned from him that he intended landing ourselves and cargo at Zikinzir, which would be sufficiently sheltered in this wind to allow of it.

There is no port at Zikinzir, but an anchorage in the lee of a headland, and a landing-place under the walls of the old castle. To this beach we rowed time and again, the skiff loaded to the gunwhale with our cargo of cotton and of guns. Ivy had netted its toils over the battlements of the castle, and creepers of the wild vine trailed their long fronds over the cliff's edge above us, tentacles of that inland jungle of Asia which, flushed scarlet with autumn, seemed reaching out for fresh conquests beyond Asia's shores. I could not suppress a twinge of apprehension, as we rowed over the glistening undulations of the cove, at the prospect of the journey I must make through that entangled forest.

A few wretched inhabitants of the place had gathered on the shore to watch our work, and these creatures we now employed to carry our cargo into a hut which I had appropriated. We had brought with us sufficient victuals for our supper – one seaman remaining on guard aboard the sloop – so that we were able to establish ourselves in tolerable quarters upon our beach-head on this hostile shore. For my own part, rejoicing to find myself once more independent of the gas-lamps and constables upon which the humdrum "civilised" world relies for its security, I delighted in this first bivouack exposed to the hazards of war. Too long had I "kicked the heel of idleness on the carpet of impatience" at Constantinople, until I had all but forgotten my true allegiance to a soldier's life, and had, indeed, entertained pipe-dreams of quite another order, in which had figured a fair English rose to bring my supper to a cosy fireside, whilst infant voices lisped and prattled about my chair. Now all such supports, with the gas-lamps and constables aforementioned, were left behind like the chocks which will support a vessel on the shore, but which cannot support her once she is launched upon her own true element, the deep.

My bargain with Nogai, the rascally Circassian skipper of the sloop, had been that the consignment of cotton stuff should be his, in return for landing myself and the arms safe upon the Mingrelian shore. The *bez* and *chivit*, which are worth but fourteen piastres the piece at Constantinople, will fetch twenty-five piastres at Kutais, and are, moreover, the currency of the country, the coin in which the value of guns and horses, and all other necessaries of the mountaineers' life, may be measured. Accordingly, next morning, he set out to discover a buyer for his cotton, whilst I took another direction in search of sufficient ponies to carry the guns into the mountains.

The rifles I had brought from Trebizond were the 1855 Enfields, the most modern pattern in use anywhere in the world, which, having competed successfully in trials against the Minié and Lancaster, have been adopted by the Army. Each weapon weighed 9lb 3oz, and threw the Pritchett bullet with its boxwood plug, which was a development from Minié's expanding bullet. My rifles (as I had ascertained by prising open a case) were of the short pattern supplied to the 60th and Rifle Brigade, having a 2ft 9in barrel, beautifully bronzed, and a sword bayonet. I had altogether six cases of these rifles, as well as ammunition for them, and four mahogany-and-iron-bound boxes of Pigou and Wilk's best powder weighing 30lb each. It will be readily calculated from the above data that I required three baggage ponies to carry a weight of 10 stone each, a reasonable load so long as they were not expected to run from an enemy.

My hunt for cattle was a weary business. At one village they swore that all the horses had been carried off by bashibozuks to replenish Mustapha Pasha's transport animals, which were dying wholesale in the swamps about Batoum. At another I met with such louring looks from the menfolk hanging about the huts, and such very cool courtesy from the headman, that I half expected to be laid hold of, and sold for a trifle to the Abasseks. At length, after two days of such work, I came upon what I needed in an *aul* built upon stilts over a marsh, where all the inhabitants were busy beheading and skinning frogs – that is to say, the women and children were thus pleasantly engaged, whilst the men lounged in their doorways, armed to the teeth and smoking like steam-engines. A party of these gentry condescended to lead me to a corral, where I was invited to take my pick of animals which had, I suppose, been stolen in a foray just previous. With three ponies for my guns, and another for the Imeritian frog-skinning youth whom I hired to look after them, I pushed back to Zinzikir.

I entered the hut in which we had stored our goods to find myself plunged in a scene, over the disgusting details of which I must draw a veil. Suffice it to say that part of the hut had been converted, with the aid of my bedding, into a couch of more than matrimonial width, upon which were disposed, in a state very nearly of nature, no less than three young misses of the native race, whose attentions were directed upon the person of my miserable skipper, Nogai, sprawled like a pasha in their midst. Nor did he seem inclined at once to explain himself to me, until my boot convinced him of it – the girls meanwhile had sprang into a giggling huddle among the cases of guns and powder.

Nogai's first question was, "Should I like to buy of his wares?" A cut of my *kourbash* answered this enquiry, and another persuaded him to tell me the story. Provided with capital in the form of cotton cloth, he had lost no time in setting himself up as a slave-trader, and had purchased the three females, who were about fourteen years old, from their relations in the first *aul* on his road. Why should I be angry? (he asked) I had been out buying horses, he out buying slaves; what was the difference? He would ship them below decks in his sloop to Samsoon, and with one trading venture would have restored his position in the world. Would I not (he repeated) care to take one of the young ladies off his hands at a discount, as the companion of my journey into the mountains?

I laid down my whip. How could I inculcate the very grammar of a morality into a mentality so debased? I merely told him what feuds and conflicts – what corruption and misery – is perpetuated in these unhappy lands by the continuance of slaving, and bade him leave me. From the door, driving his captives before him into the night, he indicated my cases of guns and boxes of ammunition piled about the floor.

"And will my poor country be at peace," said he, "so long as you *feringhees* carry the materials of war into its heart by every road?"

His words stayed long in my mind, as I sought sleep on the couch where had lain so lately those three young ladies now tossing below decks in Nogai's sloop on their voyage into a life of luxury and ease at Constantinople or Grand Cairo. What harm, after all, had Nogai done? He had not offended against the laws of his religion. He had bettered the girls' chances of rising in the world. He had relieved their parents of want, and had put into circulation enough sound cotton to clothe a dozen villages.

And then I thought of the arms and armed men being unloaded by the power and wealth of European nations upon this poverty-stricken country; the materials of war entering by every port, to replenish the poison-fangs of that serpent, tribal warfare, which crushes and envenoms its heart. I seemed to see Ismail Bey's cargo of weapons discharged upon this shore as the very seeds of evil – dragons' teeth which would grow up a crop of ills perpetuating anarchy in the Caucasus. Was that not his plan, his and Herr Novis's, to perpetuate the anarchy which would frustrate Sir D— F—'s intention of trading across the isthmus?

If there be any distinction between Sir D—'s intention and his adversary's, between good intentions and evil, it is that Sir D— intended arming one superior tribe (Rachinskiy's) to whom was entrusted the work of pacifying a corridor through which Europe's goods, and good influences, might pass; whilst his adversary's intention was to feed tribal dissensions by throwing in weapons amongst them indiscriminately. I saw this, as I lay awaiting sleep, and I resolved that my weapons at least should be placed in the hands of that one chosen tribe. Only thus could I rebut Nogai's charge, and, separating myself from the mere gun-runner in Ismail Bey's pay, place myself on the side, if not of the angels, then at all events on the side of "progress through trade", that watchword of our enlightened century. So resolving, I rested easy.

I could not help calculating, though, before I slept, that Nogai had obtained an extraordinarily handsome price for his cotton. We can reckon the twenty-seven inch piece at about twenty-five piastres, and a young female at, say, 5000 piastres (which I have heard quoted as the rate), so that in acquiring no less than three fair ladies in exchange for his cargo, he had struck a pretty bargain.

*   *   *

Next morning before dawn I was on my feet, and seeing to the loading of the ponies and the arrangements for the march. The boy I had hired from the frog-skinners, whose name consisted in some unpronounc-able number of Imeritian syllables, but whom I christened "Tack" after a favourite dog, seemed a sharp lad eager to be useful. With the sun as yet a rosy flush behind violet-coloured snow-peaks to the north-east, and the forest ahead of us as black as night, we left the lonely castle of Zikinzir on its sea-cliff, myself at the head of the little caravan of three laden ponies, whilst a fourth carrying Tack and our stores brought up the rear.

I had calculated that, without mishaps, we would be three days in reaching Prince Rachinskiy's headquarters at Alatstchinsk. How I should be received by the Prince – or, indeed, by his daughter – I hardly knew. I brought no Treaty signed or sealed by the Queen of England, which they had seemed to expect me to obtain. But I brought an undertaking from young L— O—, whom I had met knocking about Pera (and who claimed a mighty influence in the matter), that Omer Pasha's army should join up with Rachinskiy's forces somewhere about the Tsiva river; and I brought six cases of the Enfields for which, I knew, the mountaineers would sell their souls – having sold their grandmothers long since for the trumpery muskets they carried. Would the Prince be satisfied? And the Princess Mazi? Hoolaghan at least would surely be relieved to see me back, for he and I had drawn lots as to which of us made the journey to Constantinople, it being pretty clearly understood that the other remained behind as a hostage. Or so I had thought, expecting to be that hostage if I lost the draw; when Hoolaghan had drawn the short straw, though, I had seemed to detect something like a smile of complaisance pass between himself and the Princess.

We plunged into the forest. I was glad of the cover of trees, for I feared that our peacable-looking little convoy would become the mark of every robber and *âbrek* in the region, not to speak of the troops of *bashibozuk* roaming upon one side, and Cossacks on the other. For the first few hours I expected to be attacked at every turn in the road, and kept myself in a state of high alert. But, I don't know how it is – perhaps the soft air of autumn, the mazing trees silently shedding their leaves upon a carpet of leaves already shed, perhaps the blue peeps of heaven amongst the high branches, perhaps the easy stride of my little horse – conspired to lull me into a kind of waking dream, which those who have made long journeys on horseback will recognise, wherein I pondered long and deeply upon the days that never will return, and how it had come to pass that I was engaged upon such work as this, instead of taking my ease as the respected Squire of R—w, or perhaps serving the nation in Parliament. But *sic visum est diis*, and it don't do to repine. There was no turning back.

We had been climbing through forests all the day, skirting the plain of Redout Kaleh, and at evening we came down upon a valley where ran a broad rapid river, perhaps a branch of the Rion. It had to be crossed. I rode into the water, but was instantly in difficulties. The incident served to waken me from my trance-like musings, and I collected my thoughts. Downstream towards the plain I would not venture, so we turned upstream to seek a crossing-place. The flanks of the valley were clothed with forest, ours in deep shadow, the other gilded with the setting sun. We had clambered perhaps a mile along the ever-steepening hillside, on a path like a goat-track, when I saw below us a bridge. An unstable, makeshift affair of ropes and broken planks, the slender span crossed an abyss between two precipices of limestone. Down to it we scrambled. Trailers of wild hop and vine had reached along the bridge's ropes, and hung swaying in the disturbed air above the rapids.

Then I saw the horsemen on the other side. Though distant from us the bridge's length, I could mistake no detail of their appearance. *They wore armour!* Each wore a chain-mail surtout over head and torso – I could see the links glint in the sun as they turned their little ponies – and each carried a long sword at his side. In the mouth of the tunnel-like track into the forest behind them I counted four of them waiting for us to cross, though more might be concealed amongst the trees. Now, these warriors, I had reason to believe, were the very tribe to whom Ismail Bey had bade me convey the Enfields – the worst set of ruffians in the Caucasus. And I was determined that the Enfields should reach Rachinskiy.

The roar of the cataract rose like a hoarse exhalation out of the chasm between us. To attempt retreat, with my laden ponies, would have signalled pursuit and certain death. I must advance.

The structure of the crazy bridge shuddered as my pony put her foot upon it. I urged her on with the flat of my sword, but left her head quite free. I turned to find the others following, little Tack hunched up like a monkey amongst our provisions. I pretended the most absolute unconcern as to our reception on the further bank – and was indeed sufficiently occupied in getting safe across, and in hoping that one of the cases of rifles would not become entangled with a tendril of vine, and swing the whole ramshackle contrivance to destruction a hundred feet below.

My pony scrambled at last onto the smooth boulder where the bridge was anchored, and I found myself surrounded by these grim apparitions of the Middle Ages. Their chain-mail gave off a curious metallic susurration, or steely whispering, as they moved, something like the scaly rustling of so many serpents. I saluted them in Turkish – to which, rather ominously (as my readers who have themselves encountered wild tribesmen will recall) they made no reply, their dirty bearded faces louring at me through the apertures of their mail headpieces. To fight or fly was equally in vain. As they milled about me whilst my ponies stepped one by one off the bridge I expected at any moment to feel a sword-cut disabling me. One of them, a ruffian on a black horse, tapped the wooden case on the nearest pony with his sword and looked at me in fierce interrogation. What use to lie?

"Rifles," said I in Turkish, adding in the Mingrelian dialect, "Rifles and ammunition for Prince Rachinskiy."

He indicated the box to a follower, who was off his pony in a jiffy and prising up the lid of the crate with his *khingal*. He pulled out an Enfield and passed it to his chieftain. My nerves were strung taut, we were hemmed upon the smooth limestone above the chasm, and when the fellow who had dismounted now seized my pony's bridle I knocked him away with the flat of my sword. Instantly he wheeled upon me, and struck my sword such a blow with his own that the weapon was wrenched from my grasp and, sailing upward in an arc, flashing and turning in the evening light, ringing yet with the blow it had received, fell amongst my enemies. It had been my father's sword – the only possession of his that I had inherited – and to be disarmed of it seemed to presage coming evil.

"For Prince Rachinskiy?" now enquired the chief of these brigands, displaying the greased rifle.

"The Prince," replied I grandly, "has formed an alliance with the seven kings of Feringhistan, who send as a gift to His Highness these weapons. Soldiers – an army – will follow by this road and will avenge any ill done to the Feringhee envoys or the presents they bear."

I saw that my Pumpernickel-like tone took effect. Whilst the mailed Abhasseks were wheeling and turning in the *mêlée* these savages love to create, working themselves up to fall upon us with their swords, I added loudly to the irresolute chieftain: "Take the rifle you hold – "

"I shall take it, never fear," said he with an ugly smile, "it is our custom to take, mark you well, and who don't like our custom may amend it – if he can."

"Take the rifle," I repeated, looking upon this Black Knight as fiercely as I knew how, "use it against the Prince's enemies. His Highness shall know that I made a gift of it to a great warrior of the Abhasseks. Now, clear our road, for we must find shelter ere set of sun."

Well, it did not go off just according to Cocker. Nonetheless, having supplied a rifle each to the horsemen – and a fifth for some absent party of high standing – we were given passage over the great rock to which the bridge was anchored, and allowed to pass into the dusky recesses of the forest. Behind us, shots echoing in the gorge told a tale of target practise. My sword had been restored to me, and was again at my side; but, I don't know how it was, I felt that my grasp upon it had been weakened, as though the weapon was no longer an indivisible adjunct to my identity, if a mere savage in armour could knock it from my hand. Despite this pang, I was relieved to have escaped the ambuscade with the loss of five rifles, and pleased too with the steadiness of little Tack, who had stood to me like a trump.

It was that night – or perhaps the night following, for the chronology of our journey through the forests is confused in my memory – that we found ourselves hospitably received in an *aul* in a clearing. It was a collection of wattle-and-daub huts thatched with stalks of the Indian corn which was cultivated all round the village, up to the margin of trees. A furious dog hurled himself at us as we rode up the mud street, clinging to the tails of our ponies in his rage, and this canine alarum soon brought dirty faces and dark eyes to every doorway to watch us pass. The *khedkhota* of the *aul*, when he was produced amongst a group of greybeards under a large Turkey oak, in a space amongst the huts which served for village green, insisted that we were Russians. Nonetheless he had us quartered in a barn, and sent us a present of melons. Perhaps he sent, too, the half-witted youth who came to play to us on a rude lyre, whose twangings and twitterings, obnoxious to me, seemed to delight the soul of little Tack as he watered and fed our cattle. It was now that I made an uncomfortable discovery as to Tack.

It seemed that, whilst paying as I thought for a night's lodging and a few provisions at the frog-skinning aul, I had inadvertently *bought* my young companion. He now considered himself as belonging to me absolutely, and so could not be persuaded to concern himself in the least degree with an independent future – though of course I gave him his freedom instanter. Thus the lesson, that whoever enters the savage regions is made to comply with the customs of the country, whatever may have been his prior intentions. As the brigand at the bridge had asserted, "It is our custom to take – amend it if you can". I had amended their custom no more effectively than I had amended Nogai's, for I had allowed the brigand to take my rifles, and found now that I had bought a slave. Well, I was still determined to pursue Sir D— F—'s good intention, to pacify the region for trade, rather than to sow weapons broadcast and so propagate anarchy, but I saw very clearly, as I lay down to sleep in the barn, the difficulties of the task in face of the "customs of the country". *Video ameliora, proboque; deteriora sequor.*

So passed three days of our journey through those mighty forests. We had skirted the plains, and were now, I calculated, somewhere above Kutais (for I had recognised Mount Chramli showing his glittering fangs of ice to the dawn), and feeling our way up the headwaters of another branch of the Rion towards Rachinskiy's mountain kingdom. The silence and solitude of these regions is of a profundity unknown to the little woods and hills of Britain; league upon league of silence, century upon century of solitude, bury those remote forests under a snowfall of time. Here generations of beech and oak stretch back their genealogy through the centuries, untroubled by any action of mankind since old Noah's keel grated on Mount Ararat.

It was, therefore, with surprise that I heard far-off the axe-strokes of woodcutters resound from steep to steep of the valley into which we rode. It may be remarked that the Caucasian woodman makes no use of the saw, employing only his axe to fell, split, and square off the timber, thus occasioning much waste (as Robinson Crusoe lamented in a like case). The work seemed to be going forward ahead of us, and above the track we followed. When the axe-blows ceased, we too paused, and listened. Into the silence came all at once a rush of sound and fury which I can best describe as the roar of a gigantic sledge as it comes tearing and crackling down an ice-slope. In an instant it was past, and gone below: a resounding crash signalled its arrival in the depths. Silence returned. Shortly, the axe-strokes began again above.

Little Tack, knowing nothing of these forests, was as mystified as myself; I could see that he expected the *padishah* of all the *djinns* of Mount Kasbek to rush out of the trees and seize him by the ear. Pushing cautiously on, we came in a few minutes upon a glade slashed down through the forest from the heights above like the track of a landslip. Curious to explore, I rode out upon it: or attempted to, for the scoured earth and stones of its surface was so slippery that my pony at once came down on his side, and would inevitably have tumbled away to destruction, taking me with him, had he not very fortunately caught his saddle against a stump of shattered chestnut a yard or so downhill, which enabled him to scramble upon his legs again. I had got off him, and crawled to safety.

What was this *djinn*'s sledge-run, though, and how were we to cross it? Reconnoitring below, I discovered an indentation running across the avalanche-track (if such it was) which I hoped would afford sufficient footing for the ponies and ourselves. I considered roping them, but our cord was of inadequate length and doubtful strength. The axe-strokes above had again ceased, though I had hardly remarked the fact. Foolishly, I did not connect the tree-felling above with the "avalanche-track" before us.

We were well launched on our crossing before disaster struck us. Tack had reached the further side, drawing one pony after him, when the second pony slipped and fell. I was yet upon the nearer side, and was in hopes that the pony would get upon his feet again and continue, when that dreadful sound – the hurtling onrush of a sledge on rough ice – burst upon my ears from above. From the heights, in a roar of scattered stones, came pitching down upon us at racing pace an enormous tree-trunk. I watched in horror as the pony saw its danger. Down upon us the trunk rushed in a cannonade of stones like a war-canoe shooting rapids. I saw the fallen pony struck as it struggled to rise. In the same instant the standing pony behind it was hit, and rushed to destruction, both of them hurled away with such force that they pitched head over tail down the glissade like a couple of dead rats kicked down a gutter. After the crash of the great trunk's arrival at the bottom, silence. And then, out of the dazzle of the sun where it peered over the steep above, came the harsh laughter of the woodcutters. I unslung my rifle, for it would have relieved my feelings to have placed a bullet amongst them; but up there in the dazzle of light they might as well have been the *djinns* of Mount Kasbek indeed for all that I could see of them.

It was a long climb down to the spot where the tree-trunk and the remains of the ponies had pitched up amongst boulders and timber on the river bank. Both animals had been pretty thoroughly flayed in their descent, though in one remained a quiver of life which I extinguished with a ball. The cases had been torn open and the rifles scattered, smashed and twisted, down the slope. Fortunately one of the ponies lost had carried the rifles taken from me by the Abhasseks; still, nineteen more Enfields were lost here.

On the river bank I made a curious discovery. I had before noticed traces of igneous material in the rock formation of the locality, and I now found pieces of coal – undoubted coal, though not perhaps of the veritable Derby Bright quality – loose among the stones forming the primitive slipway from which the woodcutters launched their logs downstream. I put a fragment or two into my pocket, wondering as I did so under what circumstances, if ever, I would draw them from that pocket again and lay them before Sir D— F— as evidence that an exploration of the region's natural mineral resources would repay his investment.

That night Sleep tarried long ere she came to my side, though we were lodged in a comfortable enough shed. My mission was failing fast. Of the thirty-six weapons I had resolved to carry to Rachinskiy, there remained but twelve, and I was not yet at Rachinskiy's borders. Indeed, I had begun to ask myself, where might Rachinskiy's borders begin, for I had hoped to be within them before this, yet the villagers that evening had affected never to have heard of him, much less to owe him an allegiance. Yes, my mission for the pacification of the region was failing fast. My cargo of cotton had been translated into slaves. I had lost two-thirds of the Enfields. However, the discovery of a seam of coal might be set on the credit side. The presence of coal would make the construction of a railroad-line through the isthmus a very much sounder speculation; and the owner of a coal-mine may be pretty sure of finding friends at Capel Court who will turn him into quite a comfortable little king. No use in showing Rachinskiy my find, yet that igneous substance now reposing in my pocket could well bring pros-perity and civilisation to his kingdom with an effectiveness which the Enfields could not match. I, however, was bound to return to

Rachinskiy. With or without treaties, and rifles, and prospects of trade, however empty-handed, I must keep faith with Hoolaghan, and return to Alatstchinsk. Supposing Hoolaghan was not a hostage, though – supposing he and the Princess had employed my absence to forward their own intrigues? Well, I could only perform my promise, and return, as Regulus had returned from Rome to Carthage. On this resolution I slept.

When I enquired next morning for the road to Alatstchinsk, which town I conceived to be at no great distance, my interlocutor conceded inadvertently what direct questions had not elicited, namely, that Prince Rachinskiy was known to be mustering a strong force at Alatstchinsk. Deceit is second nature in this country of treachery and misrule, and a direct question will always be countered with a lie. The *khedkhota*'s intelligence, however, was followed up by a cool demand for twice the payment I had last night agreed for our lodgings. He had been from home, he said, and I had imposed on his underlings. His hand rested on his pistol as he spoke. My reply was, to laugh at his beard and order out Tack, and our one remaining packhorse, upon the march.

We had not cleared the village fields when, with a rattle of weapons, there sprang up from amongst the Indian corn a dozen or so of the young bloods of the place to bar our way. They milled about us in an insulting way, demanding their money and whipping themselves into a sufficient fury over their grievance to rob and murder. It was necessary to act rapidly. We were close to the village, so that the men had not troubled to catch up their horses to intercept us. If we could break through their ranks without wounding or killing a man, we might make a run for it – and perhaps get clear, too, for they would not pursue us very far if they had no blood-injury to avenge.

Accordingly, seeming ready to bargain, I took out the purse of *paras* which I always keep in readiness to answer the endless importunities for *baksheesh* of Eastern travel. The whole purse was not worth sixpence I suppose. I opened the string and put in my hand. The hubbub decreased as all eyes watched me. Suddenly taking out a fistful of *paras* I sowed them broadcast amongst the men around me, the little light coins pattering down like fish-scales on heads and clothing and road. At the same instant I set spurs to my pony, lashed Tack's mount and the pack-animal with my whip, and scurried away amongst the rocks and wal-nut-orchards. Not a shot followed us. Looking back from the fringe of forest I saw, as I had calculated, that every man's hand was turned against his neighbour in the grand hunt for *paras*, and the fury into which they had been whipping themselves to murder us had found expression in as first-rate a free-for-all as you might find at a Tipperary horse-fair.

We soon steadied our pace, and followed our track through the sparser forest of sweet chestnut and hazel which here clothed the uplands. The night had been cold, and the large leaves of the chestnuts, rusty and tooth-edged as saws, had dropped from the trees into deep shoals, allowing windows in the branches above through which the sunlight chequered down upon us as we rode. Through those same windows we saw snow-peaks above the forest. One of these peaks I now recognised as a landmark visible from the tower in which I had been confined. We had not far to go.

The nearer we drew to our journey's end, the more certain became I that, to assure myself that my rifles might be employed for peace-keeping and the furtherance of Sir D——'s purposes, I must make it my concern to place the rifles in hands I had first approved. In short I must judge Rachinskiy's intentions to act honourably before I gave him the Enfields.

It will sound risible, no doubt, to a reader with one foot on the fender of his library fire, and a world of English comforts about him, that a poor wanderer struggling over the Caucasus with a parcel of firearms for a savage princeling, should concern himself with "honour" and "good faith", and other ornaments generally thought to be very much above the station of so abandoned a mortal; but, I don't know how it is, the significance of those weapons had increased for me in proportion as their number had dwindled. I believe I would have sold my life in defence of that last dozen of Enfields, and chests of Pigou and Wilks' powder – a fact I never would have believed of myself when I had undertook the mission at Stamboul. As their number became token, so the token augmented its consequence to me. The right use of my burden, I believed, would alone justify my journey. I must discover how the land lay at Alatstchinsk, before I gave Rachinskiy the rifles.

It was for this reason that I hid them. Not far from the tower in which

[71]

I had been the Princess's "guest" there lies a valley, suddenly come upon, in which a waterfall spouts over a crag and, after a break upon a ledge, plunges seventy or more feet into a gorge. Concealed by the falls is a cavern, accessible only by a dangerous scramble across rapid water. Now this cave occurred to me as a hiding-place for the Enfields, and accordingly I set a course across the hills to hit off the falls.

It is necessary that I should here reveal the circumstances of my first acquaintance with this hiding-place, else a future portion of my narrative will be rendered unintelligible by an omission which delicacy would otherwise urge me to insist upon.

I had been out riding with the Princess a short time before my departure for Constantinople – better mounted than myself, and surrounded by her Persian greyhounds, she was ever ahead of me on such excursions, whilst I was ever spurring to keep her in view – when she had vanished as if the earth had swallowed her. Casting about the folds of the hills, I had suddenly come upon the falls in their hidden valley. There on a turf shelf above the smoke and thunder of the rift she sat her horse like an image, waiting for me.

"Come," she called, her voice high and clear through the Cerberus-like roar of the falls, "come, I will show you a secret."

Before I was well out of my saddle she had left her dogs with her pony in the shade of three Caucasian oaks which stood nearby, and had set out across the rapids. The falls, which were of no great volume at that time of year, made first a leap of ten or twelve feet onto a ledge some two or three yards wide, then leaped down clear over seventy feet of sheer rock. It was along this limestone ledge between the two falls, horribly narrow and swept by a racing current, that the Princess was darting from stone to stone ahead of me. Her dogs, which I had never trusted, snarled at my heels as I walked down to the river, but came no further, though looking with longing after their mistress. I was soon stumbling through the rapids behind her, the stream so swift and cold that an aching chill penetrated in a moment to the very marrow of my shin-bones. She seemed immune to cold. On my left hand the river plunged seventy feet into its tumbled pool seething half-seen through mists of spray: on my right, the lesser falls spouted and spattered in my ear: whilst the furious current tore at my footholds. When I looked up from my work of wading, the Princess had again vanished. Half-way along the ledge, heaven knows how, a thicket of holly had taken root on a rocky islet suspended between the cataract's two leaps. To this life-preserver in the tumult of waters I scrambled, and soon stood, drenched with spray, amid the shining wet leaves of the holly. I saw then that the islet led back into a cave half-veiled by the tumbling water. Watching me through "the dangling water-smoke" was the Princess. I stepped, as she must have done, through the icy shock of the falls, and found myself in a dim stone cavern filled with the hollow clamour of the cataract. The Princess stood with her back to me, cutting with her whip at the ferns which had taken root round the lips of the cave-mouth. Her riding dress, loose pantaloons and a long tunic, had been as thoroughly drenched as my own, and the blue material clung to the outline of her figure. By the conventions and usages of intercourse between the sexes, she was at my mercy; and yet, I know not how, I never felt myself more in her power than at that moment. "So," she said, turning, and running her whip between her fingers, "you find your way. Now I show you more."

Of the cave there was indeed nothing more to show than my first glance had taken in. Ample room there was to hide an arsenal of weapons – if one could transport them across that sloping ledge between the two falls which I remembered scrambling along behind the Princess.

Tack and I found the falls without difficulty. Due to an exceptionally dry season – which was to be continued until the fatal floods of November – the wasted river was less of an obstacle now, in mid-October, than it had been in June, and little Tack and I soon had the remnants of our cargo of arms stacked against the back of the cave, where we strewed a covering of ferns and loose scree over them.

*   *   *

That evening Tack and I rode down into the town of Alatstchinsk, where I had arranged long since to rendez-vous with Rachinskiy when I should return from the West. As we approached the little wooden town through gardens and orchards on the slopes of its eminence, I confess that my heart beat uncomfortably quick at the uncertainty of our reception, though all was cheerfully enough lighted by the setting sun.

Guardian ranks of beeches wore their autumn facings of shabby gold as we rode between them towards Rachinskiy's palace.

In my absence I had built a castle of hopes upon Rachinskiy. I had met him but once, when he had granted me an audience before my departure. Freedom from the Russian or Turkish yoke: the military strength to pacify his kingdom: the encouragement of trade with the West, and the encouragement of a native manufactory to supply that trade: these had seemed to be the Prince's objectives, and the objectives of his daughter Mazi.

But, how very small a town Alatstchinsk in reality was, as Tack and I rode through it! How small a town to nurse such pretentions! Of course, before I had gone away to the West, it had seemed quite large enough for its purpose, a capital in proportion to its provinces; but now I found it a mere village. The beeches overtopped the wooden houses, which were raised on stilts, like hen-coops, above the dust and rubbish of the road. Was this the seat of government on whose behalf I had negotiated with Lord Stratford at Therapia, the *entrepôt* of trade through which I had urged Sir Daniel Farr to build a railroad-line to the Caspian? The woodsmoke of cooking-fires rose into the windless evening light. Our three unladen ponies scuffed through drifts of fallen leaves into the town square, and we came upon the palace.

I had forgotten that it was but half-built since Paskievich had burnt the town in '29. A scaffold made of unbarked branches, and sundry rude ladders and piles of planks, crippled one wing of the plain wooden building. At the gate lounged a group of armed men discussing a bottle of *vodky* which they passed from hand to hand. One of them, after taking a swig and wiping his mouth, led us by an arch into the palace courtyard, where we got down. I saw that little Tack's eyes had grown as round as gooseberries at the magnificence of our surroundings, whilst his mouth hung open in frank astonishment. I was comforted at this: it is, after all, upon persons such as Tack from the frog-skinning *aul* at Zinzikir, rather than upon persons such as myself from London, that the capital and palace of a local prince should impose its authority. There is no call for the nigger king to build himself a Versailles, when a little hunting-box will do the work of brow-beating his subjects quite as well.

As I reflected thus, we were brought indoors, and a servant undertook to show me into the Prince's presence. Tack I put in charge of another servant, with orders to see him fed and quartered, for he had come through the journey like a good 'un, and I intended keeping him by me. When my arms were demanded of me I gave them up, smiling at the recollection of Lord Stratford's attaché's exquisite dismay when I had handed him my sword at Therapia. I was led down a dark passage with a creaky floor, in which passage unwelcome callers were no doubt assassinated, and found myself announced into the audience hall.

It was a large, raftered, comfortless chamber like a tithe-barn, with raised benches against the walls. Its only decorations – if wreaths of greasy smoke and a strong smell of pig be excepted – were trophies of arms. At its further end two chairs, covered in rugs, stood near one another before a crackling fire, their high backs concealing their occupants. Round the sides of these chairs two heads now protruded themselves, and two faces regarded me. One was that of Quin Hoolaghan in a disarray of fair hair and whiskers: the other was the swarthy, heavy-lidded countenance of Prince Rachinskiy. It was when they got upon their legs and collided that I realised they were drunk.

They had collapsed back into their chairs with a hoot of merriment, but now staggered upright again. Hoolaghan started towards me with the *chibouk* in his hand trailing out smoke and grasped my shoulder – whether to greet me, or to steady himself, was in doubt.

"Well, well, well," he said, "well, well. You've come back, so, you reliable man. Devil a bit did I believe we would see you again. I never thought it. Did I now, Prince dear? Did I ever believe we would be seeing his dear old phiz again, did I? Come now, my man, come on in to the fire with you now. This is the Prince, you know him I think? No ceremony, he's a good Christian man, so he is. Now – a little toddy? Take a little toddy will you. A *vodky todky*. There you are. If I had a lemon I'd put it in for you, but the place is so damp all the lemons have grown beards on them like Jews." He had leaned close to confide this news to me, with a beaker of the fire-water, and now he stood back. "No, never one of me believed you'd be back, once you was at Const – Consta – Constable. But herself did, mind. Oh, yes. Sure of it, so she was. He'll be back, she said, just as if she'd laid a spell on you. Well, right for her. Right for the Princess."

During all this discourse the Prince had been clutching hold of his chair to arrest his swaying, and regarding me with that dulled and stupefied expression, at once contemptible in a man, and alarming in a despot who may order any barbarity on a whim. The glance of his half-closed eyes fell on me balefully. Now he said thickly in Turkish "Where is the army?"

A peal of laughter from Hoolaghan greeted this sally. Spilling toddy generously about the hearth the Irishman repeated, "Where *is* your army, indeed my boy? Is it left at the gate is it? Sit down, sit down now, and tell us which army you brought with you. Sit down, sure the Prince doesn't mind if you sit or stand."

As a man will with a boon-companion, Hoolaghan seemed to suppose that the prince shared his own mood and character. I however, stone sober, thought differently, and preferred to stand until the Prince told me otherwise. He seemed to me as dangerous as a drugged snake. Facing him I answered his question:

"Sir, Omer Pasha's army of forty thousand men marched from Soukhum Kaleh ten days since, and approach Your Highness's kingdom by way of the Ingour River. With him are English officers whom I talked with at Constantinople. They count upon Your Highness's forces to join them against the Russian enemy."

"So, they come!" The Prince held out his glass, into which Hoolaghan slopped liquor. "They come!"

I don't know that I have ever seen a more malignant look of satisfaction on a man's face. One might have supposed that he was a spider, and Omer Pasha's rumoured approach was the trembling of a fly at the extremity of his web. He lowered himself back into his chair, drinking, spilt liquor glistening down from his mouth into his beard. Hoolaghan too reclaimed his chair, put his pipe in his mouth, and looked ready to snooze in the heat of the fire. I stood by the hearth regarding them for a moment or two. In the stillness a rat ran across one of the rafters bridging the room and disappeared into a crack in the plastered wall. I bowed to the more or less torpid Prince, touched with my foot Hoolaghan's long boots stretched out to the fire, and walked out of the audience-chamber followed by the guard who had brought me thither.

What best to do? I had built, as I say, a castle in Spain upon this prince and his progressive intentions. Now I find a half-tipsy savage carousing with an Irishman in his rat-infested hall – this is "the baseless fabric of my vision"! Should I leave at once, secretly, tonight, and ride for the coast, and take ship to Constantinople and the West? There came into my mind the neatness of Miss E— F—'s arrangements in that pasteboard-looking little dwelling by the Bosphorus, which seemed from this remove to be the acme of all I had forfeited. "Would God no Argo ere had winged the seas (thought I) to Colchis through the blue Symplegades".

I was striding down the dark passage with my regrets, and intending a walk in the open to decide my course, when I collided with a rustling apparition hurrying the other way. My hands were upon the creature's shoulders – its own soft hand was on my arm – she gasped – it was the Princess Mazi. The warmth communicated by her touch still throbbed in her voice when she spoke:

"Oh! It is you! I had heard, and was running quick. Really you have done it, you have come!"

"I'm told you trusted me for it."

"So long. So so long away. You have – " She looked at me enquiringly, hesitantly, in the half-light of the passage where we still stood close together, "You have seen the Prince? Yes, you have seen how he is. Come. You are hungry?"

She led the way by corridors and stairs into regions of the "palace" where bare boards were a good deal ameliorated and feminised by carpets and wall-hangings. Indeed the room into which she brought me at last was a pleasant little curtained parlour with a bright fire winking and glinting its reflections into picture-glass and furniture. Dozing in her chair, her knitting in her lap, sat old Hannah.

"See, Hannah, who is come!" The Princess had not the scruples I should have felt in wakening the old woman. "Wake up! You must fetch some foods. Some rice, some *kabobs*, some wine. You will drink wine? See, Hannah, he is come!"

I had not particularly remembered Hannah as my ally, yet now she clasped my hands and looked up into my face with a tearful satisfaction, before she was bustled off to roust out the victuals. Left alone with me, the Princess's rush of animation lost pace a little. She brushed a strand or two of her inky hair under her cap, and folded her hands on her plum-coloured skirt, and composed herself on a sofa. I went to the fire.

"I have not been in so cozy a boudoir since I left the Bosphorus," I said, merely to have something to say.

"Oh! So, Captain, you were in many boudoirs on the Bosphorus? Is it what has kept you so long away? So long away from my father?" she added quickly.

I recounted to her the thousand delays and dissemblings and deceits attendant upon any business a man might try to prosecute at the Ottoman capital, and described the slow hours I had passed in kicking my heels between Pera and Therapia and Stamboul. I found that she had little notion of the geography of these places, and no standard by which to conceive of the extent of Constantinople, or of the multitude of its people. That a woman should appear to be an accomplished lady, and talk French and play upon the pianoforte, and should yet suppose Piatigorsk to be as great a city as London or Paris, was ever surprising to me. I had in my baggage Murray's *Handbook for Turkey*, brought out the year previous, and I undertook to show her the maps next day.

Attendants had meantime brought food, and placed tables, and made all ready for me to eat. I learned from them that Tack was already fed and cared for below. These servants the Princess now dismissed, and told Hannah too to retire into the room giving off the boudoir, which was perhaps her bedroom. "Go," she said, at a look of protest from the old woman, "go in to bed. But you may leave opened the door."

I was now made to seat myself before the savoury messes smoking in their brass platters on the trays, whilst the Princess herself poured wine into a goblet for me. She then took herself off to a low chair beside the fire, in which she sat with her legs drawn under her, and looked into the flames.

Although the purpose of my journey to the West had often enough been discussed by us, she did not now question me directly as to its results. Perhaps she supposed that I would consider her father the only proper recipient of my news. Nevertheless, since it was with herself, on our rides together from the tower, that my plans had been formulated – it was with her that I had been intimate – I told her all. I told her of my meeting with young L— O—, who was even now with Omer Pasha's army ten or twelve days march inland from Soukhum, and with whom I had made a *rendez-vous* for the Prince's forces on the Ingour river. I told her of my talks with Sir D— F—, and of his anxiety to foster a trading route through the Caucasus which might eclipse the Trebizond monopoly. I told her of the favour which Lord Stratford (the Great Elchi whose fame had reached even to Piatigorsk) had offered towards the scheme for pacifying the Caucasus and for promoting trade – and I confessed what little practical use his Lordship's favour had been.

I say that I told the Princess all, but, as I talked, I debated with myself as to whether or not I should tell her also of my visit to the *konak* of Ismail Bey, and of my acceptance, despairing of help from any other quarter, of the poisoned gift of gold and guns offered me by that testudineous old creature in his vault of treasures.

I had not decided upon my course when a scream burst from the room into which old Hannah had retired. It was the scream of a child. I thought myself quickly upon my feet, but the Princess was before me. In the doorway of the room her rushing figure met the white rushing apparition of a child. This she swept up into her arms, and kissed, as though the open lips of love should swallow down that little atom of nightgowned fear which had screamed out. Now the old nursemaid could be heard calling out of the dark: "Is the captain not away, ma'am? I canna come out if the captain's not away."

The Princess spoke thrillingly: "Go back to your sleep, I shall keep Shkara with me. My dear, my darling," continued her vibrant tone to the child, as she covered the nestling head with kisses, "be at peace, be at peace." Her woman's figure seemed to complete itself in the burden of the child, her woman's nature to be expressed in solicitude for her offspring.

Her offspring? Yes – that it was her child, I had not a moment's doubt. Yet never had this infant, nor her marriage, been revealed by the least allusion. How little, after all, I had known of her! Tightly the little arms clasped her neck, gently and carefully, as she sat down, the Princess eased their embrace until the child turned its head, and looked into the firelight. With an anxiety I could not help, nor explain, I studied the small face. That same sleek dark hair as was her mother's surrounded the ivory-white oval, the black lashes, the reddened lips. Were the child's eyes so narrow, even aslant? – or was it the effect of sleepiness? I seemed to catch in the slant of those eyes a hint of the wastes of Tartary before she closed them, and again buried her face in the lovely curve of her mother's neck. She was five, perhaps six.

"We have suffered so much of worry," her mother began in a low voice when the child had sighed, and lain still. "She slips never well. Never she slips all the night. Sometime she bump her head, bump! bump! against the wall. Or she wake screaming."

I could have nothing to say to this. Our earlier discussion – wars, treaties, trade – seemed suddenly remote, the distance from council-chamber to nursery, which she had crossed at a stride, into mysteries where I could not follow. To myself and my journey there seemed no chance of her attention returning. I rose, saying that I would retire to the quarters which the servants would have made ready for me. She spared me one white hand from clasping her child, and over this morsel, dropped so to speak from the feast of love, I bent my lips.

Although there had been much to concern me in my reception at this wild Princeling's "palace", and many immediate questions to worry over, the speculations which crowded my head, as I sought sleep in a guest-chamber that night, centred upon the narrow-eyed infant which had now materialised at the heart of the matter. I remembered of course the Princess's tale of her father's attempt to marry her with a Mizurskiy chieftain, in order to secure the Mamisson pass; had the attempt perhaps not wholly failed? Who was the child Shkara's father? The corner of a curtain – a curtain of European clothes, French accent, civilised manners – seemed to have been lifted, admitting a blast of the *semoon*. I looked over the Mamisson to the unhallowed wastes of Tartary which lie beyond the *pylae Caucasia* of Pompey, the gate at the end of the world with which he had hoped to shut out barbarism. Was barbarism to creep in by means of this child's Tartar blood?

*   *   *

Next morning I was sorting through my packs and saddlebags in a courtyard adjoining stables and kitchen quarters when Princess Mazi came out to me.

"I did not know that you had a daughter, Princess," I said, for I had awoken with that night scene still much in my mind.

"Shkara is too young to come on horse with me to the tower," she replied. It was reasonable, for I had been "confined" to the tower

[80]

before my departure. Ere I could take the matter further she said eagerly, "You find the map?"

"The map?" I was non-plussed. "Of the Caucasus?"

"No, no – you have told me last night you are having the map for Constantinople. The hand book?"

"Ah, Murray's *Handbook* – indeed, yes, you shall have it when I – "

"I will take him now. That is him, please?" Her eye had lighted on the red volume, the only book, indeed, in my baggage – perhaps the only book in Mingrelia – and she snatched it up.

"I have your physic," I said. "Drugs and draughts and potions all complete I think. Now," I added with a smile, showing her the medicine-chest I had brought at her express request, "you will be able to set up for a witch again, Princess."

"Ah," she said over her shoulder, walking off with Murray's *Handbook* clasped to her bosom, "send them in to Hannah, please."

I confess to disappointment at the cool reception for the store of drugs which I had been at pains to put together at Constantinople to replenish her long-exhausted stock – a stock which had first secured her ascendancy over other palace women and palace quacks when she had come from Piatigorsk. Advised in my choice by Mme Misseri, by steamer and sloop and pony over some thousands of miles I had carried opium, quinine, sulphate of zinc, seidlitz powders, calomel, tincture of catechu – a hundred and one of such "magic" substances as a modern Medea might require for her spells – and instead Medea had walked off with Murray's *Handbook* under her arm!

How gratified Mr Murray would have been to learn what a customer he had upon the mountains of Mingrelia! She cared nothing for what Murray had to say of Caucasia (which is little enough): no, no – it was at the section describing Constantinople that the volume was ever open for the Princess to pore over, and for Hoolaghan or myself to answer a catechism upon. The maps of the city would be unfolded twenty times a-day, and she would require to be taken, in imagination, a walk down from Pera to the Golden Horn, or to hear the band play outside the hotels in the Piccolo Santo, or to stroll to Droyschmann's for an ice through the Grand Bazaar, or to take a steam-ferry upon the Bosphorus from the Galata Bridge station – in short, to spend her time just as I had been obliged to fret mine away in those weeks of idleness which, though exasperating at the time, had now, in retrospect from a wooden "palace" at Alatstchinsk, something of sweetness even to myself. The scale of the maps she could not comprehend; thought we were "pulling her leg" when we asserted that from the Seven Towers to Pera was five English miles, or an hour's ride on one of her ponies through streets of houses all the way. Hoolaghan, indeed, did "pull her leg" a good deal in depicting the marvels of Byzantium, taking, as I thought, great liberties, which I supposed to be allowed to him on account of his position (so often assumed by an Irishman) of "court jester".

Hoolaghan's cheerfulness altogether was wonderful. Though groaning a good deal over his breakfast on account of headache – a penalty of drinking *vodky-todky* which seemed to surprise him afresh each morning – he would rapidly recover his good humour, joking with the Princess in his easy way if she was by, or teasing Hannah if she was not, or showing the child Shkara how to play at cat's-cradle, or how to cast the shadows of animals upon a wall by manipulating the hands before a candle-flame. He could devise a game to amuse Shkara out of a couple of sticks, if need be, for his mind had that trivial turn to it which only seeks to amuse, never to learn or to instruct, so that the pastime of a game was as necessary to him as it was to the child. In this fashion he drank with the Prince, and pored over Murray with the Princess, and played with the child, making himself the equal of each and the critic of none. For months he had been satisfied to play the rôle of everyone's friend whilst I had been gone, and of course the whole household thought him a very fine fellow in consequence.

Perhaps it was the ambiguity in Hoolaghan's position, perhaps it was that I conceived that the Princess had not told me all she had told Hoolaghan as to Shkara, but I did not feel myself immediately inclined to confide in anyone at Alatstchinsk the secret of the hidden Enfields, or to tell them of my discovery of a seam of coal. I had determined that my influence and my gifts should be used for the pacification which would secure trade, and I could not as yet be sure of Rachinskiy or Hoolaghan or the Princess.

Many "audiences" were held between Rachinskiy, Hoolaghan and myself. The Prince would squat cross-legged on the wide bench running round the walls of his durbar-hall – the chairs in which he and Hoolaghan caroused at night were removed by day – whilst I sat cross-legged not far off and Hoolaghan, who said he couldn't sit in that fashion, lounged or sat as he liked. But we were never alone, and never uninterrupted for five minutes together. In and out would scamper groups of excited savages, quarrelling in screeches, or clamouring to the Prince *en masse* for a ruling on some vexatious point, or bawling out a budget of news at him. Meanwhile the humble, and diseased, and destitute, crept in and out at the mercy of kicks and ill-usage from any officers of the court who could spare a moment from their quarrels. The fire of chestnut-wood, which was ever kept in a blaze, volleyed out a perfect fountain of sparks and explosions, adding to the uproar and threatening to burn down the whole palace at a moment's notice. The hall had not the settled atmosphere in which to devise a strategy or plan a campaign. I began to suffer the same impatience with vacillation and irresolution that I had suffered beside the Bosphorus. Fifteen days had now passed since Omer Pasha's force had commenced its march from Soukhum: even at the snail's pace of an oriental army, they must surely now be upon the Ingour, if not beyond it.

"Let us send scouts, at all events," I begged the Prince.

"Is it yourself would go with them, just?" enquired Hoolaghan.

"If the Prince wishes it," I replied. Did Hoolaghan want me out of his way for some purpose?

The Prince's sluggish brown eyes watched us. He had a mud-coloured skin much marked by the smallpox, and a roll of fat above each eye which imparted a look of petulance to his glance – of calculation and petulance. However, he agreed to despatch a flying column into the plains to gain intelligence of Omer Pasha's movements. With this I had to content myself.

"Why in heaven's name is Rachinskiy so devilish cool about throwing in his force?" I asked Hoolaghan when we were alone.

He laughed. "Wait till your man wins down there," said he, "and then old Rachinskiy will send down his rapparoos to put in their hands with the pillaging there'll be."

"Well, I shall go down to Omer Pasha myself if he don't soon commit himself, I shall indeed,' said I.

"Aye, well, you will so, I suppose – if His Highness allows it to you," he added. To this insinuation I made no reply, but walked off.

What Hoolaghan wished for from his position at Rachinskiy's side I could not determine. Perhaps, having stumbled upon a berth where life went on pleasantly enough from day to day, according to his notions, and where his wants were "all found" – as the advertisements for servants say – perhaps he required nothing more, except that I shouldn't upset the apple-cart. I do not know. His cheeriness was, as I say, wonderful – when it was not exasperating. For I had no intention of living out my life as the dependant, or the prisoner, of such a petty tyrant as Rachinskiy, who would not have thought twice about having our throats cut, if he conceived that our usefulness to him had ended, which he certainly would conceive once Omer Pasha had left the country.

Hoolaghan's apple-cart was to be upset, however. The Prince's scout came in three days after, to report that Omer Pasha's army of Turks was encamped on a plain near the village of Ertiscal, within a day's march of the Ingour. It was now or never. I exerted all my eloquence to end the Prince's procrastination of action, and to exhort him to commit his forces to the campaign. I succeeded in part: a detachment of seventy horsemen was put under immediate orders to make contact with Omer Pasha. At first the Prince intended that "Colonel" Hoolaghan should have the command, and that I should remain at Alatstchinsk; but upon my protestation that my arrangement for the rendez-vous had been a personal one with young L— O—, he ordered that both of us should ride with his irregulars, and command them jointly.

2

Then began a pleasant interlude. Still the fine autumn weather continued, the country we crossed was wild and beautiful, our mission was an active and a romantic one. Hoolaghan, too, was an amusing enough companion for such a venture, whose carefree good humour induced a sense of *joie-de-vivre*, whilst command of such a rascally set as our "Mingrelian Lancers" (as we dubbed them) was a novelty to be enjoyed. I could not help comparing my present high spirits, as we jingled down towards the plains, with the vexed and apprehensive state of my mind as I had toiled up with Tack from Zikinzir. When I said as much to Hoolaghan he replied,

[84]

"My dear man, you were the weak one then, and now you're the strong. There's all the difference in life between the two."

There was his philosophy "in a nutshell": to be comfortable on the side of the strong. Well, it had carried him safe through a good many tight places, which is more than may be said for many a philosophy more profound. I heard a good deal of his history, on the march by day and over our camp fire by night; but he was in the habit of so contradicting at night what he had related as a fact in the morning, that to construct his biography would have puzzled me sorely. Was the old stone house which he described as the scene of his childhood, on the lake shore in County Clare, was it a considerable estate, which he had forfeited by taints of Fenianism, or was it a famished little Irish holding unable to support his eleven brothers and sisters and himself through the famine times of the '40s? Had he spent his youth fighting the evictions and burnings of the absent landlords in the West, or had he passed it in dancing with those very landlords' daughters at the Dublin Castle balls, and in hunting over Tipperary, and in running up debts he could not settle for horseflesh and faro? By another account, he seemed to have held a commission in the 43rd Foot, which he had sold out in disgust in 1849 – "for d'ye know, I never saw a corpse?" – and had then set out on the travels which had put him aboard the Varna steamer on which I had met him in '50 with Lord V— and poor F—. Whether debts or disgust had occasioned his quitting Europe, I do not know to this day. Since then he had been in Persia, where he had found employment under the Matamet at Shuster in putting down a revolt of the Bakhtiari, and had risen (so he said) to hold a colonel's command. He had a thousand good stories, but they were as random as a handful of gemstones loose in his pocket, for no thread of purpose, no general intention, no moral apparatus, linked together his experiences, or strung his gemstones on a cord. His philosophy as to the comfort of siding with the strong he had perhaps learned from early comparisons between Dublin Castle and the cabins of Clare, and had certainly continued in fighting for the Matamet against the mountaineers; but I wondered as to the strength of his present position.

"And how did you come to choose your side in these wars in the Caucasus?" I asked him.

"I did not," said he with a laugh, lying back on his elbow with his long legs stretched out to the fire, and the stars coming out over his head, "I thought, would I maybe try my luck with the Russans, indeed; that was the first fancy I took."

"In the Crimea, you mean?"

"No,no!" said he, "faith, that's not a war at all for a man who may choose his war. That's a terrible business, I believe. No, it was against this fellow Shamyl I thought would I have a run, over in Daghestan there," he jerked his thumb over his shoulder, quite as though we were upon one tennis-ground, and Shamyl's match upon another next door, "but, when I came to look into it, I couldn't see which side I'd be taking at all. There's never one of the two is odds on to win. When I made out that, I was for coming away out of it. And indeed, riding away I was, when I fell into our Princess's net. Fell hook and line. As you did yourself I suppose."

There was that about Quin Hoolaghan which made it impossible not to become intimate with him, though experience of such natures as his has taught me to entrust no secret to a man who is loyal only to himself. I was neither so frank nor, I hope, so contradictory in my yarning as was he, yet I was encouraged by his easy intimacy to speak of the past. Such were the confidences that his sympathy elicited – for he censured nothing he heard, the recipe *par excellence* for extracting confessions – that once or twice I was on the brink of confiding in him altogether. As it was, I told him of the hand Ismail Bey had had in mounting my expedition to Mingrelia. I told him of the incidents of my march, but not of my intentions – I showed him my gemstones, so to speak, but not the cord of purpose they were strung upon. He laughed heartily at Nogai's rapid conversion of the cotton cargo into female flesh-and-blood. The tale of my wanderings with Tack, and of the ambuscade at the bridge, amused him too.

"And what became of the rifles?" he asked carelessly at the end.

"I – I hid them."

"Hid them did you?" He looked at me with a half-mocking glint in his eye. "Had you the idea of a rising in your head, had you? Of a coup d'état? To knock over old Rachinskiy? Was that the idea you had in it when you hid the Enfields?"

I laughed. I never had harboured so wild a scheme.

"I've considered it," said he. "A little kingdom. I've been on the look-out for a little kingdom all my own since I saw some of those Bakhtiari gentry suited so snug with the little kingdoms they have to rule in the mountains. A Paradise they have of it! I swear you couldn't come closer to heaven on this earth. Now, consider how it would be, to reign in old Rachinskiy's shoes."

" 'To reign is worth ambition', eh?" said I, Milton's words coming into my head.

"Aye, well worth ambition."

"Even though they are the Devil's words, and he speaks of ruling Hell?"

He was not disconcerted. He shifted his back more comfortably against his saddle-bags, and balanced his tumbler of *vodky* on his knee. "Faith," said he, "heaven and hell – I believe there isn't a sixpen-nyworth of difference between the two of them, that we'd recognise, you and I. Not if you subtract away all the clap-trap of morality and look at them plain."

"Ah, if you take out morality, of course," I said. "Take out morality, and all's one at once. Saint and devil, advocate and adversary, we've no light left to steer by, if you put out morality."

"Whisha, Vinegar," said he, "whisha – the longer the years you and I live in this wild world, the surer we must be that there ain't one straw to choose between a saint's plan for the world and a devil's plan for it. I gave up morality when I looked about me in County Clare in the hunger times, and couldn't tell if it was God or the Devil had brought innocent creatures to that pass."

I could say nothing to this. He went on, "I've served all sides, I suppose, and this one thing I have learned, that I'll trust no heart but my own. It has the only workings I understand. What's in the other fellow's, when he wants to tell me who is my enemy and who is my friend – what's in your Sir D— F—'s heart, or in Herr N—'s, when they give you out orders – why, dear man, we've no more idea of it than what's in the moon. I'll take no orders but what I give myself, and I won't look far down the path ahead of me, if I find I'm well suited where I am – not far enough to see if it leads to heaven or hell anyway."

I recollected that we were on our way together, very probably, into an action, when one likes to be sure of one's friends. "And how should you like to have your back against a man with your views," I asked him, "if it came to a fight? A man who acts by no rule but his own advantage?"

"Bless you," said he, kicking the fire into sparks, "I'll tell you what it is though: I'd sooner have my back against a wall than against any man living."

After a pause, during which he sipped and smoked contentedly, and I resolved to depend upon him not at all in the coming action, I asked, "And have you decided to take on Rachinskiy's little kingdom for yourself? Have you and the Princess got up a plot together?"

"Ah," he said, "here it wouldn't do. With Constantinople taking an interest in the place, for trade and the like, it wouldn't do. We shouldn't hold it, not with a hundred Enfields." He turned on me suddenly. "Where did you hide the rifles, though?"

"There were few enough left in the end."

He gazed at me, his good humour unruffled by my refusal to tell him. "Now," he mused, "where the devil would he hide them? In a hut? No. In a cave? Aye, in a cave. Now, where is there a cave? I have it! Under the waterfall – you've hid them under the waterfall, ain't I right?"

I was taken aback to learn that the cavern under the falls was not a secret between myself and the Princess, as I had supposed. But I would not show him my chagrin, and made no reply. As soon as he had found out where the rifles were concealed he dropped the subject, and took up some other. He was incapable of silence, words seeming to appear on his lips at the very instant a thought flew into his head. I had expected there to be a difficulty as to restricting the quantity of liquor consumed on our march, but he was as content with one tumbler of *vodky* by our camp-fire, as he had been with twenty in Rachinskiy's hall. With a drunkard he drank, out of good fellowship and the desire to please his company; in a monastery no doubt he would have risen at five and read Mattins, and dined off bread and water, if it would have persuaded the monks to vote him the best fellow going.

On the third day of our march we had come down upon the plains of the Ingour, and were feeling our way through its swamps and thickets as we proceeded down its stream. The discipline of our wild troopers had improved wonderfully under the simple British expedient – unknown in Eastern armies – of paying the men promptly in coin. Hoolaghan had been thoroughly infected with the oriental system of witholding pay, and allowing the soldiers to live off the land, taking what they required by force, and thus perpetuating to the end of time the feuds and ill-feeling between one tribe and another; but I would not have it, paying the men their money from my own store of gold acquired of Ismail Bey. In this way I carried out my plan of devoting to worthy ends the means put into my hands by that evilly-intentioned source at Stamboul. Our troopers, in consequence, purchased their requirements from villagers eager to do a trade with the *nizam* on these novel terms, and, moreover, attributed to me as their paymaster, rather than to Hoolaghan, the superior command. Word of our coming spread ahead of us, and women and children from the *auls* would come out to our camp with a basket of eggs to sell, or a sheaf of Indian corn cobs, or a scrawny cock tucked under an arm, as soon as we had pitched our tents.

I was contemplating this scene with some satisfaction on an evening we had encamped close to the Ingour, thinking that such a picture might serve for an illustration of how a warring country may be pacified by honest trade, when Hoolaghan, who had been out posting pickets, rode up to the door of my tent shouting out that he had heard a number of single shots down the river, which he proposed to reconnoitre. I at once sprang up and said that I would accompany him. Little Tack, who had promoted himself to be my orderly, and interpreter, and general dogsbody, of course gallopped after us.

The sun was sinking as we rode out of the camp into a low country of swamp interspersed with the stubble of Indian corn and patches of tangled forest, towards the village of Roukhi. It was not easy to determine the main branch of the Ingour, which divided and sub-divided itself into a perfect network of channels and oozing marshes, but we kept to our course southward, and strained eyes and ears for sight or sound of "the military". I checked Hoolaghan's pace by holding up my hand.

"The last thing we want to do," I said in a low voice, "is to ride into a Russian outpost."

"I don't know that at all," he whispered back, "would you not as soon join in with the Russian as the Turk, if we was to run into him first? For I know Rachinskiy don't give a shilling which we do."

I smiled, not knowing if he was serious; but I determined that I alone would command, in the event of battle, even if Hoolaghan must be put in irons to effect it. Very soon afterwards, as we picked our way by a woodcutters' path through a scrub of willow and alder, a deep-throated bellow arrested us. It was surely the shout of human throats? We were shocked to a standstill, our rifles raised. Another ragged huzza, a cheer from a hundred throats, resounded through the woods, and another, and another yet, cheers like a salvo of shells bursting above the swamps. Hoolaghan and Tack looked at me uncertainly; but I had let my rifle drop on my saddle-bow, and I smiled at their alarm. I knew the meaning of those "huzzas", which I had heard at sunset before, in the valleys of Koordistan where the Turkish *nizam* was encamped. "It is the Turkish army cheering the Sultan before it eats his dinner," I told them. "Now we have but to get through their pickets, and we are at home."

It is a matter of fact that we never saw a Turkish picket, and were into the camp before we had realised it, where a couple more of sunburnt and bearded horsemen with their native servant excited no attention. Outside one of the first tents we came upon, pitched by a little wood, we discovered the agreeable *vignette* of young L— O— himself, swinging back and forth in a hammock formed by placing a blanket over the thick tendrils of a vine which hung between two trees, whilst his supper was a-cooking nearby. Hoolaghan and I dismounted, introductions were effected, and we were soon discussing an excellent bottled stout which was, apparently, amongst the stores which the European officers had insisted upon dragging up from Soukhum. I quite thought that Hoolaghan, who had not seen a bottle of stout since 1849, would break down altogether.

When I had met with L— O— at Constantinople I had of course taken *cum grano salis* his pretention to authority in Omer Pasha's command – he was the cocksure type of young Englishman who supposes that by writing a letter to an important personage he has become that personage's confidant, though his letter may not even have been answered – but I was dismayed now to discover his true insignificance. If Omer Pasha's force was to be directed towards pacifying Mingrelia, it would not be because L— O— wished it. He was in that state of high excitement which the crack of a few rifle bullets is apt to induce in a civilian, and was fire-eating retrospectively over some sketching expedition he had made to delineate the enemy's defences across the Ingour, so that we could not have obtained useful intelligence from him, even if he had possessed it. How it was that Omer Pasha had expended twenty days in covering the fifty miles from Soukhum Kaleh, which appeared to be the most fatally significant feature of his present situation – for the exceptionaly rainless autumn weather could not extend forever the campaigning season – this conundrum L— O— could not expound. For my part, having perhaps led L— O— to suppose, at Constantinople, that Prince Rachinskiy would field a formidable force against the Russians, I did not quite like to confess, now, that Hoolaghan and I represented but seventy irregular cavalry to throw in against the enemy in the battle expected on the morrow. For this reason I did not seek an interview with the High Command, or with any other of the several Englishmen in camp, Colonels Simmons and Ballard and Mr Longworth among them. After a supper of sardines and other luxuries, and a pipe by his fireside, L— O— led us back through the Turkish pickets and bade us farewell, swaggering to the last, a perfect arsenal of brand new weaponry disposed about his person, the amateur campaigner to perfection.

Hoolaghan and I rode circumspectly upriver to our own camp, as anxious to avoid patrols of *bashibozuks* as of Cossacks, and eager to put our squadron into trim so that we might be in the saddle at first light. I opined that we should send a despatch to Rachinskiy advising him that his cavalry would be in an action upon that day; but Hoolaghan replied, that the Prince could do nothing to assist us in the fight, and that he certainly would do nothing further until its issue was decided, when he would ally himself with the victor. His seventy irregulars, and ourselves, he was ready to sacrifice "to test the water". Hoolaghan made no criticism against Rachinskiy in this, merely perceiving – and probably perceiving correctly – how a savage prince would behave. What makes a fellow of Hoolaghan's stamp so widely liked, especially by rogues, is that he makes no judgement against anyone, and lacks, indeed, the moral apparatus to form a judgement. Strongly as I might contend his view, that we may not unravel good from bad, I was obliged to concur with his assessment of Rachinskiy's Machiavellianism in this case, and so sent no despatch to Alatstchinsk that night.

For any pretty and sequential account of the Battle of The Ingour I must refer my reader to the works of some of those devotees of Clio who, never having seen action, seem yet possessed of wings to carry them above the smoky confusion of the fight, and to place them upon a calm vantage point from which the Olympian muse clearly discerns, and as clearly describes, the phases, and crises, and turning-points, of battle. A plain soldier, I can only tell what I saw. *Arma virumque cano* . . .

At an early hour of the morning of November 7th we observed the dust-cloud and glitter of the Turkish force advancing from the woods where we had left them the previous night, and marching across some open ground towards the swamps and thickets of the river. Resolving to attach ourselves to the left wing of this advance, we forded a branch of the Ingour, as we knew must be done in order to come to grips with the Russians defending its main course, and rode cautiously along the thickly wooded isle between the two streams of the river. Seeing infantry deploying ahead of us, I left Hoolaghan with our squadron and rode forward to establish our identity. Fortunately Colonel Ballard was in command of these riflemen; he had seen sufficient service with the Turk to be surprised by nothing, let alone by an English gentleman popping up his head out of a swamp and offering him the swords of seventy Mingrelian Lancers, so that he merely asked where the river might be forded. Where we stood upon its bank, this main stream was perhaps a hundred yards across; fast, heavy water running over a bottom of sharp stones. The Russians opposite were keeping up a warm fire upon Ballard's *toffunchees*, who were, however, well placed in the cover of the wood. Bullets sang and cracked about us, or smacked into an oak's trunk, or clipped off a branchlet overhead which floated down through sun and shadow. I had agreed with Ballard to send scouts upstream in search of a ford, and was about to ride off, when there swept into the wood perhaps two hundred Turks at the run, chasing a stout, grey-whiskered old party, all of them scampering along like dervishes and yelling out "Allah akbar!" at the top of their lungs. It was a Turkish attack! – and we were in their path; as, indeed, was the river.

Ballard was perfectly astonished to see these ragged warriors actually overrun his own men's positions and charge through them down to the water's edge, where they began firing off their rifles at the Russian battery opposite without a thought of concealment or cover. Of course they dropped like nine-pins, and might have been decimated had Ballard not succeeded in persuading the old Turkish *bimbashi*, who must have been seventy at least, to withdraw his heroes into the wood.

I rode off at that, and occupied myself for the next hour in trying various points of the bank for a ford. A mile upstream, a number of islets divided up the main stream, and I found that a man could wade from one to another of these, until a mere twenty yards channel separated him from the Russian bank. How deep and rapid was that channel, I could not tell, though little Tack, who had stuck by me like my shadow, volunteered to turn guinea-pig to discover. I reported my find to Ballard, and then returned to my men, who were amusing themselves with rifle-practice at the Russians opposite.

Time passed, and the position seemed unchanged, no crossing having been made in our vicinity. The rattle of small-arms and the occasional boom of artillery continued without check or crescendo. The sun being high, I gave permission for my people to consume whatever provisions they had about them, though myself refusing the viands Tack had procured for me, it being my habit to eat nothing during a battle. Hoolaghan said, "'Tis all ballyhoo, to my mind, the fear of being wounded on a full stomach," and he ate away as if he was on a Maidenhead picnic.

We did not then know that Omer Pasha had effected a crossing of the river lower down, and was marching upon the Russian position from the South; full of impatience, I had ridden over to Ballard again, when we saw columns of men marching upstream through the thicket behind us. On Ballard sending to enquire, we learned that Colonel Simmons had been granted permission to cross the river above, by way of the islets I had reconnoitred, and that this was his force. Determined to attach myself to him, I rode rapidly back to my squadron, and, putting myself at their head, led them upstream towards the ford. It was now about 4 pm.

There is no soldier braver than the Turk, and no soldier worse commanded. At the ford was a scene of utter confusion. Men struggled from isle to isle, the press behind pushing those in front up against the final channel, and in some cases pushing men headlong into the swift, deep stream, who were swept off their legs and carried away. Even the fact of Colonel Simmons having Captain Dymock as his aide, and a Polish officer as his interpreter, could not prevent the Turkish officers spreading contradiction and panic on all sides. It seemed however that the Russians, almost as incompetently commanded as the Turk, had not prepared against an attack in this quarter, for we were not fired upon.

Colonel Simmons was, very understandably, in a state of some excitement, and, on my applying to him for permission to lead my squadron of cavalry first over the final channel, he made it clear that I might "Go to the D—l and take my d—d savages with me" for all he cared about it. I took this for a permission. Clearing a way for ourselves through the crush we reached the river's edge. The water looked twice as swift, and the stream twice as deep, as it had appeared to me when I had reconnoitred the spot with no immediate need to plunge in. The current rushed and foamed amongst rocks which looked horribly slippery, whilst many an eddy showed where sunken snags awaited us. I was obliged to delay, with this horrid prospect before me, until Hoolaghan reported to me that all my people had pushed their way across the islets, and were in place behind me.

Aut nec(k) aut nullus (as you may hear the Melton swells say when cramming a green quad at the Whissendine). With a rousing Hurrah! we plunged in. My little pony was a trump. Though I could feel the current almost float her, and though her struggles to keep her footing were more the contortions of an eel than a horse, she *would* have the honour all to herself of being first ashore, and pushed up the enemy bank full of going just ahead of Hoolaghan and three or four more in the first flight, all of us flinging off the water in fountains. Now the infantry were in the water behind us. I saw one or two poor fellows swept away, but their comrades struggled on regardless, and soon our bank was crowded with bedraggled Turks scurrying about in the trees to rejoin their units.

Impatient for action, our blood roused, Hoolaghan and I led our wild horsemen in a gallop through some open country beyond the woods, to find if we should sweep up any Russian outposts or skirmishers. This proved a mistaken manoeuvre: we were at some distance from the river, and considerably scattered over the country, when heavy firing from the woods signalled that Simmons had engaged the enemy. By the time that we had rallied our Mingrelians, and sped towards the scene, we found that the fun was, alas, over, the battery taken, and the Russians already fled through the woods, as their track bestrewn with knapsacks, greatcoats, muskets, etc, showed. Expecting that my cavalry would now be given the important work of following up and harassing the flying enemy, I sought out Colonel Simmons.

I found him walking among the silenced guns of the Russian battery, surrounded by heaps of the dead which the Turks were already stripping. He formed a picture of the melancholy office of a commander, even in victory. His own losses had been triflng – a mere fifty or so Turks killed – but all sense of triumph was extinguished by the tragic death of an English officer on his staff, Captain Dymock. This catastrophe was, no doubt, the cause of his somewhat curt refusal of my request, to which he added some opprobrious comments upon the character and usefulness of Caucasian light cavalry altogether.

I therefore withdrew. I met with Hoolaghan, as anxious as myself to find work for my people, who had not as yet blooded their lances, except upon some unfortunate villagers. In crossing the field of battle we came across a Turkish *yuzbashi* occupied in stripping the corpse of a Russian officer. I would have expressed my disgust by knocking the creature down, but Hoolaghan, noticing that the Russian's sword was a particularly fine one, had ordered the *yuzbashi* to prise the weapon from the dead man's grasp so that he might try its weight. Evidently the Russian, though fearfully mangled, had been a man of rank and wealth, for the sword was a valuable one. Whilst the Turk was taking the scabbard also from the corpse to give Hoolaghan, I enquired news of the action in which the battery had been taken. His account was so confused that I supposed him to have "led from behind" in the usual Turkish style, but he related one fanciful incident which I scarcely knew whether or not to credit: at the height of the battle, seemingly, the Polish interpreter on Simmons' staff, Hidaiot, had stood up in his stirrups and exhorted the Russians to abandon the field, his Polish cloak and red, fur-trimmed cap (as well as his excellent Russian) convincing the soldiers that a Russian officer was thus urging them – "Fly, my children, fly; you are surrounded and outnumbered by these infidels!"

Whether Hidaiot's ruse had been the cause of it or no, a vastly

[95]

superior force of Russians had certainly fled, abandoning their guns into Omer Pasha's hands. He himself had not crossed the river, nor had he ordered any pursuit of the enemy; the cavalry, indeed, had remained unemployed all day. However, the Ingour might be counted as a victory for the Allies, and I complied with Hoolaghan's suggestion that he should ride immediately for Alatstchinsk so as to apprise Rachinskiy of the fact, and thus secure him to the Allies' cause. I was, I confess, a little uneasy at the alacrity with which Hoolaghan dashed away to the Prince, or perhaps to the Princess; but so long as I had the seventy Lancers in my pay, I felt myself reasonably secure against treachery.

That night, once I had seen my brave people well-established in their camp, I joined L— O— in a very polyglot circle round a blazing wood fire close to Omer Pasha's headquarters, where the snail's pace of the advance to date, and today's failure to pursue a defeated enemy, were very heavily criticised by officers of all nations. We ate our rice, and smoked our pipes, and drank our brandy and water, and wondered at Omer's dawdle, when he had seemed in the summer so awfully anxious to obtain Pélissier's permission to bring his army to the Caucasus for a swift and decisive campaign. Now he had been in the province a month, and had covered but fifty miles. The idea of him relieving Kars at this pace was ridiculous. The weather, moreover, was certain soon to break, and the plain would then dissolve into a mud-bath.

As we officers talked and smoked on one side of our great fire, to its opposite perimeter of warmth were brought wounded men for whom nothing more could be done, Turk and Russian alike, who were laid there in the fire's glow on pallets of Indian corn straw. Never were Europeans so patient under suffering as these poor souls. When a fresh bough was flung crackling upon our fire, and the flames leaped high, they lighted very terrible wounds, and blood-soaked stumps, and ghastly faces. But the sufferers lay mute as their life ebbed, neither moaning nor crying out, until they died, and were silently replaced by another torn body hurrying to the grave.

Of the fight for the passage of the Ingour, my abiding memory will ever be of the great fire hollowing and reddening a space under the trees, its flames lighting upon one side officers of many races who had been drawn to this wild spot, and had survived the fight to warm themselves at the fire, whilst upon its other side were laid down to die the poor peasantry of both armies, like so many faggots which the flame of war consumes. As the fiery sparks gushed upward among the oak-boughs, and expired in blackness above, it did not seem over-fanciful to suppose that I was watching the souls of the dying mounting into eternal light.

*   *   *

If Omer Pasha made the mistake of dawdling forty-eight hours on the battlefield, he compounded it by passing five days of inaction at the town of Sugdidi, not ten miles further into Mingrelia. Chafing at the delay, and finding that my irregulars were to be controlled only with increasing difficulty as they came in contact with the marauding propensities of the Abkhasian horsemen attached to Omer Pasha's army, I determined to return to Alatstchinsk and consult with Rachinskiy – from whom, by the by, I had, perhaps ominously, received no message.

Alas! the country through which we rode showed a very different face from the welcome it had afforded us a week previous. "Dim eclipse disastrous twilight sheds": war had eclipsed its sun. In place of women and children eager to sell us fowls and eggs, we found deserted *auls* where not a cock crowed, or villages where louring eyes stared at us in silent hatred, or mere heaps of blackened ruins. In one village it was the Abkhasians who were to blame, in another the Cossacks, in a third it was the inhabitants themselves who, fearing Turkish rule above all possible calamities, had fired their own houses and withdrawn into the mountains. Money now was useless to supply our wants: either we took by force, or we went hungry.

I was oppressed by all the circumstances of my position. If Omer Pasha's army did not reach at least to Kutais before the weather broke, there to establish itself in winter quarters, I saw no hope for it; and what chance of that snail-like force covering the fifty miles to Kutais in time? Mouravieff would take Kars, and would sweep Omer into the sea on his return, and such of the Mingrelian tribes as had assisted Omer would be punished and dispersed. British influence, and any prospect for British trade, would stand at nil. As for myself, if I stayed in the Caucasus I was likely to become a prisoner of the Russians; and, if I did not stay, to which of the four corners of the world would the wind condescend to blow me?

As I sat with my melancholy thoughts at my tent door on the second evening after the Ingour, I heard a cheery shout from the trees across the brook, and the rattle of a horse's hooves on stones. I looked up to see Hoolaghan in the act of clearing the water on his little charger, which he pulled up before me in the lather of foam usual to an Irishman's mount.

"Holloa, old fellow," he cried as he sprang down and threw the reins to Tack, "by Jove, 'tis cold though!" He held out his hands to my fire. "A bite of supper, is there? And, Tack my boy, a drink too, for it's chilled through I am, and a dry dinner never was a lucky one. Now then," said he to me, "what a game I've had finding you!"

My spirits had unaccountably lifted at the sight of him. He told me that Rachinskiy had billetted himself in a village ten or a dozen miles off with his "army" (which amounted to no more than two hundred and fifty horsemen, according to Hoolaghan's estimate). The prince had marched down from Alatstchinsk upon hearing of Omer Pasha's victory on the Ingour, but indecision, and caution, had again seized him upon Omer failing to follow up his success. It was just as I had feared. The country would only support the Allied invasion if it pushed ahead and established a *de facto* rule over these provinces. I said so to Hoolaghan.

"Well, that's the truth," he said, taking the tumbler Tack put into his hand. "Did you see how the place is all broke to flitters as you came through, did you? Not a roof on a house nor a cow in the barn."

"I did," said I with a sigh, "it's all in confusion."

"There is another side to the coin, though," he said, attending carefully to his dish of *pillau* and not looking at me.

"To which coin?"

"To the coin of confusion," said he. "There's advantage in confusion, could be, if a man has spirit enough to seize his chance."

There was a silence between us. "What do you mean to say, Hoolaghan?"

He looked full in my face over the fire, and I couldn't tell if it was the firelight in his eyes, or laughter. "For your coup d'état I mean," said he.

"*My* coup d'état, Hoolaghan?"

"Listen to me, Vinegar," he said, sucking his fingers clean, "do a couple of bright fellows like you and I want to serve our lives away under a dolt like Rachinskiy, do we now? – who'll be sure as the devil to get us killed entirely in some little brawl over sheep – or if he don't get us killed fair and square in a fight, he'll have a knife pushed in at our backs – do we now? Look how it is, now, listen: you saw the sad road the country was gone, coming through it? 'Tis anarchy, no less. Well, with your seventy fellows here, and fifty more would come away from Rachinskiy with me – why, with a hundred and twenty men at our back, we'd be a power in the land, so we would. A power that would hold Alatstchinsk easy. We'd make our terms direct with Omer, direct with Constantinople, by God! We could too. Direct with your Sir D— F— or with Ismail Bey, whichever of the two would suit our book best."

I kicked the fire. "They're tribal people, Hoolaghan," I said. "They ain't going to attach themselves all of a sudden to an Irishman and an Englishman, you know, and give up their chieftain."

"Have you not been listening, dear man? Did I not say we'd take Alatstchinsk? Of course we take the Princess too – of course we do. She'd come in with us at the run."

"And her father?"

"We knock old Rachinskiy on the head easy enough. What matters he, if we have the daughter? Why, one of the two of us could marry her, quick as wink, and make it all square with the tribe that way."

It was preposterous. There he sat, eager as a boy who sees a hole in the wall of the orchard he thinks of raiding for pippins, while his horse cropped the grass behind him, and the wild Mingrelians moved about under the trees, or sat before their own fires. Eager as a boy – and yet I had heard him speak the Devil's words. "What matters he, if we have the daughter?" There had echoed in my mind the identical words spoken in my ear in the hot room of a *hammam* in Damascus almost five years earlier. "What matters he, if we have the daughter?" Then the "he" spoke of had been Sir D— F—, and "the daughter" Miss E— F—, and the suggestion, put into my ear by Herr N— himself, had been to carry off Miss E— F— as hostage for her father's non-interference with Herr N—'s corrupt empire. I recognised the Tempter's words in Hoolaghan's mouth. If no course lay open for Vinegar save to accede to them, perhaps the time had come to put an end to Captain Vinegar's career.

The rosy glow which follows sunset gilded the air, in which a keen frost could already be felt. Tack's plaintive songs, no doubt com-memorative of the frog-skinning *aul*, rose amongst the trees. Was Hoolaghan serious with his devilish idea, I wondered as I listened to him expand upon the life we would lead as co-rulers of a province enriched by the Caspian trade; or was he a pawn of Rachinskiy's seeking to make me commit myself to a treason he would then reveal to his master? In either case, it was the Tempter's voice I heard.

*　　*　　*

That was the last fine evening of autumn, the moon full. Next day early the rains began. By noon, as is the way with wet weather, you would have believed it had rained for months, the slippery ground cut about by horses' hooves, the tracks splashy, rain dripping from black branches overhead, streams running full. I saw no purpose in attaching my people to Rachinskiy's force, which could only have multiplied the difficulties of his commisariat, and increased the depth of the mud into which we were all at once plunged. Hoolaghan returned to the Prince with a message to this effect. In truth I had become attached to the command of these rough mountaineers, very much as I had once been attached to my Tyari mountaineers in Koordistan, when I had "reigned" in my old fortress-palace at Amadyah. It is the sort of billet a man is in search of, who wanders the East. Hence the appeal to me of Hoolaghan's coup – its temptation. I had continued paying my lancers out of Ismail Bey's gold, and of course the rumour of gold, even in such a disturbed country as this, had conjured a hen and a few eggs, or a pig and some Indian corn, out of the ruins of *auls* which had seemed utterly without sustenance. By circulating Ismail Bey's treasure in this beneficient trade, I persuaded myself that I was converting that infernal metal to better use than the old reptile at Stamboul had intended.

So we moved about the country, ever alert and in the saddle, whilst I waited for news of Omer Pasha's progress, and pondered Hoolaghan's suggestion. If only Omer Pasha would establish himself in Mingrelia for the winter, the tribesmen might adhere to the Allied cause without need of our coup at Alatstchinsk.

News once again took the form of Hoolaghan gallopping into my camp. Coming immediately into my tent he threw off his sodden cloak and *calpac* and stood stamping his feet for warmth. Was it fever, or excitement, which had brightened his eye? "His Highness wants to see you," he said.

"Does he indeed," said I, noting his use of the Prince's "title". "Do you know what the matter is?"

"A couple of things." He looked sly. "Do you know how far Omer Pasha has ever come, since he had the battle?"

"How should I know? I hear nothing in these d—d woods."

"Eleven miles."

"Only eleven miles?"

"Aye, to the Tsiva river – and there he's stuck like a wasp in the jam, with the country all one bog about him."

Hoolaghan's coup would hardly succeed with Omer so far off. So, what was I to do, I and my seventy horsemen? I realised that I had come to count on Hoolaghan's coup, for all that it had seemed a suggestion of the Adversary, because I saw no other course open to Captain Vinegar. "And your second matter," I asked him, "your other news?"

"Well now, the tale goes – but how would it be likely? – anyhow, the tale of it is, that Bagration has burned his stores and decamped."

"Bagration? Burned his stores at Marani?" This was astonishing intelligence. Bagration-Mukhranski was the Russian commander in the province (and a descendant of the old ruling family of Georgia). "What in mischief has he done that for, with Omer stuck fast on the Tsiva?"

" 'Tis a tall tale I agree. But however it is, it was when His Highness heard the tale that the Russians were gone that he asked for you."

The inference was, that Rachinskiy had come down on the side of the Allies, believing that the Russians meant to abandon Mingrelia. I judged it therefore reasonably safe to ride back to Rachinskiy's HQ with Hoolaghan, leaving my people in the charge of a native *yuzbashi*. Little Tack I left, too, very much against his will: but I had not liked Hoolaghan's excitable manner, and, if I was to run my head into a noose at Rachinskiy's HQ, I did not care to run Tack's in with my own.

In a teeming wet dusk Hoolaghan and I rode into the village which Rachinskiy had seized for himself and the half-dozen lesser chiefs who officered his corps. The cabins glaring out light and noise into the night, and the rain-pocked puddles and the mud, and the dead horses and heaps of abomination piled up at every door, seemed more suited to the squalid disorder of a robbers' lair, than to the HQ of a military commander. I have seen navvies' camps better conducted. Hoolaghan of course was upon easy terms with all the ruffians who stared in our faces, or challenged us, when we had left our nags in a *syce*'s care and had tramped into the Prince's quarters. He was squatting on his rug near the fire, his black-bearded face thrust up at a man pinioned before him by two guards, evidently in process of questioning this prisoner, whose head lolled dully to one side. At a nod from the Prince, the poor fellow was supported out of the hut. As I heard his feet bumping down the steps outside, and met the Prince's malevolent eyes staring out at me under their creases of fat, I felt a twinge of pity for anyone whom he resolved to interrogate.

"You have kept yourself at a distance," he said when he had received my greeting. "Where are my horsemen?"

I explained my reasons for keeping my people separate from his. I had not been invited to sit, so I walked about as though I preferred it, and warmed my hands at his fire. I had an intimation now of danger, which I concealed. Hoolaghan, too, looked, I thought, most decidedly ill at ease; but whether with the suspicion of treachery against himself, or with the foreknowledge of an attack to be made upon me, I could not tell. At least my sword had not been taken from me, and my hand resting upon its pommel, as my father's must often have done, comforted me as a symbol of honour, should I be destined to die in this hut.

"I hear that you pay my horsemen with gold," said Rachinskiy, picking at his teeth with a dirty stick of wood. "Where is this store of gold?"

"Almost exhausted," I replied. The wash-leather bag of gold I had entrusted to Tack, knowing that none would suspect him.

"Gold sent from Roum is sent to me," he said heavily. "You were but the messenger."

"Your gold, Prince, I employed to pay your horsemen," said I. He was silent at this, rolling the tooth-pick fiercely between his blackened teeth. "Is it true," I continued, "that the Russian commander has fired his stores at Marani and withdrawn from Mingrelia."

"It is true."

"Your Highness then has a brilliant opportunity."

This seemed to puzzle him. He grunted, rather as a pig might grunt who senses that he has missed a truffle, and looked up sharp at me.

"An opportunity to unite Mingrelia under yourself," I went on, "and make a treaty with the *feringhee* Allies on the Tsiva."

He snapped his tooth-pick between two stubby fingers. "What use is the *feringhee*?" said he scornfully. "Fifty days has Omer Pasha been marching to meet me, and he has reached only the Tsiva. Now the rivers rise, winter comes, he cannot reach me. What use is the *feringhee*?"

In this one idea he had laid hold of – scorn for the European – was the danger to myself. From an envoy I would be degraded to a prisoner, if he ceased to fear the West whence I came. Knowing this of himself, had Hoolaghan made some private bargain with Rachinskiy?

"How, then, will Your Highness proceed?" I asked.

"I will proceed, Captain Vinegar, by possessing myself of the arsenal of weapons sent to me by the kings of Feringhistan, which you have hidden from me."

That, then, had been Hoolaghan's bargain! The dozen poor Enfields under the waterfall he had magnified into an "arsenal"! I said nothing, hoping that he would reveal his hand.

"Where are the weapons hidden?" he asked. So he didn't know that. Why had Hoolaghan not told him what he had guessed? Intent upon this, staring into the fire, I had not seen the approach of two guards, who now seized my arms from behind. They turned me to face the Prince. He had taken up a whip whose lash crept on the floor like an adder. "Where are my guns hidden?" he repeated softly.

Hoolaghan stepped out of the shadows into which he had retreated. "He shall lead me to them," he said. "Come, tell your guards to free him. Torture will only shut his mouth tighter, for he has all the folly of the English. Depend upon it, tomorrow he shall lead me to the arsenal, or you may flay the pair of us."

The Prince seemed to calculate. "Very well," he decided, "tomorrow. Mere thieves I flay – traitors do not die so comfortably. Be warned."

I passed that night wrapped in my cloak on a hut floor, its door guarded, very much in the same captive state I had first awoken to in this mountain kingdom, when I had found old Hannah looking down upon me. Now, whichever way I looked at the present adventure – whatever the outcome – I could descry no way forward for Captain Vinegar beyond the waterfall cave on the morrow. There his career must surely end – unless Hoolaghan had in mind some deeper game of double-cross than I could make out. Though ordinarily possessed of the old campaigner's trick of sleeping soundly in an unpromising situation, I confess that I slept but fitfully that night.

A circumstance of peculiar horror occurred towards morning, which I will record as showing how the anticipation of evil may affect the nerves. I awoke before dawn to hear a succession of sounds, half way between a thud and a splash, coming in to me from outside the hut. Creeping to the shutter, I looked through a crack in its boards onto the dirty, scuffling backs of pigs in a muddy enclosure. Down amongst the pigs there fell through the faint, drizzling dawn – human heads! Yellow, shaven, leaking a horrible juice, these foul tokens of barbarous victory thumped into the mud amongst the pigs, who guzzled them with awful despatch. I craned up. From a roof two crones were flinging down these disgusting objects which I now saw more clearly in the growing light. Melons! Rotten melons, which the Mingrelian housewife was sorting from her rooftop store, and pitching down to her pigs. Not heads, but fruit! And yet I was only half-relieved of my horror by the discovery, as I lay down again upon the mud floor, and listened to the thumps of the melons and the squabbles of the pigs: elsewhere in this village, so my fears told me, from some other rooftop into the jaws of other pigs, real human heads were indeed being tossed down through that drizzling dawn. My nerves had begun to be unstrung. A creature whose nerves are unstrung has no long future in Mingrelia.

An hour after, the door of my cell was flung back, I was led out into the mud of the street, and put upon my horse in the rain. To my surprise, my sword was left with me, though not my rifle, pistols or *khingal*. Perhaps they regarded the heavy old-fashioned cavalry sword, which had been my father's, as a merely ceremonial weapon, like the halberd of a Beefeater at the Tower. Hoolaghan and half a dozen horsemen soon came up, followed by a springless horse-drawn cart with solid wooden wheels. Without a word to me, Hoolaghan led us out of the village. Now, there is not one of a man's accoutrements, be it his wineglass or his boots, which is not made a good deal less comfortable to him by the addition of water; and this element now came into our affairs in full measure, the rain pouring and teeming upon us from hurrying low clouds. As we crossed the dreary upland pastures, with the primitive conveyance creaking along in our rear, I said to Hoolaghan, "The cart is for the rifles, is it?"

"Shall they all fit in, do you suppose?" said he, so very much in his usual way of making a joke of things that I couldn't help laughing.

"And what will your master say to you when he finds there are but twelve of the things after all? Or have you arranged that I have the blame of it all?"

"You might, captain, you might so." Then he drew his horse closer to mine and went on, "Now, listen, will you, till I tell you what it is. Listen, and I'll tell you the truth of it."

"I'll listen," I replied, "but I don't know if I shall believe you."

He ignored this, though he usually evinced all the touchiness of the Irishman if his word was impugned. "What Rachinskiy is about is this," he said to me, low and urgent; "With Bagration gone out of the country, the whole of it is given up to pillage entirely. Omer's bashibozuks are out at the game, and those devils of Abkhasians, and Cossacks too – they're all at it, and the whole length of the land down there below is in flames. Well, Rachinskiy goes down too. He couldn't keep his boys back any way – I heard it this morning that your fellows had gone in the night – for it's loot and murder is mother's milk to these rapparoos. 'Tis the breath of life to them. With Omer at Kutais he might have stopped it, but sorra a one in the kingdom gives a pin for Omer now."

So my people had gone, and no doubt Tack and the gold with them! Of the goods I had brought into the country, only the Enfields remained. I determined, if possible, to destroy them, before they too fell into mischievous hands, and so frustrated every intention of my mission. I said, "So Rachinskiy wants the rifles, does he, to take on his foray?"

"He has set his heart upon having them to himself, since I let it slip out that you had – "

"Ah, you let it slip out, did you?"

"Holy Mary, wasn't I defending you?" said he as if hurt at my tone, "Wasn't I fighting it out for you tooth and nail, when himself was full of saying how you'd brought him nothing worth the having from Roum? 'Prince,' says I, 'didn't he bring you those rifles, a cartload of them, just the most elegant weapons in the world?' Dear man, I think it's your life I saved that day, I do so."

We splashed upward by watery tracks into ragged cloud. Was it true that he had spoken out for me? And whose side would he favour when we reached the waterfall-cave, only a short march further into the hills? I suspected that Hoolaghan, a true adventurer in this, did not yet know which way he would jump down and bet his life on the issue, as a true gambler reserves his wager until the last moments before the "off" have been given their chance to alter the odds. If I could yet contrive to alter the odds in my favour – offer him something of value – he might bet upon me against the Prince.

But what did I possess that I could offer him – stripped as I was of every possession save my sword and my bare identity?

I had ceased to question him, as the beginnings of an idea formed in my head, but silence was anathema to Hoolaghan. After a moment of it, he said, "You know the Princess is a prisoner?"

"How should I have known it?"

"She is though. All of her people up there at the old tower is served the same way. They're not chained up, but they're not let out either. It's the reason why Rachinskiy thinks I'll not run off with you and your beautiful rifles when we have them."

"I don't see it, Hoolaghan," I said.

"Ah, you don't see it! You'd light off, I suppose, would you, and leave your wife to have her throat cut, and worse, by Rachinskiy's *ferashes*?"

"So she's your wife now, is she?" said I.

"Devil take you, Vinegar – do you not believe anything at all, don't you?"

"Precious little that you tell me, Hoolaghan."

Perhaps at last I had pierced his skin and insulted him, for he dropped back, apparently to try to hurry the cart, which was heavy and awkward to drag up rocky slopes and slippery track. His surprise, and chagrin, at being distrusted, was of a piece with the perfect candour with which he told his lies. For the first time, though, I had felt a thorough disgust of the man. No doubt by "wife" he meant to imply that the Princess was his after some barbarous rite only, such as disgraces these savage tribes; nonetheless his claim upon her angered me, and I felt that we were enemies.

Nearer and nearer our straggling cavalcade approached to the waterfall, and, surely, to some climax which would finish the affair one way or another – or finish myself – in the cavern behind the falls.

V

The Sultan's Ball

THE ARRIVAL OF THE SULTAN in the ballroom of the British Embassy
at Constantinople, in the course of the *bal costumé* given on the 7th of
February, 1856, caused a crush of sightseers towards him which was
perfectly appalling to the more languid and fastidious attachés on the
Ambassador's staff. Still, it was a sight never seen before, the Padishah
at a *feringhee* ball, so that even one or two of the attachés improved their
pace a little to observe it. In his plain blue frock-coat, and scarlet fez, he
had paused a moment at the doorway of the main saloon, evidently
struck with the fantastic scene; then he had moved, causing the
brilliants with which he seemed sprinkled to sparkle, and had walked
forward through the press, and sudden hush, Lord and Lady Stratford
and their two daughters rustling along beside him, and a peacock's tail
of gorgeous pashas drawn after him. In the centre of one of the
ballroom's looking-glass walls, on a dais, had been placed a velvet and
gold chair, almost a throne, to which the Sultan was conducted. Lady
Stratford at his side was dressed as a woman of fashion of the 1720s, in
powder and pink roses: the elder daughter floated along in the white
robes and oakleaf chaplet of a Druidess: the younger wore the costume
of Mary, Queen of Scots. The history of the world, and all its legends,
had been ransacked to provide the pageant of dress displayed below the
Sultan's dais. In that scene of dazzling splendour, he was the cynosure.

Pressing in upon the pashas who surrounded him there jostled and
peered as weirdly caparisoned a crowd as ever can have been gathered
together in a ballroom. For half the fantasy was real: in a *mêlée* where
real Persians in lambskin hats stood upon the toes of mock French
shepherdesses, and a chain-mail knight upset the Armenian Archbishop, and a Crimea hero carrying two glasses of champagne pushed

between a Negro king and an Italian bravo out of Donizetti – in such a crush, who could tell where reality left off and masquerade began? Was that handsome Circassian chieftain some dull fellow dressed up, or was he one of the real refugees from Omer Pasha's failed Caucasus campaign? In a walk through the rooms every language of the East might be heard. To recognise a friend was impossible, so mazed did the brain become by dress and paint and candlelight and barbarous tongues, as well as by the fumes of champagne and the music of the waltz. For the orchestra, which had been silent for the Sultan's entrance, now struck up again, and the owner of a thousand concubines leaned forward in his chair to watch the fabled indecencies of his European allies, who clasped their half-bared women and pushed them about the room to the discordant janglings of their "music".

In shoving and craning to watch the Europeans dance, the pashas of the Sultan's suite so shook the great fruit-laden orange trees in ceramic pots which adorned the dais, that oranges in dozens dropped and bounced and rolled out among the dancers, to be kicked, or tripped over, or squashed under a heavy foot. Now the pashas laughed in earnest, clapping their hands before them and rocking to and fro like mechanical toys. It was too much for Arthur Broadbent to endure; pulling Frank Smallwood's arm he said, "Come on, old fellow, quick – it'll set off HE into one of his furies, bound to, and we shall have to stand the racket if we're by."

Smallwood made no objection to being steered towards the refreshment room by Broadbent's hand on his arm. Dressed up as an officer in Prince Rupert's cavalry, he wore his outfit as a dwarf might walk on stilts, with the satisfaction of spirit felt when outward appearance at last comes up to a man's own idea of himself.

The Sultan's appearance had almost emptied the refreshment room, save for two or three Turks stuffing down sweetmeats, to whom Broadbent certainly did not intend speaking. "Come," he said, "we should stroll about. Take a glass of fizz, and we'll walk through the rooms."

Broadbent wore no disguise: he could imagine no costume more satisfactory to his self-esteem than that of an Embassy attaché. With glasses in their hands the two young men left the refreshment room and entered a long gallery where sofas were filled with mammas, and pouffes with a crowd of their daughters, and tables were taken up by groups of elderly men whose knotted hands clasped the handles of sticks, and whose knee-breeches and glossy shoes stuck out rather stiffly, whilst they wished themselves at home. Smallwood and Broadbent walked through a cross-fire of glances from pouffes and sofas which bathed their self-regard in glory. To have something to be seen saying as he strolled along, Broadbent asked,

"And where is your savage fascinator, my boy?"

"Not here, at all events," said Smallwood. "We seem to have got in amongst the Pera girls and counting-house fellows here. She was on the stairs when I saw her."

"Dressed as a Circassian, eh?"

"The real thing, Broadbent, I swear it. Such eyes! – A flash to them, you know, and a proud way of turning her neck, and – oh, a skin like snow!"

"Somebody's aunt dressed up."

"Not she! For one thing, she was coming upstairs with that Vinegar fellow everybody fawns upon, who's just back from the Caucasus, so she certainly was a Circassian. Or a Mingrelian."

"Vinegar!" exclaimed Broadbent. "Damned Irishman swaggering everywhere! You'd think no one but himself ever was in the Caucasus at all, to hear him at it. How has he got himself up tonight? Is he king of Ireland, or king of Mingrelia?"

"Well – a Circassian chief, I suppose. There was a fellow with them, though – with Vinegar and the Princess on the stairs – who was clattering along in chain-mail with his head stuck in a helmet with the visor down, who I take it was that fellow Pitcher who used to hang about us at Therapia last year, for he was with Vinegar all through the Caucasus, I'm told."

"If your savage Princess is in with Vinegar, you've only to find the Farrs, and your work is done. They know him. Sir Daniel and the daughter know Vinegar."

"I asked Miss Enid. She'd been at Damascus, she said – which I knew – and she hadn't seen Pitcher since September, before he went off to join up with Vinegar in Mingrelia."

"Ah. Shall we find Miss Enid, though?" suggested Broadbent, brightening at the idea as they strolled through the room with their policeman-like air of supervising a crowd admitted on sufferance to exalted surroundings. "She ain't exactly jolly, but she's awfully sharp at seeing the fun of a thing. And I believe she has a dull time of it, with that bear for a father."

"Yes," agreed Smallwood, "and nothing but a pack of these yellow-looking Levantine Johnnies to talk to."

"Oh Lord – !" exclaimed Broadbent, catching his friend's elbow, "See, there's Old Mortality looking like thunder. We'd better see what's to do."

As the two young men lengthened their stride towards the gloomy figure of Lord Stratford standing alone at the further end of the gallery – no less horrified at seeing their ambassador alone in a crowd than two midshipmen at seeing their ship adrift among shoals – a pair of eyes followed them from a sofa, and watched them pass by with regret.

The eyes belonged to Enid Farr. She was not at first glance particularly noticeable among the stout mothers and insipid girls seated in this long gallery rather removed from the heat and glitter at the heart of the Sultan's Ball. She appeared to have made no attempt at fancy dress, beyond drawing a mantilla over her hair, and fastening it with damask roses. So well did the rose-petals suggest the colouring and texture of her skin, though, and so handsome upon her hair was the fine black lace, that the care of her choice of adornment was evident. Had she worn some flamboyant costume, how absurd – how pathetic – would have been her situation among these forgotten Periotes far from the swirl of fashion in the inner rooms! Her mother, Lady Fanny, would have dressed her in some wonderfully striking style; and would have seen to it that she danced with ambassadors and princes. But, alone with her father, she had chosen the roses and the lace, which distinguished her, without isolating her from the company she must keep.

She had known beforehand how it would be at the Ball, and had dressed herself accordingly. Papa was not welcome in the inner rooms. She would go nowhere in Constantinople where her father was not welcome. She was not here to exercise her mother's scornful judgement upon her father's choice of society. That had been her resolution before ever she had agreed to come out with him to Turkey, and she had kept it, turning down whatever invitations ran counter to her principle.

She had chosen Pera in place of Mayfair, and such vigils as this among the yellowish Periotes was the consequence of her own choice. She had the little house at Bebec for solace when these interminable evenings were over.

That she accepted the consequence of her choice, however, did not mean that she was bound to be content with the outer rooms, or pleased with the company of Levantines. She might not voice her mother's scorn, but she could not prevent her blood articulating it to herself. How she disdained the dreariness, and dullness, and stupidity of these rows of matrons and their daughters! All through the last months' tour to Damascus, made with her father as a pilgrimage in her dead brother's footsteps – all through the weeks in Smyrna and Antioch and Aleppo, her gorge had risen against the company they had kept. Recollection of her brother Roland's light-hearted letters to her from such towns, mocking the boorish airs and graces of Consular society, confirmed her own view as the right one, and even gave her back Roly now and then, as a companion to share the joke with. But dear papa! He was better pleased to sit in a fog of tobacco smoke in the parlour of a Greek currant merchant at Smyrna, and to compliment the ringletted daughter on the fearful sounds she drew from her piano, than ever it had pleased him to sit in a gilt chair in an English duchess's drawing-room and hear Pastori sing. As he grew older and blinder, he seemed to care more frankly for the Levantine scenes in which he had grown to manhood and power. He never ceased remarking how the Europeanising influence of the war – the influx of foreigners and of foreign manners breaking down the old labyrinthine ways of Constantinople – had altered and vulgarised the East. He retreated into his own past, and into the Levant's past. Dear, simple papa! It didn't make her love him the less, that he cared for such dull scenes and such second-rate people; but her perception of his real taste altered her love a little, by tinging it with condescension, which would have been unthinkable before she had seen him in the East.

"Ma says we'll take a house at the West End when we go," said the greasy-haired girl beside her as she licked the last smears of an ice off her spoon, "I forget the part just, but wherever's smart Ma'll go to be sure."

"You will enjoy London, I expect," Enid replied. She could not prevent her mind flying off to London as she spoke its name, like a homing pigeon released by mistake.

"You know it a bit?"

"Yes; we have a house in London. My mother is there now," she added, as if obliged to describe the scene she saw, of her mother sweeping downstairs at Berkeley Square, and out in the gleam of silk and jewels through the flutter of footmen to her carriage. To see her mother go out was a wonderful thing, the very essence of the word "London", which she and Roly had always delighted to watch from an upper landing. To be expected to go with her mother, though, was another matter ... Hauling her mind away from that disputed ground, and from London, Enid enquired, "And shall you go off to the Princes' Islands with your box of books when the spring is come? I remember you saying you doted upon reading in your garden there."

"Yes, ain't it droll, for who would ever think it, that sees me at nothing but balls and parties! I dote upon reading." Then she added, as she seemed to consider again the scene thus sketched, "But Lord, how stupid books are! Though Pa has what's best sent regular from Malta, I declare there's been nothing to read this season, except that stupid Captain Vinegar's *Journal*."

"Yes, everyone has read that, I suppose," said Enid in a controlled voice. She was entirely inured to hearing the book discussed, as it was everywhere discussed, by people who had no idea that the affecting description of a young Englishman's death from the plague at Damascus, which Captain Vinegar's book of travels contained, was in fact the account of her brother's death. In the book Roland was "F—", just as Tresham Pitcher was "P—", and none of her Pera acquaintances connected her with the narrative of Vinegar's journey and adventures. Only with Mr Pitcher himself had she been able to discuss *en plein* the coded book, when he had been at Constantinople in the autumn. Enid believed herself to be the only person alive, besides Mr Pitcher, who knew that "Captain Vinegar" had been invented by Roland and Mr Pitcher, and that his celebrated *Journal* of their travels together was the work of Tresham Pitcher. This knowledge, this secret, allowed her to listen with perfect composure to discussions of the book, as if to an irony shared with Roly alone. Now, however, her fat

[113]

companion at the ball uttered words which broke in rudely upon this secret satisfaction:

"He's come to the Ball, Captain Vinegar has, so Pa says."

"Come to the Ball? He is here tonight?" She could not help lifting her head to scan the crowd, with the eye of a deer startled by a footfall.

"Are you acquainted with him?" asked the girl curiously.

"No, no, not a bit. But – but I should like to see him, you know." And indeed she would like to see Mr Pitcher, though he might not have done what she had asked of him, and left "Captain Vinegar" behind him in the Caucasus.

"Ah, would you? I'm sure I shouldn't then," sniffed the Pera belle, shaking her ringlets scornfully, "such a horrid brute as he must be. And Pa says he knows it for a fact he ain't to be let back into England on account of the *zaptieh* being onto him for debts. Ma says he – "

"Excuse me." Enid had risen: amongst the crowd she had again glimpsed Mr Broadbent, and hoped by rising to attract his notice. Indeed he saw her, and began to make his way down the gallery towards her. Enid, in the matronly part she had played as housekeeper to her father at Bebec, had smiled upon the young Embassy attachés – whenever she had seen them – with the complaisance of a dowager, never conducting herself towards them in the manner of a young unmarried woman of an age with themselves. It was a comfortable rôle to her, impossible to adopt while her mother was by, even in Wales among the cottage people, let alone in London society. It was one of the comforts of the little cardboard-like house at Bebec, that she could behave in it like a dowager, a widow – like Roly's widow, which was how she felt. She saw Mr Smallwood swaggering beside Mr Broadbent in his long boots and his lace, and did not fail to congratulate him, as the two of them came up to her, on a costume which suited him so admirably.

"Just step this way with us, Miss Enid, won't you?" whispered Broadbent bending near, "your Periote friend is looking daggers that you don't introduce her."

"Mr Broadbent!" she said, as though shocked. She and the young attachés shared a view of Pera society, for they stood upon an equal social footing, having cousins in common through Enid's mother. But they never discussed it, for that might have led them into an awkwardness over the position of Enid's father. "But come, may I walk through

[114]

the rooms with you, if I shan't be in your way?" She stepped out from her sofa, and left the daggerish looks of the Periote belle to stab the air. "I suppose you have been waltzing yourselves giddy?" she said as she took Broadbent's arm.

"Not a bit of it," said Smallwood, "not a waltz nor a bite of supper have we had between us, ain't it so, Broadbent? Nothing but work for us, these kind of things. We've just this minute come from putting the Ambassador into his bed – and if that ain't work I don't know what is, eh Broadbent?"

"Confounded hard work. *And* it's snowing."

"I hope Lord Stratford isn't unwell?" Enid asked as they walked along.

"Not unwell, no, for he ain't sufficiently human to be unwell. Devilish tucked up though. He felt the Kars business most awfully, the way he was blamed for it you know, and he's never just trotted out sound since," Broadbent said.

"I know people do blame him for the fall of Kars," Enid said, "I know papa does."

"Your papa is a great blamer, Miss Enid, he is indeed. He seems to find a plot against him in everything – as if General Williams gave up Kars just to spite him. That HE hasn't taken offence against your papa is a miracle," Broadbent said, touchy at once if any but himself dared criticise his ambassador.

"It's the loss of the Caucasus as a consequence that papa feels," said Enid, "and if the peace comes now, as people think, I suppose the Caucasus is lost to Russia forever, and never will be pacified."

"How awfully grave you are, Miss Enid," said Frank Smallwood, "why, it's just like a meeting of Ministers, to hear you talk so."

Enid smiled at him. "Well, you know how papa cares about it all, on account of the Persian trading route he hoped for through Mingrelia. So the Caucasus is discussed with us at Bebec till I feel I have walked over every inch of it."

"At the Embassy it seems to us a puzzle that your papa don't join up with old Novis in the Persia trade, instead of squabbling over it," said Broadbent.

"They are old enemies," said Enid, her face closing, "arch-enemies."

[115]

Frank Smallwood hovering along beside them – Enid and Broadbent were arm in arm – didn't see her frown. "Arch-enemies! They're like as two peas for what I can see – at least their interests are. I shouldn't have thought those merchant fellows could afford to squabble."

Enid's eyes flashed, and the weapon of her tongue showed for an instant sharp between her teeth. Then she laughed. "You mean to say it is only you diplomatists who are to be allowed squabbles, and principles, so that you may start wars between nations?" She never openly took offence when it was forgotten that she was half-merchant herself. Not only had her mother inculcated into her the superior fitness of the aristocracy to arbitrate in all refined questions, whether the question concerned moral principles or the laying-out of a garden, but her father too had always acquiesced in leaving such matters to the nobly born: until, that is, the aristocratic mismanagement of the war in the Crimea had begun to fill his heart with an impatient and angry mistrust of the noblemen at whose hands England's wealth, and his own with it, might be squandered away. It was the arousal of this distrust of England's ruling class which had fired Sir Daniel to ignore Lady Fanny's opinion, and her mockery of him too, by coming out himself to the seat of the war, and bringing Enid with him. Knowledge of all this prevented her from showing herself to be offended by Frank Smallwood's clumsiness, and so she smiled as she satirised the diplomatist's right to quarrel over principles, where the merchant must meekly agree.

Broadbent turned the subject off this ticklish ground by remarking, "Dr Sandwith is here tonight, you know."

"Who was let go by the Russians when Kars fell to them?" Enid took up the diversion gladly. "I should like to see him above all things. How is he dressed I wonder?" She hoped discussion of the famous Kars doctor might lead to an opportunity to ask if "Captain Vinegar" was indeed at the ball.

"No need of a fancy dress when a man is a hero in his own clothes," said Broadbent. "Sandwith is a plain enough little man in a dress-coat, as you'll see by and by."

"I'm hanged if I see Sandwith as a hero," said Smallwood, piqued, "or Williams either. Kars fell after all. The Turks don't talk of Williams as a hero, I can tell you, for putting a Turk army into a Turk fortress and then throwing both away to no purpose. They don't indeed."

"Speaking of heroes," said Enid, taking her courage in her hands, "I heard it said that the famous Captain Vinegar was to be here, who wrote the *Journal*, you know. But I suppose he isn't come."

"Yes, by Jove, but he is – we was looking for you earlier, Miss Enid, to tell us if it was your friend Mr Pitcher in a suit of armour with Captain Vinegar's party – weren't we, Broadbent?" appealed Smallwood.

"Smallwood here was struck in a heap by the lady they have with them, that's what the matter is, Miss Enid," Broadbent said. "He thinks that if you was to lead him up to Mr Pitcher, the savage fascinator might notice him. Then Rupert of the Rhine here shall sweep her away – eh Smallwood? Not but what Prince Rupert ever won a campaign any more than General Williams did, so far as I recall history," he added.

"Let us find them by all means," urged Enid as she stepped out through the glitter of the rooms with her head held high on its slim neck, and the blood colouring her cheek between the lace and the roses. Who might it be within the suit of armour, she wondered? Not Mr Pitcher, cetainly, for Mr Pitcher would be in the disguise of "Captain Vinegar". Here in the inner rooms which they had now penetrated, where the music played and the crush was fierce, reality danced with fantasy, and the reflections of both danced again in the gilt-glass walls.

"There he is!" called out Smallwood in her ear, nodding towards a group of three under an orange-tree across the room. "The Irish-looking fellow with the ginger beard and the high boots – that's Vinegar."

"It's not!" Enid had spoken before she thought. That was not Mr Pitcher!

"I assure you it is," said Broadbent. "Come!"

He shepherded Enid between dancers and lookers-on. With the reddish-bearded Circassian stood a helmetted knight in chain-mail, and between them was a dark queenly woman in loose garments which might have made her as well the wife of the knight of the Middle Ages on her left, as consort to the present-day Circassian on her right. Again, rather faintly, Enid protested "I am sure it cannot be Captain Vinegar, Mr Broadbent."

Now the knight, whose slit-eyed helm had been regarding her, clashed towards them on his armed feet and raised his visor with a gauntletted hand. Out of the casque spoke a hollow voice she knew: "I think you will find that it *is* Captain Vinegar, Miss Enid, if you will allow me to introduce him."

The voice was Mr Pitcher's. So was the face, when he allowed sufficient light to reveal it to her. Who then was the other? Who was the stranger? She looked apprehensively at the Circassian, this *avatar* of a man who had never existed, finding herself led up to him by a mailed hand on her own.

"May I introduce Captain Vinegar?" said the knight. "Vinegar, this is Miss Enid Farr, whom I think you might have met for a moment long ago in those rooms you had in Half Moon Street, if you recall."

"And how could I forget Miss Enid? How do you do now, how do you do?" His grasp was firm, quite unghostly. A sunburnt, cheerful countenance looked out at her with bright grey eyes. The voice was Irish.

At a loss, she could say nothing, could only look her appeal at Mr Pitcher. Whilst the others occupied themselves with the Irishman's introductions to the dark "Princess Mazi", he drew her a step aside until an orange-tree was between themselves and the rest.

"Who is he?" she asked urgently, leaning forward.

"Miss Enid – " the armoured hand lay upon hers for a moment with the cold and scaly touch of a dragon's claw, "Miss Enid, take him for Vinegar. Take him always to have been Vinegar. Forget I ever was the creature – will you now? The truth is, I've given Vinegar away bag and baggage to the fellow you see there. Who seems to make the most of him, I must own," he added, looking rather ruefully towards the group collected around "Captain Vinegar" on the other side of the orange-tree.

Enid looked too. The attachés and another gentleman or two were arranged admiringly round the easy figure of the Irish Circassian and the tall shadow-dark lady from the Caucasus. Only the ivory of her face caught the pallor of the candles. Was she amongst Captain Vinegar's "bag and baggage" which Mr Pitcher had given away? Finding that the woman's eyes were watching her – watching her with a heavy-lidded indwelling amusement which was intolerable – Enid looked away.

"What possessions had Captain Vinegar that you gave away," she asked, agitated to find her hand still clasped by the dragon's claw, disturbed by the woman's eyes.

"His book."

"The *Journal*? – you gave away that? But you wrote it?"

"Yes, I wrote it. I wrote it at Baghdad, but I confess I hadn't understood what the thing amounted to – in the way of fame, I mean, and cash too – all the time I was rusticating on a mountain in Mingrelia among a set of savages who haven't a book between them and couldn't read it if they had. I confess I didn't twig to what I was giving up. But there, Hoolaghan – Vinegar I mean – Vinegar is a neater hand than ever I might have been at squeezing out the juice of the thing, I fancy. He seems to be. I shouldn't have been half so famous as he's contrived to make himself. Come, shall we walk a little? Is your father here? Perhaps you will dance?"

How strange it was to have a choice of pleasures before her, and Mr Pitcher by her side, ten minutes after she had been sat amongst the Periotes yawning away the hours till she should be allowed to go home! The savage princess mightn't after all belong to Mr Pitcher. But she wouldn't accept to dance quite at once. "Let us walk by all means, if you like it," she said. "If you don't mind leaving your friends?"

"Vinegar is well launched," said Pitcher a shade sourly, as he gave Enid his arm. "In the month we've been at Constantinople he's made himself very thoroughly at home in Vinegar's shoes."

"Yet you didn't come to us," she said, "to papa and me at Bebec."

"I knew you were away. I heard – besides," he went on, as if he had considered speaking of her journey to Damascus, and had decided against it, "besides, our situation when first we fetched up in the Golden Horn was a great deal less than respectable. We had been kept waiting for boats on every beach of the Black Sea with a crowd of other poor beggars – oh, for months. Such a rabble as there was clearing out of the Caucasus after Omer Pasha gave it up! It was a good deal like being in the last carriage in the file outside the opera on a wet night, by Jove, it was so confoundedly uncomfortable. And then to reach – "

"Mr Pitcher!" entreated Enid, pressing the chain-mail arm under her hand, "you say you have given over Captain Vinegar, but there you are talking just in the style of his *Journal*! Can't you tell me truly what it was like, and forget the wet night at the opera? Remember," she said earnestly, looking up at the armoured figure beside her, "remember what I know."

[119]

The casque turned so that he looked down at her. "Forgive me," he said. "The truth is, it ain't an easy matter, to separate oneself from the companion of years. The old captain protected me, you know. It's curious, but it is so. Protected me from feeling. From thinking too."

"Roly's letters show how Captain Vinegar did that to you," she said. "How he altered you. Till – " Till you could ride off and leave Roly dying, she wanted to say, but desisted.

"Now the draught comes in, though," said Pitcher, who had continued with his own thoughts. "With Vinegar gone, I must feel – I must think."

"Better suffer any draught, Mr Pitcher, than wear such wraps round your heart as that!"

"You say so. You may think so. Excuse me, Miss Enid, you have no conception of the reality. You read a book of travels, and you think it is all just so, pretty adventures – come, you do! – but books of that kind are all the fictions of such a fellow as Vinegar, a fellow concocting a yarn with himself as its hero. They are indeed. I know it. Ourselves getting clear of the Caucasus now, take that: if I was to think about it, and feel about it, Miss Enid, and find words to make you understand in plain truth – in disgusting truth – what we suffered among that rabble of savages, first in the mountains where every man had turned robber, then looking for a boat in a fever swamp, then upon the sea in our filth with the child as I thought dying in my arms – well, I shouldn't find the words for it, and I should very likely break down and weep in the attempt. You would find half the soldiers and travellers in tears in their books, if they was to write as they think, and feel. But we call in Vinegar, to write our books for us, and he speaks of 'the last carriage in the file at the opera', or some such fancy humbug as the world accepts, and the thing's done – done without tears. The only traveller I know of who's forever in tears in his books is that mad fellow Wolff, and the reason he hasn't understood that he must send out for a Vinegar to write his books is because he is a Jew missionary, poor fellow, and not an English gentleman. But there," Pitcher added, as if ashamed of the warmth with which he had spoken, "I only mean to say how uncommon easy it is to teach yourself to look at the world through another man's eyes – a man you have invented for the purpose."

She had found his vehemence exciting. She said, looking up, "But now you have given up Captain Vinegar – ?"

"Now I shan't look through his eyes any more," replied Pitcher, inclining his casque to look down at her through his own. "If I should stray, will you remind me of it, as you did over the file at the opera just then?"

"If I am by," she replied with a turn of her head.

How she hated herself, a moment after, for that instinct to show indifference! Very far from her true feeling, her shrinking from self-commital interposed its constraint, always, between herself and honest reaction. She had her own Vinegar within her, like a duenna, between her feelings and her tongue. As if to shock that duenna, she leaned a little more on Mr Pitcher's arm and said, "I so admire your costume, Mr Pitcher – tell me, did you win it by a feat of arms, like the knights in Lord Tennyson? We have trophies of armour, you know, just the very match for your outfit, on the walls of the Great Chamber of Ravenrig."

"I remember them. You forget I was at Ravenrig."

"I forget nothing, Mr Pitcher. Nothing of that time."

"What should you have said, Miss Enid, if you had known that you would walk through a ballroom in Constantinople with myself dressed in the armour off your walls?"

Encouraged by the weight on his arm, he had almost whispered the question. But she leant less upon him, and replied briskly, "I shouldn't have believed it, Mr Pitcher – except of Captain Vinegar, perhaps, if we had invented him by then. I would have believed any marvel of Captain Vinegar, even that he had stripped that suit of mail off the Black Knight of the Ford, in the proper style of the Romances. Did you come by it so, Mr Pitcher?"

"I fear not. I am not Vinegar at heart, you see, after all. I had the armour off Preziosi. Half the costumes here belong to Preziosi, I should say."

"It was Signor Preziosi painted Roland when he was here."

"As a Bakhtiari chief, was it not?"

"Yes. As a joke. Whatever they do, they cannot make Roly solemn, even with monuments and obelisks."

"He was not solemn, ever."

"You should come and see what we have of Roly at Ravenrig, Mr

Pitcher." Again the pressure of her hand on his cold mailed arm; again he responded:

"I should value an invitation to Ravenrig above all things."

But she did not issue such an invitation. She would go no further down that road at present. Instead she asked, "Who was it you brought with you out of the Caucasus, Mr Pitcher?"

"Oh," said he, sounding disappointed, "there was myself and Hoolaghan – Vinegar, that's to say – myself and Vinegar, and the Princess Mazi whom you met there, and her daughter."

"Her daughter! She is a married lady."

"As marriages go in those wild parts. But the daughter, Shkara, is a dear – a trump. She came through it all and never complained. Never gave up. I had no notion a child could have such a character for courage – well, I knew nothing of children, before. She is a trump," he repeated, and Enid saw by the light in his eye that the child, at least, had captured his heart. "Then we had with us the nurse, too," he went on, "Hannah, a very remarkable confusion of the races – a Circassian slave brought up amongst Scotch missionaries in Russia, if you will believe it. She stuck it all as a matter of course, for I don't believe aught in Creation could put out Hannah."

Pitcher talked, and Enid appeared to listen. But what she really wondered was, How old is the child? – and, how long were you with the "princess" in those wild regions? Coil by jealous coil that woman from the East had slid into her mind. Enid almost wished herself back amongst the Periotes, where nothing so uncomfortable had troubled her superior calm. She heard him ask a question about Damascus, but she did not answer. Was he condescending, bored, counting the minutes till he should regain his "princess"?

"Shall we find chairs," he asked at last, "or do you care to dance?"

"I should look for papa, I think."

"Let us dance once before we search."

"I think I should find papa."

Why could she not accept to dance, which was her real desire? For so long – years – she had truly not wished to dance that the formula of acceptance was a rusted lock. Another persona answered for her – the duenna-like *dopplegänger*, invented as social armour, answered for her in season and out.

[122]

But what was this? Mr Pitcher had led her upon the floor, despite the rusted lock, and had launched them both into the swirl of fantastic costumes and spiralling lights. His arm was about her, his coat of mail against her breast, all was shut out but their two selves and the music.

"You have been at Damascus I know," he said again, his breath close to her ear.

Asked like that, a whisper, soul to soul, she could reply: "Yes. I have so wanted to be where Roly died."

"No one called him Roly but you."

"No one. I loved him so." Tears heated her eyes.

"He loved you. Damascus was of comfort?"

"There is no comfort."

"Time."

"I hate time. I hate time for filling in the voids with – with oblivion. As the mist comes down upon you in the hills where you had a view. I want the view. I want to see him clearly always."

"It is not possible. Time does not allow you that." When she said nothing to this, he added gently, "You must let time bury the dead."

"But it is so unfinished!" she broke out close against him as they danced, "his death is such an unfinished thing. I mean that my idea of him dead is so wanting in completeness that I don't even believe it. I thought Damascus would make an end to it. I thought I would see it all clear. But I don't."

"You never will. Make up your mind to that."

"But I must. It is as though he were unburied. Papa put up his monument and forgot. Mamma had a stained glass window made of him like one of the old saints. But I have completed nothing, not my thoughts even. It is like a book I cannot write until I see it all clear."

"You are not called upon to write the book. Only to read it."

"A letter, then – we must all write letters. It is like a letter which lies on your table unfinished. You will seal it up and send it when you are satisfied that your mind is expressed. So it lies day upon day."

"But say a servant takes it up and posts it, as it is. An end is made. Not the end you might have made, but an end nonetheless."

"Yes," she agreed sadly, after a moment's thought. "Perhaps after all that is the only end there is. Perhaps."

[123]

He left a silence, and then he pressed her hand and asked, "Is the letter posted?"

"The letter is posted," she lied, and leaned her whole supple self against his armour, and closed her eyes, and danced.

*   *   *

When the music of the waltz ended, Enid's physical self was recaptured like a truant by her mind, and the captor spoke severely: "Mr Pitcher, I must ask you to find papa for me without further delay."

"Come then," he said, smiling, "we will find him directly. How does he get about without you, by the by, now he is so awfully blind?"

"He has Wicker." She was stern with him, as she had failed to be sufficiently stern with herself, and would not answer his smile. By that lie as to the posted letter – by her aroused blood which had made her lie – she had broken faith with poor unburied Roly. Remorse grew stronger like a grey dawn amongst burnt-out candles. This was reality, all else was false.

Pitcher said, "I suppose he's infernally savage over the Caucasus failure, your papa?"

"Very savage, as you call it. Everyone is to blame."

"Well he shan't blame me, at all events. He shall blame Vinegar if he likes. Now, there's an advantage to having given the Captain away!"

"I know." The thought had already occurred to Enid, whilst they were dancing: Captain Vinegar should be held to blame for failure in the Caucasus, while no such fault would impede an invitation to Mr Pitcher to come to them at Ravenrig – for old time's sake, of course. Now, in her stern mood, she said, "But I fancy papa suspected a fraud over Captain Vinegar from the first, and only went along with it whilst it fitted in with his schemes. Now it don't anymore, he may call the bluff."

"But there ain't a sniff of fraud about Vinegar now. There he stands as plain as you please, and over here quite separate stands I!"

Despite her plan of being severe Enid couldn't prevent herself from laughing, and her spirits lifted as they used to do. The turn of events was just how Roly might have developed his joke, first inventing Captain Vinegar, then fusing him with Mr Pitcher, then at last dividing him off again into a real personage appearing out of the Caucasus with

[124]

his motley retinue quite as wonderful as anything in fiction. Laughing, with her hand on Mr Pitcher's arm, she did not hurry him through the rooms in their search for her papa. Then she saw Sir Daniel.

"Look! There is papa!"

Her fingers closed tight on the chain-mail arm. For the short figure of Sir Daniel, with the back of his plain dress-coat towards them, was addressing itself to Captain Vinegar under the orange-trees.

"He's there before me!" exclaimed Pitcher. "God bless my soul, but Vinegar goes fast to work!"

Vinegar's group stood where Enid and Pitcher had left them twenty minutes earlier. The two attachés were still there too, Broadbent listening to Sir Daniel with his thumbs in his waistcoat pockets, Smallwood intent upon the princess. Wicker, who stood respectfully apart under an orange-tree, saw Enid first and touched Sir Daniel's arm.

Sir Daniel did not turn, and Enid stayed Pitcher's approach, she hardly knew why, by the pressure of her hand on his arm. She had noticed that the "princess" had observed Mr Pitcher and herself returning: she wished that the creature might have seen them dancing together, too. How she disliked the sickly pallor that passed for "beauty" among these Eastern females, and how wonderfully unbecoming it would appear in Wales!

"I did not think he would make his way in with your father before me," said Pitcher again, watching the group.

"If you have given up Captain Vinegar and all his belongings," said Enid, "what have you kept back for yourself, pray?"

"My freedom," said Pitcher without hesitation, as though he had thought out the bargain long ago, and was content with it.

"The freedom of the East?" It was a phrase papa used.

"Freedom to go home. Vinegar is bound up with the East. That is why I gave him up – him and the East together. I shall go home."

"And what shall you do there?" She did not look at him, nor he at her.

"I have an uncle who owns an estate in Kent – but that is only one among many possibilities. I might – my word though," he broke off to say, watching the group under the orange-tree, "it's certain I gave away a good deal in giving away Vinegar. Look at the fellow! Look at your father how he listens! And those Embassy men fawning upon him, who

[125]

wouldn't leave off their breakfast when I went to them at Therapia last year. Shall we join them?"

"Wicker will bring papa to us." She did not want Broadbent and Smallwood to see her with Pitcher, in case they perceived also that she had betrayed herself with him. So they waited, watching.

Whether it was the name of "Vinegar", or whether it was the character inside the name, which was all his own, Quin Hoolaghan's "Captain Vinegar" certainly had surrounded himself with attention, and good humour, and laughter, as he lounged under the orange-tree in his magnificent costume of a Circassian chieftain. Evidently wishing to hear the end of whatever tale the Irishman was telling, Sir Daniel had shaken Wicker's hand off the sleeve of his coat, as he leaned on his stick to listen.

Enid said, "I'm glad to see him enjoying himself a little."

"Roland always said your papa hated a ball."

"He only came because he wouldn't offend Lord Stratford, whom he says is the one gentleman in all of politics and diplomacy who properly understands the importance of commerce – only papa puts it a great deal more forcefully."

"Do you see Lord Stratford much, then? Do you go to Therapia?"

"Not I. But papa goes there to talk now and then. Lord Stratford is the only man whose view he cares about. With the rest of them here he's dreadfully savage. With the army people, whom he blames for the failure in the Caucasus."

"He tells them so to their faces?"

"Of course to their faces. There is nothing of the coward about papa. But if any man could make papa alter his view of a thing, it would be Lord Stratford, who has been at him hammer and tongs to give up his enmity against Herr Novis, and to make them go in together for the Persian trade, instead of cutting one another's throats over routes and tariffs and railway-building plans."

"It would be sensible, not a doubt of it."

"Sensible! It would be sensible if there never was to be any wars or quarrels any more, I suppose."

"Two merchants, though. They must have very much in common. Interests in common, I mean to say." He was watching Vinegar's group, and hardly attending.

"Just so! Two merchants! Lord Stratford from his Embassy looks down and sees a pair of merchants squabbling over shares like a couple of rough boys fighting over a sixpence in the gutter, and he don't see why they can't agree to take threepence each and go along quietly from under his windows. When merchants quarrel," she went on, touched on her raw place, "he don't see warring principles, and enmities shaking the heavens, as he would see if two generals, say, or two diplomatists, was to fall out with one another over a trifle."

"Ah," Pitcher agreed, "it is the aristocratic prejudice, that. To regard 'principles' as their prerogative, because the necessity of money-making don't confuse their ideas as it does with the commercial classes."

"I believe papa would spend his last shilling to bring Herr Novis down."

"It may be so," Pitcher said. "I wonder though. I begin to wonder. Ah – he is coming to us at last."

A final burst of laughter among Captain Vinegar's listeners had released them, and Sir Daniel allowed himself to be walked up to his daughter under Wicker's guidance, and to have his hand shaken by Tresham Pitcher. Though he took the short steps of a blind man on a strange territory, he seemed to look keenly through his gold eye-glasses into the open visor of Pitcher's helm to make out his face.

"So, papa," said Enid softly, to fill in the awkward pause which contrasted with the air of brilliant amusement surrounding Captain Vinegar, "so – you have met the savage Princess, have you?"

"I have met a native woman," he replied in his strong flat voice, "she has been brought up to me, that's to say – for I don't set out to meet such creatures at my age."

"Hush, papa!" Gratification at her father's plain words flushed Enid's heart. "She is uncommonly beautiful, I do assure you."

"What is uncommon," said he no less loudly, "is to meet with such a one at an Embassy ball, where she has been brought in by some gent who knows nothing of the East, and nothing of custom. How do the pashas feel, to see their women here, amongst ours? Eh? But custom is all at Jericho now, since the war. Anything may be done."

"She is truly a Prince's daughter, Sir Daniel," said Pitcher, "I can promise you so much as that."

Sir Daniel turned his blind countenance towards the speaker and told him earnestly, "Whatever she may have been in Mingrelia, Mr Pitcher, she should be an odalisque here, or she should be nothing." He spoke with emphasis. "Such roses cannot be picked in the wilds and brought indoors without their thorns becoming a danger. I was young in the East, sir, long ago. Whoever has brought this greasy creature out of savagedom will learn his mistake, depend upon it – unless indeed he puts her away mighty sharp into a harem, where he limits the damage she may do. Now then. You, Mr Pitcher, you might have learned by the example of your little slave-boy, which Captain Vinegar was just telling us of in his droll way. I never knew before, by the by, that Vinegar was an Irishman: ain't that strange now?" The look he directed at Pitcher's casque had a sudden sharpness about it, as though he saw a long way into that millstone with his blind eyes. "Ain't that queer?" he repeated.

"What slave-boy is this, Mr Pitcher?" asked Enid.

"Oh, a long story."

"But an instructive one, Mr Pitcher," said Sir Daniel. "Mr Pitcher, my dear, bought himself a slave-boy when first he landed at the Caucasus – "

"By an accident, sir. I had no thought of buying – "

"But buy him you did, sir, and he *was* a slave. Well he served you, too, by Vinegar's account of it."

"He was a fierce little fellow," said Pitcher. "Too fierce – ferocious! When we came down out of the mountains and had to live amongst others, in a hut in a swamp, there was no taming him to fit the life. Fights without end he got himself into – he had no notion of not taking what was wanted, and killing to keep it. He near had us all killed. He had the hut burnt over our heads. Vinegar may make a droll story of it in a Pera ballroom, but, my word, at Soukhum he'd have given worlds to be rid of little Tack. But on he came with us to Samsoon, and to Sinop, and each stage went worse with him, he grew fiercer as he understood the ways of the place less, and his savage pride and his savage honour grew the easier to upset. There was a row with the *zaptieh* at Sinop at last. Tack conceived that he had been insulted, and stabbed a police-man. To save his life he had to be got away. There was a ship, a merchant I knew, but Tack wouldn't see his chance, wouldn't go. So – " He paused.

"So – ?" Enid feared the story's outcome, and how she would feel.

Pitcher sighed. "So I sold the little fellow. I know it sounds an odd thing, telling it here. Outlandish. But selling was all Tack understood. He believed that he belonged to me, and it was only if I sold him that he would go off in the merchant's cutter to Trebizond to save his skin. So I sold him for the price of the passage to Trebizond. I daresay he's a pirate by now, and as jolly as a tick, cutting throats wholesale."

Enid said nothing, examining her feelings. She was aware that the barbarous Asia of such stories was only the width of the Bosphorus away, across the strait from Bebec, where she had once come upon those half-eaten grapes on a stone. Mr Pitcher had not really behaved shockingly – in Asia.

Pitcher said, "You have obliged me to tell the story, sir, but I hope Miss Enid won't come down too heavy upon me, or give me away to the Wilberforce fellows."

"You tell the tale, yes, Captain Vinegar – I mean to say Mr Pitcher – aye, you both of you tell the tale, you and Vinegar, but you ain't profited by it, neither of you, not a scrap. That is what I remark upon. Now we must go away, my dear, for the Sultan and his Lordship took themselves off to their beds long since."

Pitcher detained him. "How should we have profited by the story of little Tack, Sir Daniel?"

"What? You should have served the woman you brought down with you from the mountain the same way, sir."

"Sold her?"

"Papa!"

"Aye, sold her to your Sinop merchant, you might have shipped her back to savagedom where her use is. I hope you mayn't regret it, Mr Pitcher. Come now, Enid."

Pitcher walked with them towards the stairway, down which the crowd thronged. The habitude of a few hours made the extravagant costumes seem commonplace. Enid did not take Pitcher's arm. At the head of the stairway he said to Sir Daniel, "Do you go home soon, sir?"

"Home? Ah, to England. Aye, if they allow it to the French to push through their confounded peace, before ever we have a dot of benefit from the war, yes, I shall go to England in disgust, I shall."

Enid took courage to speak: "Perhaps Mr Pitcher will come and see us in Wales, papa, if he isn't too much occupied with other affairs." She was always much bolder towards a stranger when she spoke from within her family circle to him, with her brother or father on her arm.

"Aye, if he cares for it. Come to us in Wales, Captain – Mr Pitcher – come to us at Ravenrig when you are weary of civilisation once more, and try if we cannot find amusement for you among the mountains."

VI

London

'VINEGAR! Just stop half a moment will you!" Pitcher had come out upon the landing of the London hotel, and looked over the bannisters onto the crown of Quin Hoolaghan's hat as it revolved down the stairway below him in pursuit of a porter grasping his baggage.

"Hallo there – goodbye to you, dear man, goodbye!" The hat tipped back to reveal Hoolaghan's cheerful face looking upwards. "I didn't just know where to find you," he claimed. "I've a cab below, so I'll be away now to my train. Goodbye!"

"Stop!" Pitcher hurried downstairs and caught up with his friend in the entrance hall. He had not waited to put on his coat when Hannah had run in to him to say that "the Captain" was decamping, and now he stood in waistcoat and shirtsleeves by the prosperous, frock-coated figure of "Captain Vinegar" in the hallway of the hotel in which they had been established since arriving in London earlier in April. "Now," he said, "just give me a moment of your time, will you, before you rush away from us again. It's so confoundedly hard to catch up with you in this life you lead at the Clubs and the ballrooms! You'll be sure to be back, now, by Monday night next? For we can't leave them alone here, and I must be gone from this on Tuesday to run down to my uncle at Rainshaw."

"Oh, I'll be back for that easy, never a doubt of it. I've to speak in Liverpool on Friday, but I'll be back again Monday, easy. Is the cab here for me?" he enquired of the porter.

No cab waited, so Pitcher and the reincarnated Captain Vinegar strolled to the doorway and looked out into the street. Pitcher still retained his sense of watching from afar, as if in a dream, the wheeled traffic and fashionably dressed figures thronging a street of brick and stone façades. Vinegar, on the other hand, seemed to take whatever befell him as a matter of course, and accept its reality. He dropped on his feet, like a cat. It was extraordinary to Pitcher how quick off the mark he had been. "These lectures you give," he asked, "you had them settled before, did you?"

"There was a Liverpool man at Misseri's with us, and he asked would I give them a talk or two up there."

"Little Haddon, you mean? You didn't tell me he'd asked you to lecture."

"Ah, but you didn't care to talk with Haddon, you see, for he ain't just a gentleman. But he has Liverpool pretty much in his pocket. He's a good fellow, too, for he wants me to counter all the gammon that's been wrote about the east end of the Black Sea. He showed me a piece in one of the journals full of tales would stop any Liverpool man sending his boats there – the air so dark you never could take an observation – the sea so deep it never could be sounded – fogs perpetual – never a safe harbour in the length of it – "

"The truth, in fact."

"Not the truth as Sir Daniel Farr wants it told. Not the truth as I shall tell it. No, no. I'm to stand for trade. Trade and expansion is the ticket I'm to stand upon."

"To stand? Do you mean – "

"I do so," said Vinegar defiantly, tucking his thumbs into his waistcoat as he looked out at the London traffic jingling by, "I believe I may stand for Parliament at some time or another, so I do. 'Tis a life I'd like well. You know they made me a member at the Addington? Well, a couple of fellows came up to me there tother day and put it to me square. If I had Haddon behind me, they said, I might come in for one of the boroughs up there easy. My Irish blood would stand well with the mob, do you see."

Irritated, Pitcher said, "I should take care with Vinegar's Irish blood. He had none of it before."

"Well, he has it now, and it's the making of him entirely," retorted Vinegar.

"Nothing is made yet, that I see," Pitcher said, looking down at his feet, "I wish it were. To have nothing settled in Mingrelia is one thing, but to have nothing settled in London is quite another. The money

[132]

goes out day by day, and we're no farther on, that I see. Not a yard."

"I don't know why you're so devilish glum and gloomy, my boy," said Vinegar, "haven't you the world at your feet? Go out and have a little fun. Go out and give the child a run in the air. Yesterday I took her to see the Tower, and didn't we sit up the two of us on the top of an omnibus eating winkles with a pin, as jolly as two sailors? Faith, she's – "

"Have a care, Hoolaghan, or you'll undo it all. If you try and have the Addington *and* the top of the omnibus, you'll undo it all."

"Dear heaven," said Vinegar, looking round for eavesdroppers and speaking low, "why will you not call me Vinegar? That's how you'll undo it all. Now then," he went on, "where is my cab? I shall miss my train to Manchester if we don't look sharp."

"To Manchester first, eh?"

"Indeed yes, I'm to speak there tonight on the Eastern Question. The Eastern Question and how it affects the trade in cotton prints, that's what the good creatures of Manchester want to know all about, before they will support Sir Daniel and his Mamisson Pass ideas."

"And you're the man to tell them! It's very wonderful," admitted Pitcher, shaking his head and laughing, "when you think of our hut in the swamp at Soukhum, it's very wonderful."

"Sure, won't the will that'll carry a man through the pickles you and I have been in – won't it make light work of finding a few words to say to a hall full of Manchester merchant-men? Won't it carry him into the House of Commons too, by heaven? I believe it may. Look at these fellows about Bond Street, now," he said, taking Pitcher's shirtsleeved arm and indicating the crowd in carriages and strolling on the broad pavement, "will you look and see? They haven't the cutting edge to them of a plank. You and I could walk over their necks into their places any day. Any day. Now, there's the cab come."

"And you'll be sure and be back by Monday night?"

"Don't fret, dear man. Not but what the Princess may be let stop here alone, for what I care. But I'll be back. How are you for tin?"

"Badly. You?"

"Oh, I've a little."

"Borrowed off the Jews?"

"Dear heaven, the Jews are well enough, their bills lie light enough upon me. No," said Vinegar, his face darkening, " 'tis your friend

Crabtree is worse than all the Twelve Tribes together, dunning me for the trifle I borrowed of him at Constantinople. And I thought he was a gentleman. Never mind, it'll all come right," said he, crossing the pavement to the cab. "Did I tell you Buckle and Stourpaine was bringing out a new edition of my book? The sixth."

"Are they just." Of *my* book, Pitcher thought, watching Vinegar's portmanteau put on top of the cab.

"They want another book out of me too," said Vinegar as he climbed in. He dropped the window and spoke through it: "Suppose you just jot down the Caucasus part of the thing, and I have the selling of it, and we share the money, how would that be now?"

Pitcher shook his head. "I'm finished with Vinegar. Enjoy yourself in the North."

"Whatever point of the compass I go to I shall enjoy myself. Goodbye to you now, old fellow, goodbye."

The whip flicked, the hansom joined the traffic, and Hoolaghan's Captain Vinegar was carried away. Pitcher stood in his shirt sleeves watching the cab until it disappeared. There went his invention, his creation, his chance of fame.

*   *   *

At first Tresham Pitcher had been inclined to be jealous of the invitations and interest which Vinegar's arrival in London had elicited from the fashionable world. He had thought that the accolades might have been his, if he hadn't given Vinegar away. But he soon saw that it was to Hoolaghan's manipulation of the character that fame accrued. To himself in Vinegar's guise would have come no membership of the Addington Club in Pall Mall, no invitations – either from Mr Haddon to lecture in Manchester or from countesses to dine in Mayfair – nor any of the public acclaim which Hoolaghan's Vinegar had amassed in a few weeks.

On the steamer home from Constantinople Captain Vinegar had rapidly acquired the character of such a rattling good fellow, such a popular man, that Tresham had felt quite sick about it, especially since he had no companion to share the joke of the thing with. Of course the Princess Mazi knew that Hoolaghan had taken on Vinegar's name, but it had surprised her apparently no more than if they had switched costumes at the Sultan's Ball. Perhaps everything surprised her equally, perhaps she understood nothing: it was impossible to fathom her reactions to the world she had been thrust into. Thank heaven she spoke French. Her French, and her English with its French accent, glossed over (to the respectable ladies on the steamer *Ino*) the true facts of this woman put down amongst them. "A Circassian Princess, you say? (For she had become Circassian rather than Mingrelian as the Caucasus receded, for everyone knows where Circassia is.) How perfectly delightful! Of course, she has been brought up in France?" So the passengers on the *Ino* accepted her, and her daughter Shkara too, who never spoke, and old Hannah with her reassuring Scotch accent. Not a soul on board suspected Pitcher and Hoolaghan of having brought aboard at the Golden Horn a basket of serpents.

There was a Queen's Messenger aboard, a Colonel Turtle, doyen of the English passengers, with a vast experience of the East, whom Tresham had watched anxiously at first in case he should sniff out something of the mountebank about Vinegar, or something fishy in the Princess's party, and so spread unease through saloons and cabins. But Turtle fairly drank down Vinegar's tales of Persia and the Caucasus – "You must give us another book, Captain, I beg of you" – and behaved with blind gallantry to the Princess. Also on the *Ino* was an Eastern Agha, on his way to Tunis by way of Malta. With his veiled odalisques, and his black servants, and his hideous eunuch, he siphoned off upon himself all the tremulous alarm of the English matrons, and lent to Vinegar's party, by contrast, quite an everyday appearance.

Tresham had not become so integrated with the company aboard ship as had Vinegar and the Princess. Having given away his character, he was not sure how to appear to this society. What was his own past, and what was Vinegar's? So he spoke little, taciturn companion to Vinegar's colourful party, a tall, heavily-built man attenuated and lined by the ordeals of a mysterious past, his eyes so habitually narrowed against the suns and dusts of the East that the most inquisitive lady could never quite make out their colour to her satisfaction. When the *Ino*'s passengers looked up from the draughts-board, or from the fluttering pages of a novel, they were used to seeing Mr Pitcher's figure at the rail alone.

He stood at the rail like a man between two existences, in limbo. He felt the blue rollers of the Aegean swell successively under the steamer's counter, and lift her, and thrust her, and shudder away broken-crested in white spray to the south. He heard the wind in the shrouds, and the bubble of the wave-crest at the rail, as he watched the ancient islands passing, the low stony hills, the turf above foam-skirted promontories. The hooves of Centaurs had worn the turf thin on those islands. Ulysses had watched these dark-blue wave crests bubble into foam. Across this hard blue sky the sun was drawn by Phoebus Apollo. So the legends – the legendary history of the ancients which he knew so well – suggested itself out of the wind and the islands and the sea, as a shaft of evening light brightening across a churchyard throws into relief the lettering on worn stones, and makes legible the names and histories of buried forebears. Deities and mysteries and legends crowded into his mind. Sea and sky and islands became animate to him in a way that the landscape of the East, the mounds of Assyria or the desolate steppes of Tartary beyond the Caucasian gates, had never been. That sense of connexion, tinged with nostalgia, which every man feels towards the scenes of his childhood, he had been educated to feel towards antiquity. He was coming home. The Aegean, the haunted sea across which the *Ino* drove her furrow towards Malta, gave him back in place of Vinegar's adventures his own true inheritance.

Having become again a man formed by his own history, having become Tresham Pitcher in place of Captain Vinegar, Tresham was again trammelled and inhibited by that history. No, he could not look upon the Conduit Street crowd at the hotel door through Hoolaghan's, or Captain Vinegar's, contemptuous eyes, as men with no more of a cutting edge to them than a plank, upon whose necks he might walk into whatever place he pleased. This crowd was the settled English upper class. Vinegar might walk into their clubs and ballrooms by the same act of will which had carried him into pasha's palaces and tribesmen's fortresses in Asia; but Tresham Pitcher could not. He did not think that he possessed a will superior to these men and women in the street. Made aware by disdainful glances that he had infringed the rule which forbids any class but the labourer's to appear in the street in his shirt-sleeves, Tresham retreated into the hotel.

He loved the settled comfort of the place. He loved the soundness of it all, and the square brick houses you could see through the windows, and the stone-paved streets, and the gas-lamps making night as safe as day. Perhaps the tall houses opposite limited the view, but he wished to see no further view just now than those well-painted sash windows, and window-boxes full of hyacinths, and chimneys smoking with a cheerful tale of warmth and dinner. So he thought as he stood at his bedroom window looking out. He had earned his share of the comfort consequent upon gas-lamps and constables, which Vinegar had professed so to despise, and he wished to trample upon no man's neck, if he might only be allowed his place in the crowd. He put on his coat in front of the glass. He had grown a stone heavier since he had come home, and he liked the comfortable stoutness of the image in the mirror, though it made his Pera-made coat a little tight.

Money was tighter than coats, though. It had shrunk his resources very severely to put the party into decent clothes and keep a hotel roof over them thus far. Hoolaghan had a guinea or two in his pocket always, perhaps advanced from the publisher, perhaps the outcome of buying a little horse cheap and selling him on dear, perhaps borrowed from the moneylenders at fifty percent interest against a bill due in three months. When he had said at the hotel door that he had "a little", he meant he had sufficient to carry him to Manchester, probably; and in Manchester he would rely upon some minor feat of legerdemain to produce the return half of the railway ticket. Tresham took up his hat, and crossed his room to the door.

Cramped and half dark the hotel rooms were, what with the smoky light and heavy curtains and a great deal of ponderous furniture, but there was a comfort he liked well about their unruffled calm, and enjoyed as he walked down the long silent corridor with here and there a little gas-jet hissing like a guardian serpent at the sanctuary door. He remembered looking down into one of the saloons of the Ino through a deck-hatch, drawn to it by piano music: he had a bird's eye view of morocco sofas and stuffed chairs, and pampas grass in a brass vase, which had prefigured all the respectable little parlours of England lying ahead of the *Ino* at journey's end. Through the deck-hatch issued

[137]

piano music, to be scattered by the wind. His mother's Clapham parlour, to which he was going at this moment from the hotel, was not unlike that saloon. Journey's end! – he hoped not. He would pay a visit to Laidlaw Villa, and come away. It was not journey's end. He walked down the passage towards the sitting room shared with the Princess's party.

What Tresham found reassuring about the hotel – the heavy sedate order of it all, the bells, and chambermaids, and bathrooms – had quite knocked the Mingrelians off their balance. It was strange: in Alatstchinsk the Princess had seemed to surround herself with European comfort, eating at a table, furnishing her parlour in her father's rat-ridden wooden "palace": at Misseri's, and on the Ino, she had seemed quite at home with western ways: but her powers of adaptation had failed in face of this London hotel. She had never behaved, nor looked, so little "like a Christian". Even her complexion, moonlit marble in Tresham's memory of her in the Caucasus, had a sallow sort of look in the London light, like straw paper. As for Hannah, she lurked about like a prisoner, and was utterly cowed by the Irish chambermaids. Was it the size of the place? Was it London at the window? What was it?

He opened the sitting room door and went in. The Princess was upon her little feet at the window – looking out through the lifted lace curtain with what thoughts, he wondered – and she turned in her quick nervous way. She was dressed to go out, in a bonnet and a half-veil and a dress of some brown stuff. Awkward: he didn't mean that she should go with him to Clapham. Yet all in the same irritated instant his heart went out to her, for she had dressed herself so carefully to pass unnoticed in the street. That plain brown dress drabbening her figure, and the little veil over her enormous eyes, made him think of royalty venturing out in a town patrolled by regicides.

"Well," said he, taking the hand she always offered in greeting, "well – he is gone."

"I have watched," she replied, letting her eyes fall upon him with such a gaze as shrivelled away the veil.

"Ah." Had she dressed herself to go to Manchester with Captain Vinegar, and not at all to go with himself to Clapham? Was her bag packed next door? Uncertainty was a familiar element in all consideration of the Princess and Hoolaghan: he never knew how they stood to one another. He disengaged his hand, moved out of range of her mysterious eyes.

Tresham had puzzled over the connexion between Hoolaghan and the Princess Mazi as long as he had known them. Once, in the open cutter running from the Mingrelian coast to Samsoon, he had settled the question, as he thought. It was night, very cold, the wrapped figures of refugees crammed from gunwhale to gunwhale of the little boat, when the beam of a lantern swung in a seaman's hand had shown him for an instant Hoolaghan and Mazi where they huddled close to one another, and close in talk. When the lantern-beam wavered elsewhere, Tresham had been left with an insight. They were intimate, but they were not lovers. What they shared was the intimacy of accomplices. The lantern had shown him a pair of accomplices on their way from one field of operations to another. That was what kept them talking together in the black of the night on the cold broad sea.

Nonetheless, he remained uncertain. The idea that the Princess might have dressed herself to go off to Manchester with Vinegar, as his lover or as his accomplice, served to persuade Tresham that he should like her company himself at Clapham after all. She would be the necessary stranger to restrain his mother's emotion at this first meeting. Besides, a Rachinskiy Princess was after all rather a brilliant prize to show off at Laidlaw Villa. Shkara too he would take. He had crossed the room to the table where the child was turning the pages of a picture-book silently.

"Good morning, dear Shkara," he said, laying his hand on her thin straight hair with all the love he felt for the little girl. She stopped turning the pages, crouched mouse-still under his hand. "Come," he said, suddenly cheerful, "we will all go up to Clapham, shall we? Shall we, Princess? You know I am going up to see my mother?"

"Is there a graveyard near to her house?"

"A graveyard?"

"For to walk in while you talk with your mother."

"No, no, you shall come in. A graveyard! There is a common, but you shan't walk in it, you shall come in. My poor mother – I will like to have your company." He rather dreaded the maternal tears, the clinging hands, the inadequacy of his own response. The Princess would shield him. The more he thought of taking her, the more he liked it.

*　　*　　*

It had seemed to Tresham Pitcher impossible, and undesirable too, to bring the Princess out of the wild Caucasus into Europe. But Hoolaghan didn't see it – he never did see that one person was much different from another – and he thought that she would do as well in Europe as anyone else. So they had agreed to bring her, and had ridden from the waterfall cave to the tower among the mountains where she was. The scene at the tower had been so confused, horsemen spurring this way and that, mist blowing over the grey walls, flight and treachery everywhere suspected, that it hadn't been clear whether the Princess Mazi was prisoner or commander. Having just given away the identity of Captain Vinegar to Hoolaghan, in exchange for Tresham Pitcher's life, Pitcher was himself disoriented and bewildered. Hoolaghan issued the orders, and gave out the dozen Enfields they had brought from the cave. Then in a rapid rush of footsteps came the Princess running to him. "You take me? I think we leave them all, then we go quicker I think, then my father will not know I am escaped." "Leave Shkara and Hannah?" "Yes I think." Looking into her face, Tresham saw there a desperate eagerness like lust. "There is no question," he said harshly, turning from her, "Shkara and Hannah come with us."

That glimpse of her ruthlessness tainted Tresham's feelings for the Princess with apprehension. The woman who would leave her only child among savages so as to delay her father's pursuit of herself would surely commit any barbarity. He would have left her, but Hoolaghan – the new Captain Vinegar – had insisted that she was their *laissez-passer* through the disturbed country to the coast. Of course they were accomplices, as the lantern-beam in the cutter had revealed. Each was a part of the other's stock-in-trade, and so they had stuck together, the Mingrelian Princess and the Irish adventurer.

It was Shkara whom Tresham grew to love during their flight from the tower to Constantinople. Aboard that same cutter to Samsoon he had recognised it. He had taken the child from Hannah, who was sea-sick, and had wrapped her up with himself in his cloak under the gunwhale. Inside the cloak little hands had sought his neck, a warm head had settled against his heart; a sigh, then the peace and stillness of a child's trust enclosed him too in angel wings. No child had ever slept in his arms before. He understood how old Hannah had sat long hours on the mud floor of the abominable hut in the swamps of Soukhum, so still against the wall with Shkara sleeping in her arms that the red eyes of the rats had twinkled round her feet. No doubt Shkara thought herself in Hannah's arms in the boat, but if she had woken, or struggled or cried out, all his pride and glory would have been dashed in pieces. Was there no picture, no ivory carving, of Jesus asleep in Joseph's arms during the flight to Egypt?

He had revealed to no one how dearly he loved the child. Such a breach into his heart exposed him awfully: it put him at the mercy of a barbarous mother. As he sat between mother and daughter in the growler on its way to Clapham, he thought of all this. Shkara looked out of the window through wondering dark eyes, asking no questions, her "horse" clasped under one arm. Somewhere she had acquired this piece of driftwood, perhaps on the beach at Soukhum, which either by chance or by rough carving possessed four stubs for limbs, and a knob for a head. She loved it with a solicitousness which she showed for no human or animal creature. Aboard the *Ino* one of the English matrons who sat knitting under an awning amidships, like so many Britannias queening it over the waves, had knitted for the toy a pair of trousers, taking it for a naked doll which required decent covering. Not unkindly, Shkara had refused the present, saying, "It's a horse, and it doesn't have clothes." Tresham had been for some reason secretly pleased by this rebuff, though he had apologised to the offended Britannia.

It had amused Tresham to see how the Princess had insinuated herself amongst the ladies aboard the *Ino*, so demure, her eyes downcast, so ready to be instructed. He had watched her from the ship's rail, the sea seething past: "So glistered the dire snake," he thought. A following wind ruffled the wave-backs, and swelled the white sails, and drove the steamer's smoke before her, hurrying the *Ino* on towards England. There was a wounded lieutenant aboard, a pleasant quiet fellow travelling alone, who perhaps lacked courage to attack the Princess Mazi direct, and so instead took Shkara on his knee, and drew animals for her amusement, and told her English nursery-rhymes, and showed her the letters of the alphabet. He was always at it. Tresham, outraged to see Shkara made a catspaw, walked away up the shuddering deck to the mizzen shrouds. As he stood watching the toppling wave-crests surge by, nursing his anger against the lieutenant, he felt a hand thrust through the crook of his arm from behind, a hand which spread its fingers over his sleeve like the tendrils of a vine-creeper. It was the Princess claiming him. "Round and round you walk. What you think of? Our friends watch you go round, and they wonder. Mrs Trotter say you leave your heart behind." "Mrs Trotter attributes all human actions to the influence of Aphrodite." "So, what you think really as you go?" That she was the "dire snake"? That he feared her? The clasp of her hand on his arm communicated the pulse of her savage blood into his. "Come," she said, "Shkara is asking for you, come." It was a lie, but he went with her.

The growler climbed the familiar hill towards Clapham, and he answered the questions the Princess asked him about himself, and his childhood, and his family. If he thought he had opened the door into his home only wide enough to admit a refugee, he found that he could not now force it shut in face of the retinue of questions and intimacies which streamed in with her. But she was mistaken (he told himself) if she thought that the door of Laidlaw Villa was the door to break down so as to get at him. Next week he would escape her and go down to Rainshaw. His step-uncle's old house amongst its oaks rose before his mind's eye, tranquil, the mild light touching its façade, or glinting in window-glass – journey's end, beyond reach of pursuit. And Shkara? He put his hand over her where it rested on the cab seat beside him, and felt her fingers flutter like trapped wings. She had tried to break down no doors, but she was within his heart wherever he might go.

"Here we are!" He saw the sooty trees fringing the common, saw the railings, the gate between laurels, the path straight to the front door. At a window his mother no doubt watched for his return, exhausted with her own emotion. "Here we are," he repeated, with resignation.

Having paid the driver the half-guinea he asked, Tresham lifted the familiar gate-latch, kept Shkara's hand in his own, and followed the Princess's cloak and bonnet up the path towards the silent house. How it would erupt into tears and blessings and embraces when he pulled the bell! And how he dreaded it! The door opened. Not his mother but

Meg, the old Scotch maidservant, stood at the top of the steps with her hands clasped.

"Meg! – dear Meg!" He ran up the steps to grasp her hand. It was not enough: he must embrace her, knocking her cap sideways. Expecting emotion in other people only, he was shocked at its strength in himself.

"O, Master Tresh!" She half-wept, half-laughed.

He felt the patter of the heart in her thin body. He was home. Old Meg, his first friend! Now that his heart was breached, he longed to see his mother. But Meg had stiffened, and drawn back, and was looking at his two companions at the bottom of the steps.

"Master Tresh, is the lady – is the bairn – ?"

"Meg, this is Princess Rachinskiy, and Shkara her daughter."

A curtsey and a granite countenance; then Meg turned to lead them indoors. Whilst they put off cloaks below, she had mounted the narrow stairs, limping a little. Tresham heard her open the parlour door, and heard his mother's voice: "Is he not come even yet, Meg?"

"Aye, he's come. There's two come with him."

"Two with him?"

By now Tresham had run upstairs and was in the room, coming towards her chair by the fire. She laid her worn fine hands on the chair's arm to help her stand, and said,

"Ah, Tresh, in you come, and most welcome." She kissed him drily, closing her eyes, and repeated "Welcome. We didn't know if you would be so soon."

She was so slight, so old, so fragile to touch. The skin of her cheek was like a withered petal. He was rather horrified by the change in her. He introduced her to the Princess Mazi and to Shkara, who looked up with earnest questioning eyes into her face. In response Mrs Wytherstone stooped and kissed the child with affection, or pity.

"You are most welcome, too," she said, holding Shkara's shoulders for a moment in her hands.

It was a gesture which showed Tresham that his mother saw into his heart, as she had always done. In gratitude he put his hand under her arm. Her perception and her tact communicated her love for him through the medium of what he loved. He had forgotten her tact. Meanwhile the Princess stood apart, a shadow against the window.

"Shall we all sit down?" suggested Mrs Wytherstone, indicating a seat to the Princess. "Do you sit there, Mrs – Mrs – "

"Princess, mother. Princess Mazi."

"Ah, I am a little old to begin with princesses and curtsies. Would it do if I was to call you 'Madame'?"

"Pray, pray call me Mazi, or what you please," answered the Princess humbly as she took the offered chair.

"Her name means 'the moon'," said Tresham. He felt more responsible for the creature here in his mother's parlour than ever he had done before.

"The moon. Fancy. Now," said Mrs Whytherstone, "we will have our tea, I think, directly. Tresh, would you just call out to Meg? Or shall the child run down to her? Little girl, will you run down to the kitchen and ask the kind woman there if we may have our tea?"

Tresham looked at Shkara, surprised. He had never thought of her as an ordinary English child to be sent on an errand. What would she do with his mother's orders? Carefully she put down her wooden toy – the same that she had found on the beach at Soukhum – and ran off through the door. It was easy.

"Sit down there, will you Tresh," said his mother, putting him into her own fireside chair and herself taking a stool nearby. Across the fire Mr Wytherstone's chair was left unused; indeed, it did not look as though it was much sat in at all. But his mother's chair, Tresham saw was a little fortress stocked with supplies to withstand the siege of loneliness. Book, sewing, a solitaire board, all spoke of hours whiled away without company. Tresham made these observations whilst he asked about the family, his two stepsisters, his stepfather, and his grandfather McPhee.

"Is he still up there in Wester Ross, and well?"

"He keeps on about the same as ever," his mother replied, as if change were unexpected and such a question surprising. "He was down to Edinburgh last summer, but you will have heard of that."

"How can I have heard of it, mother? I have been away from England six years." She did not seem to appreciate the extent of his absence. He had expected to be overwhelmed with tears and emotion – had dreaded it – but she spoke as if he had been a week at Boulogne. Well, he mightn't complain of the lack of what he had dreaded.

"So! Is it six years? Then I daresay it is longer gone by than summer last that your grandpapa was down to Edinburgh. Meg," she enquired of the servant who now came in with a tray, "Meg, is it last year the Minister was down to Edinburgh?"

"Bless you madam no! Three years come Whitsun. It was whiles we had Miss Eliza here poorly, mind, and the bairn is going on three now. Put the milk down there, child," she finished coldly to Shkara, who had carefully carried in the jug. Tresham smiled at the child.

Whilst the tea was served out, and he sat by the fire in the quiet of the room listening to Meg and his mother disputing domestic dates, an image came into Tresham's mind of how an iron hoop, such as boys beat along the road, may be kept upright and rolling onwards by rapid strokes on its rim; but let the strokes fail, and the hoop will stagger, and reel, and soon collapse into stillness and silence in the grass by the road. Pulse by pulse, instant by instant, such lives as those of Hoolaghan and Captain Vinegar are kept upright and rolling by the iron strokes of the will. Here in this room was the silence and stillness by the edge of the road. Let Hoolaghan or Vinegar lose momentum into such a backwater, and they failed utterly; tottered and fell like the hoop. But Tresham believed that he existed here; in his childhood home, in his mother's chair by the fire, he found that he existed. Sustained by a context, and by antecedents, it was not necessary to construct and support his character instant by instant as a traveller in remote lands must do, keeping up the momentum which alone preserves existence by strokes of the iron will driving himself onward through alien scenes. If he sat on here in his mother's chair, or went down to Kent to his step-uncle's house, it was not he himself – not Tresham Pitcher – who would cease to exist, but Captain Vinegar. And "Captain Vinegar" he had long since given away to Hoolaghan, in the waterfall cave, in exchange for Tresham Pitcher's life.

"I do not know what is his plan," the Princess's voice aroused him from musing. He came to himself. His mother never would know how very long he had been away, and how very far from home. He smiled at her, and she repeated her question:

"And will you soon be off again?"

It was asked with seeming indifference, as she carried her tea cup from the tray to her stool by Tresham's side.

"Never," he said. "I shall never go back to the East."

She looked into his face eagerly; and then sadly looked away. "Ah," she sighed, "so you think. So your father used to think, when he was home safe from his scurries over the world."

"I shan't go back ever," he repeated.

The two women were silent. The child played on the hearth. Presently Mrs Wytherstone said to the Princess, "Do you know, when he was a boy he ran off from his school down to the navvies' camp in Kent. Oh dear, do you remember it, Tresh? It was only a few miles, and he was back with us in a day or two, but oh! the pain of it. You can worry but once, with such bitter pain as that. I never worried over you all the time you were in the East, as I did that once you were in Kent."

"I am to go down into Kent again on Tuesday," said Tresham, "to Rainshaw, you know. I shall stop for good this time."

"Yes, so you say."

"I shall, mother. You see if I don't."

"Well Tresh, I hope you may."

The exasperation of attempting to convince his mother came back to him from childhood. No course of action, no development of character, is allowed to a child by its mother, except what may be predicted from nursery precedents. That was a condition of existence in this context of home and antecedents, where no acts of will were required to keep the hoop of a man's life upright and in motion. He said earnestly to his mother, "I am to live at Rainshaw. I am to come into the place after Uncle Marcus' death. I am, mother. I told you of it in my letter."

"I hope you may," she repeated, "if you have built upon it."

"It was promised me ever so long ago, in a letter Uncle Marcus wrote me to Damascus. I don't suppose he will choose to go back on his word."

"It is so much better to be sure of a thing, before you count upon it for your happiness."

"And why am I not to be sure?"

"Eliza and her little boy have been down there such a very great deal."

Now, Eliza was Tresham's step-sister. Neither she nor her sister May had ever been asked to Rainshaw, before Tresham had left England: and Eliza's marriage to a Mr Walter Roach, of Sydenham, had seemed to confirm her in the downward social spiral which would carry her further than ever from her Uncle Marcus' notice.

"Have they, by Jove!" Tresham rubbed his chin. "Well, I suppose I may depend upon my uncle's word, and upon – " Upon the fact that he was a gentleman, which Walter Roach most certainly was not. True, Uncle Marcus' response, on receipt of Tresham's announcement of his arrival in London, had been an enigmatic note dictated to his house-keeper. True, a letter or two written from Baghdad, and another from Constantinople, had been all the communication he had held with his step-uncle since he had received that letter from him at Damascus seeming to offer him the inheritance of Rainshaw. Still, he had not supposed that arrangements would have been altered in his absence. He looked at his mother. He had not supposed that she would have grown so much older while he was away, either. "I believe I may depend upon it," he finished.

"If that is what you want," said his mother, turning the rings unquietly on her finger whilst she gazed at Shkara playing with her "horse".

"So – " the Princess leaned forward, one white hand laid on her bosom. "So, there is some thing not sure about it in Kent?"

"Pray don't concern yourself for me," Tresham snapped at her. He had not known that she was aware of his expectations. But she was. She had found it out somehow. He remembered the thrust of her arm through his on the *Ino*, claiming him in front of all those Britannias knitting amidships. Now there she sat by his mother's fire, her black eyes steadily upon him. "So glistered the dire snake – "

"Let me just fetch something I have put by," said Mrs Wytherstone, rising impulsively and leaving the room.

The Princess, still leaning towards Tresham, asked in her low voice, "Where is the husband?"

"At business," said Tresham shortly.

"What is this business?"

"He is a tea-merchant."

"And the other wife?"

"Other wife?"

"Yes, the mother of your sisters. Is the woman in kitchen?"

"What?" Was it possible that this barbarian believed that two wives would share a Clapham villa with one husband, the discarded wife to

[147]

work in the kitchen? What seep of the outlandish dark had he admitted with this woman into the citadel of home? He felt his flesh creep under her gaze. And how horribly desirable she was to him in his mother's parlour, like an actress in a church. "My stepfather's first wife is dead," he said as coldly as he could, fearful that his feelings and desires would leak into his voice and let her know her strength.

"Now," said his mother, re-entering the room, "now, child, here is a doll I had put by, which you shall have if you care for it."

Watching her stoop by the child and put the pretty German doll into her hands, Tresham started forward. "Oh mother –!"

"Yes Tresh?"

He was sure it would be rejected. He was aware of a crisis in his feelings at bringing these two Mingrelians into his home. But the toy was not rejected. Shkara tucked it under her arm, and went on playing with her wooden "horse". With a little laugh his mother resumed her seat on the stool, turning it towards the Princess's chair and beginning to question her about Shkara and about herself.

Tresham sat back. This was what it was like to be at home. He had put off coming home – had dreaded his mother's emotions – because he had not accurately remembered its comforts, which balanced its constraints, and had forgotten his mother's composure and tact and self-dependence, which contained her emotions. He listened to the talk. His mother had got upon the subject of her travels from Italy with himself after his father's death at Rimini. It was her saga – her Aeneid. How would that journey sound to the Princess Mazi's ears? He remembered Mazi preparing their rice in the sodden dark of the hut at Soukhum, while the rain fell in torrents on the mud outside: Mazi sunk by necessity into one identity with all the other women in the huts in that swamp, an identity shared with his mother in that inn-yard long ago at Dôle, where she had despaired of feeding himself and of paying the fare in the diligence next day. Yes, he thought, they know one another at bottom, as all women do. He could let them talk.

He rose and went to the window looking over the back garden and over the immense smoke-laden stretches of London below the blackened trees at the garden's end. He stood listening to his mother's voice. There by the fire the child played, there the silver on the tea-table glinted. Supposing he were married – to Mazi. Suppose they lived together at Rainshaw, all was settled, and from their quiet lives among the Kent oaks they had run up to London. He tried on the idea like a pair of slippers, and took a few paces in his imagination. It would secure Shkara to him. Certainly he loved Shkara. Didn't he even rather love the idea of marriage, if it would secure Shkara?

Through the hazy vastness of London below wound the coils of the river reflecting the wet light of the April sky. Near the Tower he could see sails creeping upon the river, white topsails. *There lies the port, the vessel puffs her sail.* A scene aboard the *Ino* came into his mind. Steadying himself against the windward rail, watching the violet cliffs of Turkey across the wild blue sea, there had suddenly dashed into view another vessel. He had heard the wind drum in her taut canvas, and the seas crash on her quarter, so close she cut to *Ino*. A felucca, lateen-rigged, cutting suddenly so close to the English steamer as the swing of a sword-blade! Her prow slashed through the seas, her bird-beak figurehead hunted through the sky, her sail curved slim as a gannet's wing. Her crew lay barefoot and turbanned against the steep pitch of her deck, watching Ino through eyes black as gun-muzzles. A pirate-ship! A Turkish pirate after them from some cove among the cliffs, a great fire on the beach, a cave-full of captives; slavery, or service in the pirate felucca. Ah, piracy for me, he had thought. His heart had leaped up at the whiff of such freedom. Adventures! He thought of Nogai's cutter running arms from Trezibond to Zikinzir, returning him to Asia and to adventure, and his heart yearned after the felucca striking white fountains from the Aegean as she sailed close-hauled for the shadowy isles, rapidly past, soon vanished. She was gone, and part of himself went with her. "Captain Vinegar" went with her.

So there was no part of Tresham Pitcher left, surely, to yearn after those distant sails crowding London's river, as he watched them from the parlour window of Laidlaw Villa? The slippery-wet light of April gleamed out suddenly on London between dark clouds. He was home, and would stay.

VII

Rainshaw

1

THE MAY BREEZE BLEW SOFT from one slope of the parkland at Rainshaw to another, and ruffled the lake between. From its crest the old many-windowed house looked over the water through the fans of broad oaks to the slope where Tresham Pitcher was walking with Shkara. Round them the beeches were in tender leaf, sheep and clamorous lambs were scattered over the turf, the greens and blues of spring shone in the sunny air. The oaks, though, were as yet leafless, and cast the black lattice of winter shadow on the grass. Tresham had found himself avoiding these netted shadows, as if they were the webs of a spider which lurked in each crooked oak. Now he stood looking down upon the valley.

"I saw them make the lake," he told Shkara, thinking of the scene. Under the trees the labourers' women and children had gossiped and played. The barrows had cut yellow tracks from the claypits to the dam along either slope, and only a rushy stream had wound through the valley. And he himself had been young.

"Are you very old?" Shkara might have read his mind, looking doubtfully from his face to the lake among its reeds and trees.

"I must be." For it seemed very long ago. The gulf of a whole life opened between this "now" and that "then". The whole life he had led out of England – the life of Captain Vinegar, so to speak – severed him from that other self which had watched the lake made. He looked across the valley at the house. Why was it that Rainshaw appeared from here a perfect picture, the very house of a traveller's dreams of rest and quietness; and yet, within, the dream was dispersed, and the place seemed not quite the happy mansion it appeared to be from afar? The gulf was uncrossable. Over there stood the simple views of England and childhood, the close horizon to the church, or to the chestnut woods which rimmed the park. If only he might school his eyes not to search beyond the quiet English woods in hope of a wall of ice-mountains piercing the heavens. If only he had not seen the Caucasus, if only he had not felt his heart lift to the chinese-white peaks of Circassia as they had appeared from the deck of Nogai's cutter setting sail from Trebizond! Did Shkara look for the Caucasus behind the chestnut woods? Or was she content? "Do you miss the mountains?" he asked her.

"What was under the lake?"

"Under it? Well, there were rushes, and a stream, and two oak trees. I helped cut one of them down."

"How did you do it? From a boat?"

"It was before there was water in the lake." He watched her try to see things as they had been, a lake without water in it. But she could not cross the gulf. The rector's power had worked with nature's, just as nature's briars as well as the fairy's spell engulfed the Sleeping Beauty's palace; and his lake, his creation, had so sunk into the landscape that she could not imagine it away. She gave it up.

"Can we go in the boat again?" she asked.

"We can."

"Now, can we? Can I do the oars?"

He took her hand. He loved her for giving up difficult lessons and declaring it a holiday for them both. She clasped his fingers, just as her arms had first clasped his neck in that open boat on the Black Sea. But now she did not think it was Hannah's arms she slept in, now her fingers didn't flutter within his grasp like a trapped bird's wings, now trust and fellowship united their two hands. They walked down together to the lake shore. There, in an inlet among reeds, shaded over by alder and hazel, stood a boathouse. Within lay the lovely craft waiting silently. Into it they stepped, rippling the shadowed water till it lapped the piles of the jetty. Shkara sat in the wicker-panelled stern seat and took up the rudder-strings as he had taught her. They smiled at each other as he leaned on an oar to propel the boat onto the lake. Out of the dark mouth of the boathouse they shot, into light glinting on the lustre of

[151]

varnish, gleaming along the dripping oar, where the sun flashed down onto the lake through beeches. He fitted oars into rowlocks with a rattle which echoed off reeds and sent a coot scuttering away across the water.

"Now," he said, sitting down to his work, 'steer where you like in all the seven seas."

"The castle?"

"The tower? Very well, to the tower." He reached forward for his stroke. Before this day he had kept her away from the grey tower glimpsed down the lake, and they had rowed to the cascade, or to bays and inlets which they had given fanciful names, and had imagined as the scenes of pirate exploits. Now let the smile of spring and of childhood – the clamour of the lambs and the shaken sunlight under the beeches – preserve him from the past, and what he knew of the Palmyra Tower. He might cross back over the gulf, if she would keep hold of his hand. A stroke drove the boat out of the creek's shade into open water which the breeze wrinkled and made to chuckle under the forefoot.

How suddenly large the lake became, seen from the water, and how high above it frowned the Gothic outline of the house against the sun! They seemed to be far from any shore, under scrutiny from hostile windows. There had been no boat on the lake when Tresham had last been at Rainshaw – only since his seizure had the rector taken to being rowed about his lake by a servant – so that this altered, waterborne perspective of the house had surprised him, and even now chilled him a little. Just then the clock upon the stables struck eleven, the notes soaring out like cannon-shots from the hilltop to bracket the boat with the almost visible splashes of a bombardment. The clock tower was new. When Tresham noticed it, his step-uncle had said, unusually expansive as to his motives, "Yes, I made up my mind at the age of sixty, when my repairs here were pretty much complete, that I would try how it was to hear a clock strike away the hours. If I am not to be content in my old age, why, bless me, I shall deserve to be reminded of it each hour, I shall indeed." And was he content? Tresham guessed that the clock's tongue would very soon have been silenced, if Uncle Marcus had not liked its message. He had always been used to control his surroundings absolutely, making and breaking what he pleased.

Clock and boat were new to Tresham, but the tower had been there before. The tower had been built when first the lake was made, a stone turret where the lake's furthest and narrowest winding would just lap its foot. The rector had built it of ragstone taken from "repairs" to the parish church, which stood in his park, and his design had followed Wood's engravings of the tower-tombs at Palmyra, of which he had a folio amongst the books of travel in his library. The Palmyra Tower, indeed, had been intended to house his library of travel, with a comfortable upper room looking down the lake in which he might have read and pondered upon distant scenes; but the site and the building had proved too damp for this purpose, and so the tower had stood empty.

Empty, save for one wretched tenant. When (to the rector's hearty satisfaction) the railway-building works had been abandoned beyond his woods over the hill, certain stray creatures who had followed the navvies into the parish had remained, for want of any place else to go, and it was one of these women, with her infant, who had crept into the Palmyra Tower. Here she had lived most miserably until, taking her child in her arms, she had walked out into the waters of the rector's new lake, and had drowned them both. Tresham had dug her grave. By chance, on a visit, he had entered the church to find his step-uncle reading the Burial Service over her coffin, and the sexton Fettle too drunk to dig her a grave sufficiently deep. On that visit, too, before leaving for the East, he had entered the Palmyra Tower. He remembered now, as he rowed Shkara towards it, the January wind launching flotillas of shrivelled leaves onto the lake water, and the scrape of the tower door as it opened. What had he seen within? Rats scattering from an oozy shape, a stench of death, a spreading stain, leaves creeping over the floor. He had shut the door quick, and run away.

Now, as he rowed up the lake facing Shkara and the dazzle of the sun on water, he was aware of the Palmyra Tower growing taller and darker in its trees behind him. He was aware of another scene too, his approach to that other tower, at Palmyra itself: an Arab child hastening along the scree of a stony slope towards one of the tombs, carrying a basket whose weight almost unbalanced him: how he himself had dashed across the dry white valley, and slipped between worn stones into the tomb: and what he had found there, what he had touched in the basket. Now the two towers made a double image arising among the trees behind him. He kept his eyes on Shkara. As Perseus directed himself by watching his dreadful objective in the mirror of his shield, so he watched to see the tower's approach mirrored in the child's eyes.

The lake's shore closed in on either hand. Entangling stems of water-lilies caught at his oars. The boat slid into shade over the veiled water. Leaf-shadow fled over them, dappling her face made anxious by steering. The stem grated, shuddered over snags, stopped – stopped as if the claws of a Medusa had grasped its prow behind his back. "Look!" she cried. He turned.

The tower was a ruin. Parapet stones had fallen, fissures zig-zagged like lightning-strikes through mortar and masonry, ivy clasped the shattered walls. It was a ruin, picturesque. The grey shafts of beeches rising around it supported their canopy of May leaf overhead, and ladysmock grew among the fallen stones. The Medusa was slain, and he looked at Shkara as full of love and gratitude as if her hand had destroyed the double-imaged tower which had haunted him.

"Can we land? Is it empty?"

"Yes. It is empty. I think so."

He stood up, measuring the long step to the shore. Strange how unwilling he was to wet his feet in this English lake, when he thought of the rivers and marshes of Asia he had waded. He hesitated, rather pleased with a fastidiousness which seemed to settle him into English ways. There was a splash behind him. He looked round. Shkara had jumped in.

"Oh, it's deep! It's cold!"

She splashed ashore, and ran up to the tower's door squelching mud and water out of her button boots and draggled skirt. It was where the woman had drowned with her child. There flashed upon Tresham's mind the image of Shkara drowned. Destroy the past, and you have the future to fear. Love gives hostages to fortune. He made the long step to the root of a beech tree, and followed her up to the door. Any one of the hours hoarded within that clock can kill what you love.

It was a heavy door, nailed, with a rusted iron ring-handle which she pushed at. "I can't open it."

"I expect it's locked. I expect it's dangerous." He didn't try the door, looked up at the threatening stonework. "Let's leave it."

"I want to see in."

Well, he thought, if she has killed the Medusa, the tower will be empty. If she has not – he grasped the iron ring and pushed the door, which grated inward into darkness. She walked straight in, eagerly. There was nothing in the world she feared.

"It is empty!" She sounded disappointed.

He followed her. Yes, seen through her eyes, it was empty. But he noticed that her leaking boots had left footsteps staining the stone floor with water as those of a drowned *revenant* are said to do. Through his own eyes, he could not help seeing that.

2

A week ago, in London, with the day at hand for Pitcher to travel down to Rainshaw on his own, there had been no sign from the North of Captain Vinegar, no news of his return from Liverpool. Pitcher's suspicion was confirmed by this silence. On the Black Sea he had glimpsed their accompliceship, which had lasted them well through the weeks at Constantinople; but on board the *Ino* it had been dissolved. That promiscuous thrust of the Princess's arm through his, as he had stood by the *Ino*'s rail, had signalled her switch of allegiance. He knew it in retrospect. At that moment she had turned for her support from Hoolaghan to himself. On the boat her attention, and her weight on his arm, had rather flattered him; but he had not reckoned up what a very real weight her dependence upon him in England might become. He had in truth regarded her as more or less belonging to Hoolaghan, until it was too late. Even shared with Hoolaghan, the responsibility had seemed light – all responsibilities shared with Hoolaghan weighed light – but on Pitcher alone the Princess's party weighed awfully heavy. He couldn't afford to leave them indefinitely on their own at Limmer's hotel, even if he could have hardened his heart sufficiently to leave Shkara to fade away in those dim plush rooms. What could he do? Could he take them to Rainshaw? And then there had come back into his mind the idea of marriage he had had in his mother's parlour at Clapham.

He wrote off to Uncle Marcus:

Limmer's Hotel
Conduit Street, London, W

May 9th 1856

Dear Uncle Marcus,

Whilst I am anticipating most keenly the fulfilment of my engagement to come down to you on the 14th inst, I must apprise you of a circumstance which may very probably affect my independence.

I contracted, whilst in the wildest recesses of the Caucasus, an obligation and an attachment to a Princely family of those parts, the Rachinskiy, whose ancestry may be traced back very readily to the old Colchian kings – perhaps to Aeetes himself – and, upon the break up into disorder of that country, consequent upon the fall of Kars and the retreat of Omer Pasha, I found entrusted to my protection a Rachinskiy Princess and her infant child. I escorted this Lady through many dangers as far as Constantinople, where her high position and royal blood ensured her reception by Lord Stratford and numerous noblemen of all countries into that brilliant society; and I have accompanied her to London, where she finds herself half-exile, half-refugee, and largely dependent upon my protection until she shall decide her course of action.

I believe you would not wish me to abandon at a London hotel this victim of war – victim, indeed, of a British policy which ended the war without thought of its courageous allies amongst the peoples of the Caucasus, now mercilessly preyed-upon by the Cossack – but whether or not you will be willing to extend to herself and her small daughter the hospitality you have been generous enough to offer to myself, I cannot presume to anticipate. I will, however, wait in hopes at this address until I receive word of your decision.

Your affectionate and dutiful nephew,
T. Pitcher

PS. Having received the education of a French lady of good family, the Princess Mazi speaks that language, and English, as

[156]

well as I do myself, whilst a nurse educated by Scotch missionaries ensures that the manners and language of the child are all that may be desired. T.P.

Having sent this letter, Tresham waited. Bored with kicking his heels about the West End and the Park, with nothing to do and no acquaintance, he wondered what his feelings would be if Hoolaghan should choose to reappear, and make it unnecessary for him to take the Princess's party with him to Rainshaw. He thought he would wish to take them all the same, if Uncle Marcus would have it.

The truth was, Pitcher had no other prospect. He had no acquaintance in London, no club, no life to take up again: all the society he had known before starting for the East had been his fellow-clerks at the Inland Waterways, whom he had despised, and a few rich young men, intimates of Roland Farr, who would undoubtedly have despised him had they not been deceived into taking him for "Captain Vinegar". Having been removed from a fashionable school, aged sixteen, as a result of his stepfather's losses in the Railway Bubble of the '40s, Tresham was ready to read a contemptuous knowledge of this humiliation in the eye of every man he saw lounging at a club window in St James's, or riding his hack through the park. Of course they had forgotten him: but if they had been reminded of his existence, they would at once have recollected his history. Pitcher recognised rather bitterly this penalty of a settled society, that a man cannot escape his past.

He had no other prospect but Rainshaw. It was not a certain thing at all, but he counted upon it because he had nothing else. On his last visit he had been promoted downstairs from an attic bedroom into an elegant pair of rooms lit with wax lights, and with a clock set ticking above the fire, surely so that he might consider himself his step-uncle's heir? To the rector's half-suggestions that he should stop in England, Tresham had retorted that he wouldn't lie all his life under a plum-tree in hopes of the fruit dropping into his mouth, for at that time all his pride and self-esteem had been fixed upon making his Eastern journey. Though the rector had growled at this, Tresham believed that he wasn't displeased. Then had come the letter which Tresham had read at Damascus, written after his uncle's seizure, offering him the

[157]

inheritance if he would return. He had not returned at that time; but now he had come home, and still the plum-tree stood, and still the fruit hung upon the bough. He debated his chances with himself by the hour as he walked the London streets or stared out of the hotel windows.

He thought about Mazi a good deal in his loneliness, too. Wouldn't Uncle Marcus prefer that he should be married, if he was to come down and bury himself at Rainshaw? And wouldn't a Circassian Princess for wife mark out his character as something very singular amongst country gentlemen in Kent, with a whiff clinging about him of the old romantic life? – a touch of Captain Vinegar, like the crossed feet of a Crusader knight which remind the rustic parish that their squire has fought under Kings and Popes in half-fabulous Eastern lands? Despite having given up Captain Vinegar, he shouldn't have liked that element in his character, and in his past adventures, to have gone quite unrecognised amongst the Kent bumpkins.

Whilst he waited for the rector's permission there came another letter for Tresham. It had been sent round to Limmer's from the Foreign Office and was addressed in a lady's hand. Tresham opened it in the hotel foyer when the clerk handed it to him; but when he saw "Bebec" on the letterhead he carried the letter upstairs to his room to read with an eager anticipation of pleasure which surprised him.

Bebec
                                                          April 29th 1856

Dear Mr Pitcher,

    I know that you will forgive the intrusion of a letter which I am desired by my father to write to you on his behalf. I have asked him, Should he not prefer to dictate it, since it was to concern a business matter, but he would not agree, saying that "a grown woman" might surely write to an old family friend "on her own hook". You will hear the vigour of his voice in these phrases, and know that I report his words faithfully.

    Papa wishes me to enquire whether you are still in communication with your travelling companions, Captain Vinegar (!!) and the Mingrelian female whose father was a mountain chieftain of the Rachinskiy tribe? For Papa wishes

[158]

that an offer be conveyed to them, which you will recognise as falling into the category of "forlorn hopes". I am afraid that Papa designates both "Captain Vinegar" and the mountain woman as the type of agent to be employed with no scruple as regards their safety. No doubt you recall the terms of employment offered Captain Vinegar in the past!

It appears from Papa's intelligence that the Rachinskiy chieftain is dead, most likely murdered in a brawl over pillage, and that, were Papa to seize upon this opportunity to restore a legitimate chieftainess to her "throne", with a strong escort of bashibozuks under Captain Vinegar's command, he might even yet pacify a sufficient portion of the mountains to bring the Mamisson Pass under his own and Mr Novis' control. I forget if you knew that Papa and Mr Novis have, since the peace, formed together a Transcaspian Company to trade into Persia across the Caucasus?

What Papa wishes, in his own words, is that "Mr Pitcher fish my proposal under Vinegar's nose, and see if he be tempted to bite at it". Or (Papa adds) perhaps you know of another man sufficiently reckless of danger, or sufficiently in love with adventure, to attempt the rule of a barbarous kingdom and its savage "queen"?

We shall be home quite by the end of May, and Papa asks if you would be kind enough to address him at Ravenrig if anything can be done with regard to Captain V and the lady in the case. Should Mr Novis make a similar, or any other, offer, Papa would be glad to hear of it. He does not yet know quite how far he may depend upon his new partner.

There! My commission is done! To write "upon my own hook" I hope I may second Papa's proposal that you address him in person at Ravenrig when we are come home, and so renew a family friendship which revives the past, and Roly's memory, in quite a heart-warming way to

     your ever sincere friend
     Enid Farr

Tresham stood at his window with the letter. Twice he re-read the last paragraph, as if to savour again the touch of Enid's soft hand in his at the Sultan's ball, before turning his mind to the chief business of the missive. Shocking to him was the casually conveyed notice of Sir Daniel Farr's alliance with his adversary Herr Novis. How could an enmity of thirty years standing, if it ever had been based upon a moral principle, alter itself in a few weeks into an alliance?

Not that it concerned himself. The twists and turns of plot and treachery and devil's compacts spinning out their spiders' web over the East no longer touched him. He sighed, and shook out the letter, and considered its proposal. Yes, Captain Vinegar with a regiment of bashibozuks could very probably pacify the Rachinskiy territory sufficiently for caravans to pass through it, even for a railroad to be built. To take up such a commission, for such a pair as Farr and Novis made together, would be an adventure indeed. He thought of old Rachinskiy's "palace" at Alatstchinsk, wondering if it might be made sufficiently "royal" to please a European's taste for kingship – his own daydreams of ruling in Koordistan, which had formed the second part of Captain Vinegar's *Land March*, might be made into a reality in the Caucasus. Then there was the seam of coal he had discovered, and had divulged to no one. The plan might succeed. Or it might be a sentence of death. To attempt to open the Caucasian Gate was to pass from one world to another. Still, even if it was certain death it would make an adventure to ring down the curtain on "Captain Vinegar" in style. Behind the thin London houses across the street he saw again the far-off silvered peaks of Circassia above the wastes of the Black Sea, and felt Nogai's cutter lean upon the wind as she sped towards them . . .

It might be done. His own Captain Vinegar might have played the part. Was Hoolaghan's Vinegar, though, not a horse of a different colour? – a speaker at Manchester meetings – a Member of Parliament – a profiteer from share-issues – a frequenter of clubs and country-houses? So it had seemed in these weeks in England. Yet Tresham remembered a certain conversation with Hoolaghan, whilst the two of them had been riding down from Alatstchinsk with their Mingrelian Lancers before the Battle of the Ingour, when the idea of ruling in Rachinskiy's place had been put forward by the Irishman. He had been on the look-out for "a snug little kingdom all my own", so he had said:

[160]

at the same time he had pooh-poohed all moral distinctions which might appear to divide right rule from wrong. He had agreed with the words Milton put into Satan's mouth, which Tresham had quoted, "To reign is worth ambition, though in Hell." Tresham remembered him with his long legs stretched out to their bivouack fire, and his tumbler of *vodky-todky* balanced on his knee, chaffing him for supposing that there was a ha'porth of difference between Farr and Novis, in a moral way. If Hoolaghan's Vinegar failed in his English ambitions, would a shaky throne in Mingrelia tempt him East again?

And what of Mazi? – what would her response be? He well remembered her as the savage princess mounted amongst her chain-mail warriors and hunting dogs in the court of a stone castle under misty mountains. He well recalled the eagerness with which she had fallen on Murray's *Handbook to Contantinople*, too, and her desperate desire to quit Mingrelia with himself and Hoolaghan, even at the cost of abandoning Shkara at the tower. What future Mazi wished for herself was not clear to him. However – and here Pitcher's mouth set in a hard line – she would be the necessary consort to legitimise any Captain Vinegar who ruled her tribal territory, and the Captain Vinegar who was sufficiently iron-willed to control a regiment of *bashibozuks*, and a tribe of mountaineers, would hardly even enquire what were her wishes in the matter, or attend to her views if he heard them.

He therefore decided to say nothing to Mazi about Enid's letter or its proposals. Let him discover first of all whether she should be his own consort in the little Kent kingdom of Rainshaw. There would be time enough then, when that question was settled, to tell her of her father's death, and to inform Hoolaghan of Sir Daniel Farr's proposal.

After two days came the rector's reply. It was a mere note, dictated to his housekeeper Mrs Poynder, giving off-hand acquiescence to Tresham's request, and advising him of the proper train to take so as to be met by the Rainshaw carriage at the railway station. The note was neither warm nor cold.

But the train was not met by old Branch with the Rainshaw carriage when Tresham and his party arrived in Kent. His situation on the country platform amid luggage and dependents, when the London train had steamed off among the orchards and left them, showed with awful clarity to Tresham the responsibility to which he had committed himself by bringing a Mingrelian and her child, and her Circassian slave, out of polyglot London, where any oddity passes notice, into the depths of Kent to be peered at and speculated upon by every porter and carter and hanger-on at a rural station. He did not care for it. He stamped about the platform, and shouted at the station-master, in a style the porters found very different from the diffident manner in which he had enquired for the Rainshaw gig on his two previous visits. "Comes of getting hisself married I reckon," said one of these bearded porters to the other as they enjoyed the scene through the luggage office window. "Shouldn't wonder but he's caught a Tartar," agreed the other, studying the lady's stern eye.

At last, in the station fly, with a luggage-cart promised to follow, Tresham and the Princess Mazi and Shkara set out into the hopyards and orchard's at a snail's pace. It was a mild day, windless, hazy, and the orchards blossomed marvellously all about the lanes, rosy clouds of petals, as if from the sky of some baroque picture which had settled onto the dark Kent landscape, lighting it with their colour. Tresham refused to be gladdened, nursing the grievance, as it seemed to him, of his responsibility. Thus far his whole journey with the Princess, from the stone tower under the misty Caucasus to Limmer's hotel, had been a flight coincidentally shared. Now, since leaving Limmer's this morning, he had voluntarily begun a different journey with her. That was what kept him silent through the slow hour among the lanes behind the plodding horse.

If it had sounded a note of warning, that Branch had not met the train – a sign of change at Rainshaw – then Mrs Poynder's greeting to the caravan of trap and luggage cart, when it drew up on the gravel sweep under the stucco'd and battlemented south front of the house, echoed the same warning note. She stood rather grimly with her hands clasped together on her skirt in the shadow of the pointed Gothic porch which the rector had added to his mansion along with its stucco and battlements and lancet windows. Rather than welcoming them, the inclination of her head acknowledged that they had arrived, and must be accommodated.

"Ah, Mrs Poynder, I'm glad to see you, and to be here!"

Tresham stepped out of the vehicle and took both her hands in his.

He was prepared to distance himself from his dependents if need be. The housekeeper curtsied.

"And how is my uncle?" he continued, letting go her hands.

"Poorly." Her lips emitted just the word, and snapped shut. She was looking past him at the Princess Mazi accepting the driver's hand to descend, and at Shkara standing forlorn on the gravel, and at Hannah peering out of the luggage cart like an old hen from a hencoop.

Tresham introduced them. On board ship – at Limmer's hotel – even at Clapham – the title "Princess" had kept a little of the dazzle of Scheherezade about it. But here he might as well have introduced her as a "sorceress" or a "giantess" and hoped to convince Mrs Poynder of her station. Then there was a difficulty with Hannah: Mrs Poynder would expec to call her Mrs Something-or-other, and what was her surname? Very likely a Circassian slave was obliged to rub along without a surname. When he had bungled his way through these difficulties there remained Shkara standing alone twisting her fingers.

"Come, Shkara," he said, holding out his hand to take hers, "Mrs Poynder I know will stand your friend."

Still holding the child's hand he followed Mrs Poynder into the house. Here was the pillared hall scented with woodsmoke which he remembered, the dark shapes of chests and presses against panelled walls. A door lay open into the library. Expecting to see his step-uncle stooped over his writing table, or standing at the lectern outlined against the lancet window at the room's end, Tresham looked in. The library was empty, tall shelves of old bindings rising above mahogany drawers. It was empty and silent, with that peculiarly deep silence which he now remembered as characteristic of Rainshaw. Above the fireplace was the painting which he had so often thought of. There it glowed, unchanged; the evening light, the classic scene, temple and sea and blue mountain, "the crisping ripple on the beach". In that picture was perfect peace. He had thought of it so often that he almost expected its painted scene to be the landscape onto which Rainshaw's own windows looked, and its umbrageous trees to shade him here, as well as shading those figures in Arcady from too fierce a sun.

"If you please, sir – " Mrs Poynder summoned him, and conducted them upstairs from the staircase hall, dresses rustling against the balusters, feet creaking the polished treads, her voice ascending above:

"I've put the little girl up top in Master Marcus's room."

"Is that my step-sister Eliza's child, Mrs Poynder?"

"Her eldest. Such a bright little lad. You, sir, is put in them rooms just across."

"Ah, where I was before. And the Princess?"

"If the ladies come along of me."

Mrs Poynder opened for the ladies a landing door which gave upon a steeper stair ascending to regions above. Up these their steps receded. Tresham entered his own rooms. "Master Marcus, indeed!" he said aloud to himself in disgust. Before he had left England there had been no intercourse between the rector and his nieces, who were Tresham's step-sisters. Now Eliza, or more likely that counter-jumper Roach from Sydenham whom she had married, had come pushing forward her son into Rainshaw – a son they had called "Marcus", too, to toady the rector. "Master Marcus's room!" He wondered if the pair of rooms he had been put into was known as "Mr Tresham's". There was a comfortable little sitting-room, then two steps down into a bedroom beyond. In old times they had been the nurseries of the house, a fact which somehow pleased Tresham, as though he was made an honorary child of the place by inhabiting them. He looked at the pine overmantle of the fireplace, where his stepfather's initials had been scorched into the wood with a poker, a childish exploit which Uncle Marcus had once instanced to Tresham as an early example of his stepfather's propensity to make retribution inevitable, but to call it misfortune. "How could he be so great a fool as to burn in his own initials, and not expect to be flogged for it?" The rector's contempt for his brother Adolphus, which he extended to the "Clapham girls", had been the foundation of his intention that Tresham should inherit Rainshaw, or so Tresham had understood it. And now came "Master Marcus" simpering into the picture!

He went to throw open a window as a relief to his feelings. But the Gothic ogee, into which the windows had been altered by the rector's "repairs", seemed to have prevented any letting-in of air, and he gave it up. He could see the jackdaws quarrelling in the elms at the lawn's end, but he could not hear them. The silence which lay thick as dust within the house had robbed the view from its windows of sound too. He opened his door, expecting luggage to be brought up. The long arched passage stretched away to a closed door at its end. Not a voice, not

[164]

a footstep. The small commotion of his arrival had settled back into the listening stillness which possessed the house.

He would go downstairs and find Uncle Marcus. He would ask after luggage, enquire for little Tom the hallboy, animate the place with his voice and his activity to disperse this silence which listened like a spy at the keyhole. So he trod heavily down the stairs and entered the hall. A corpulent servant who had been lounging with an arm upon the mantleshelf now made himself busy with a pair of iron tongs amongst the smouldering logs.

"Tom?" enquired Tresham, "Is it Tom?"

"Yes sir, Tom it is. How are you keeping? Fit I hope?"

"How do, Tom – I'm glad to see you." Tresham chose to overlook the fat youth's free manner of questioning him, since probably he saw no visitors to teach him his manners. Tom had been a child at his last visit. "I hope I find you all well here, Tom."

"Mustn't grumble," said Tom from the grate, "all work though. And in course since squire was took bad a deal of it ain't my work, not properly speaking. You take the morning work now – "

"Thank you, Tom. Is the baggage upstairs?"

The servant's half-lounging manner was checked by this sharpness. "I'll look after it for you, sir."

"Where is my uncle?"

"I put him into his business-room. Want him wheeled in here?"

"Do you see after the baggage, which I'm sure is wanted upstairs." Upright as a ramrod – upright as Captain Vinegar, and as fierce – Tresham waited by the fire until Tom had left him. "Wheeled", he had said; so, the rector was helpless. Tom's familiarity, and Mrs Poynder's surliness, were alike the manners of servants who had taken the upper hand in the household. They confirmed suspicions first aroused by the non-appearance of Branch with the carriage at the railway station. "Wheeled": a picture formed in Tresham's mind, as he stood a moment more by the faintly hissing oak logs on their ashy hearth, of a lolling invalid in the power of servants in this silent house, who had conspired with Eliza Roach to put up her child as their master's heir. He walked towards the door of the business-room, one of many doors which gave off the hall.

"What's that? Who is it? Come in," called out a testy voice in answer

n the panel. In he went. Behind the rent-table sat his step-
wers open, ledgers spread, calculations evidently in progress;
ed up from his figures, a pen in his left hand, stern eyes irritable
e florid face capped with white hair.

"How do you do, Uncle." Feeling obliged to explain his presence, Tresham added, "You were expecting me, were you not?"

"Expecting who?" He peered. "Ah, Tresham, it's you is it – why don't you say so! Bless my soul. Of course; just so; yes, yes. You are welcome, most welcome. Now I recollect it all, of course." Instead of standing up behind his round table, a movement of his hands propelled him out into the room in a wheeled chair, and brought him close to Tresham, to whom he extended both hands. "And Branch met you according to plan, I suppose, at the railway station?"

Tresham felt the grasp of those thin old hands gladly, a true welcome to the house. "No," he said, "the fact of it is Branch didn't meet us. I thought he should, but he didn't. So we came in the fly, and had the baggage and the servant come after in the cart."

The rector stared for a moment, his fleshy lips pursed, as if at a conundrum which required solving. "Didn't meet you?" he wondered. Then his face cleared: "Oh no. Oh no. I daresay he met you, only – only you didn't see him, you know. Such a pity. Wasting your money on the fly. Is it ninepence a mile nowadays, as Mrs Poynder tells me? Is it really? Well, I warrant it's a trifle to you, eh, whatever it is? A trifle. Now then – for it comes back to me – weren't there to be ladies coming? And children, and all that sort of thing? I suppose the railway travel has knocked them up has it? Are they lying flat? It is best to lie completely flat when the nerves are affected. Flat as a herring."

"They are upstairs. Uncle, you will remember from my letter that there is a – a Princess, you know, from the Caucasus mountains, and her child."

"If they have been used to the Caucasus, then I should say the railway speed will have shocked them like the very mischief. I'm told the tunnels are enough to kill you with fright, at the speed they dart along. I won't do it you know. I won't go up to London since the coach is taken off. They come down to me, but I won't go up anymore. But Branch drove steadily I hope? Yes, he's a steady man with the carriage, Branch. I won't have him drive me above four or five miles an hour, you know."

"I'm sorry to see you in a Bath-chair, uncle," said Tresham, seeing that the Branch question would lead him into difficulties if pursued.

Again the rector stared. Then he seemed to become aware of his position. "Oh, my chair, this." He looked down at his hand resting on the wheel. "Quite unnecessary! They choose to make an invalid of me amongst them all."

"But you was ill, I know, and I'm sorry for it."

The rector seemed impatient with this line of talk, and had soon shuffled Tresham out of the room so as to return to his ledgers, with a promise that "we shall meet by-and-by, when you are all a little better after your frights."

3

The rector chose to ignore a good deal that was puzzling to Tresham about his circumstances. Why had Mrs Poynder written to him, at the rector's dictation apparently, when Tresham had seen his uncle with a pen in his hand? Did the servants keep letters from him, opening and answering them in furtherance of their designs?

He was not an invalid, for he could, and did, walk slowly about his garden and into his park; yet at times he would allow himself to be pushed about the walled garden's gravel paths, or even inside the house, as if he were helpless. Branch, for instance, had always been a crabbed, gingery creature, and now he was old as well, possibly consumptive, a withered little stick of a man fussing about with a broom in the stables, encased in so many wrappings and comforters that hard work was impossible to him. From criticism he took refuge behind a torrent of complaints. Had he or had he not met the train? He leaned on his broom. "I told him that off wheel weren't going to take no more, but he wouldn't listen. Pushes hisself off when you tells him summat. And in course that come off first rut we was into." "Just today, on your way to the station?" "No – ! Bless you, that were back along March. Today! Well, I ain't a wheelwright, never was. I told him. But he won't fetch in the wheelwright, see. Don't like his politics! Jaunce, that is. Then there's some can't do no wrong far as squire sees. You seen Fettle have you – Fettle as was sexton back along? Don't give him nothing if

[167]

you want my advice. I'm charitable, mind, but you can't do nothing for his sort. Drink." He put his thumb to his mouth and tipped back his whiskery, nutcracker little face, while the malice gleamed out of his watery eyes. Tresham walked off, and could well understand his uncle avoiding such disagreeable company.

Avoidance of what was disagreeable to him perhaps explained the rector's ellipses round reality. Less unpleasantness – less that caused him discomfort – was caused by playing the part allotted to him by his servants than would have resulted from enforcing his discipline upon them. And so he had outwardly tolerated much apparent change, and much laxness and decline from old proprieties, whilst inwardly perhaps determined to believe, like a *roi fainéant*, that no real or significant decline had taken place. This, after a few days at Rainshaw, was Tresham's belief. Though it was still his uncle's kingdom, the vigorous days of his "repairs", or of his lake-making, seemed now impossibly beyond his authority.

One May morning, with his dependents well settled into the house, Tresham was accompanying and supporting his uncle down the slope of the park towards the lake. There, in a dell under four oaks, a stream had been dammed to form a sheep-dip, and the squire wished to see the work which was being done upon it. He had Tresham's arm, and leaned upon it. He wore a low round hat, a black coat, and very white linen. Bluebells patched glimpses of the chestnut woods, and the blue lake itself gleamed between alders and beeches as they descended. Tresham said, "I saw a capital show of swallows about the lake when I was down last evening with Shkara."

"They don't come to us," replied his uncle, just as if he had said he saw no swallows last evening. After a pause he went on, "They never do come about a house where there are no children, do you see. There used to be crowds of them about – flocks of them – in old days. Dolly and I used to shoot at them I am afraid, when we were boys. But now – now you won't see a swallow about the place ever, I suppose."

Tresham saw suddenly and vividly the Arab boys on the walls of Aleppo slinging stones at the swifts as he and Roland Farr had ridden into the deep shadow of the Antioch gate. Unexpected, such scenes interposed themselves between his eyes and England, with a knife-cut of nostalgia. He remembered the brilliant dazzle of the light, and his horse a little lame under him, and the satisfaction of the long hard ride from the Orontes accomplished. He blinked his eyes so as to dissolve that half-alluring Eastern scene, and said almost impatiently to his uncle, "Look, though, sir – look, there are swallows over the lake now, ever so many of them, see!"

"You don't say so!" The parson paused, shaded his eyes. But, as Tresham saw the Aleppo swifts, perhaps he saw only the swallows of his youth. He walked on. "There are martins, of course," he said, "but if these are swallows they don't belong here, do you see. I don't suppose we've a swallow about the place now that belongs."

They soon came into the dell under the oaks where two bricklayers were repairing the outflow of the sheep-dip. They had dug down through the dam to reach the culvert, whose half-round tiles they were renewing. One of the men had been whistling as clear as a blackbird under the trees, but ceased when his companion indicated the rector's approach. Both men touched their foreheads with clay-yellowed forefingers.

"The work going ahead all right, Bob?"

The older of the men replied, "Powerful lot of they half-rounds have broke, like."

"But these are our own," said the rector, stirring the heap of broken tiles with his stick, "these don't break surely?"

The man shrugged. "Didn't ought. Who you got down along the kiln there now doing that?"

The rector shuffled his stick-point evasively. "Job and Angel from over Thorn Hill took it on."

"Ah!"

"They were both apprenticed to old Barge, – they should know the work."

"Apprenticed. Should."

"Well, I couldn't let them go on the parish, Bob, you know that. Is the work very bad?" he asked, almost humbly, looking at one of the tiles made in his own kiln.

" 'Tis bad, squire, but we'm make do."

"Well done, Bob. I will send word to Job he must mend his ways.

Then we shall see. Good morning to you, Bob, and you Jem, good morning." With this, content, the rector took Tresham's arm and walked him away. "Two men back from the war," he said, "not wanted over at Thorn Hill farm, which they ran off from to go for soldiers in '54, so I put them into the kiln to start it up again. They'll learn, I daresay. And I like to build with my own bricks," he added, "always did."

The war in the Crimea – that was its effect upon Rainshaw, and upon the squire: two men from the parish come home needing work and their places in the community again. Walking beside him, Tresham's head teemed with ugly images of the stripped dead, their flesh so white, strewn about the field of the Ingour, and of the transports groaning with wounded as they thumped up the Bosphorus in the darkness. He remembered the wounded of all nations brought to die beside the great fire under the oak trees, after the battle, and the sparks gushing upward into darkness.

They walked down the stream from the sheep-dip, the rector clearing its channel of leaves with his stick. Was it possible, Tresham wondered, that these unpeaceful images ever would cease to disturb him. Looking into a pool of the stream, whilst his uncle poked at the dam of leaves which had caused it, he thought of the lines, "O fountains! When in you shall I myself eased of unpeaceful thoughts espy?" The leaf-dam broke, the pool sank away taking his image with it. They walked slowly on towards the lake shore.

It was extraordinary how completely Nature in ten years had adopted this foster-child, the rector's lake. As the feelers of the sea-anemone close upon an irritant, so the green grasp of Nature had fastened upon what had been introduced into this valley. If the water ran inland up many a shady creek, the land seemed to run out onto the water on the green pads of lilies, whilst willows and alders, bulrushes and reeds, vaguened the lake's margins where they had taken root.

"It has sunk wonderfully well into the landscape, Uncle," said Tresham as they approached the whispering reeds.

"I took care that it should be so. I took care to discover the ways of providence in the matter, before ever I commenced upon the work. Shall we sit a little here? I have had a seat made, do you see, and the alder trimmed away so that I may look out upon the water. Yes," he said, seating himself in the very centre of the slatted bench of chestnut wood, so that Tresham was not left space enough on either side of him to sit down, "yes, I asked them to see about it, and they have attended to it." He spoke with satisfaction, as though his wishes were not always so well observed, and pushed his round hat forward to shade his eyes from the sparkle of the lake.

Where the alders had been lopped in front of the seat their stumps bled a red sap – as red as the blood from sword-wounds, Tresham thought. Confound such images, ever breaking in! "The alders will grow again quick as wink," he said.

"I daresay. I wouldn't have them rooted out, if they choose to grow here. But it don't go against Nature to trim them, I suppose. Against the natural order. You may check a growth that don't suit, without denying it room altogether. So I believe. You know the *Bacchae*?" The rector turned with this question, looking up at Tresham standing behind the bench.

"I do." He tried to remember something of Euripides' play.

"First-rate it is. I look into it – oh, ever so often. Indeed I have a copy always down off the shelf on a table somewhere, to save stretching, you know."

"Why do you ask – about the *Bacchae*?"

"Oh. Why did I ask? Ah – the alders; denying them room you know. What if Pentheus had chosen to join forces with Dionysus when the new god came into his kingdom – chosen to direct the savage new-comer, and put his power to a use – what might the two of them not have achieved together! Eh? The civilised king and the daemonic Phrygian pulling together in one harness. But no, Pentheus wouldn't have it, he would stand out against his visitor, and see what became of him!"

He clasped his hands on his stick and contemplated with grave complacency the lake formed by a union of himself with Nature, a wiser Pentheus.

"But Uncle," objected Tresham, "there are powers – forces – that you have stood out against. The railroad. Steam. That is a savage power enough."

"I could not allow them here. The railways. The navvies." He spoke sternly, jarring the ground with his stick. "The disruption to our life here. I could not have it. Disruption to the natural order, do you see,"

[171]

he continued in a milder tone. "Well – it is like the war in the Crimea for disruption, they go hand in hand for disorder, the war and the railways. Ructions and upsets, and the common people flibberty-gibbet off about the world for no good reason like a set of gypsies. Job and Angel here are but two of them at sixes and sevens on account of the railroads and the war, I assure you. Of course there's discontent, when principles are called into question by any fellow who can read a railway timetable."

"You mean the principle –"

"I mean the principle of aristocratic government, Tresham, upon which the health and order of this country is founded," said the rector earnestly. "The principle of aristocratic government has been called in question because of the bungling of our commanders in the Crimea. That's the truth of it. Mismanagement – a few noblemen mismanaging affairs. By their sad bungling, paltry persons at home have allowed a principle to be called into question. That is their crime, Raglan and all the rest. And sedition finds its way down to us fast enough, depend upon it. The railways bring it, smoking and stinking and shaking all things to pieces." He said nothing for a moment, staring across the water with unseeing eyes which certainly did not remark the swallows which, despite his denial of their existence, sped and darted over the lake. When he went on, it was with the hint of apology which confesses a personal irritant behind a general diatribe: "I have a creature come about the parish, a wheelwright, Jaunce he calls himself, who never could have taken hold of men's minds here before the Crimea and steam travel, never could have done. Wretched fellow."

He pondered Jaunce's crimes for a moment. Tresham recognised that he had been wrong in supposing that all the war had meant to his uncle was two out-of-work labourers come home; their re-employment – their re-admission into the system – was part of a larger than parochial design of the rector's to combat the adversary of misrule and to uphold the principle of order. Now it was Tresham's own view of the Crimea which seemed the narrow one. Certainly deference to the idea of aristocratic rule had been eroded by the war: he thought of Sir Daniel Farr's impatience with a system he had never before questioned. Could it be that Sir Daniel's own "principles" had depended upon his deference for an aristocratic ideal – for honour and probity – and that this leaguing of himself to Herr Novis had been a consequence of the disgust and disillusion with which he had viewed aristocratic incompetence at first hand in the Crimea? The rector was continuing meanwhile with the case of the wheelwright Jaunce:

"There's a pair of cottages below the lake there, below the dam, just over the road out of the park – oh, a wretched place, not mine. This Jaunce took one of them if you please – no need of it, he's a dwelling of his own elsehwere I'm told – but he took it particular so that he might complain to me that if my dam there should break, and my lake should escape, why, then his cottage and the other would be overwhelmed. What do you think of that, eh? For impudence?"

"It would be uncommon awkward."

"My dam shall not break." He struck the ground with his stick as if adjuring the earth to obey him. "It was built upon the proper principles. No one has understood waterworks so thoroughly as the Romans, you know, and I took my ideas from them. Well, Jaunce has made his calculations, and I have made mine. We shall see whether an impudent agitating wheelwright or the Romans are in the right of it. Yes. Poat of course is in with him, foolish fellow – you recall little Poat my curate I daresay? – pretending to me with his eyes rolled up to heaven that the cottagers dare not sleep in their beds for apprehension of the flood! All humbug of course."

"I suppose any dam may break, though. Here's a vast weight of water kept in against it's will, so to say. It may break out some of these winters I suppose."

"Then I should be guilty. Then I should be to blame. Yes," said the rector humbly, "if my lake should drown the man, wretch as he is, I should be to blame."

"Jaunce wouldn't be the first person your lake has drowned."

"Ah, the railway woman. Didn't you bury her with me? How did that come about, now? – such a strange thing as you digging her grave? One's memory becomes littered with such isolated curiosities, you know, once you have grown old enough to have forgotten the con- nexions." He considered this for a moment. Then he said, "She would have hanged herself in one of my oaks if I hadn't made a lake for her to drown herself in. Poor wretch, she had no business with us here. I took nothing to do with the railway people, never would. They were not my responsibility, coming in from outside as they did."

[173]

"As did Dionysus," murmured Tresham sotto voce behind him.

He turned and looked up. "What is that you say about Dionysus?"

"The railway was a power from the outside, Uncle, like your daemonic Phrygian in the *Bacchae*."

He faced the lake again, contented. "Ah, the *Bacchae* – what a play it is. You prefer the *Medea* I suppose. You must have thought of it a good deal when you was at Colchis there, and upon the Phasis – the Rion, do they call the river nowadays? It is Euripides' understanding of the savage mind that is so wonderful. Medea! All barbary is in her. 'My serpent I slew for you' – do you remember? Thinking that her treachery to her own people will *recommend* her to Jason! What he understood so well, poor Euripides, was that the moral ideas of civilisation are not written by God upon the conscience of the savage races. It is well to notice that, if we are not to be torn in pieces like old Jason."

"It was Pentheus who was pulled in pieces by the women, surely."

"The maenads pulled off Pentheus' head, granted; but Medea pulled Jason's heart in pieces and left him living – is that not crueller? I think so. To kill her own children because he loved them! Was anything ever conceived more barbarous? How did he know the savage woman's heart so well, I wonder – Euripides. Well, Athens I suppose was under siege from barbarism in his day. From disorder."

"Disorder!" said Tresham, suddenly impatient with his uncle. "Sir, is civilisation, and principle, and religion, and everything else, simply no grander a thing than order?"

"Order is the foundation of all else. Try and do without it, and you'll find how long aught else will stand. Look to 1848, when we let in disorder. Not here, thank God, but elsewhere. You have seen the effects of disorder in your travels, I suppose. Hungary. The East."

"Yes, and a good deal that is worth seeing comes of it, in my experience," said Tresham impulsively, with a kind of loyalty to his memories.

"Oh, worth seeing for a traveller. But you wasn't looking to inherit a settled estate in such lands I suppose. No" (he went on, when he found Tresham silent at this home thrust as to Rainshaw) "no, the railway that was building here came to nothing you know. It never was built, and the woods no doubt have grown over their cuttings and their works just as if they had never been."

[174]

He folded his hands upon his stick with satisfaction and considered the prospect of parkland and water into which his ancestors and himself had directed the powers of Nature. Standing behind him, it occurred to Tresham to wonder if the malacca stick between his uncle's knees was the same stick which had figured in a long-ago incident he had so often thought of, and he asked, "Do you recollect at Clapham once, Uncle, when you stopped a cat from killing a sparrow? You hooked your stick about the cat's neck just as she sprang. My word but it was sharp work to watch!"

"I shouldn't wonder." He chuckled. "I shouldn't be surprised. I never did care for Dolly's cat. Fancy you remembering that, though, for I haven't been at Clapham in a dozen years."

"I was watching you from my window. It made an impression. I was cramming Xenophon and looking out, and I saw you come between the cat and its prey."

"I daresay I chose to let pussy know there is a providence pays heed to the fate of sparrows." He turned his head to look at Tresham. "I should do the same again, if I was to see a sparrow in peril from such another feline."

"Suppose the cat was too strong for you," said Tresham, thinking of the steam-power the rector sought to exclude, or his lake bursting the dam. "What then?"

The rector pushed himself upright on his stick. "When that day comes," he said, "it will be I, and not the cat, who is obliged to learn the will of providence. Come, there is the clock, give me your arm and we will go up."

Obeying the summons of the rector's clock, whose sweet bell now regulated the labourers' day all over the estate, they left the lake and began to climb the slope of the park to the house.

*   *   *

Towards the Princess Mazi the rector had at first showed a polysyllabic courtesy as elaborate as the net in which a gladiator entangles his adversary's weapons. His coldness he dressed up as respect; treating her as if she was a superior being, he kept her at arm's length. Tresham took note of this, but he saw also how quickly she had penetrated his defence. Very soon she had gained the intimacy of being allowed to push his Bath-chair if he chose to ride, or to support his arm if he preferred walking, on a dozen little expeditions a day to visit his vine-house, or his garden, or his wooded walks.

Watching them cross the lawn together below his window – the rector leaning back in his chair with an air of pampered enjoyment, Mazi leaning forward solicitously to catch what he said as she pushed him – Tresham found that he could hardly reconcile the Mingrelian chieftainess he remembered among her dogs and mailed warriors, with the lady he saw on the Rainshaw lawn. But he knew that it was the vigour of the wilderness that she instilled by touch and voice into the veins of the old man: she had not changed. What she might have achieved in Mingrelia by dint of armed horsemen a-clatter in the courtyard of a stone castle, and by kidnap or murder, she would attempt in an English country-house by pushing a Bath-chair across the lawn, and letting her hand rest on its occupant's arm. Touch was part of her arsenal: probably the rector had not felt a woman touch him so affectionately since he was a child, and certainly the tendrils of Mazi's fingers on his arm made him captive as effectively as her horsemen's swords had made Tresham her captive in the Caucasus. Not her ambition, nor her determination, was altered; only her weapons. So much Tresham thought he saw, anyway, watching her push his uncle into the shrubberies between the house and the stables. What was her ambition, though? To live here, with himself?

She didn't care a pin that the servants abominated her. Tom spoke to Tresham peevishly of "madam doing our work for us with squire" as if she was taking the bread out of his mouth. Mazi made no attempt to appease Tom or Mrs Poynder. Whether she had not understood the position of upper servants in England, or whether she understood it and didn't care about it – or perhaps calculated that upper servants would inevitably stand against her ambitions – Tresham could not tell. Though Tom and Mrs Poynder doubtless ran every day to the rector bearing tales of malice against her, Mazi's campaign throve notwithstanding.

Whilst the Princess made her way in the front of the house, Shkara had very soon endeared herself to every heart in the servants' hall. From kitchenmaid to housekeeper they loved her, very soon forgetting to make comparisons with "Master Marcus". Toys made by the estate carpenter for Marcus, a wooden horse on wheels, a wooden rifle, were brought out of a cupboard by Mrs Poynder and given to Shkara. Hesitantly the child would put her hand on the toy offered, stroke the mane, finger the trigger-guard, as if it were a live thing which must be enticed into her possession by the magic of touch. Then it was hers, and she loved it fiercely. She smiled, but never laughed. "Such a solemn little scrap," declared Mrs Poynder to the rector, "and what I call modest, after them stuck-up things we see." Was this a reference to Master Marcus, wondered Tresham? What they made of Hannah in the servants' hall – and what the Rainshaw servants got out of her in the way of tales and reminiscences – Tresham could not guess at. She seemed contented, though, and moved stiffly and silently about her work for the Princess and Shkara, having evidently learned from her kaleidoscopic experiences to accept variety as the condition of existence. A Circassian slave! – what would Cook say to this incursion of the Arabian Nights into her domain? Probably she wouldn't believe it, any more than she believed in the royalty of Princess Mazi, at least as royalty is understood in British kitchens. Tresham had discovered by chance that Hannah had moved herself into Shkara's attic to sleep, and, when he asked why, the child replied "Because of Yani". Now "Yani" was her name for her mother. What the move was intended to achieve, or prevent, he did not know. But old Hannah knew her mistress through and through, from childhood; knew her ambitions, and had no doubt known her to lay schemes and perform deeds which would have appalled the roughest labourer who ever entered the Rainshaw kitchen. If Hannah chose to sleep in Shkara's room to guard her, Tresham was glad.

All this time Tresham had in his possession Enid Farr's letter from Bebec, with its suggestion that the Princess should be restored to the throne of her blood in Mingrelia. He had not yet told her about the letter, having had no word still from Hoolaghan's Captain Vinegar. But he felt as though the commission put into his hand the power of deciding her future. Watching her disappear among the laurustinus pushing the rector's Bath-chair, he wondered which destiny he would choose for her, Rainshaw or Mingrelia. There was little doubt that she schemed to stay. However, if the schemes of Sir Daniel and Herr Novis required her presence on the throne of the Rachinskiy in Mingrelia, there would come a clash of fierce wills at the end.

It was an effect of the intimacy between the Princess and the rector that he turned his caustic tongue rather often against Tresham, in their conversations over the table, sure of Mazi's dark glittering smile if he made a hit against his nephew. He particularly mocked Tresham's travels, never failing to pitch in if Tresham should begin, "When I was at Palmyra –"

"Ah, now, when you was king of the Cannibal Isles – now we shall get at the truth, ma'am, if we attend – go on sir: when you was at Timbuctoo?"

"Shouldn't you be interested, though, Uncle, to hear of Palmyra at first hand, after putting up your tower by the lake there?"

"No, thankee. I have my Tacitus and my Wood."

Provoked, Tresham said, "Your Palmyra Tower has tumbled down, I see, despite Tacitus and Wood."

"Tumbled down? I don't know anything about it tumbling down."

"It is cracked, Uncle, all cracked through, and the coping fallen. It is unsafe."

"It is not all cut stone and fresh paint, I grant you. It is not a Cockney turret; no, it ain't. It is part of my landskip, if you have half an eye for such things. Time has taken a hand, God be praised, and finished the work for me – as time completes all our designs, if we are patient, and content. Time, ma'am, I have found, is a kindly power – an ally – so long as we are content."

The three of them were eating their dinner in the tall-windowed dining room, evening light between the oaks laying drifts of gold over the green of the park, the candles pale in the dimness within. Behind the rector rose a wall lined with portraits of his ancestors: against that vague host, the white dead faces peering down from the dusky wall, his own rubicund countenance and snowy hair glowed with the vigour and satisfaction of earthly life. That was old age (thought Tresham) sufficiently content to withstand the striking clock, and the hosts of dead plucking at his elbow behind him.

"No, Tresham," went on the rector, his old veined hand reaching for his claret glass, "if I want to hear of Palmyra, Tacitus will tell me how it was when I should have cared to see it. There ain't very much that a tourist scribbling nowadays can add to Tacitus that I should care about."

"There ain't many tourists at Palmyra, Uncle."

"I don't know how that may be. *You* was there, you say." His eyes looked for Mazi's smile, then he went on, "However it maybe these days, I'm content with Tacitus's Palmyra, which stands quite as clear and perfect to me as any of the scenes of my youth, my own youth. Quite as clear. All antiquity is clear, through the classics. Indeed, antiquity *is* the youth of our race, its infancy and youth. It is."

" 'Infancy'? What is this?" asked Mazi.

"*Jeunesse*," said the rector.

"*Çocukluk*," said Tresham, supplying the word in her own tongue.

"Chock-oo-look," repeated the rector, half to himself, musingly, whilst his eyes studied the Princess where she sat against the light from the windows. "No Greek in the origin of such a word as that, I'll warrant. Neither Greek nor Latin. No, the old world of Greece and Rome that was our nursery," he said, "was not where the infancy of your race was passed, ma'am. Your race I suppose came out of Tartary. I suppose so. But Tresham and I are the children of Arcady."

"Not of Eden, Uncle?"

"Eden we share with all. Eden we share with the savage races. It is Arcady which is ours alone, we Europeans. Arcadia. The vale of Tempe."

There was a silence. The last golden light flooded across the park beyond the windows. Tresham heard Roland Farr's voice speaking out angrily against him on a knoll above the ruins of Tchardourhissar, in Phrygia – "of course it ain't any use to a beastly Turk, it's our history, not his" – when Captain Vinegar had gloated over the casual destruction of the Roman theatre of Azana by the Turk. Captain Vinegar wasn't fit for a life within European civilisation, rejoicing as he did at the extinction of gas-lamps and constables, and Roman theatres too, when the barbarian decided to foreclose. There was no place for him in Europe, that was the truth. He looked across the table at the Princess, and found her eyes dwelling on him. Was there room in Europe for her? A child of Eden?

"I was at Eden once," he said, to tease his uncle.

"Oh, hark! Eden now, d'ye hear, ma'am? It wasn't paradise you was at, I suppose?"

"There is a village above the Orontes called Eden, Uncle."

"Upon my word! Do you suppose Eden to be found upon a map, and reached in a railway train?"

"I think any place may be found by persistence."

"Small wonder you have come home disappointed, then."

"I have not come home disappointed, Uncle."

"What, having found Eden, you left it again, did you?"

"Such has been the general practice, since Adam."

The rector paused, considering this, seeming to judge its weight. Then he said, "This is poor pert stuff. Come, ma'am, take a glass of wine with me. It is the Lafitte '44," he went on, reaching down the table to fill the Princess's glass, "and I warrant they didn't know of such a vintage as this, in Eden or in Arcady. It is worthy of a libation to older gods."

The stream of wine glamed red into her glass, and she watched it with so ardent a gleam in her eyes that Tresham felt his blood quicken towards her. Desire, or fear? He saw his uncle leaning over her with the decanter like a moth into the flame of her. He was her prey; softly as her hand enclosed the claret glass, her claws encircled him. Well, let him make a fool of himself, thought Tresham. "Pert"! – to be called "pert", as if he was a schoolboy! He – Captain Vinegar – called "pert" by a used-up old cleric in this slow house. A position of dependence here, such as this, would be intolerable to him. He had known it would be so. There would be no respect for the man who came and sat himself down under the plum-tree with his mouth open. He would not be called "pert", though, by any man, be he the owner of ever so many plum-trees.

"Sir," he said, "you speak as if every objective of humanity was behind us. You speak as if absolute perfection was attained in classic times. As if nostalgia should be the filter of every thought. And as if there had been no advance made whatever since Aurelian knocked down Palmyra and we left off minding the sheep in Arcady. You have called me pert, which ain't very civil, and perhaps you will only call it pert again if I say that I believe that the goals of the human race lie ahead, and may be found by travellers. May be looked for by travellers at least. I don't for the life of me see how it is that a man born in this century don't believe in progress."

"I wasn't born in this century," returned the rector, leaning back in his chair in the candlelight, "I was born in a better one."

"Then you have had all the more opportunity of seeing the progress made in this one."

"Progress!" He puffed out his lips. "Penny post and steam travel I suppose."

"If you wish. If you see nothing else. Nothing more."

"It is you men of this century, sir, who see nothing more," said the rector. "There has been but one advance since we was expelled from Arcady."

"What advance?"

"You ask me that?" He looked at his guest in surprise, or contempt.

"What then?"

"The coming of our saviour Jesus Christ into the world." There was silence. In it Tresham remembered the rector sustained in his pulpit above his parishioners by faith like the Ark on the flood. He believed. Perhaps faith is impossible except as part of a fabric of conservatism as close-knit as the rector's. Tresham also remembered that the question he had asked himself, long ago in the church in the park where he had seen his step-uncle float secure on his faith as the Ark on the water, had not been the question, *Is it true?*, but the question, *Can I believe?* He had thought that the answer was *Not yet*, and so he had gone away on his travels. What would the answer be now that he was home again? The rector added to his statement of faith, in a voice quite without the asperity which had cut into Tresham before, "If our beginnings were in Arcadia, it is the coming of our Saviour which enables us to set our course towards Paradise. Now, ma'am shall you eat some nuts? They come from my own woods, and should be sweet."

"Thank you, I will try some. But, sir, will you tell me one thing what is change about man from Jesus coming?"

Again there was no doubt or hesitation in the one forceful word the rector uttered: "Revenge."

"Revenge?" echoed Tresham, drawn into questioning such certainty. "By Jove, I should have said revenge was as strong a motive in human affairs as ever it was."

[181]

"Yes," said Mazi, "explain to me too, if you please, how you think that revenge is disappear."

The rector put his fingers on the table's edge and looked from one of them to the other. Evidently (thought Tresham) he was not wondering what to say, he was wondering whether it was worth saying it to this audience, or whether he shouldn't rise from the table and go into his library and close the door. Deciding to speak, he said rapidly, "The knowledge that revenge is of the Devil, Satanic, is written on the conscience of a Christian as it was not written on the pagan conscience. Now," he went on more slowly, sitting back with his wine, "consider the *Bacchae*. There is a scene in the play when the captured pagan god Dionysus in Pentheus' hands perfectly resembles the captured Jesus in the hands of Pilate. No, there is no blasphemy in the parallel. Each god calls out of his captivity to his Father for deliverance. Jesus – why, Peter has denied him in the courtyard, now his own Father denies him on the cross. Won't interfere. Gives him up to death and ignominy. Forsakes him. That is what becomes of Jesus Christ's petitions to his Father. But how different is the case with the pagan god! Dionysus calls out to *his* almighty father, to Zeus, and down tumbles the palace of his captor in an earthquake! Down tumbles his prison and sets him free, where all that the Father of Jesus Christ was able to manage was to rend the veil of the temple. Not much. So, are we to conclude that Zeus is the more powerful god of the two? Is that the lesson? No. No, the lesson we are to learn is that revenge – vengeance in this world – is no longer the weapon of Almighty God. Everywhere in the pagan world vengeance was rife. Jehovah deals in vengeance every whit as cheerfully as Zeus. But here is something new. Here is the strength of humility shown us. This is what is altered above all else – altered in man's moral conscience – by Christ's coming: revenge is condemned, and humility triumphs. Humility triumphs," he repeated on a rising note, his voice quiet and reflective.

Tresham looked at him. He spoke with the same assurance of faith with which he had delivered that sermon Tresham had heard long ago. It was all of a piece. He believed. The wholeness and order and peace of his uncle's life was sustained by faith. He thought of the motto inscribed over the new Gothic porch: *nisi dominus domum aedificaverit vanum est labor.*

[182]

"But excuse me please," put in Mazi, leaning forward, "but is necessary for honour, to make revenge."

"You confuse pride with honour, ma'am, I think."

"Pride too is necessary, and honour, with our peoples," she asserted.

"I fear your people are pagans, ma'am, that's the truth of it. We mayn't expect grapes from thistles. But you can see it, ma'am, I suppose? Your people's shortcomings are plain enough to you, I daresay, from the vantage-point of your education amongst the French, and your travels abroad?"

"I am proud of my race, sir."

"Just so – but a Highlander may be proud of his race, I suppose, without designing to use against us the knife he carries in his stocking, when he comes down off his mountain wilds and sits at our dinner-table. The weapons of barbarism become ornaments, ma'am, when a man – or a woman – chooses to come down off his mountain-top. And revenge is the weapon of barbarism. The weapon of Satan."

" 'The unconquerable will, and study of revenge'," Tresham quoted.

"Satan's very mind!" agreed the rector. "Will – the devilish will and pride that seeks to reverse the decree of providence. The pride that ain't able to submit itself to the hand of God. Humility accepts the hand of God. The order of God – it must."

"Humility, yes," said Tresham, a bitter smile thinning his lips as he looked at the rector. Here sat the squire among his silver and his portraits and his claret, absolute ruler of his kingdom. Humility! "Though an archbishop, now, ain't particularly a humble man, I take it, nor a good many Christian kings."

"When humility succeeds," said the rector, "succeeds to power, why, of course it must sit in the place of the proud. It is obliged to rule. But still a man may rule humbly, under providence. Under God's order. I am not sure of it, but I believe so. I hope so. Put out the candles, will you Tresham, and perhaps we will go into another room, if you don't mind taking my arm, ma'am."

4

It seemed that the Princess was always at hand to take the rector's arm, or push his Bath-chair, or sit by his side in the drawing-room or the wistaria-covered summerhouse. Uncle Marcus had quite lost the reclusive traits which Tresham remembered – the book-rest on the dining table, the skull-cap and shabby coat indoors, the habit of avoiding discussion today by promising it for tomorrow – and appeared to bask in Mazi's attentiveness like his stout old pigeons strutting and cooing on the ledge of their dove-cote in the sun. Though he saw little of her alone, her graceful submissiveness made the house pleasant to Tresham, too, and he was content to let time pass in this way.

Surely it was a period of probation, whilst they settled into their places? So Tresham wanted to believe. The rector would speak, when the time came. Meanwhile the lethargy of inaction such as he had never known, and a regular timetable strange to him as well, suspended in him the very wish for action. It was pleasant to idle the spring weather away, Shkara his companion in the boat, or in walks through the woods which the full-leafed sweet chestnut now made secretive and shady. He would have liked to have procured her a pony to ride, but he did not care to precipitate discussion of how long they might be there, which the question of a pony might bring upon the *tapis*.

If the future didn't come any closer, the past at any rate receded. When a scene from his Eastern travels occurred to Tresham's mind's eye now, it belonged increasingly to another life: to Captain Vinegar's life, in fact. He actually read now and then a few pages from Captain Vinegar's *Land-March*, of which there was a copy in the library, with astonishment. The fact that events had not happened in reality quite as old Vinegar had arranged them, and dramatised them, put a further distance between himself and that past wandering life. Reading, he would hear again the creaking gush of the Tigris waterwheel which poured its stream over the Residency garden-house at Baghdad where he had sat writing the book, and his own adventures began to seem as fantastic as Scheherazade's tales. The Caucasian gates were indeed at the far ends of the earth. Here at Rainshaw only the present existed, and Rainshaw's own past; and the only future which seemed credible was an extension of the present. He could hardly imagine a different life.

Because it was agreeable, as well as seeming inevitable, he was taken very much by surprise when Mazi first ruffled the water.

He and she were walking down through the park to church on the second Sunday of their stay. The soft west wind had dropped, and the church bells rang loud in the still, dark air which had succeeded it. Ahead, in the gig, had gone the rector with Shkara on his knee; the servants, including Hannah, had walked down a little earlier, as was customary. The question of church-going had been settled very curtly by the Princess the previous Sunday, when Tresham had made rather a hesitant enquiry. "Of course we go to the church," she had snapped. "Shkara and Hannah too?" "Of course all. We are Christian as much as you." To his uncle's enquiry Tresham replied that the Princess had been brought up a Christian at Piatigorsk, and Hannah by the Scotch missionaries at Arras. Whatever beliefs lit their souls, cloaks and bonnets matched them in with the Rainshaw congregation.

The park road curved downhill towards the church, passing not far from a pond in a cluster of oaks. Voices came over the grass. Under the trees two or three boys were setting out fishing-lines.

"Once I was here," said Tresham to Mazi on his arm, "when my uncle stopped his gig and sent me across to take up the boys' lines – to show them he knew the mischief they was at, he said. Now he don't see them, or don't trouble maybe, and the boys don't hold their tongues as we pass even." He was amused by it, and spoke lightly.

"Old fool!" The violence of her voice jolted through her arm into Tresham, and shocked him. "Old stupid man can't stop all people doing how they like wiz him! Just how they like!"

"Come, my uncle –"

"Oh – your oncle!" She turned her fury on him. "He can't stop them all one bit, so wiz you he is *bravache*! Wiz you he makes a sport, what is in his power. All in the house are laughing, all servants. 'Yes Oncle – no Oncle'! I want to kill him – kill him!"

Hatred jabbed her fist in and out of the crook of Tresham's arm, appalling him, yet making him feel the intimate pulses of her blood, her soul's nakedness so close and fierce. He grasped her fist. "They are only boys fishing," he said.

"Oh! Boys fishing! I would beat them, flog them – but you do nussing! A man would not be a dumb ox like you in my country to let all

[185]

be take from him. Stupid man! Let go my hand! Hannah say to me 'Wait, the Captain is strong man, will find good way for us.' Captain –! Yes was captain, is now gentleman, and does nussing. Let oncle stupid pig spit on you. Ach!" She had withdrawn her arm, but she pushed it under Tresham's again with this final shudder of her passion, for they were almost at the church, the bells loud and furious overhead, and she evidently considered that they should approach its gate arm-in-arm.

The Order for Morning Prayer contains in every line remedies against the confusion and disquiet which filled Tresham's mind as he entered the Rainshaw pew, and knelt down beside this terrible creature. He listened to Poat's voice spinning out the words into the dark spaces of the church; and their music, and their familiarity to him from old times, quietened his mind. "*As it was in the beginning, is now, and ever shall be, world without end, Amen.*" Yes, the words built out their fragile bridge over the abyss. Would it bear his weight? Could he trust the weight of his unbelief to it?

The rector rose, and was assisted into the pulpit by a sexton or clerk, the procedure watched with an unfeeling eye by the curate Poat from his reading desk. Tresham noticed that the wing had been broken off a carved angel on the choir-stall nearest the pulpit steps, and recalled the letter he had received at Damascus, whose postscript in Mrs Poynder's hand had recounted this mishap. He had read that letter smoking his *narghileh* amongst the striped bolsters in the caffé beside the Barrada with the harsh burnt taste of Turkish coffee on his tongue – and he recalled how remote and miniaturised Rainshaw had seemed from that distance, a doll's house peopled by toys, irrelevant to reality. Events, the adventure to Palmyra, had rapidly carried him off on the full current of life, and the English letter had been dropped amongst the refuse of the caffé – though it had offered him the plum, if he would come back and lie under the plum-tree . . .

He watched his uncle in the pulpit as he thought of these things. In the orifice between pulpit and sounding-board, the rector spoke like a tongue in the church's dark mouth. Faith sustained him there. In old days Fettle had helped him up the pulpit steps, then Fettle had disappointed him. The angel's wing, too, on which he had depended, had broken off under his weight. But there was someone else now, the clerk or sexton who had assisted him today. His faith produced them.

And is it true, what he believes? Yes (thought Tresham) for here it all stands in order, the creation he believes in; stands in the Order of Daily Service, and sustains him.

The presence of faith so close made its want in himself the bleaker. He heard the wind in the waste land beyond the gates. Watching his uncle, it was as though he looked in through a window pane from a winter's night at the fire brightening another's hearth. He stirred unhappily in the pew. No place pictured in the imagination fulfils those expectations of it conceived from afar. Rainshaw did not: even seen across the breadth of its own park, the house proposed an idea it did not fulfil. For it was into the Arcadian painting in the library that he expected to step when he entered the house, into the golden declining light of summer on temple and shore, "where falls not hail, nor rain, nor any snow". So it would be if he could break in through the window pane to that warmth he saw from the night. The fire would not burn so bright if he sat by it. There is always reality, unavoidable, wherever a man goes; every figure he hurries after in the crowd will present, when its touched arm causes it to turn, not the beauty imagined but the skull-face of reality. To break in through the pane before the fire cools – to catch before it can vanish the image of beauty hurrying away in the crowd – to force reality to be contained within the imagination's dimensions – that was the quest which might keep a man on horseback all his life long with his sword in his hand. That was hope, which he had once possessed. Hope was the quest, faith its objective. The obelisk explains the vista.

Or a man could capitulate. Neither armed and mounted on the quest, nor sustained by faith, he could doze time away in the squire's pew, the plum having dropped into his mouth – the narcotic plum. And who would doze beside him? He stole a glance sideways at Mazi. Demure, pliant, attentive, she turned her face upwards toward the pulpit. But her eyes! Unfathomable, glistering, seeing what scenes? Mild she might seem, but passion and savagery had only withdrawn into her eyes, where they dwelled in the dark like snakes coiled into a water-jar, to wait for the night. He did not know her, could not trust her. He had thought, aboard the *Ino*, that she had transferred her ambition from Hoolaghan to himself; but he had learned now that he was not her ambition, nor was any man living: he was only the temporary vehicle of her ambitions and desires, carrying her in pursuit of whatever game she was after. He thought of the little ponies trembling and sweating under her when her dogs had pulled down a deer after a wild hunt through the Caucasian forests, and one of her attendants cut its throat. What was her quarry now, God knew. The whiteness of her face beside him stared with a dead white pallor. In the midnight blackness of her coiled hair he saw a purplish hue, like the purple tint in grapes, or coarse wine. He feared her with a touch of horror. He could not live with her here. He looked stealthily about the church as if he was the groom trapped into marriage. He looked up at the windows.

Like an angel sliding down a sunbeam through the painted glass there came into his head – came to his rescue – Enid Farr. Suppose she sat by him in the Rainshaw pew! Brightening thoughts arrived in his mind like a dowry she brought with her. He remembered the *mash rabyah* at Bebec where they had sat hand in hand at peace hearing the wailing cry of a *kaikji* float off the dark Bosphorus. "Remember the promise" she had said. He felt her beside him in the pony-chaise that snowy day on the moors above Ravenrig: "You speak as if one summer was all we might have". Here summers innumerable – the Arcadian summers in the library painting – promised themselves in succession. Mazi stirring her foot on the hassock by his own caused him to banish Enid and the alluring summers like guilty thoughts from a marriage bed. He hated her. How might he tiptoe away, though, from the serpents coiled down into those terrible eyes?

When the service was over Tresham waited alone for the rector, taking a turn in the churchyard after Mazi and Shkara had walked away up the road behind the sabbatical flock of servants and villagers. A draught came suddenly cold round the grey church walls, and he gave up looking for the grave he had dug for the navvies' woman and walked back to the porch door.

The rector had come out, and stood with his hand on the gate whilst a farm-boy put his horse into the gig. "The wind has changed," he said to Tresham, "I feel the east in it now as I never used to. You shall drive me if you will. Stop a bit though," he added softly, as Poat emerged from the church porch in his black cassock and low hat, "stop a bit till Poat is gone by, or he'll want a lift up the hill." Out loud he called, "Good day to you, Poat, good day to you – you will read Evensong I take it? Very well. Walking, are you? Good, good: I recommend it. Off you go, don't wait about for us, we shall do very well now."

The odd thing about this speech of his uncle's, thought Tresham as he took up the gig's reins, was that it was delivered as though his curate's behaviour had been utterly different from Poat's actual manner on the occasion. The rector had spoken as if some absolutely humble creature had approached him requiring instructions, and had stood waiting until dismissed: really Poat had walked past with hardly a glance in their direction, his black gloved hands folded before him and no very amiable light glinting in his round glasses. Certain fundaments in the rector's kingdom did not admit to change. There must be order. A subservient curate, like a coachman who obeyed orders to meet the railway train, he must have. No facts were allowed to upset these articles of faith. The bell of the stable clock began to toll.

"Ah, only twelve, what capital time we are in!" cried the rector jovially as they trotted away from the church and its two or three cottages. "If I allow that ass Poat to preach, why, we are kept sitting under him till any hour! How he loves the sound of his own voice! He's an Oxford man, would you credit it? He is though. Only Oriel, of course. Never knew a plainer instance of the unhappy effects of the Varsity on a second-rate man."

"How is that, Uncle?"

"Put a second-rate man through the Varsity, and ever after you'll find he ain't properly submissive to his superiors in intellect. Makes him pert, you know, without adding a jot to his parts."

All who disagreed with him were thought "pert". A pulse of irritation and impatience beat in Tresham's mind against the old man. "I remember once you had fears Poat might go over to Rome," he said.

"Fears! My dear boy, those were hopes – at least if I compare them with some of the other freaks Poat has taken. Mind, I never want him put into the living here when I am gone: mind that now." This he said earnestly to Tresham, tapping him on the arm with his malacca. Then he went on easily, "I shall tell you all about his follies some of these days, so that you may judge of it yourself, when the time comes. About his doings at the school here, dammee, when I came very near sending him away. Very near."

"I wonder you didn't, if he's a trouble to you." This reference to keeping Poat out of the living was one of the oblique mentions the rector sometimes made of Tresham's future position at Rainshaw, and Tresham found his irritation increased by such morsels of plum dangled over him.

"If I turned Poat off, I should only have to accustom myself to some other curate's freaks. We should make do with what providence sends us. Besides," he added after a moment's thought, "as matters stand at Canterbury these days I should find myself hooted about the Close by the Puseyites if I ran there complaining of Poat. No, no, best make do and mend. Make do and mend, under providence. By jove though, but this east wind is getting up its strength," he said, chafing his hands, as a sour cold gust scudded over the dun parkland and rattled the oaks overhead. "Puts us back into winter, an easterly at this time. I abominate it – for the lambs, you know."

"Yes, the lambs suffer I suppose," said Tresham. He was hardly listening, thinking if he shouldn't say something which would require the rector to make his intentions plain at last, when his uncle said,

"Mrs Poynder enquired of me this morning, Tresham – enquired if I knew how long your Madame Rachinskiy was stopping on, and the child, you know, and Mrs – Mrs Whatsername, the servant. The nurse."

"And myself?" Tresham looked at his uncle, the desire hot in him to be done with hints and to have the matter out. "And myself? Does Mrs Poynder want to know when I am to be sent packing too?"

"Mrs Poynder knows you are welcome to stop, Tresham."

"To stop upon what grounds, Uncle? What is to be my standing here, if I stop on?" He rattled the reins in his agitation until the old horse threw his head about in protest and shook the gig. "Of course I must ask, though I wish it had not been necessary." He looked at his uncle. Mazi had said You are in his power, he plays with you, all the house laughs at you.

The rector took off his hat and replaced it again, looking away over the colourless park. His face was strained, chilled through by the easterly. "We will talk about it all some of these days, Tresham," he said in a tired voice. "Of course I am anxious that – anxious that –"

"Anxious on what score, Uncle? What makes you anxious?"

The old man turned stiffly full upon him and looked in his eyes. "I am anxious that you have become entangled with a deceiver. With a mountebank. That is what I am anxious about."

Tresham was silenced. Remonstrances formed on his lips, but he did not utter them. His uncle's view tallied with his own. What surprised him, was that his uncle should suspect the Princess's *bona fides*. "But I thought you had taken a liking for her, sir," he said.

"Taking a liking for a woman doesn't make her any less of a mountebank," said the rector, "though there is many a fool believes it does. She amuses me. I do like her – I have come to like her company. But we do not know her, Tresham. We cannot know her nature. Tell me, for you have seen her father's kingdom – tell me, is it possible that a woman could remove herself from there to here, come among us here, and not dissemble her instincts, her true feelings? Is such a transplanting possible?"

"I have transplanted myself."

"As a traveller merely. Could you live your life there, Tresham, that is the question – there at Colchis, at her father's court? Could you?"

"I –"

"No you could not. That's to say, you could not unless you was ready to deny your nature and become a mountebank – an adventurer – *déraciné* as such men are who live among the savages. And so it would be with her if she came to live among us here." He watched the gig wheels turning for a moment. "What does she want of us here, do you suppose? Have you considered it?"

Tresham shrugged the reins. "A refuge? Peace."

"Pah!"

"Then what is her ambition, Uncle?"

"Assuredly a wealthy match. But that is not the whole of it. There is something more. Who is the child's father?" he suddenly asked.

"Oh – a mountaineer from some other tribe. A match made by her father."

"Undoubtedly still living. And connected with her ambition in some way that I have not been able to fathom. She has fallen out with her father of course. Never trust a woman who has quarrelled with her father," he added, "it is a sound rule."

"Even such a father as that? A savage on a mountain?"

"No matter. A girl who quarrels with her father, or a man who

[191]

quarrels with his mother, runs counter to the natural order, and wants watching. I question any number of the village girls, do you see, who have come to grief, gone to the devil in one way or another, and if they tell me they cannot live with papa – no matter if papa be the blackest villain in the parish – then I expect any viciousness from them. So it is with this woman. Any viciousness. She would commit any barbarism. Why, if it would serve her turn to lop off your head as you slept by her, do you suppose any moral check would stay her hand? Not an instant. She would snap her fingers at the most solemn oath. The truth of it is," he finished with a sigh, "our law is not written upon her conscience, as I have learned from her own lips in a hundred ways. She must be sent away, if you are to stop."

Tresham said nothing, looking ahead at Rainshaw revealing itself window by window as he drove round the curve of the carriageway. There floated the ark for Noah and such creatures as he chose to save. "She must be sent away." She must drown, just as if she was to walk out with her child into the rector's lake, because she did not belong to his order. Her anger would be terrible. Her revenge even. His blood chilled. Better to be in Kent than in Mingrelia, at all events, if her fury was to be aroused. Driving the gig towards the stable-block he said, "So I am to tell her that she is to take herself off, am I, bag and baggage?"

"I will speak with her," the rector said, "I will ask her what she intends. Perhaps she will go to her home after all."

Hope that it would be so, and shame at his part in it, warred in Tresham's heart. But there was Shkara. "But the child," he said, "it is uncommon hard on her, whom everyone loves. Perhaps she might be left with us."

"The mother leave her child?"

"Wouldn't she though! She would have left her on a mountainside, but for me."

"And you would put yourself in the power of a woman who goes against even the instinct of the savages? She is worse than savage, worse than a barbarian." Shaking his head, he got down slowly out of the gig in front of the stables, and walked away on his stick into the east wind swirling up dust around his fluttering coat-tails. *"I could kill him."* Yes, Kent was safer than Mingrelia for the bearer of such orders to quit as the rector intended giving the Princess, thought Tresham.

He took the horse out of the gig shafts himself and led her into a stall, since no work was expected of the men on Sunday. Supposing Mazi could be sent away, and Shkara kept on. Would Enid Farr, say, object to such a child brought up in the house? He felt under his hand the sweet cool ripple of the mare's neck as she drank from her bucket. It seemed possible that he might after all come to possess everything he wanted.

Uneasily, filling the stables with its creaking, the weathervane on the clock-tower swung and veered in gusts of the rising easterly. The ironwork of the weathervane displayed the date 1848, the year of revolution in which the rector had completed his "repairs" to Rainshaw.

<h1 style="text-align:center">5</h1>

What happened that afternoon in a fold of the park was never exactly known, or never revealed. The rector could neither speak nor write any account of the tragedy, for he was found propped against an oak near the lake, absolutely paralysed by a second seizure; and the Princess Mazi, who ran up to the house perfectly distraught, with news of the catastrophe, would say only that she had discovered her friend and benefactor in this grievous condition in the course of her walk.

Tresham, however, believed that he knew that Mazi and his step-uncle had set out together down the slope of the park from the garden after luncheon. He was almost sure he had seen them walking away from the gate out of the shrubberies, the Princess's pliant figure leaning to one side to support the rector's weight. But Tresham knew, and he alone knew, that his step-uncle intended telling the Princess that afternoon that she was to quit Rainshaw. For this reason he did not divulge what he had possibly seen, nor would he second Mrs Poynder's opinion that "she" (the Princess) was deeper in the tragedy than she would tell "else how had squire gotten hisself down to his lake, I'd like to know, with the poor old gentleman scarce fit to take two steps alone?" To have revealed that he might have seen the Princess and the rector leave the shrubberies together, though such might have been the simple reaction of a man who had not lived so much beyond the influence of gas-lamps and constables as had Tresham, would have complicated the catastrophe without the least chance of reversing its effects. There was no mark of human violence on the rector's person: the straightforward explanation of the accident satisfied enquiry. Besides, Tresham could not be certain. Under clouds pushed low over the park by the east wind, and under the trees, the light was so poor that the two figures he had glimpsed through Shkara's attic window might have been those of two villagers collecting sticks under the oaks on a Sunday ramble.

*   *   *

It was more like winter than May, the rector thought. See how the confounded easterly takes the colour out of things! – the green out of the oak-bud, the blue out of the water, the life out of the grass. There was a good deal more east wind nowadays than ever there used to be. How such a day chilled and nipped him, and obliged him to lean heavily on Madame Rachinskiy, her warm little arm under his. Too heavily for what he had in mind to say to her. It was hardly gallant, to lean your weight on a lady's arm whilst proposing to turn her out of your house. Well, well; the day for gallantry was past – long past, to his surprise: for he had always supposed that he would marry "by-and-by". All his life he had supposed as much, and now he must accept that he would not marry, and would not produce an heir of the body for his possessions. He could hardly say that he regretted it. The upset would have been terrific: worse than a new curate. "Would to God we could raise seed to ourselves by other means", says old Jason in his disgust at Medea. Well, now it was too late for regrets on that score.

It was his susceptibility to Madame Rachinskiy's solicitude – and to her beauty – that had made him realise, as the mere passing years had not, his own superannuation vis-à-vis the sex. Having recognised that fact, it followed that he must attend to the inheritance of Rainshaw, always hitherto postponed to be settled "some of these days". Should Tresham Pitcher have it, his brother Dolly's stepson, not related to himself by blood, or should it go to Dolly's daughter's son? If it descended by female blood through his niece, of course her husband would in effect possess the place during his son's minority; and that beastly humbug Roach was not by any means a gentleman. To set up such a jackanapes in a gentleman's place was to confound natural order, and affront every creature placed under him in the parish. It wouldn't do. Men would only bear the weight of the king's chair on their shoulders so long as it contained an anointed king. Young Pitcher was gentlemanlike, and had spirit – but could he be counted upon? Might he not sell up the place lock, stock and barel, and gallivant off in search of adventures again? Certainly with such an unsettled and uneasy influence as Madame Rachinskiy at his side, drawing him away God knew whither, he was not to be depended upon to keep up Rainshaw. She must be sent away, if Pitcher was to settle here.

How her arm supported him, though! How her vigour warmed him! Any man might be infatuated with such a witch. He himself was not so old but that he felt the moon-draw of his blood's tide towards her body, smelt the brimstone of her skin and hair, looked into her pagan eyes, when she lifted those heavy lids, as if into the eyes of an enchantress. He must tell her, though, that she must look for her future elsewhere – look for her prey, rather. If she asked why? "I fear thee, woman." Yes, Creon's words were the truth. "I choose to earn thy hate." Yes, that too, if need be. Once they were out of this damnable east wind in the hollow of the park, and had crossed the footbridge above the Palmyra Tower, he would tell her his decision. He feared her, not for himself, but for the harm he believed she would bring upon what was dearer to him than life, his ordered kingdom.

The rector had stopped for a moment with his companion to consider designs for the bridge required to span the stream feeding the lake where they approached it – temporarily a plank and a handrail sufficed, but he promised himself the pleasure of "repairing" it in masonry – when the deep and savage bark of a dog came to his ears. He broke off thinking of the bridge (or had he been speaking aloud to the woman: he found it hard to distinguish thought from talk, living so much alone) and listened. In a pause of the wind came the mutter of sheep. He looked over the stream, up through the beech trees to the grass beyond. The sheep over there were clubbing together, packing, running. Again the deep-throated bark.

"Come! There are dogs among the sheep!"

Pushing off Madame Rachinskiy's arm, for the bridge was narrow, the rector made best pace across the plank with stick and handrail. Alone now, his anxious heart drove him up the slope to succour the sheep. He saw them in the open park, sombre woods behind, the wind cold in his face from the east. The flock was in a pack rapidly milling, whirling in a vortex of hooves and fleecy backs over the withered turf, lambs scrambling, ewes galloping. Two easy-paced swift dogs drove this huddle of panic before them like spirits of the wind driving a sand-storm over the desert. A confused babble of fear and the rattle of hooves arose from the stampeding pack; deep thrilling barks from the throats of their hunters. Out of the rush and rabble of sheep a straggler broke free, fell, struggled to rise on kicking legs. A dog leaped upon her. Another ewe dropped back lame, fled crooked, lost. Lengthening his stride, a dog pulled her down. On rushed the flock, dropping its victims into the savage jaws, its track marked with blowing fleece and the jerking huddles which the dogs left dying to hunt the living. Now the pack was driven towards the rector. He heard like panic in his ears the drumming rush of its hooves beat nearer. He was alone. He looked for help.

There stood the woman, on a knoll to view better the chase. The wind blew out her dark clothes and her crow-black hair. She stood thrust against the wind like the figurehead of a ship, her face white as death, and as pitiless. The old man's thin shout for help stirred her pity no more than the clamour of the sheep.

On rushed the terror-possessed flock. The dogs' long strides carried them along as easily as barbarous horsemen harrying a rout. Now they were close enough for the rector to see the blood and saliva running from their tongues. Fury seized him. With the energy of fury he struggled uphill from the dell of beeches into their track. He shouted, he roared. His rage carried him near enough into the flock's line for him to strike out a dog with a flash of his malacca stick. The crook hooked for an instant in the dog's legs – hooked, jerked, broke – and down went the man smash on his face on the ground. Away raced the running battle: but the rector lay still. He lay on his face still as a fallen statue, a hand reached out with his broken stick, his hat at a distance, the wind stirring the grass and his white hair alike.

When he was seen by Tresham, however, he was propped against an oak's trunk a little way from the grey water of the lake, his hat and his broken malacca beside him. It was here that the Princess said she had found him. Tresham, having run down from the house, knelt and took his cold hands. The Princess stood looking down.

"Is he not dead?" she asked.

"No."

"Will he die?"

"I don't know what will happen." Tresham touched the grey cheeks wet with tears which the east wind had squeezed out of the old man's eyes.

"Now is yours, all. Now he can do nussing more against us."

"I don't know what will happen," repeated Tresham. "Go to the house. Tell Mrs Poynder. Tell Tom to find Branch and come down with a hurdle."

"You do go. Is better I stay here wis him."

"Pray go at once."

When she had gone, he said aloud to his uncle, who breathed in painful gasps, his eyes fixed open: "She never will be mistress here, I swear to you."

It was the plaints of motherless lambs heard in pauses of the shrill wind that alerted Tresham to the sheep-killing. He left his step-uncle and ran up the slope. Dead ewes he could see strewn about the pasture, lambs trotting between them and nuzzling the corpses, the rest of the flock grazing indifferently at a distance against the hard black rim of the woods. He counted more than twenty dead. Of the dogs there was no sign, nor were they ever again seen in the parish.

Tresham walked back towards the rector carrying the broken-off crook of his malacca stick, which told the tale of his attempted interference between hunter and prey, and of its failure. Then he sat down close to his step-uncle to wait under the tree, having wrapped the paralysed body in his own Sunday coat to preserve the life in it if possible.

There was a dry, sour, shrilling of the wind in the leafless oak, and the cold lapping of the waves among dead reeds shrivelled out of mind all thoughts or memories of summer. There were no swallows. Dreary clouds hurried ahead of the gale, darkening the air, spilling out gleams of a harsh light onto the water. The vague margins, the dead rushes, the unclear light, all served to merge water and sky into one element, wherein brooded above, and was reflected below, the sombre double-image of the house. It would never now be his.

[197]

VIII

London

1

ONE SUNNY AFTERNOON in the last days of May Tresham Pitcher
looked down from an upper window of Limmer's hotel into Conduit
Street with the gloomiest thoughts possible revolving in his head. The
sash was up, so that the jingle and tramp of traffic, and the crowd's
bustle, came up to him like the clamour of a river out of a gorge. He
looked down into open carriages, and upon spread parasols shading
fashionable occupants, and upon the cockaded hats of footmen behind;
upon the rapid gleaming roof of a private closed carriage dashing along,
upon the glossy quarters of horses, and onto top-hats innumerable with
bonnets and crinolines depending on their arms. Into this river of life
the May sunlight slanted down through the smoke and dust of London.
Here were the iron hoops beaten along the high road by the clang of
blows upon their rims. Purpose – volition – kept upright and in motion
the iron-shod hoop of every life in the street below, from the grandee in
his carriage to the ragged boy darting through the crowd by its side. All
was action, and the hurry of life. He watched the spectacle, his nerves
drawn tight by it.

There was nothing he could do, of the sort of things this crowd did.
He could throw himself down from the window, and stop the West End
traffic with the five-minute wonder of a man's death, as John Sadleir,
MP, had done by his suicide at Jack Straw's Castle a month or so since;
but to join the West End traffic was beyond his power. For five years,
more or less, he had lived by the quickness of his wits and actions
through scenes and ordeals in which all but two or three of the West
End crowd in the street below would have perished. Put such swells as

[198]

those along the loopholed walls of the Castle of Amadyah, under Captain Vinegar's command, and see how long they would hold off an attack of the Koords! Why, he would rather have the servants off the boxes than the gentlemen out of the carriages for such a real-life purpose as that. So he judged the Bond Street crowd by a standard which licensed his contempt, as he thought, for their superior ways. Having peppered the crowd below the window with his bitter feelings, Tresham turned in towards the sitting room.

It was upon a higher storey, and was smaller, than the sitting room they had occupied before the visit to Rainshaw. Even so he could not afford this lodging for many more days. In a corner, quietly, Shkara played. What game was she devising, cross-legged on the floor so earnestly addressing her driftwood "horse" which was clasped in her lap? Indeed what language was that low murmur of words? And what were the thoughts in her head? Mute anguish in a child grieves the onlooker as complaints do not, and Tresham could hardly bear to watch Shkara.

Her compliance with the decree to quit Rainshaw had touched his heart sharply from the first. Whilst the Princess had raged at him for not contesting Mrs Poynder's request that they should leave the stricken house, and whilst Hannah had moaned and muttered over their portmanteaux, Shkara had gone away silently to her attic. The pain in her suddenly widened eyes had showed Tresham a bleakness and emptiness ahead which Mazi's fury had obscured. He went towards his own rooms in the house, and was at their door when he heard the tap of the child's shoes carefully descending the carpetless stairs from above. He opened the door onto the back stairway, and there stood Shkara with an armful of the dolls and toys which Mrs Poynder had provided for her. "I couldn't carry the horse on wheels," she said, "but I'll fetch it next." "Oh Shkara!" he bent down to her, "you may keep them surely!" She withdrew the hand which he had clasped and continued her journey downstairs, looking with caution over her burden to be sure of each step she took.

Watching her descend the stair, and watching her play now with her scrap of driftwood, Tresham understood how deep into her soul the uncertainties of exile had entered. She expected to relinquish what she loved. That expectation in a child harrowed his heart. Besides, in her

[199]

armful of borrowed treasures on the back stairs he had seen what he too must relinquish. She at least had her driftwood "horse", into which she could doubtless imagine the character of a Pegasus, to spirit her away from the prison of reality. What had he? He walked about the room, in which Hannah was sewing at a table, her mouth clamped, her eyes glinting. As in a glass reflecting her mistress's character but not her looks, Tresham saw in Hannah his fear and distrust of Mazi ungilded by Mazi's attractions. She was an old savage, and he hated her. What was he to do, amongst them all?

In effect, as the Princess had repeatedly screamed out at him in her rage, Tresham had allowed himself to be turned out of Rainshaw by the servants. With his uncle stretched out in his bed upstairs, where only the doctor and the servants hurried in and out, Tresham had found his own stock downstairs sunk to nothing, like a duff railway-share. He had been dependent on the rector, for his position in the house. No sooner had the rector been put into bed, having been carried up from the lake on a hurdle by himself and Tom, than Mrs Poynder had come to him in the library, where he had been walking up and down and feeling himself to be useless. She had entered the room with a rapid, important bustle, not troubling to knock at the half-open door. "I suppose tomorrow will be convenient for you to remove, sir, as this is Sunday and no railway trains. Oh, that it should come on a Sunday!" She wrung her hands and turned up her eyes to heaven.

"Tomorrow? – well – are there not matters to be attended to for my uncle, Mrs Poynder, that I might attend to? Or help with?"

"Laws no sir. Branch is gone for Dr Wibley, so that's took care of, and Mr Poat he looks in Sunday evenings regular. It's strangers, sir, I shouldn't want, in case that frets him."

"If I was to take the Princess up to town, I might come back, you know, for I feel you should have someone by of the family to turn to."

"It's not the foreign person only sir. It's not as if you yourself was family, sir, not properly speaking, and I shouldn't feel it right to the real relatives, not to have you about with squire in that way as people might say he'd promised one thing, and other people might know he'd meant another, and if he should take and die –" Her voice rose, her head went down into her apron, she hurried from the library.

So it was over. He stood in front of the painting over the fireplace. He had travelled in that landscape, knew the streets of that distant port, the shade of those trees and temples, the chasms of falling water in those hills. This was his country. He had counted upon it. The picture must be relinquished, with the lake and woods and park melting into mist below the library windows. *Must I thus leave thee, paradise?* He went upstairs to inform Mazi, and to blame her.

"But for you – but for you!" he said angrily, when he had told her Mrs Poynder's sentence of exile. "At all events, we are to go away tomorrow, all of us. That is the result of your afternoon's work."

"My work? What can I do? Is dead when I find him, the old one."

"He is not dead now."

"Dying then."

"I doubt it. At all events, you had better pack," he had said, leaving the room. She had come to her door to hurl abuse after him, calling him *châ* and *tagoumghia* for his feebleness in giving up what she had won for him by her actions, shouting out *oukha mouké*, and other worse expressions in the Mingrelian tongue, its barbarism ringing out weirdly through the passages of Rainshaw, such volleys of harsh syllables better matched with the clash of swords or mailed feet in a stone castle. Knowing the language, he had been able to reply in kind: it was at the finish of this savage shouting-match that he had found Shkara on the stair with her toys, her resignation to their exile a sharper knife in his heart than all Mazi's rage and passion.

Tresham had been permitted by Mrs Poynder to enter the room where his uncle lay to take leave of him the following day. It was large and full of light, its bow window commanding the landscape as the bridge of a ship commands the sea, a room bare of any clutter of possessions, ascetic by comparison to the rest of Rainshaw. The rector's form was stretched out unstirring in the shadow of his canopied bed. So silent was the room, so still did the form lie, that it was a shock to Tresham as he approached the bed, to see the living eye roll within its socket, as a prisoner might implore through the window of his cell. Whether the imprisoned soul screamed through its aperture, or was content, there was no way to tell. Tresham remembered the rector's philosophy, that the apparent ruin by time and nature of his Palmyra Tower had not ruined its builder's purpose, and he wished now with all his heart that his uncle's creed would withstand as well this apparent ruin of himself. Then he came away out of the bare room, at whose windows the east wind still jarred, and they were driven to the railway station. Here, in complaining that he must return in the evening to the station, Branch let out the painful news that Eliza Roach and her husband had been telegraphed for by Mrs Poynder, "to see all about it with Reverend Poat," as Branch expressed himself with spiteful satisfaction. Tresham had put himself into the train, and had let one bushy-bearded porter slam shut the carriage door whilst another jangled the departure-bell, as if they too were in the Rainshaw servants' plot to hurry him off the scene forever.

Now he stood two days later looking wretchedly down into the clatter and rattle of Conduit Street. Clang! Clang! went the imperative blows to their iron rims which kept the hoops upright and rolling down there. How was he to go on – how was he to wrest money to live – from this landscape of smug slates and smoking chimneys intersected by ravines full of rushing life? He suddenly was seized with nostalgia for the thick sweet smell of a slow Eastern street, for its patched tile-roofs, its heaps of ruin, its idlers smoking against tumbledown mud walls in the sun, its sleeping dogs. But the urgent rattle of London came up to his ears like the ticking of a clock to a man who must make up his mind before the hour strikes. What was he to do?

One prospect offered a hope: Hoolaghan had reappeared. A letter left for "Captain Vinegar, Addington Club, Pall Mall" had been answered by a note asking him to the club next day: "My dear Pitcher, come along here tomorrow and we will dine, and have a jolly time together, and exchange news. I am full of plans! Ever yrs affecty, Quin Vinegar."

Though Pitcher had taken some care with his appearance before walking down to Pall Mall next afternoon, he was aware before he reached the Addington that any fellows on the steps of the St James's Street clubs who had noticed him, had noticed also that his frock coat and his trousers had been put together in Constantinople, and had sneered at the figure he cut. At any rate it was with his sensitivity irritated by imagined sneers that he approached the colonnaded portico of the Addington. As he faced its vast steps, on which men lounged in the sunshine talking and joking with one another, there came into his head the lines,

> . . . as bees
> Pour forth their populous youth about the hive
> In clusters . . . Or on the smoothed plank
> New rubbed with balm, expatiate and confer . . .

It was fallen angels Milton described thus. Marks of these clubmen's devilhood appeared to Tresham in their glossiness, and their disdain, and their self-satisfaction. Their eyes picked him in pieces as he walked up their steps. He broadened his shoulders, and frowned, and looked fierce at them through Vinegar's eyes – when he saw Captain Vinegar himself calling down to him from the shadowed doorway of the club:

"How are you, my dear man?" Hoolaghan had run down and seized his arm. "What a lark, eh? – this club, ain't it though? Come on now, come in. Dear heaven but I'm glad to see you, hanged if I amn't. We'll eat our dinner directly, shall we now? They do you uncommon well here, I hope you'll agree. Faith, old fellow, ain't it a lark though, such an elegant place as this is? – after the holes and corners of shebeens the pair of us have ate our dinner in?" He laughed, squeezing Pitcher's arm.

Pitcher was carried, almost, by the warmth of the Irishman's grasp, through a tall chill vestibule full of servants and hooded chairs into the pillared dining-room, where a servant walked before them to a table against the room's vast wall.

"We'll have a pint of sherry at once," Hoolaghan told the man as he sat down and flapped out his napkin. "Now then, will this do for you? We're snug here, and can talk easy. 'Tis only the members sit down at the long table there in the middle, unless it's a fellow we all know comes in, and 'tis political talk all the while, and who's to be in the Ministry and who's to be out."

Pitcher spread out his napkin on his knee and watched the sherry poured into his glass. Hearing Hoolaghan describe the club as a "lark" had altered his view of it – had annexed a fortress of pride and privilege to Hoolaghan's happy-go-lucky kingdom. He began to enjoy himself, and warm himself in Hoolaghan's sunshine.

"Now then, dear man," said his host, "here's confusion to the enemy!" He drank off his sherry, and leaned towards Pitcher. "Tell me now, for I thought you was gone down to your cousin's in Sussex – wasn't that your plan of it?"

"To my step-uncle in Kent," corrected Pitcher a trifle coldly, for the casualness of Hoolaghan's memory showed him how little his own affairs mattered to his host.

"Just so. Well?"

"There's been a row, and that plan is sunk."

"What happened? Here, fill up your glass, man, and take some of these plovers' eggs onto your plate, and tell me all the tale of it."

"Well –" Hoolaghan's indestructible good humour, and open countenance, and general air of pleasure at finding himself fallen upon his feet into his present comfortable surroundings, had the effect of ameliorating Pitcher's adversities in his own eyes. He told the story of his visit to Rainshaw almost light-heartedly, as if the catastrophe to his inheritance, and to his uncle, were but minor reverses in a life of adventures.

"Ah, but what monstrous bad luck the old gent should just run out the wrong side of the post when your money looked safe!" said Hoolaghan at the end of the tale. " 'Tis a certain berth I thought you had there, it is so. Envied you indeed – wished I might have an old cousin down in Sussex for myself, by heaven. And now 'twill all go to your sister, so? Is she married, is she? Ah, 'tis pity, for I might have come courting her else. Well well. Affairs of mice and men, eh my boy?"

Pitcher could not have the subject quite so easily dismissed. "It's the Princess's future worries me, you know," he said.

"Aye, it would be. True for you."

"I suppose her future must concern us."

"Devil a lie in it."

Both men looked at their wine.

"I don't know where you are lodging?" Pitcher said.

"Ah, 'twould be no use – a couple of rooms." Hoolaghan made a gesture belittling them.

"Would there be rooms in the same house you could take for her?"

"So long as you're at Limmer's she's snug enough, ain't she?"

"But she hasn't a ha'penny piece, Hoolaghan – how the deuce do you think she's to stop there?"

"Jesus, will you call me by my right name?" whispered Hoolaghan urgently over the table, looking about him like a conspirator. "You'll have the whole box and dice of it come unstitched!"

"Vinegar, then. How do you suppose she's to stop at Limmer's, eh, if she hasn't the tin? And there's Hannah, and the child."

"So there is too. 'Tis a puzzle right enough." He put his cheek on his fist, as if in thought. "You could sell them I suppose," he said.

Pitcher laughed. It was so gravely suggested. "They would fetch us money at the Slave Market at Stamboul, if we was there. Do you miss it, ever?" he asked.

"The Slave Market?"

"The East. The life we had of it."

"Miss that?" Hollaghan's eyebrows formed twin arches of surprise. "Faith, I do not indeed! Why would I miss such a life as would have killed most fellows entirely? The East was only ever a roundabout road I took to lead me here. Aye, acushla, but the road to Pall Mall out of County Clare will take a man through some terrible spots indeed, so it will, and the very length of it, and the windings to every step of it, makes him most awfully glad to arrive. It does so indeed. I wouldn't go back for a mint of money, not I. Now then, dear man, here's our beefsteaks, and potatoes, and claret – will you look at that, and wish you was sitting cross-legged among the fleas at Alatstchinsk, and scraping a *pillau* out of a dirty bowl with your finger ends? Dear Lord, don't talk to me of the East!"

Pitcher waited until their plates and glasses had been changed, and charged with food and wine, before he drew out of his pocket Enid Farr's letter and smoothed it upon the tablecloth by his place. Then he said, "But I must talk to you of the East, Vinegar, in spite of what you say."

"Talk away, dear man, talk away all you please."

"The truth is, Captain Vinegar was made for the East. Made for living out of a couple of saddlebags and ruling a wild kingdom and all that style of thing. He was. You'll find it all in the book there, his character. The fact is, he's out of place on the West End pavements, and railing up to Manchester, and going in for Parliament. That ain't his way." He looked critically at Hoolaghan. "You've altered him. You've changed him. Where's his beard? – all travellers have beards.

[205]

There's too much of the exquisite about those whiskers you've given him, and those dandified stripes on your trousers. You've got upon the wrong tack, that's what it is, going in for trade, and the hustings. You have indeed."

Hoolaghan laughed. "Lord love you, Pitcher, whatever was the Captain to yourself but the jaunting-car that took you to the fair? Now 'tis another kind of a fair we're bound for, he and I. Now he's like myself, is the Captain, not a traveller at all, not he. He only ever travelled away from his native Ireland because he was driven to it by a squall from Dublin Castle, and wasn't he tacking up towards Pall Mall every minute he was gone? Now he's swallowed the anchor, or swallowed the tent-peg, or whatever it is your Eastern traveller swallows down when he gives up bedouins and bivouacks to live snug in St James's. Beards, is it? – faith, if beards aren't ten a-penny with all the Crimea fellows home! Beards and Eastern adventures too, the pair of them is a drug on the market, bad luck to them, and the Captain must hunt upon some other line than that if he's to be ahead of the pack of them all. It's Crimea heroes have tooken the shine out of the fair, it is so. Try and tell a young lady at a Ball of our bit of a scrap on the Ingour, now, and she'll yawn in your face, confound her, and go off to dance with some rapparee with a beard like a bush who has told her he was in the night attack on the Great Redoubt. And a publisher is worse than a young lady," he added. He stared into his wine for a moment. Then he recovered his good humour, and filled up his fork with food. "Ah, 'tisn't all care and dismay though. We ain't beat yet, the Captain and I, no by God! Now, what is that letter you have there, that I see you want to read out to me?"

When Pitcher picked up the letter from Enid Farr he realised he could not read out to Hoolaghan its suggestion for "fishing under Vinegar's nose" the proposal that the Captain and a company of bashibozuks should set up Mazi as the puppet-queen of the Mingrelian kingdom under the suzerainty of Farr's and Novis's Trancaspian Company. Only a reckless adventurer (Enid had implied) would swallow the bait of that uncertain throne. Pitcher must be subtler, for his host at the Addington looked no reckless adventurer nowadays, rigged out in the identical bushy whiskers and wide cravat of the other London dandies lounging and drawling about the centre table of their handsome dining-room. How might he persuade the Captain to go out to Mingrelia, and take the Princess with him, from such a crib as this? It must be attempted, though, if he was to be rid of Mazi, the incubus on his soul.

"The letter is from Sir Daniel Farr," he said, "and contains what would be a most attractive proposal, to a man of sufficient spirit."

"About slate, is it?"

"Slate? No, it is not. What slate?"

"They've slate to any amount up there at – Ravenrig is the Welsh castle called? – and a quay all handy. But his wife wouldn't let him quarry it out, for fear of spoiling her view. That's what a shipping fellow in Liverpool was telling me. I should like it fine to get in there and see the place, if Sir Dan'll have me. There's money in slate this day."

Slate, and Liverpool, made the Mingrelian scheme sound as improbable as Sinbad's voyages, but Pitcher nonetheless leaned forward and sketched out over the table Sir Daniel's plan in alluring colours.

"Do you mean to offer the chance of it to me?" asked Hoolaghan when he had done. He picked up crumbs of bread off the cloth and ate them.

"To Captain Vinegar I do."

"I suppose it would be a grand thing if I was to be hanged else. But dear man – heaven and earth! – after the rigs we've been at to get ourselves out of those terrible mountains, would you mean me to go back?"

"You would be pretty much a king this time."

"Aye, a king in Mingrelia!"

" 'To reign is worth ambition'."

"Then why do you not take up the crown of the place yourself, Pitcher?"

"It is offered to Captain Vinegar. He has the name. He's made for it. Think of the fame of the thing, when it came to be known! Another book would come out of it."

"Aye – published posthumously."

"I didn't ever know you shy at a risk," said Pitcher, filling both their glasses with claret. "Time and again I've heard you say that a quick death's better than a slow life anytime."

"In Mingrelia maybe so. Here in Pall Mall death seems a much more uncomfortable state of affairs, where such pains are taken on all sides to dodge it, with pills and doctors and police men. You feel in England now you have the right to a long jolly life of it – at least if it weren't for the confounded duns and Jews that bully you half to death over bills. You know that brute Crabtree? He's at the blessed door half the time, waving his bill for the money we had of him at Constantinople. Lord, but a bill at three months in them old days weighed as light as no bill at all! 'Tis heavy enough now."

"You would be rid of Crabtree in Mingrelia."

"Aye, and you may light your nightshirt to frighten off the hiccups, if you don't mind burning to death for it." He drank off a bumper and set down his glass. "No no, dear man, the Vinegar I am sees his way to do well enough in England this day, thankee. He's got irons in the fire in cotton, thankee, and slate too if Sir Dan comes round. Would you –"

"Slate!" exclaimed Pitcher, "cotton! What's slate and cotton to Vinegar? What did you want of him, I wonder, that you use him so?"

"A car to take me to the fair, as you did yourself. And I've another book wrote like the last."

"But I wrote the last."

"And didn't I write this one?" smiled Hoolaghan. "Or I nearly have it wrote. I have the half of it wrote, maybe, or the third. A quarter, at least."

"And what is it about?" asked Pitcher rather morosely.

"Oh, 'tis adventures, yours and mine, just as I scribble them down. Look now," he said, an idea striking him, "would you rough out a chapter or two yourself, would you? – of the time you brought in the rifles from Trebizond, maybe? If you can put on the Captain's style again. They want it quick, to have it into the shops and the libraries before the Crimea fellows sit down round the inkwell."

"There are royalties from the *Land-March* still, I take it?"

"Just a few. But this –"

"They might be used to clear the Princess's account at Limmer's, since the money is jointly ours and then we can look for a lodging for her; whilst you think over Sir Daniel's plan for Mingrelia. Eh? How would that be?"

"You're well enough at Limmer's," said Hoolaghan airily, "if they don't dun you I should stop on at the least till they do. Then we'll think. Isn't there the house of your family, too, would take you in? – your mother, so, would she not take all of you in till you see how it is?"

"Never!" Pitcher flashed out the word with anger, and dropped his fist on the table. "No doubt it is what the Princess expects, having brought down Rainshaw about my ears. No doubt it is what she waits for, up in her room at Limmer's. But by heaven she shan't have it! She shan't triumph absolutely, and trample upon everything of mine. I never shall take her to Clapham to lodge."

Hoolaghan stared, Pitcher's hatred for the Princess surprising him. "Well," he said, "you must just please yourself. There's always her throne vacant, in Mingrelia, if Clapham don't suit. Tell me now," he went on, "in the letter you had, did Miss Enid say at all when herself and Sir Dan might be home? For I've a proposal to make."

"To Miss Enid?"

"Ah, faith, not for her hand, bless you! – though I'd think of it, too, if she'd look at me, for there will be a power of money will go with her I suppose, in the dowry line. Hadn't I the notion she was sweet upon Captain Vinegar once?"

"Whatever brings into view her dead brother she's sweet upon."

"That's you, my boy, is it not?"

"Yes."

"So? Well, well, is that the lie of the land, is it? Small wonder you wish the Princess out of your road. Well, however it is." He looked narrowly at Pitcher across the table. "However that is, my own proposal is for Sir Dan and his slate there at Ravenrig. Would we ever take a run up there together, would we, when the two of them's home? Lay our siege to the castle, eh, I at the slate mine and you at the gold mine? Wouldn't that be your way out of your disappointment in Sussex, now, to carry away the daughter before papa goes to smash, as he will, or goes to the devil with Novis?"

"And the Princess?"

"Confound the Princess! My word, but I wish we *could* sell her. Why did we ever bring her off with us, once she'd served her turn in getting us through to the coast?"

"It was your doing," said Pitcher. "You wouldn't see what a fish out of water she'd be outside Mingrelia."

"A snapping great fish too, with a tooth like a shark. Once I was on the boat, though, I saw it wouldn't do – on the *Ino*. Then you took her up. As well take up a Bengal tiger. Lord, Lord! – is there no other fellow you could hit upon would take her off your hands? Wasn't Crabtree always wanting to squeeze himself up to her at Pera? Try Crabtree."

"And then there's the child."

"I recollect you was thick with the child. No, devil take it, I see no way out of your difficulty, old fellow, but a trip to Mingrelia for yourself after all!"

"It's you should take her back, Captain Vinegar, not I."

"Whisha, 'tis only a joke I intended. She'll do well enough by and by. I'll try if something mayn't be got up between herself and Crabtree, for I see him often enough, bad cess to him. Come now, have you ate your fill? Will I send for a jam pudding for you? More wine?"

"Thank you, old fellow, nothing more. It was a good dinner. You're well into the swim, belonging here. An odd apprenticeship you've served for it, adventuring in the East."

"Sure, I learned to leap in an empty saddle and cut a way through the ruck of the crowd. It's no different here."

"This crowd looks worse work to cut through, when I look down into Conduit Street from my window."

"Ah, but you are trained to respect, dear man, as the English are and we Irish men are not. I believe a Barbary pirate's shackles don't rivet a man closer to his bench and his oar than an English man's respect for a lord ties him down in his place to row the nobleman's boat for him. Indeed I don't. Look about you here, at the way the peerage is toadied."

Pitcher looked round the solemn room full of murmuring diners whose mutters ascended to the lofty and elaborate ceiling like prayers into the dome of a cathedral. Here was the respect and order which Uncle Marcus had subscribed his life to. "Even since they've been so drubbed in the papers for bungling the war, are they toadied?" he asked.

"Oh, it's freed a fellow or two who never had his heart in licking their boots anyway, that's all. A fellow like your Sir Dan, now, he'll be freed to act as he pleases, and devil take what his wife's noble relatives say to it. This scheme with Novis is a sign of it – he'll be after the money now, and be hanged to the principles. You watch if he won't. Now," he said, nodding his head towards four grave-looking men round a table against one of the Corinthian columns, thick as forest oaks, which supported the ceiling, "now, see old Vauchurch over there? Sulina-mouth Vauchurch? Remember we met him on the Black Sea coming from Varna in '50? First time you and I met, when you was travelling with Roland Farr."

Pitcher turned in his chair to see Lord Vauchurch – then faced rapidly back. "By jove! He mustn't see us together!"

"Why should he not?"

"Because *I* was Vinegar, at Varna in '50. He'll twig you ain't Vinegar at all, when he sees me."

"You think a grand creature like that will remember a face off a Black Sea steamer? Not he! It's the fame of a name he knows, not the face of a man. Come and you'll see."

Hoolaghan rose and walked Pitcher through the room arm in arm. At the table by the column he stopped, as if surprised:

"Ah, good day to you, my lord."

"What? Oh, Vinegar is it? How do, how do."

"I'm dining with an old acquaintance of ours from Varna days, my lord. Do you remember Captain Hoolaghan here?"

"Good day to you sir –" the peer held out two fingers to Pitcher, who shook them – "Hoolaghan, eh? Yes, I recollect it perfectly. You was very fierce upon me about my Irish tenantry, Captain Hoolaghan. Well, well." His cold stern eyes having been laid for a moment on Pitcher were closed, the stately head turned, the eyes re-opened to shine with a milder light upon "Captain Vinegar". "Now then, Vinegar," said he, "if the question of the Dobrusca should come up in the Chamber, as I was saying to you t'other night at the duke's, I should like to know where I can put my hand upon you, so don't dart off on some of your adventures again, eh, without telling me of it. Do you go down to the Derby tomorrow? Perhaps you'll join me?"

Tresham Pitcher, as he stood by and listened to plans made for a party to Epsom, identified in Lord Vauchurch's solemn person at that moment, all his resentment against the world for not recognising in himself the real Captain Vinegar, and for not dismissing Hoolaghan as an impostor.

It was a fortnight after the Derby, and a wet day, that found Tresham's mother, Mrs Adolphus Wytherstone, looking out of her bedroom window through the downpour at a four-wheeler which had arrived in the roadway before her front garden at Clapham, its roof heaped with luggage.

"It is them, Meg," she fretted out to the servant behind her; "Oh, why will they come?"

"Dear madam, 'tis only for the week." The old woman came to the window and looked through the wet pane.

"What will cause them to go away after a week, pray?"

"Mr Tresh will have some of his giddy plans. Did he ever stop above a day or two? An hour or two? And the foreign lady seemed respectable, madam, and the child quiet, bless her."

"I'm too old for it Meg."

"Too old to greet your boy home to you? Fie, madam!"

"It comes too late. I am used to him gone away now. Six years and hardly a word. Too long. At the first it was cruel enough, dear knows, when Mr Wytherstone sent him away to India."

"Oh, madam, he never did, the master. Mr Tresh was off without any sending. And madam, the worst taking you ever was in over the bairn wasn't the India time at all, it was when he ran off from his school down to the navvies in Kent, do you mind that?" She tried to decoy her mistress away from the pursuit of unhappiness, as was often her task these days; but she failed.

"I say he was sent away," repeated Mrs Wytherstone imperiously, "and that broke my heart. He was sent because he was all I cared for, and you know that's the truth. So. Now," she said, peering through the rain, her voice peevish, "why are they not coming in, if they're to come? Oh, Meg, will you look at the beggarly figure Mr Wytherstone makes of himself in the road there!"

There was a difficulty arisen outside Laidlaw Villa. Blocking the garden gate stood a coal-cart drawn by a pair of horses, from which two men as black as sweeps were at work carrying in sacks through the rain to tip them into a coal-hole opened up in the paved front garden. From the box of his four-wheeler the cabman shouted orders to move on their cart at whichever of the coal-heavers emerged from the garden with an empty sack. But the men appeared as indifferent to his oaths as they were to the angry face of Tresham Pitcher poking out of the growler's window.

Beside the coal-hole, under a gloomy umbrella, stood Mr Wytherstone counting off the sacks as they were delivered into his coal-cellar, quite as aloof from the humanity of the black-streaked coalmen coming and going under their loads as he was from the black coal rushing into the orifice by his boots, unless a wayward lump would spill out and seem like to escape, when he would round it up with a magisterial foot, and kick it below with the rest. Nor did he attend to the curses of the cabman, taking them no doubt for a street row taking place outside his iron railings, and outside his domain. He stood there, a wintry figure anticipating winter, while the rain fell heavily through the still June air and danced on his black umbrella.

Tresham said angrily over his shoulder to his three dependents crowded into the cab, "Counting his coal! Heaven and earth, must he count his confounded coal while the whole world waits for him?"

Rage abounded; rage at all the circumstances of his life suddenly abounded, and spilled over. He leaped out, clapping the cab door back. Striding along the pavement he met one of the coal-heavers at the gate with his empty sack. "Remove your filthy waggon out of my way!" he shouted in the man's face.

The man ignored him, chucked down his sack, prepared to take a full one on his back from the waggon. Tresham stepped up to him, strong, angry, fearless. With a thrust of his hand on the man's chest he pushed him back so that he lost hold of the sack, which spilled coal on waggon and street. The cascade of spilling coal was satisfactory in Tresham's ears as he saw the coalman's face come up slowly level with his own, anger afire in the eyes. The rain made rivulets through the coal-dust, streaking the man's face and chest like savage warpaint, his teeth white, rage heaving the breath in his bull-neck. He swept off his cap and glowered. Tresham hoped he would strike. He craved the outlet of action in the midst of his frustrations. He stood toe to toe, willing the man to strike, so that the Vinegar in himself could strike back. Then came the spokes of an umbrella poking in between him and his opponent, and his stepfather's voice:

[213]

"Pray don't interfere with the work. What are you about? What are you at?"

"Stepfather, I have the Princess and the portmanteaux and I don't know what else in a cab there, and this –"

"Tresham, you have left us alone these six years, I think you can spare us ten minutes longer whilst my coal is got in, I do indeed. Now then, fellow," he went on to the coalman, peering out suspiciously under the rim of his umbrella, "get along with your work, there are four more bags due."

"And the bag he been and spilled?" growled the coalman, blinking the water-drops off his eyelashes and smearing a black hand over his chin. "Look what this mug done," he said to his mate, who stood behind Mr Wytherstone's umbrella, "he done that for nothing."

"You knocked him have you?" asked the mate, sidling round the umbrella so that Pitcher was caught between the two coal-heavers.

"You shall be knocked yourself if you don't clear that cart out of my way," said Pitcher.

"Oh, do pray get along with your work!" fussed Mr Wytherstone, again interjecting his umbrella, his sense of danger evidently so atrophied by a life in the tea-trade that he was unaware of the threat with which the air was charged. "If there is a bag spilled, you must bear the loss, mind, for I won't. What comes about in the road is no affair of mine. And you, Tresham, sir, you must bear a wait for your baggage, pray, until my coal is got in, so you may as well make up your mind to it and walk indoors to your mother."

As he went back to the four-wheeler Tresham was aware that he had been defeated on all sides. Where there might have been Vinegar's action, and Vinegar's victory, there was climbing down and turning away, and umbrellas instead of swords. That was the way of things at Laidlaw Villa. His stepfather called after him,

"Don't let the driver have more than seven shillings, mind. He'll ask ten, but don't you give it him, or we shall all suffer by it. Seven is an ample sufficiency."

*   *   *

The weather improved. Within a few days the Princess and Hannah

[214]

and Shkara, together with Tresham, had settled into Laidlaw Villa for their "visit" more comfortably than either Mrs Wytherstone or Tresham himself had expected. This success was in the main owing to Meg's energy and concern. It had been the chief care of Meg's life, ever since she had come to Mrs Wytherstone – which had been on Mrs Wytherstone's return to England with Tresham after her first husband's death, though she had worked for her father in Edinburgh before that – it had always been Meg's concern to make the world and its inhabitants appear to her mistress in an agreeable light. To this end she altered facts, libelled enemies, promoted what was friendly, and utterly subordinated her own wants and feelings to the grand cause of making all comfortable about her mistress. So, now, she did not allow her mistrust of "the foreign lady" to show itself, and concealed her affront that a heathen like Hannah should speak in a Dumfries-shire accent. She spoke well of them both to Mrs Wytherstone, and cheerfully, as she bustled about the house.

Mrs Wytherstone nowadays was never cheerful. In the past her activity in keeping house, as well as graphic memories of her earlier unquiet life as wife to an officer in the King of Naples' army, had kept at bay a natural melancholy and an ever-increasing discontent. With Tresham and two stepdaughters to care for, she had been busy: for the roof over her head, and the security of sufficient money, she had been grateful. In those days her gratitude to Adolphus Wytherstone had been heart-felt enough to masquerade in her mind as love. But the children had gone one by one, Eliza to become Mrs Roach at Sydenham, May to pursue one good cause after another, and Tresham to march to India. Tresham's going away – to the navvies' camp in Kent when he left school as well as to India, later – had almost broken her heart at first. But there is a moment when patience, too painfully stretched by the responsibilities of love, is snapped; then relief may be felt, and unwillingness to suffer so again by partings and absence. Tresham had gone, and her heart was probably a little harder from that day on.

With the house empty of children, she had come face to face with Mr Wytherstone for the first time, and face to face with her own true feelings for this cantankerous tea-merchant. She found that she disliked him. The discovery, that she had slept twenty years in the bed of a man she disliked, mortified her enough; but what added to her shame was the realisation that deep in his cold heart he loved her with a boy's vulnerable passion, and depended, in his blindness, on her loving him.

She didn't hate him; she only disliked him, and thought him ridiculous, the way he would stand out in the rain whilst coal was tipped into his cellar, where a more likeable man would surely have watched through the window, if he must count his coal-bags at all. He was stupid, she thought, and slow, and everything he did annoyed her. Particularly his complaints irritated her. For twenty years he had complained of being ill-used by the custom of inheritance which had put Rainshaw into his elder brother's hand, dwelling upon it as if it was an injury which he alone of all mankind had suffered. Now he showed a propensity to crow, as if a stroke and paralysis were his brother's condign punishment for having profited so long by primogeniture. She had always tried to show indifference to Tresham's prospects of inheriting Rainshaw, repeating some dismissive phrase about cups and lips, but the irritation with which the whole matter of Rainshaw was fraught, and always had been, was much exacerbated by Eliza having driven up to the door in a cab one Sunday evening, triumphantly excited by news of the catastrophe at Rainshaw, to tell her that Tresham had been turned out of the house "with his Turkish lady". The cup had indeed slipped from her son's lips – or had been dashed from them by the madness or criminality of this woman from the East – and she found that she cared a good deal about Rainshaw after all, if Eliza's fat little Marcus was to have it.

The sad truth was, that every aspect of life now irritated Mrs Wytherstone, and she assumed that all prospective happenings, too, would turn out disagreeably, so that poor Meg had a hard task in sweetening her temper, and in trying to point out among the clouds the rainbow at least, if not the sun.

*   *   *

One morning soon after Tresham's arrival at Clapham he was sitting in the summerhouse which gave him a view up the garden to the back windows of Laidlaw Villa. Into the walled oblong enclosure of gravel and tile-edged flower beds the sun poured its full June heat, heat which stilled bees, and baked earth, and lay heavy with scent on the midsummer flowers. At the centre of the garden, where gravel paths met, a stone pond had been created. It was a round stone basic filled with water, having a stone island in its midst whereon stood two stone cherubs with their arms about one another's shoulders. In the water, amongst slimy weed, swam one or two goldfish (when the heron had not outraged Mr Wytherstone by stealing them) and over the lip of this basin, looking for these goldfish, hung Shkara attended by Mrs Wytherstone. Shkara leaned out over the water: Mrs Wytherstone sat on the raised rim of the pool, with her skirts arranged around her, and restrained the child with a hand through the tie of her dress. Tresham watched them with contentment from his chair in the summerhouse. It was satisfactory to provide Age with Childhood to care for; Shkara completed, to his eyes, the image of his mother seated there under her shady hat, which would otherwise have been solitary and sad. He thought that she must be grateful to him for the child's company.

These notions spiralled drowsily out of Tresham's mind, the heat of the day, and a cigar, and a shady chair, providing him with the dreamy repose of *kef*. Troubles for once were stilled. His stepfather had gone to Mincing Lane, the Princess was indoors – much of her time was passed upstairs alone – whilst his mother and Shkara provided a pleasing image for his eye. He was well-exercised, too.

On first returning from Turkey Tresham had rather relished allowing himself to grow heavier, even fat, his fleshy face in the glass signalling an end to Eastern hardship and short commons. Since the calamity at Rainshaw, though, the sluggishness and complacency of growing stout had seemed to him all at once out of place, and from Clapham he had taken to rowing for an hour or two each day in a skiff hired from a Battersea boathouse, walking rapidly there and back from Laidlaw Villa. To scull over the crowded river made him feel himself a particle of its purposeful current. Long ago he had rowed away from London up the Thames to begin the journey by the waterways which had carried him at last to Ravenrig, and he thought of that remote time often as he sculled amongst the river's traffic. The journey had penetrated into that dark, cold, thorn-thicketted heart of old wintry England which had lain about his imagination as a child, through which the knights had ridden in search of the Grail: he remembered scenes from his own journey as if he had taken part in that quest. Like a legend in Malory was the burying of the two halves of a tramping navvy, who had burned himself to death on a lime-kiln, in the hard December earth of a Warwickshire wood. It was neither more nor less true than the incidents in Malory, or the tales his mother told of their journey together from Italy after his father's death. In the state of *kef* his mind wandered over all these fabulous landscapes equally.

He had come back thoroughly exercised from the river an hour earlier, and was lounging in the summerhouse with his cigar and a writing-desk on which he had begun to scribble down in these last days, at Hoolaghan's suggestion, the account of Captain Vinegar's adventures between Trebizond and Alatstchinsk: "It would be but a poor specimen of the sons of Albion whose bosom did not expand to find himself bounding over the fabled Euxine in a piratical little sloop, the snow-clad mountains of Circassia his destination, and adventure amongst the mountaineers his purpose . . ." So it began: the pen now had slipped from his hand as he gazed and pondered in his chair. The pool in the centre of the garden was a new thing, not there in Tresham's childhood. He fancied his stepfather had made it in rivalry, or imitation, of his brother's lake at Rainshaw: or perhaps to demonstrate to the world the cramped scale of his life and prospects compared to his brother's. Ah, on such a shimmering day of heat as this, imagine the lake at Rainshaw! Instead of the Thames, imagine gliding over the veiled water in the shade of beeches, the dipped oars leaving glistening rings to widen silently, Enid's face before him intent on managing the tiller-ropes, her figure close, her form tempting as he reached forward for his stroke – and themselves alone in tall cool rooms in the house, alone forever, mounting the stairs together, entering their paradise. He blinked, and stirred. It was a surprise to find Enid in the boat with him. How difficulties melt away, in a seat in the shade on a June day! He looked up the garden at the sooty brick of the house.

A movement at an upper window caught his eye. The Princess's face looked down through the reflecting glass, faint as the moon through cloud. Her face had that magic attraction of the moon, he thought, which rivets the attention, and is not without fear. Impossible to sit idly under that pernicious gleam. Enid and the lake melted away. He had promised – he had promised to do a thousand things, to busy himself looking for lodgings, and seeking employment, and bringing into dreary existence a future he had no appetite to live through. Mazi was part of that future. What other resource had she but himself? Even so he might have looked for a means of casting her off, or throwing her upon Hoolaghan at least, had it not been for the child. He got to his feet and stepped into the heavy sunlight, to take shelter with his mother and Shkara from the baleful moon-beam directed upon him from the window above.

"Ah, Tresh dear, I didn't care to disturb you when I saw you writing, with so much to think of and plan for as you have," said Mrs Wytherstone, rising from her seat on the pond's rim, "but pray could you attend to this child? She will lean over so, whatever I say to her."

"Certainly," said Tresham, nettled, "I thought you was pleased to play with her."

"Hardly playing," replied she, "dabbling into foul water after fish that don't show themselves. I don't know how the nursemaids on the Common suffer it, I don't indeed."

"Suffer what, Mother?"

"The tediousness of little children's pleasures."

"I thought you cared for children. I'm sorry you have suffered." He threw away his cigar and sat down on the pond's rim, as if to take on her duty. To have so misread the scene from the summerhouse, and to have thought that she was grateful to him for the child's company, was what galled his heart and vexed him, for it seemed to make fool of him. He had thought that maternal usefulness would have made her happy, but he was wrong. In what else about her might he have been mistaken, he wondered, looking up at her against the sun's dazzle?

She had loosed the strings of her wide-brimmed bonnet, which she now took off altogether. Shaking her grey hair as if to be free of all memory of constraint, she held up her face to the heat of the sun, eyes closed, a smile on her lips.

"Ah, the blessed sun!" she exclaimed, "is it not wonderful to feel its power? For years after Italy, do you know, I didn't care a pin for the sun – for the heat. Now I believe I only live from one hot day to the next, and am dead in between. Ah, the heat of Naples!"

"I don't suppose Italy's hot, compared with real heat," he said rather

[219]

scornfully. "Anyone who has ridden from Palmyra to Damascus in the *semoon* won't care much for the sun, I suppose."

She ignored this, still basking her face in the sun with closed eyes. "I was thinking just now of the day we came up the Val d'Aosta," she said, "with the diligence, and how hot we were on the top where we had seats. Do you remember all the people with the goitre we saw, and all the cretins, in the villages? Ever so many. And so hot the sun was. When we stopped for the horses you played in the brook. There were little fish there under the stones. I was so worried about food for you that truly I thought should I not try catching a hatful. I was so worried." She had opened her eyes, which were fixed on the distant scene. "Not unhappy, though," she added; "that is the odd part of it – not unhappy, not sad even."

He knew just what she meant, and had shared in her feeling a hundred times on his travels, of worry, and apprehension, and hardship, which only served to intensify, by banishing boredom, the sharpness and sweetness of the moment. Fear, a thousandfold more than mere worry, guarded that wonderful region of intenser life which might only be entered on tiptoe. He knew exactly her meaning, but he wouldn't share the retrospect with her. What was the journey she harped upon, but a mere ride in the diligence from Rimini to London? To *him* she harped upon it, who had travelled over half the deserts and mountain-ranges of the East, which she seemed hardly to care about.

"It certainly always sounds as though you enjoyed the journey,' he said, just as if he didn't understand her meaning at all.

"It was a grand thing to have the task before me each day of winning through to the day's end," she said; "it was a grand satisfaction. But I wouldn't be poor again so as to have it. Indeed and I wouldn't go on that journey again so as to have the satisfaction of it. No," she concluded with a sigh, putting on her bonnet again, "the chance comes along and may be seized upon, but you cannot repeat it for your pleasure. Though you may hanker a little after those times when life grows dull after."

"Life isn't bound to grow dull."

"But it is," she said rapidly.

After a moment she went on, "It is bound to grow settled, and dull. The things you care for cannot be done, and the people you care about cannot be seen. That is how it is, ever after. After you are young. And then, you know, what breaks through the dullness, even, is hardly welcome any more. I wish it were not so," she added plaintively.

"I wish it were not so with you." He had got to his feet; now he took her arm gently.

"And you, Tresh?" she asked as they began to pace slowly along the gravel walk away from the pool and Shkara. "Is anything settled?"

"Settled and dull?"

"There are worse woes to complain of than a little dullness, if things are to be well settled, and secure. I know it, though I cannot always quite accept it."

He said nothing, wondering how he could protect her from worrying on his behalf. The gravel crunched underfoot, and the scent of the clipped box by the summerhouse underlay the heat. No doubt she worried over him, and felt herself useless to help him. "Nothing is settled," he said. "Nothing is even begun. I don't know what to do." The instinct for self-pity in the child towards its mother made him franker than he intended. "I don't know where to turn."

She was studying the gravel before her feet as she walked, her head bent down on her folded hands. "Because –" she began – "because, Tresh dear," she went on, looking suddenly up at him, "I must ask when you think of leaving us, do you see."

Tresham stopped. He looked into her eyes. Where he had imagined concern for himself, none existed. "So," he said, "you are turning us out?"

"I haven't spoken to you before this because I wanted you to feel you had time, Tresh, without a giddy rush, and regrets. But –"

"But now time is up, is it?"

"It must be so, Tresh."

"You were uncommon keen that I should stay, once."

"But you went," she said.

"And this is to be my punishment, that I mayn't come back?"

"If growing up is a punishment, yes. It is not only what you are to do to earn your living, it is Madame Rachinskiy, too. What I feel doesn't signify, but your step-papa feels the difficulty of it, the two of you under his roof together and no –"

"What am I to do about her, pray? She is an incubus!" he said intensely, beating his leg with his fist.

[221]

"I don't know what you are to do. Of course she dotes upon you, that is obvious," said she with a mother's scorn, "following you about with her sheep's eyes. But do you – care for her in that way?"

Tresham sighed and turned away, plucking a leaf from the shaped box. "I suppose I rather – but what's the point of talking?" he said fiercely again, pitching away the leaf. "When are we to go? Directly?"

"I wouldn't have asked it," she explained, "but that Eliza sent to see if we will take in her little Marcus and his sisters here, with their nursemaid, whilst she runs down to be with Walter at Rainshaw. She thinks it a sad house just at present for children there, with the poor rector on his death-bed."

"You don't mind seeing after the little Roaches, then? It is only Shkara that wearies you."

"Don't speak bitterly, Tresh. How should I feel for a child of that woman, what I feel for Eliza's children? She is so – so foreign to us."

"And how do you suppose I am to feel, with the Roaches flocking down upon Rainshaw like so many crows? Isn't May there too, sitting at Uncle Marcus's side?"

"May is a nurse, Tresh, it is natural she should go to her uncle."

"Natural! Yes, greed is natural enough – and then a little bitterness is natural in me, I suppose, to have Rainshaw taken from me. No doubt they will alter the will amongst them all, if ever there was a will. And the heir is coming here, is he, to turn me out of this house too?"

"Marcus is your step-papa's own grandchild, Tresh, his own flesh and blood. Of course he must feel for him as he cannot feel for a child from the ends of the earth. But if you and Madame Rachinskiy were to be married, of course then it would be different again. And –"

"That would make it al right, would it? However ill-matched we was?"

"It would make all respectable, Tresh, and that signifies with your step-papa – whose house this is," she added with emphasis. "You know I have never considered the house here mine, yours and mine."

"Why not?" he asked, interested in this aside.

"Because we found your step-papa and the girls already living here when we came to it from our travels."

"I didn't know you felt that." He looked at her in surprise. "So many years ago we came – all my life almost. I thought this was our home."

"A great deal was over and past when we came to rest here," she said. "The greater part, if we don't reckon by time only."

"And I thought this was my home," he repeated. Had that early wandering life in Italy formed him more than he knew, the heat of the sun, the little fish under the stone in a clear brook, black cypress against blue distance, tolling bells, cupolas, ruined temples, the cretins at cottage doors in the Val d'Aosta? – all that his mother had told him of, which he thought he could not remember? Was that why he had cared so for the country about Kutais, which had reminded him of Italy? Was that, not this, his true home? His mind escaped into the idea of Italy, out of this close-walled garden, as a swallow pent in a room finds by chance the open pane, and is in an instant fled away into freedom. Is the image of paradise put into a recess of the mind by impressions received before consciousness wakens? He hardly remembered one Italian scene: had the images nonetheless waited to be developed in his mind by the catalyst of other landscapes, Azana in Phrygia for instance, a stork spiralling down out of heaven to its nest crowning a temple's column seen against far snowy mountains; or Palmyra outlined with skeleton grandeur against the desert at sunset; had these scenes and a hundred more, and even the painted landscape in the library at Rainshaw, chimed with scenes already stored in recesses of his memory, where they represented to his imagination both home and paradise? "It is strange that I have never forgotten Italian," he said.

"My dear, not strange to me." She had, as ever, followed his line of thought, read his mind.

"I wish I hadn't lost father's sword," he said, taking her arm. "I didn't care when it went over the waterfall, when little Tack and I were pulling out the Enfields, as I told you, and Hoolaghan kicked it over the falls. But I wish I had kept it."

"Yes, you told me." There was no response from her arm in his. She could not understand (he thought) that the Val d'Aosta led to that waterfall cave amongst the Caucasus; or she would not follow him there. She would not look in the direction of ideas that required of her the trouble of altering her fixed view of things, or extending her horizon beyond the Italy she remembered.

So they were parted, though arm in arm; she to walk on behind the diligence up the Val d'Aosta, he to watch his sword kicked over the rock-edge of the waterfall cave, where the leaping water caught the blade, and whirled it in an arc, and dashed it down into the abyss. A window rattled up in the Clapham house behind them. A voice shouted:

"Shkara! Shkara!"

Mazi's voice. Tresham turned. The child was not to be seen. Then amid the quaking water-lilies in the stone pool her sleek head arose. He dropped his mother's arm and ran, angry and alarmed. From above came Mazi's voice like guilt on his head: "I thought I trust you – why you let her fall?"

"She didn't fall." He reached out his hand to Shkara who was wading through the water-lilies towards him. "You jumped – why?"

"To catch the fish," the child said. With a smile of delight she held up a wriggling goldfish.

"The little beast!" exclaimed Mrs Wytherstone. "Put it back this instant, pray, and run in to Hannah, do you hear? Oh, such a trial as children are. Now she will take in the dirt everywhere!"

Weed and slime streaked Shkara like a drowned child as Tresham lifted her from the pool, horrifying him. His mother's words precipitated his decision. "I'll take you in," he said to Shkara, gripping her hand. To his mother he said roughly as he walked off, "You may tell step-papa that we won't trouble him beyond tomorrow."

"Where shall you go, Tresh?" She was anxious at once, following him up the gravel on which Shkara's footprints left glistening wet marks.

"The Princess shall go into lodgings while I go down to Wales."

Once he had decided, he saw his way clear. But he could only decide under the duress of imperatives. He led Shkara indoors.

IX

————•————

Ravenrig

1

TRESHAM HAD NOT PUT THE PRINCESS into lodgings, for he had not been allowed to do so by his stepfather. He had however come down to Wales himself, and was now riding along the sea coast within a few miles of Ravenrig Castle. The means of arriving at Sir Daniel's Castle, which he had begun building ten or more years earlier in a remote valley opening to the sea, had been developed very much since Tresham's last visit. Then, there had been several changes of train, several waits at junctions, before the final long drive over the moors; today, Tresham had left the Holyhead Mail on the Menai Strait, and had taken a passage in one of the slate-boats plying between the railhead and Sir Daniel's quay below his slate quarries in the vicinity of Ravenrig. Evidently Sir Daniel had overcome, or had ignored, his wife's opposition to having the slate quarried from her "view".

By this altered physical approach, Tresham found his ideas about his destination made less clear than they had been to him in London. As he rode along the seaside track on a Connemara pony borrowed from the quarry-manager, he was uncertain of his position in relation both to the Castle and to the road he remembered across the moor from Pentre Bridge. He was obliged to recognise what other alterations ten years might have made. The traveller supposes that what he leaves behind remains static, to be picked up again on his return, though the example of Ulysses' homecoming should be ever before him.

The moorland road of those past days had dipped suddenly down at last through an oak wood onto the very chimneys and towers of the then unfinished castle whose vast works dammed with masonry the wooded valley which wound towards the sea. Tresham supposed that the track he now rode along, which followed the sea coast over cliffs and beside beaches of shingle, would lead him to the mouth of the Castle valley. He would know the mouth of that valley by the white stone cottage which had stood a few yards from the shore, on the bank of a stream. He was anxious to orientate himself. He hoped for the self-confidence in relation to Sir Daniel which familiarity with the great contractor's surroundings might impart, and he looked out for the white cottage as he came over each headland.

He had not recognised the neighbourhood of Ravenrig from the deck of the slate-boat heading in towards Sir Daniel's quay over a glassy swell until a deckhand had pointed out to him the obelisk on its hilltop, which he said Sir Daniel had erected to serve as a sea-mark for his slate ships. A sea-mark! Tresham recognised (from Enid's description) the far-off glint of stone on the mountain as Roland's monument – the obelisk which had materialised as the focus of Sir Daniel's "Wistas" cut through the Ravenrig woods. Perhaps he had had its function as a sea-mark for his slate ships in mind all along. Tresham had studied the coastline through a glass borrowed from the skipper.

The hills above the quay presented an arresting and gloomy spectacle of commercial destruction. Quarried into, and sliced open, the mountain seemed chained upon the seashore by the tram-rails fastened over its flanks, and seemed too to groan aloud with the clanking of waggons and the screech of their wheels, and all the multitudinous sounds of work which rolled and echoed among the hills. The slate boat thudded in over water which reflected the dark steeps. The deck-hand standing by Tresham pointed out the whitewashed hut perched at a great height among the cuttings and quarries, from which hut, as they watched, a bugle blew a faint alarm. At once such a silence fell on the gigantic workings, that from all that coast only the wash of the sea on rocks was heard. Then came a spurt of smoke or dust vented out of the whale-grey mountain; followed the crash of the blast, and the echoes of the explosion rumbling off cliff and water. Soon the clatter of all the Lilliputian works on the fettered mountain began again, and in a few minutes the slate-boat had slid alongside the quay. Here was bustle and activity at close quarters. Tresham forgot the impression gained offshore, of a groaning Titan, a defeated mountain, chained down and tortured upon Sir Daniel Farr's orders. He went ashore.

He was in the little port an hour, while the quarry-manager's office found him a pony. During that hour, as he walked about the quay and watched the work, it was the bold and imaginative scale of the enterprise which impressed him. Nothing was so distant, or so deep buried in the earth, but Sir Daniel would take it to market if he chose. The formidable character of "the great contractor" rebuilt itself in Tresham's mind amongst his works. The London idea of "poor Farr" overwhelmed by debt and rivals, which Hoolaghan as well as his stepfather had put into his head, melted away in face of this grand actual enterprise between the mountains and the sea. Here work went forward at his orders – onto this remote seashore, silent since the Creation, was directed the energy and noise and bustle of human life – just as his will had driven railway cuttings through the virgin hills of Europe, and had put trade, and immigrants, and soldiers, into the clanking steam-trains which had followed his venture. Why shouldn't such energy carry trade through the Caucasian gates too?

Walking an hour on this quayside amid Sir Daniel's works, it seemed to Tresham that if Sir Daniel had resolved to push trade across the Caucasus by way of Mingrelia, then success would follow that venture as a matter of course – as the steam-trains followed his navvies.

Finding him a riding pony took time. A boy tried to sell him fragments of quartz with veins of gold in them, kept like a great mystery in a knotted cloth. Tresham laughed, thinking of the coins and trinkets he had been offered by Arab boys in the ruins of ancient cities. Gold must be the object of all travellers' researches, according to the natives of Wales as of Babylonia. "Do you suppose," he said to the uncomprehending Welsh child on the quay, "that if there was gold worth mining in these hills, your master would not have had it out of them before this?" He threw him back the quartz. In his carpet-bag he had the fragment of coal which he had picked up among the Mingrelian hills, carefully preserved to show to Sir Daniel.

At last a fleabitten Connemara was produced with an apology for delay. Ordinarily, he was told, a guest for the castle who came by sea was met by a carriage at the quay. He replied that his visit was altogether too urgent an affair to have waited for such arrangements to have been made.

Urgent to himself it certainly was. There had come upon him in the last days a very pressing sense of being driven into a corner. From Rainshaw he had been forced to retreat to London, and to Clapham; now he was driven back upon Ravenrig. The thread of track leading along this remote coast, between mountains and sea, signified to him, as he set out on the grey pony, how narrow a path forward was left him. His own mother had ejected him from Clapham! However, the jar to his ideas of that fact had opened his eyes, and he had seen with opened eyes what discord and jealousy inhabited Laidlaw Villa. When he had told his stepfather that he intended putting the Princess into a lodging, and himself travelling to Wales, Mr Wytherstone's reaction had been immediate and violent. Standing in the vestibule with his door-key still in his hand, just come in from Mincing Lane, he had rasped out, "Into a common lodging? Princess Rachinskiy? You can't do it."

"I haven't the alternative, sir, for I can't take her to Sir Daniel Farr's uninvited."

"She shall stay here."

"My mother says she needs the place for your grandson."

"Needs a fiddlestick!" He dashed down his tall hat on a table. "It is my house, and she shall stay here."

"If she ain't welcome I don't choose –"

"I say she is welcome, which is enough for you I suppose. Let us have no more humbug, pray." He took up the newspaper, then, and walked into the parlour. The subject of "the Princess" (as he liked to call her) was not resumed until ten o'clock that evening, when he came down from his study to the parlour again, to take tea and sit in his accustomed chair across the fireplace from his wife.

By then Tresham had done a little watching and speculating on his own part, considering his mother and his stepfather from a detached viewpoint which the jar of his mother's inhospitality had opened his eyes to. At dinner Mr Wytherstone made sure that the Princess sat by him. He pressed food and wine upon her, even talked to her on subjects beyond his usual hobbyhorses, and always called her "Princess', in contrast to his wife's "Madame Rachinskiy". Mazi responded with the concoction of charms of which Tresham knew she was mistress, the demure, downward-inclined head interspersed now and then by such a flash from the black eyes that their target believed he had seen into her soul. Having watched Mazi's attractions exercised upon his step-father, Tresham observed his mother. Was jealousy behind her attempt at turning Mazi out of the house? It would not have occurred to him before that afternoon to have imagined jealousy as a motive behind his mother's actions – unless it were jealousy of himself.

When, at ten o'clock, Mr Wytherstone had tramped downstairs into the parlour, and had taken a cup of tea which he stood stirring next to the Princess's chair, he had cleared his throat and announced, "I want to hear no more talk of the Princess leaving us, mind. At least until Tresham is returned from Wales she shall stop. She shall not be put into lodgings. If we are dull here, why, let us take tickets for the theatre. I have been thinking of it. What do you say, Princess? Ristori has a new production, should you like to see Ristori?"

"I can't suppose Madame Rachinskiy would be amused by going to the play with us, Dolly," interposed Mrs Wytherstone from her tea-table.

"Then let her say so." He turned his creaky smile on Mazi.

"Oh," she responded, "please, I would love to see him once, if –"

"It is a settled thing!" He parted his hands like a magician. "I will take tickets tomorrow."

"Pray don't take one for me, Dolly," said his wife sharply, "I shan't go."

"As to that, my dear, you must just please yourself."

Listening, Tresham felt himself become suddenly – painfully – an adult in his view of his mother. He saw a sulking, peevish woman jealous of the infusion of vigour injected into her husband's veins by their visitor from the East. He looked at Mazi. How far down that road would she go, to secure her wants? Well, if she chose to sing for her supper after that fashion, she was welcome to it whilst he was gone into Wales. He took his tea and went to the window looking out over London flaring up its gas-lights into the sky.

"What profit do you expect from running about Wales, eh Tresham?" called his stepfather across to him, still half genial from his encounter with Mazi's eyes.

Tresham did not turn round. "I go to discuss plans with my old friend Sir Daniel Farr, sir, who is just home from Constantinople."

"Invited you down, has he?"

"He always welcomes me."

"Ah. Don't need to tell you to tread cautious, then, where old Dan's concerned."

"I don't know what you mean, sir."

"Don't you? Don't you now." His stepfather had come over towards him, and stood raising and lowering himself upon his toes beside Tresham, as if determined still to overtop him, and overawe him, as he had done when Tresham was a child. "Don't know about that rogue Sadleir I suppose, either, who took the prussic acid route out of his difficulties – don't know about Hudson going to smash – don't know nothing about Farr, oh no." He left a pause, but Tresham drank his tea and would not ask what information he had about Sir Daniel which might connect Farr with the bankrupts and suicides he had mentioned. His stepfather's natural waspishness made it certain that he would drive in the sting. "Plunging mighty deep is Farr, they tell me," he went on. "Over his ears into Manchester prints now, with some wild scheme about the Caspian. And slate. And shipping. Oh dear, oh dear!" He shook his head.

"He ain't mistaken the line yet, in his ventures. And it ain't a wild scheme at all, the Manchester cotton, for he –"

"No, no! – just to send it clean across the Caucasus, that's all, where there's a war on! No, no, not wild – you know best, of course, and it ain't a scrap of use advising you, never was, nor telling you what's common talk on 'Change, if you'd bring yourself to listen to that instead of tattling at the West End clubs."

"What is common talk, on 'Change, step-papa?" asked Tresham of the peppery man bobbing up and down on his toes before him.

"Why, what I've said, only you wasn't listening. How Dan Farr plunges deep as ever he did, though his touch for the thing's gone. Plain reckless now. He won't cry quits till he's brought it all down about his ears I suppose. Such a smash as there'll be then!" He laughed drily, walking off and stooping by the Princess's chair to set down his tea-cup. He was thin and somehow spidery, stooped over her in black, the candle-light glistening among thin grey hairs on his scalp; but really he was the fly, Tresham thought, and Mazi the spinner of webs.

"And will Miss Enid be at her father's, Tresh?" enquired his mother, turning from that spectacle of spider and fly to address him with

[230]

affected interest. Before he could reply she had added to Mazi: "Do you know Tresh's friend Miss Enid Farr, Madame Rachinskiy?"

"The Princess knows her well, from Constantinople," put in Tresham.

"And is that one now at this castle?" asked Mazi, turning a suddenly malevolent face upon him.

"I don't know." He had turned away, but it had not prevented the ferocity of those eyes from penetrating his brain. He had known perfectly well that Enid was to be at Ravenrig.

The idea of Enid at his destination had given point to his journey. Indeed she almost seemed to be its objective, when he tried to resolve what other purpose there was in travelling to Wales. She stood like a sea-mark in his imagination – like Roland's white obelisk above Ravenrig – with the confusion of other motives and purposes rising behind her like the orderless Welsh mountains behind the obelisk. He needed her to direct him into harbour. In her company, and in her father's, at Constantinople, Tresham had felt buoyant and optimistic, sure of his future: it was perhaps the desire to recover this optimism, and to find it fulfilled, that really directed him towards Ravenrig now. "You speak as though one summer was all we might have" she had once whispered to him on the road above this sea-coast, as if holding out the promise of more. To assert his belief in those future summers he had made the journey towards Ravenrig as a pilgrim towards the sacred sites, where faith so abounds, that it may be drunk at the springs, and inhaled of the breeze.

As he rode, he looked out for landmarks. He was anxious to recognise his surroundings, and to catch his bearings, and to be as a man revisiting old haunts. To put himself upon easy terms with Sir Daniel and his family, he claimed familiarity with the landscape about the Castle.

The grey pony ambled along the path by cliff and sea shore with his carpet bags tied before and behind him on the saddle. This track would surely lead him, he thought, to the mouth of the wooded Ravenrig cleft, down which he had walked to the sea with Enid and Roland one December morning long ago. Then he had climbed the sand dunes to look out across the winter sea whilst brother and sister had spoken to a white-haired old man at the door of his cottage by the stream. The sea

[231]

beyond the dunes had seemed to incarcerate Tresham like a prison moat. He remembered that at that moment a sudden idea had rushed into his head – connected somehow to the wicker basket in the old man's hands – that he, Tresham Pitcher, was a changeling. Strange idea! It was almost as if it were true (he thought) for he had escaped over the moat-like sea not long after on wings borrowed from "Captain Vinegar". He wondered, riding above that same sea now, what his flight had achieved? Still the sea affected him with an unquiet longing to travel over it until the mountains of a magic kingdom rose beyond.

Could he not rest? As he looked out across the glistening calm, where summer cloud-shadow rested in violet patches on the blue, he willed his mind to see these waters joined and mingled with Aegean and stormy Euxine, with the Bosphorus straits and the brown flood of the Tigris at Baghdad, so that by looking on this one sea he could look on all the world's seas, and so quieten that uneasy ambition always to look over horizons, which he had felt when he had topped the sand-dune long ago. Had he not brought the essentials of Trebizond or Baghdad home with him, a hundred strange cities possessed in his mind like pictures to hang upon the walls of a snug English home?

Alas, he knew they were as far away now as they had been when he had never seen them, across that sea at the foot of the Welsh cliffs. He had not brought them home like trophies; he had left part of himself in each, part of his heart. Trebizond! He saw the pirate sloop with her cargo of arms run up her sail in the roads below the town; worse, he felt the draw of the wind as she left the ancient city perched like a stork's nest above its ravines, and struck off over the swell for the ice peaks of Circassia. He felt the reality of it like the heart's longing of the prisoner for freedom. That was life. You cannot hang life on the wall of your cell, and hope to be content with its image. As he looked out over the Irish sea from his pony's back, on the cliff path, he saw the broad grey shiver of the wind steal across it like the ruffles fanned upon water by restless wings. He could not be content with the images of life that the stay-at-home hangs on his wall.

There lies the port: the vessel puffs her sail:
There gloom the dark broad seas . . .

[232]

He rode over the headland, wondering that he didn't recognise landmarks even yet from that visit ten years ago which stood out so clear in memory. At the door of the stone cottage in the valley Enid and her brother had looked into the basket which the old man had held with the kind of precious care with which a sleeping child is carried, whilst he had climbed the sand-dune to see the sea breaking on the beach. Only later – years later – had he wished that he had looked into the basket, to see what the old man carried so tenderly, rather than satisfying his desire to see the sea. Surely not lobsters, as Enid had pretended? Well, he would find the cottage and ask the old man. If his choice had been wrong then, he would repair it now.

He was half way down the slope of the headland before he realised that he had entered that same valley. There rose the sand dune, closing it from the sea and the sound of surf: there ran the stream among its rushes, away inland curved the silent, wooded valley; but where was the stone cottage? No trace of any building remained. Nothing stood, not one stone upon another, not the chimneystack even above a heap of ruins, which would have signified a natural collapse. It had been destroyed: he was too late, too late to ask the question.

He crossed the brook where memory placed the lost habitation, and there he saw nothing but sedge and reed, and the lick of the stream on its stones. Wait: in a pool amongst the reeds he spied a coracle afloat, the bobbing round basket tethered to a ring set in a grey stone, its painter now dipping in the stream, now tautening to fling off sparkling water-drops as the craft tugged in the current. He pushed the pony amongst the reeds to look in; but the vessel was empty. Unless the sedge concealed a watcher, it was unattended. Having hesitated, he rode on. Across the stream, the track which he had so far followed now joined another from the shore and, turning away from the sea, both lost themselves in a broad gravel walk laid down under the beech trees clothing the lower flanks of a valley which wound inland between high bare outcrops of moor.

Here it was cool and shady, the light netted in many green veils of foliage before needling down upon mossy roots ridging the wood's floor, and upon the flecked grey of his ambling pony's neck. He remembered a track under the trees, and himself walking on one side of Enid's pony whilst Roland walked upon the other, and the snow melting off the hills. The gravel of this new grand avenue, he now noticed, was deeply indented by the weight of a pair of broad wheels. Having seen these ruts, he at once connected them with a grinding, stone-crushing creak which echoed back to him along the valley. He surmised that some vastly heavy contraption was crawling towards the Castle from the sea.

He glimpsed the object first at a distant turn, but it was gone from view before he could make out more than a huge shrouded shape attended by a pigmy crowd, crawling forwards. He kicked his pony into a trot to catch up the creeping cortège. At its centre there creaked along a wheeled cart of the design used for conveying coffins, greatly enlarged; to this was secured a monolithic object which, corded down and shrouded in sacking, rose above the bent backs of a dozen or so men hauling the cart forward with ropes, or pushing its wheels.

"What is it?" asked Tresham of one of the men as he reined in beside this colossus on its way to Sir Daniel's castle like some siege-engine of old, or like the wooden horse towards Troy.

"*Sgriflech*," answered the dark little workman briefly.

"What? Is that Welsh you speak?"

"*Faen*," went on the man, "*muth ar chwarae ar fwrdd â phelau ifori*."

"Does no one of you speak English?"

If they did, they would not reveal it. In no recess of the Ottoman Empire would Tresham have been so debarred from understanding a group of labourers as he was from understanding these Welshmen. He rode close to the cart and pulled aside a corner of sacking to see for himself what the object was. It was a glistering stone, dark grey. It was slate, a colossal slab of slate cut from the heart of the mountain. Hands reached up and covered the corner he had disclosed, like a secret. He looked into the men's faces. They were a dark set of creatures, little and active as trolls, going urgently at their work of dragging this splinter of native rock towards the Castle. The mountain's groans, as he had heard them from the deck of the slate-boat, re-echoed in the creaking wheels. He spurred on ahead, with the feeling that the Castle should be warned, the guard called out, a defence prepared.

Although he had of course expected to see Ravenrig in front of him when his pony cleared the beechwood, yet his first glimpse of the castle took him aback. So large, its façade shut up the valley from slope to slope with a monumental weight of stone and tower and slate and twisted chimney. It was silent, too, utterly silent: the whole still valley seemed crushed into silence by its presence.

Presently, as he rode forward again, his eye separated the impact of the façade into its details; separated bastion from bay, rose by way of oriels and turrets to a fretwork of carved stone; mounted upward again into an intricacy of corbelled towers and slate-capped steeples, to wander among battlements and ranked chimneys and gilt weathervanes, until it finished upon a flagpole on a slender tower, which overtopped the rim of moorland showing above the woods and slopes of the valley. The castle was complete, which he had last seen half-built. The once wild valley, too, had felt the hand of authority. Broad terraces of gravel and turf extended towards him, guarded by balustrades which supported gigantic urns, terraces dropping by stone steps from one lawn to another, these lawns edged by canals and gravel walks, the whole well-ordered plan picketted by the clipped shapes of yew against the precipice and moor which looked down upon it over the beechwoods. The river, whose loud-running water over its stones he so well remembered, had been removed from its bed under the trees and compelled to gush through the stone mouths of lions and flicker in geometric pools. The valley, like the slate-mountain on the sea coast, had been conquered. Even the seasons could not alter or affect this landscape of stone and gravel and yew, Tresham thought as his pony carried him past the silent terraces towards the silent castle. Above, there sounded the faint intermittent creak of a weathervane turning in some wandering free air not felt below; and, like its echo, the creak of the axle of the slate-cart approaching under its colossal weight.

He dismounted before a deep-arched doorway and jangled the iron bell-pull. He waited in the shadow until the bell's clangour and its echoes had been consumed by the silence, and then stepped out into the hot, heavy air of the valley again. No one came. He looped the pony's reins through an iron window-grille, unstrapped his two carpet-bags from the saddle, and entered the deep archway, where his footsteps sounded extraordinarily loud. Leaving his bags on a stone bench, he went in at the open door.

The space into which he found himself plunged was immense, and

[235]

cool and lofty. Even the size of the castle's exterior had not prepared him for such a church-nave of a chamber as this. Walls decorated with tapestries soared upwards until, at a tremendous height, a timber roof vaulted between them in the dimness of shadow. At the hall's further limit, across a coloured lake of Turkey carpet, rose a double staircase whose twin curves supported a minstrel's gallery backed by a vast dark painting, and ornamented with trophies of arms. Narrow and tall lancets pierced the walls, by which fell light in sunshafts through church-like shadows. Here the light touched a face in a tapestry, there it glowed in the ruby glass of a lantern affixed to a newel-post, or glinted on the outline of steel armour. The silence and stillness and vastness of the shadowy space magnified the buzzing of a bee against a window, somewhere high above Tresham's head, into so furious a commotion that he turned and looked up.

Above the arched door by which he had entered rose a round-headed Gothic window of painted glass. The figure in the window, against which the bee bounced so angrily, was that of a knight in armour who leaned on his sword in a grassy orchard. His helmet was in his hand, his head bare, the light of the sun making a halo of his golden curls. It was Roland Farr.

The narrow lights had imprisoned him into an angular gauntness, from which the well-loved face threw down an appeal to Tresham, as a man caught amongst thorns might beg for release without moving a limb, lest the briars tear him worse. Poor Roland – it was Tresham's first thought – poor Roland caught in such thorns. Against Roland banged and buzzed the trapped bee.

Tresham walked further into the hall to see the whole window clearer, and his friend's face. It was not the armour he was trapped in – that he wore as lightly as fancy dress at a ball – but the window. The discipline of the leaded panes made a saint of him, or a martyr. Dear Roland! The tears started into Tresham's eyes, remembering the dying candlewax face bubbling with sweat, the lips caked black with blood and vomit, where he lay on his ledge in the verminous mud wall of their lodging at Damascus. There he stood now in the window, resurrected, in the armour someone had thought fitting. Light falling through Roland in his window fell in confused and violent colours like bloodstains on Tresham's hands and clothes and face as he stood looking up.

[236]

Confused emotions, too, flooded his mind with feeling. Before he could separate remorse from guilt, or love from nostalgia, there came a shuffling footstep approaching the gallery above the hall's further end by unseen passages behind it. Who was this? What spider had felt the trembling of his web, and now came out to investigate it? Tresham faced the approaching footsteps, and waited.

There appeared a figure which grasped the gallery rail. He seemed old, angular, gaunt. He hesitated, his hand on the bannister of the staircase, seeing someone standing in the midst of the hall below. Tresham thought, Is it Roland? – Roland aged by death, faded by long imprisonment in the leaded panes? For he had a look of Roland, a resemblance.

"Who is it?" came a thin, uncertain voice.

"I am Tresham Pitcher. I am expected, I think, for I telegraphed."

"Ah, of course," said the other, some apprehension apparently quieted. He began to shuffle down the stairs, and Tresham went towards their foot. "Pitcher, yes, so it is, so it is. Now I see you, of course. I am Edmond Farr – do you recall we met? When you was at Ravenrig before? I shouldn't have known you, I confess, but I had the advantage, so to say, by knowing you was coming." He held out his hand.

It was the eldest of Sir Daniel's four children. Still, thought Tresham as he took the bony hand, Edmond couldn't be above thirty at most, yet he looked fifty, the skin of his face papery and pinched, eyes dull, hair lifeless, his figure stooped and inordinately thin – almost as attenuated as was poor Roland by confinement in his window. Edmond's hand lay in his like a few sticks as he shook it. He remembered that the elder brother never had seemed energetic, that his father had appeared contemptuous of his solitary shooting expeditions after the snipe and wildfowl of the mountains. Edmond had seemed to attend in those days on his mother in upstairs regions, appearing behind her on the stairs with her white dog under his arm, when the family was already assembled in a drawing room. All this came into Tresham's mind as he listened to Edmond tell him that the castle party had gone picnicking on the moors. "Even my father has allowed himself a half-day's leisure," he said, a sly grin at the floor seeming to disparage Sir Daniel, and to invite the visitor's sarcasm.

"No half-day for you, though?" said Tresham, ignoring the invitation.

Edmond smiled and parted his hands, as if the idea of himself upon a family picnic was absurd. "I am so much alone about here," he said, "a great deal too much alone to care for a party to the moors."

"And Lady Fanny is gone picnicking?"

"Oh Lord, mamma ain't here! Mamma is in Berkeley Square. Mamma is in Berkeley Square until Goodwood, you know, and then she goes down to stop at my sister Lucinda's in Scotland for – oh, ever so long. A month. You knew Lucinda was married I suppose? – I daresay you was there."

"No I wasn't," said Tresham, "I have been much abroad."

"Ah." Edmond stared, and Tresham saw that he believed his visitor to be much more intimate with his family, and with society, than was the case; Edmond making the assumption common to solitaries, that all but themselves live in society and know one another. "Yes," he said with a sigh, "Lucy was married October three years to Lord Trumbelow. You know him? Was you at school with him? Everyone knows Trumbelow – except me, who wasn't sent away to school, do you see."

"I don't know him."

"Ah, is that a fact?" It seemed a fact in Tresham's favour, for Edmond's wan eyes brightened a little. "He's well enough, I daresay, and mamma dotes upon him, for he goes about everywhere, and is a convenience to her, but the truth is a man must keep himself more in the swim of things than ever I did if he is to be easy with such a fellow as Trumbelow is. I went down a time or two and shot with him in Dorsetshire – partridges, a pretty fair sort of manor – but the house was full up with a noisy set of fellows I couldn't see the point to. Betting you know. They would bet upon anything – anything, and lay you the odds in a jiffy, though they was stupid enough in the general way. But then – I suppose it ain't – any more stupid than stopping in Wales buried in a book." He smiled awkwardly at his boots.

"Miss Enid is here I suppose?"

"Enid is here." If Tresham had hoped that Edmond would rattle away as garrulously about Enid as he had about Lucinda's husband, he was disappointed. After a pause Edmond went on, "And Captain Vinegar is here."

"What?"

"Vinegar. I thought you would know."

"Captain Vinegar here! Is he by Jove!" Tresham was shaken. He recalled Hoolaghan suggesting that they should run down to Ravenrig together – and suggesting too that he might have taken an interest in Enid himself "if I thought she would have me". Hoolaghan's words came back to him, together with the Irishman's voice and manner. Captain Vinegar! "How long has he been here?" he asked, suspicion in his question despite himself.

"They'll be back directly." Into a vaulted passage, whose mouth opened below the double stairway, Edmond had turned away from his visitor. "Would you care to see some of the castle?" he asked over his shoulder. "It wasn't completed, I take it, when you was last down in poor Roland's day?"

"I should, if you please." He caught up with Edmond. Why was Hoolaghan here? He did not know quite why he was here himself: to find Hoolaghan on the ground before him made it necessary to define his own objective. He felt as if he had been entered for a race, without knowing what direction to run in, nor what prize he ran for. He said to Edmond, "There was a strike of workmen building the castle when last I was here, and I went upon the roofs with your father to tie down some tarpaulins to keep the snow out. It was winter, there was a storm. But you don't remember that, I'm sure."

"Father does though. Father was speaking of that when we heard you was coming to us."

"Ah, was he?" Tresham was gratified. "And Bounty was here, the architect," he remembered. He had been much struck by coming upon Bounty's drawings for the castle, floor plans which allocated to every enclosure its function, the word "Sewing" or "Lamps" or "Billiards" having been inscribed in a firm hand upon each of the hundreds of vacant spaces within the projected building. Imagine the confidence – the will – to fix such order on the vaprous air of a Welsh valley, as to call stone rooms into existence out of the void, allot each its name and function, and to set going the machine for living according to plan! It had seemed to him magnificent. Then, it had been a projection of will, and faith, into the future, with the vast structure rising half finished, half roofed, the strike of workmen throwing upon Sir Daniel's shoulders the

[239]

whole weight of sustaining his intention, to build a castle here. Now the machine was in being, and Edmond guided him through its mechanism. Doors were opened, silent rooms looked into, the shapes of dust-sheeted furniture and bagged chandeliers discernible in the shuttered half-light. It was like investigating the interior of a hibernating monster, a mammoth under the ice, its heart scarcely beating, its shallow breath the fluttering of butterflies trapped at forgotten windows, or against skylights, or in fanlights over doors. "When is the place brought all to life?" he asked as he followed his guide.

"Oh Lord, when mamma comes it is all opened up. She brings down a party, you know, oh, forty or fifty of them, in September. August it used to be, but she said the grouse weren't worth coming for. Poor papa's grouse! That was after Lucinda had got Trumbelow and Scotland, where I suppose the grouse are a great deal better. I'll show you the library."

He opened a pair of mahogany doors and they stepped through the doorway. Long and high and dusky stretched the interior before them. The windows narrow and few, the walls slatted with shelves mounting between carved columns to the timbered roof. Every shelf was empty. The effect was of a shocking void, a robbed sanctuary.

"Upon my soul!" Tresham exclaimed, "did he buy no books for it?"

"Oh, papa bought books right enough, or had Bounty buy 'em for him."

Edmond said nothing more, standing as desolate amid the mouths of the shelved walls of that gloomy library as if he were the owner of a columbarium emptied by some treacherous stroke of all its murmuring doves.

"What has happened? Where are the books now that Bounty bought?"

"He wouldn't have it that I should buy a book now and then for his library," said Edmond, as though he hadn't heard the question. "Papa's children may wait till they are a hundred years old, before he might be persuaded they was old enough to do anything in the world of that order, particularly if it was a thing he ain't able to perform himself, as he certainly ain't able to choose a library. So Bounty bought for him. Bounty chose. Old Bounty worked up a regular system: what was worth the having he kept – the gems he kept – and what was dross he put here.

Dross by the yard we had here, though the bindings was handsome enough for papa, and the effect of it all was pretty, I suppose, with the firelight from the two big chimneypieces, and a few hundreds of wax candles, the two or three evenings a year mamma's party came in here. I lived in here a good deal, but no one else. Not a soul else ever took down a book, I believe. Come, we'll go out, if you please."

"So, where are the books now?" Tresham walked out, and Edmond closed the doors behind him.

"Sold. Papa sold them."

"That's a pity – for you."

"It don't signify to me what papa does." The erratic smile darted across his face. "I have a useful little library fitted up in a tower, which papa don't twig anything about. Now, should you like to look in the chapel? – though it ain't in commission either, any more than the library, for papa closed the chapel down too, as far as closing's possible for chapels."

"Why did he close it?" Tresham looked into the chapel through a pair of doors Edmond had opened without going through them himself. An impression of marble and gilt drowning in a twilight of purple glass repelled him. Here dwelt the civilian Death of wax flowers and prayers and black crape which Tresham feared as he had never feared a sword-thrust. He quickly withdrew.

"Papa closed the chapel," said Edmnd as he shut the doors on it, "just as soon as mamma had engaged a chaplain for it. Poor dear mamma – I don't believe she had any more thought about it than she might have thought about engaging a hermit, if papa had taken a freak to build a hermitage – or a cookmaid for his kitchen – but papa wouldn't have her chaplain. Oh dear no, came down very strong, wouldn't have a chaplain at any price. Played old gooseberry with the poor little fellow mamma sent down from Town, some curate or other she'd come upon! Dear me! I never saw papa half so savage as he was, a-stamping up to the curate as if he would eat him, and the little clerical gent 'Lady-Fannying this' and 'Lady-Fannying that', and a-walking away back-wards with his hands up, till he was driven out of the house altogether. Neck and crop!" Edmond giggled, as delighted by the curate's discomfiture (thought Tresham) as if a rival in love had come to grief.

On through the castle his Vergil conducted him, now and again throwing open in passing the door upon some silent interior awaiting the return of life. The soundless labyrinth waited for voices and footsteps to advance along its corridors as a deserted shore waits for the returning tide to pour itself into landlocked pools, and refresh them. Sir Daniel's will had commanded the Castle's creation, but he did not command the tide of life which filled, or did not fill, the landlocked rooms. Perhaps he did not care to. Nor had he cared to find the idea of a Library made flesh in the form of his elder son all the day up a ladder with an open book in his hand, or the idea of a chapel incarnate in an acolyte of his wife's choosing: what he disapproved he had struck out, drawing a line through that room's name and function, returning 'library' and 'chapel' to the void whence his will had called them. His will and his vigour had built the castle: Tresham could not forget Sir Daniel that winter's day on the roof, directing operations to confound the strikers and defy the elements so that his intentions should not be thwarted. Yet he remembered too the impression he had received from watching Sir Daniel's abstraction from them all at the dinner table, where he had sat eating an orange peeled for him by his Turkish servant, like an emperor visiting a conquered province. Not here, for all its magnificence, was centred Sir Daniel's power. Now that it was complete, how did the great contractor view his creation? – as a plaything he was tired of? Tresham's heart turned rather uncomfortably over at the prospect of his impending meeting with the lord of the castle, into whose hands his own future seemed unaccountably to have fallen. Edmond brought him suddenly out of the labyrinth by a door onto the gallery above the long and high great chamber where they had first met. With a gesture towards the hall's further end he said,

"See old Roland in his window there?"

"I saw him." It was the most casual reference to Roland and his death that Tresham had yet heard, and he hardly knew how to reply. He looked at his old friend locked into his window by the glazing bars. The summer shone through his face from without. "I saw him, yes," he repeated.

Edmond said with his weird smile, "I always think he looks as if he was leaning on his cane at the rails by Rotten Row, do you see that? With his hat just took off to a lady, and his steel suit so uncommon well cut. He don't look like a knight with a sword, not a scrap. Papa commissioned it," he went on, "but I'll wager mamma set to work on the glass-painter, don't you know, to have Roland set down in Hyde Park for his heaven."

The confidential way in which Edmond shared his ideas about his family with him made Tresham a little uncomfortable, as if it committed him to Edmond's side before he could see where his own advantage as to taking sides might lie. Therefore he did not smile at Edmond's fancy, but said, "I haven't met Lady Fanny since Roland's death. Was she –?"

"She took it hard. She took it hard. But mamma is wonderful. Mamma is wonderful the way she will twist a thing about until it suits her taste, don't you see, like a scrap of ribbon she might pick up and somehow twist into a bow just to go right on her bonnet. Bless me yes, we are all bows on mamma's bonnet, more or less. Dear mamma! Do you know she said the other day – said it quite *en serieuse* – that Roland had always pined to go into the Guards. Well! Can you imagine it? Little Roland."

Little Roland! That was his elder brother's view, who will not allow the young sibling to leave off being a child. Tresham knew – he alone of all of them knew – that Roland had grown up by a hard path out of childhood in the course of their journey together, to die a man at Damascus. Before it had destroyed him, the journey had forged his character. He had won the spurs that he wore in the window. But no one here at his home would allow that he had grown up away from them all. Family ties had enmeshed this image of Roland in his prison of stone and glass.

"I daresay we all of us possess the dead jealously," Tresham said as he thought of his own image of Roland alone with himself in a caravanserai amid the wastes of Anatolia. "We can make the dead do as we like at last. They disappoint nobody, the dead don't – not as the living do."

Edmond too gazed at Roland. "Yes, I half envy him," he said, "the way he's out of all the rows."

What were the rows? – what quarrels divided this castle, emptied chapels and library shelves, left the dwelling itself empty of life for three parts of the year? The question could not be asked. To detain Edmond, who seemed ready to sidle off, Tresham asked, "Captain Vinegar came down from London did he?"

[243]

"From Liverpool he came to us. Though he had seen mamma in Town, it's true, and she had told him he might come here if he liked it. She used to be awfully stern on Captain Vinegar, you know, like granite she was, and told it about how he had been at fault over Roland's death – had killed him, she used to say – but all was mended directly they met at Epsom. That fellow in the Ministry, whatsisname – he introduced Vinegar at the Derby."

"Lord Vauchurch?"

"Vauchurch, yes. The minute she met him with Vauchurch she forgave him everything. Now he's to be taken to all our hearts, Vinegar is."

"And have you taken Vinegar to your heart, Farr?"

Edmond looked awkwardly away. "He ain't a bit what you might expect, is he, from reading his book? I'd thought of a big heavy gloomy sort of fellow riding his way through those adventures you all had, and here comes Vinegar to us now a bobbish sort of an Irishman chattering about slate – slate, if you please, as if he was ready to forget all about his travels, and go to work in a counting-house. But I daresay he ain't such small beer all through, if you know him," Edmond ended, with an enquiring glance at Tresham.

"And has Miss Enid taken him to her heart?"

"You must ask her. Enid's heart – well, there hasn't been standing space to spare in Enid's heart, since Roland died. You know he was her twin? Roly – it's for pity of Enid I ever did shed any tears for his death, her Roly. Ah dear. It caught her just wrong, wrong age, everything. Ah dear. What does Enid care for now, indeed? Her Cochins. Her Cochins! But hark – ain't that the trap on the gravel? I believe they are back."

2

It was indeed Enid's pony trap which Edmond had heard upon the gravel. She had put down "Captain Vinegar" at the castle entrance, and now drove herself round to the stable yard. Really the trap and ponies were her mother's, but her mother was so little here that Enid counted them among her own possessions (which were very few) and enjoyed driving her father and any guest there might be on an expedition such as the picnic they had just made to the moors. Papa had got down from the trap before, to speak with the men hauling his great slate up from the sea, and would accompany them to the castle. At the door Mr Pitcher had come out, but it had been her instinct to retreat, so she had left him and Mr Hoolaghan – the two Captain Vinegars – a little awkwardly together. One, perhaps both, of these Captains would no doubt follow her and disturb her peace, for Edmond was as solitary as herself and would soon contrive to be rid of their company. She gave the reins to a groom, who came out of a stable with a broom in his hands just as though he had been working, and told him to go and clear away the horse-droppings where Mr Pitcher's pony had stood tethered at the hall door. She got down on the man's arm. Could she escape both Captains, until dinner at least? Pretending, which had seemed natural enough at Constantinople where all was pretence and unreality, was such weary work here, where all was real. She would run away from it and visit her Cochins.

Alas, she no sooner had come out under the stable arch than Mr Pitcher called to her from amongst the urns and balustrades of the upper terrace. She stood still. He would come. But he would also go away again, if she waited passively for the little interval of action to be over. Like his horse's droppings, the disturbance of his coming would be cleared away, and his footsteps raked out of the gravel when he had gone. The sun had come out, and was rather hot on her shoulders and arms: she stood looking down, waiting, under her wide-brimmed hat. There lay her shadow on the paving. Just so on this stone had fallen the shadow of herself in summer's past. It was the single outline she would cast always, in all future summers. She saw Mr Pitcher's shadow come rippling over step and stone black as a bat towards her own. She braced herself as if their shadows' conjunction would be a shock.

"They have brought the Connemara I borrowed at the quay into the yard, I suppose," he said.

"Yes." It was not a bit interesting. "I was going down to attend to my fowls," she added.

"Edmond told me you kept Cochins. I should most awfully like to see them if I might walk down with you."

"Pray do."

She would not show him her treasures. It would be easy to deflect him. They began to walk in the direction of a shrubbery beyond the terraces and gravelled *allées*. They walked apart, stiffly, out of step. The presence of Mr Hoolaghan here had already taught Enid, as she thought, the truth: that she was not the free agent she had appeared to be, and had even believed herself to be, at Constantinople. No, she had come home to find herself unchanged – to rejoin, just where she had left it, her shadow on the stone. Her old character she had again put on, the everyday dress after a night of dreams and ball-gowns. And at the end of every vista stood Roly's monument, closing the avenues of her mind. She walked with downcast eyes beside Mr Pitcher. Why were men not as comfortable as her brothers, who never would have pretended that they wanted to see her Cochins?

Mr Pitcher spoke, as they walked, as if he had a perfect passion for poultry, and for this species in particular. He talked of the points of the ideal comb, and of the horrors of a vulture-hock; and defended the partridge Cochin against the Buff, and enquired if ever she had bred up a bird to weigh fourteen pounds or above – just as if he had posted down from London on purpose. Because she knew it was pretence, she hated the words and names of her avocation in his mouth. Amongst thickets of laurel and laurustinus, in shade which smelt of decayed leaves, she chose paths leading him in a circle away from her poultry. The secret which linked them, of Captain Vinegar's true identity – which had seemed at Constantinople so momentous a connexion – was insignificant to her here, where she was connected to every stone and tree by the secret bonds of childhood. For a time he kept up both sides of a conversation about Cochins, and then he asked her rather abruptly, in the midst of the wood: "Has your father spoken to Hoolaghan about the Mingrelian proposal you set out to me in your letter?"

"My letter?"

"Your letter from Constantinople."

Remembering the letter, she remembered the anxious wish which had gone with it, that it might bring Mr Pitcher to Ravenrig. She blushed, and quickened her step, and turned her head so that her hat's brim hid her cheek from him. Was it herself, who had sat writing that letter in the *mashrabyah* at Bebec?

"Your father's plan," Mr Pitcher's voice reminded her, "was that Hoolaghan and a troop of cavalry should put up the Princess Rachinskiy on her father's throne. Has it been put to Hoolaghan, do you know?"

"Papa doesn't confide in me at all as he did at Bebec. I am quite a stranger to his plans, here."

"I am sorry for that."

"I am not," she said quickly, earnestly. "I am sorry for nothing that –" That was there, and is not here, she wanted to say, and willed him to understand. "Oh, how I should dread it, if I was told I ever was to go back," she said.

"To your little house on the Bosphorus, and the waves against the quay, and the creak of the kaik's oars coming in through the window in the dusk – do you remember? And Asia just over the water?"

"Ah, how I should dread it!" Of course she remembered Bebec – the moment of intimacy between them in the dusky window over the Bosphorus which he sought to stir to life in her mind. But she knew that what had bound them for that moment together was shared feeling for Roly; feeling so heartfelt that each of them had mistaken it for love of the other. "I should dread going back above anything," she repeated.

"I believe I should dread a future in which I never was to see Asia over the water again," he said, "and never was to feel what it is to be free of Europe."

"You speak like Captain Vinegar." She dared a little smile into his face.

"Yes." He didn't smile. "So you don't know if Hoolaghan has agreed a plan with your father?"

"Mr Hoolaghan seems to think more about duchesses and countesses than ever he thinks about Mingrelia."

"You mean London has turned his head?"

"No, no – at least, it may have done, but I mean to say it is slate he has taken into his heart. 'Duchesses' and 'countesses' are the names given to different colours of slate, Mr Pitcher. Oh, Captain Vinegar has it all off by heart, I promise you, just as if he was looking for employment. Captain Vinegar –"

"Let us call him Hoolaghan between the two of us," broke in Mr Pitcher rather impatiently.

"Then who is to be Captain Vinegar?" she asked, "for I have come quite to believe in him, just as Roly did, at the end."

He did not answer her, and they walked on some way in silence among the laurels. She was stealthily bringing him back upon the castle, sure that he would have forgotten the Cochins. Because she had continued to think of Roly through the silence since she had spoken his name, she said without preamble, "Roly came to hate Captain Vinegar, you know."

Mr Pitcher stopped short at this, turned to look down at her. "Hated? No, no: never hated. He was a joke between us. He was –"

"Hated," she repeated, as one who strikes again with a weapon put fortuitously into her hand. She had not looked for this satisfaction, of revenging herself on Roly's persecutor, but it was sweet. "Oh yes – I have his letters, you see," she said.

He stared for a moment, then seemed to accept the fact of Roly's hate, and walked slowly on between the laurels. "Someone to hate is necessary on a journey," he said. "We invented Vinegar."

"You didn't hate him, Mr Pitcher."

"Do you, Miss Enid? Do you hate Captain Vinegar?" He looked intently at her.

"I think I hate deceit."

He looked ahead through the thinning trees at the castle to which her circuitous path had brought him. "Ah well," he said sadly, "didn't it all seem to be such a first-rate lark, though, when we set him in motion? – You and Roland next door, do you remember, in that pair of rooms we took in Half Moon Street, whilst your father gave old Vinegar his first commission?"

"I do remember."

"And he did come to see the fun of it, you know, Roland did."

"Before he died of it."

"Oh yes, of course he is dead. He is certainly dead."

"And you and I are grown up, Mr Pitcher, which is perhaps worse – as far as larks are concerned," she suggested.

"As far as deceit is concerned," he agreed rather bitterly, "yes, for the living suffer by finding it out, which the dead are spared."

They had emerged from the shrubbery, their tour through the woods having brought them out only upon the other side of the stable block. As they walked towards the corner of the upper terrace where they had met, Enid said, "Up in his stained glass window Roly has gone on with his larks, though. Have you seen him up there? Brave Sir Roland. It only

[248]

ever will look like Roly at a Fancy Ball to me – Mamma has a likeness of him – the one Signor Preziosi took – and he is in some fancy costume, Albanian I think, there too. I believe they wouldn't know him out of some fancy dress or another."

"You have to take off the fancy dress if you live, though," he said. "Or decide on a suit to wear always, at least. Roland grew up at the last, you know," he added, "but you was none of you there to see." She said nothing, and he went on, "Everyone has to grow up, if they live. There's no escape. If you die they may catch you and put you in the window in any attitude that pleases them. But if you live –"

"It's a great deal harder," she finished for him.

"Yes. If you outlive the joke of the thing." After a pause he added, "Outlive it as I have. And you have. It's uncommon hard."

She stood there looking down at her shadow on the stone pavement waiting for him to go. It was all she thought of. She waited for his shadow to withdraw from the shapeless two-headed creature which it made with hers on the stone, and leave her her own clear outline, the shadow of her childhood, as it had always fallen on this ground. Mr Pitcher's shadow stirred.

"I must see your father," he said. "Would I disturb him if I was to ask for him now, do you suppose?"

"Nothing disturbs papa," she said, "except dullness and quiet."

"I will go to him then."

He turned to leave her. As soon as she could, Enid walked lightly away to amuse herself among the Cochins.

3

When Pitcher had entered the castle, and had summoned the Turkish major-domo by pulling at a bell-rope, he learned that Sir Daniel was out, or occupied. It was a curious experience to speak Turkish to this servant in Wales. So harsh and overbearing did his habitual usage of the language sound that he felt obliged to soften its effect by inserting "if you please" and "thank you" amongst the imperatives, as he was led through the house and at last put in through the door of an upstairs sitting room to await Sir Daniel's leisure. Hoolaghan's back blocked an

[249]

open window where he was looking out. Turning when he heard Pitcher, he said,

"Come on and watch these Welsh boys work, will you?"

Pitcher opened the astragal-paned casement beside him, and looked out. "It's the block of stone I followed up from the sea," he said.

The windows gave into a courtyard below. Activity surrounded the sacked and corded stone which was in process of being winched from its cart in a cradle of ropes up the courtyard wall by means of a clacking windlass on the roof above. From each window which the great slate would pass there protruded a man armed with a mop-ended pole with which to buffer the slowly-ascending burden away from walls and window-ledges. The well of the courtyard echoed up the steady loud ticking of the windlass ratchet, and echoed up too the rapid Welsh voices calling out above and below. The stone itself as it rose gave off a curious effect of stillness at the heart of the bustle.

"Is it a statue? What are they about?" enquired Pitcher of his neighbour at the open window.

" 'Tis a slate. About the largest slate that ever was cut out of the mountain it is, too. Will you look at the weight of it now?" Hoolaghan appealed. "Twelve foot by six that creature will measure, weigh a ton easy. 'Tis a wonderful thing to grave that out of the hills, now, and bring it here, and have it in the house, without ever a scratch upon it! You'd be puzzled to find a quarry-man else but Snave could do it, devil a lie."

"But what is it for, Hoolaghan? A thing that size."

"Dear man, it's for a billiards' table."

"But he's got a billiards' table. I've seen it."

"Never a one bedded down on a slate took from the heart of his own hill. The one he has in his billiards' room there came out of the Pennant's quarries along the sea a few miles. Lady Fanny's idea of it, that was – wouldn't trust to a slate of Sir Dan's for her friends to play upon, so away she sent for the three halves to make up a table from the Pennants, who are gentry. Well, when it came twas a scrimp of a thing such as any man going might have had for the money."

"How do you come to know it all, Hoolaghan?"

"From the quarry-man there, a thorough good fellow. Wasn't he put on his mettle, though, when Sir Dan goes along to him and says he wants a slate cut out sound enough for a table for himself for the castle?

Between the two of them they cooked up a plan to cut out the block in one, the whole table-slate in one stone, to put out the Pennant's eye. Cut it they did, and here it is."

"I wonder how Lady Fanny will like it?"

"Oh, she may whistle all she will, since the war."

"I wish you wouldn't speak in riddles, Hoolaghan. What has the war in the Crimea to do with the case?"

"The way it has altered Dan's view of a thing. Why, before, if Lady Fanny gave it out that the slate for the table must come from the Pennants, didn't he swallow it down meek as milk? Now if her ladyship's friends want to play at billiards, faith, they shall play on a slate of his choosing or not play at all! I like the man for it, I do."

"You hadn't such a high idea of him last time we talked."

"High? I haven't a high idea of him at all, dear man. But I've a true one I believe, for haven't I studied him?" He drew in his head through the window.

"Why should you study Sir Daniel, Hoolaghan?" Pitcher too drew in his head to question his companion.

"If you was looking for a horse to bring you through the mire, wouldn't you study him first?" He lit a cigar. "Well then, my boy."

Pitcher watched him, wondering what plan he had. "Do you suppose we may smoke in here?" he asked.

"I make it a rule to smoke first and ask after," said Hoolaghan as he stuck his head through the open casement again to watch the work.

"So you're to make Sir Daniel carry you through the mire," said Pitcher when his own head was outside again. "What does he say to it?"

"Pitcher my boy," said Hoolaghan amid rich clouds of smoke, "you've known the man any number of years, how is it you never was down upon him yourself to put you in the way of a fortune?"

"But I was. I had Vinegar's commission from him."

"Oh, lord, I hope I shall end with better than that."

"You speak contemptuously of Vinegar now, Hoolaghan, but by God it wasn't always so. Vinegar is the horse has carried you this far, mind."

"Horses for courses, Pitcher. Horses for courses. Vinegar may be a great man in Mingrelia, never a lie in that, but he has his way to make in England, so, same as any stray captain home from the war with a grand set of moustaches and precious little besides."

[251]

"You have my book, you have my reputation –"

"Yours, is it?"

"Aye, mine! I wrote the book, confound you, I made the name! All that's required is to steer."

"Yes, to steer back to Mingrelia. Well now, I'll tell you what it is, Pitcher my boy, you may have it all back, for me. Your Vinegar don't cut through any ice much in Liverpool, nor there at the slate quarry where never a soul of them can read a word of your book." Then he added, with an attempt at lightness, "And your Captain Vinegar, if you want to know all about him at once, is rather deep in with the Jews."

"You're in debt?"

"He's in debt."

Pitcher considered this. "Very deep?"

"He'll feel it tight when the bills fall due." Hoolaghan smoked at the window. "He's a little sea-room yet to turn himself about in, if he was off over the Channel before the paper was to start flying home."

"And I take it you don't plan to leave the country?"

Hoolaghan didn't answer this, but struck his hand forcefully on the sill and said "Oh, lord, but didn't the world all seem so devilish pleasant when first we came home snug into Limmer's hotel from the ship? And I thought it was only the few sovereigns I'd need, extra you know, for a few comforts till I was settled on a perch. And my club. But 'twas all talk, with those gentry. Never a sixpenny piece did I come by amongst them, and a power of money going out the while. And the fellows in the North no more use to me neither, though they've another way of being useless, and it ain't such pleasant hanging about, in a Liverpool warehouse, as it is on the steps of the Pall Mall clubs."

"What did you hope for?"

"Anything half decent. What do fellows do? Wouldn't some of the nabobs make me a Director, or some of the railway men, or wouldn't old Sulina-mouth Vauchurch keep me by him as a secretary, wouldn't he – quarters found, all expenses paid – devil a bit would he! Doesn't he take all I tipped him on the Eastern Question, which he spouts out next day in the Lords – doesn't he take it all free and gratis, with a wave of his white hand, just as if I'd the rack-renting of half Connaught in my pocket like himself. The truth of it is, Pitcher, you made your Captain Vinegar so high and mighty there's none in the world believes he wants

[252]

paying, that's what it is. 'Tis all very fine for Mingrelia, but it don't raise the wind."

After a pause Pitcher said, turning to him outside the window, "It's just as it was before, ain't it? – before you sold out and went for a soldier to the Shah. The debts I mean. The corner you're in."

"Ah, faith, I'm a terrible case," said Hoolaghan cheerfully through his cigar smoke. "Whichever one I am, Vinegar or Quin Hoolaghan, 'tis tick and hopes I must live upon. Aye, tick and hopes, and devil a bit else."

"You could rule a province in Mingrelia, near enough, with the Princess by you."

" 'Tis a desperate remedy for debts, is Mingrelia. Herself too. Indeed and I believe I'd cut slates for old Dan in his quarry here sooner. 'Twould be honest work."

"Not work for Captain Vinegar, though. They wouldn't take him on."

"Your confounded creation don't have any proper work, devil take him," broke out Hoolaghan with the first glint of anger he had shown. "No work, and no place either, in a settled country. An Ishmael he is, and I believe I shall – but there, we shall see. We shall soon see. Miss Enid don't – but there." He curbed his temper, and concealed whatever hand he meant to play. Turning to Pitcher he said, "What plum are you after, old fellow, coming up here so sudden?"

"I've no taste for plums, Hoolaghan."

"And Dan don't hand 'em about, neither. 'I don't employ gentlemen, unless I want a scoundrel's work done for me' was what he told me when I asked him flat would he put me into the slate concern. Yet I believe he'd have me if I was to sign on for a labourer. I believe he would so. And I shouldn't mind swallowing my pride, hang it, for I should be pretty sure of rising quick. Do you know at all a fellow named Snave? Big blackish bearish sort of creature."

"I know Snave. Used to lead a gang of navvies about the world for Sir Daniel."

"Quarry manager, so he is now. I could work under Snave."

"I'll be hanged if I could," said Pitcher, "for I knocked the brute down once, on the road up above there."

"Is it a fact? Why did you do that now?"

"To teach him his place."

"You didn't succeed, then, for he's out of his place entirely now, with the whole quarry put under him. 'Tis Dan's way, to raise a man up if he shines, and it would give me hopes for myself, if I was to go in low. It appeals to me, so it does. Look at that slate now, will you," he said, pointing his cigar at the corded and sacked burden still ticking ever so slowly up the courtyard wall. "Ain't that a grand thing, now, to cut out such a creature as that from the heart of the wild hills, and oblige it to lie quiet under a green cloth indoors while you knock balls about upon it? How is that for power? 'Tis the power that has civilised the world, I believe."

"Power, yes, maybe." Pitcher watched the weight swaying in its cage of ropes, and shivered. "But I'll tell you what it puts into my mind, to see that slate hung upon the wall there. I was by once when the pasha of Mosul had took for his prisoner the chief of one of the Koord tribes, and he put him in a cage, an iron cage, and he hung him up from his castle wall. That's what power may do, in humbling what it has seized upon. With a Turkish pasha there's no pretence of civilisation and billiards about it, though. There's power and profit, and I believe Sir Daniel is all one with a Turkish pasha for that, and would sit down to as comfortable a dinner if he kept a Welsh chieftain hanging in a cage just as well as a Welsh slate. I do indeed."

Both men were leaning out of the window. Slowly, heavily, the stone swung in its cradle of ropes. The windlass was silent. A flock of dark little Welshmen chattered and gabbled in the court below, turning up their faces towards others perched at windows. By hooks the ponderous object was drawn towards the wall above Pitcher's and Hoolaghan's heads. In an instant it disappeared from their view, drawn into the castle's mouth by the hooks, swallowed like a morsel of meat. A cheer went up from below, in which Hoolaghan joined by clapping his hands, his cigar in his teeth. Pitcher, thinking perhaps of the fate of the Koordish chief in the iron cage, or perhaps of his coming interview with the lord of the castle, neither cheered nor clapped, but drew in his head. He fingered the wrapped lumps of Mingrelian coal in his pocket as a gambler fingers his final stake.

"I must go and find him, I suppose," he said. "I daresay we shall meet?"

"I daresay. They dine like Christians, at least."

Pitcher left him. With very little idea of direction he had been walking for some minutes through passages and halls of the darkening castle when a door suddenly opened ahead of him. Through it fell an unexpected sunshaft across his path from some high window behind, perhaps the last sunshaft of evening, falling heavily as if of its own golden weight it had burst open the door. Then standing on his long shadow came a footman through the doorway, who was evidently going about to light up the castle with candles. He told Pitcher that servants were searching for him to bring him to their master, who had heard of his arrival and was awaiting him. Guiding Pitcher to the foot of a tower stairway, the footman left him to mount it alone.

The stairs turned and climbed within a stone silence isolating the climber. At their head, where the sharp, burnt scent of coffee prepared over a flame in the Turkish style came like a warning to his nostrils, Pitcher found himself on the Persian carpets of a vaulted chamber. He might have travelled a thousand miles from the room where he had left Hoolaghan. The vault was dusky, very still, crowded with innumerable objects. Ikons, stone, gold, crystal, bronze – over the glints and gleams of all these surfaces and outlines his gaze travelled with the rush of a bowshot through a wood till it struck a white pure target at the vault's further end, a figure within a niche. It was not lit, but seemed to glow. The daemonic Phrygian! Was this the stone corded to the cart which he had followed through the woods from the sea? For it was the god, the Dionysus – "my Phidias" – perfect and complete. The head at last was upon the shoulders. What had been the bargain struck between Sir Daniel and his old adversary to achieve this union?

"Who is come? Is it Captain Vinegar?"

Pitcher turned at the voice, and saw Sir Daniel. The great contractor was seated in a stone chair, perhaps looted from an ancient theatre, whilst behind him stood his Turkish servant, the coloured turban conferring on master and man a ceremonial and oriental air.

"The head – how did you come by it?"

Sir Daniel chuckled. "From a stonemason, Captain. From a stone-carver, at Lady Fanny's order, for a broken thing she cannot abide. So a head was knocked up for her at Mortlake while I was gone. Now then, Vinegar," he went on, "I thought you would come yourself at last. Are you come to catch a hold of my proposition for Mingrelia? You've the Rachinskiy woman held safe, I take it?"

"I am Tresham Pitcher, Sir Daniel. Vinegar is somewhere below, watching how the Welshmen manage your slate."

"But I know your voice though, you see, Captain. The blind don't depend on the outside of a man to know him, and so we ain't humbugged as the world is. I know your voice, Captain, plain as day. Any road," he added, "if it ain't so, what's my Phidias to Mr Pitcher?"

Pitcher said, "And if I was Captain Vinegar, who went on your errand to Palmyra, would it still be your answer, that the head on those shoulders came from a stonemason at Mortlake?"

"Ah. A deep question. I'll answer you thus: things what are apart come together for a patient man. They may do. What seems to be apart, may combine if you attend to it."

"They may," agreed Pitcher. "There may be a compromise between enemies, I suppose. Or one may capitulate. Or again, there may be a bargain struck between the two of them, mayn't there, in which some third party is to be the sacrifice? I've heard of that. What there is not, Sir Daniel, is an altogether honest way of a man combining with his enemy."

He had walked up close to the stone chair, and looked into Sir Daniel's face, but the old man had left off the gold-rimmed glasses he used to fidget with, and now looked ahead undaunted past his interlocutor with the impassivity of the blind, saying: "Well enough for a young man's view, Captain, cut and dried, black and white. It don't tally with what life teaches, though. Cut and dried ain't what a long life teaches, nor yet Milton – 'the spirits damned' – how does it run – 'neither do the spirits damned lose all their virtue'. Upon my soul, though, I went a good many years fancying the devil all black – aye, and fancying that all that wasn't snow-white must be the devil's work, too, and that what went amiss in my affairs went amiss by the devil's intent. And I'd strike back – revenge was honour, I thought. 'The study of revenge, immortal hate': that was my notion of honour."

"And now?"

"Now, sir, I've learned to give the devil his due."

"And had the head of your Dionysus given you in return? That was your bargain with him was it?"

[256]

"Bargain? We are upon one side in this, Captain, he and I."

"Who is upon the other side, then, if it ain't your old adversary?"

"An older yet. The true adversary of all."

"His name?"

"Savagedom." Sir Daniel hissed out the word harshly, and clamped his two square hands on the fine-carved arms of his stone seat. "Savagedom is his name," he repeated, "and disorder, and collapse, and all the wilderness of wild nature creeping over the ruin. Aye, there's your enemy, Captain. The enemy all must combine to overcome. Savagedom. War. Ruin. Wreck. All that stalks in upon our new world out of the black heart of the old 'un, and writes an end to cities, and trade, and peace. 'Barbary' – that's your adversary, Mr Pitcher – Captain Vinegar – 'all barbary', and not a Vienna banker as I used to mistake. Ha!" He barked out a short laugh. "Youth – foolishness – vanity – made me fancy that any man who wronged Dan Farr must be the enemy of the human race!"

He had spoken with great vehemence, and now sat back. Pitcher took a turn through the close-grouped treasures of the room under the eye of the unmoving Turkish servant. What was true? Had Sir Daniel honestly so altered his ideas that he no longer required revenge for the death of his son? Or had he struck with his adversary a bargain for the return of the Dionysus' head, which would be redeemed when "Captain Vinegar" brought the Mingrelian Princess and her child ashore into the old enemy's power in Asia? He stood before a fast-ticking French clock and tried to get at the truth.

But, as with any man who sets supreme store by the possession of courage, fear was his measure of truth; what he feared most, was to him most probably true, and attracted his footsteps with awful magnetism towards the edge of the abyss. As the soldier hears the guns, and knows which way he must take towards the battle, so Pitcher knew which path he must take.

He saw that the porcelain face of the French clock had been chipped round the keyhole by a key inserted violently and frequently. Was that the clock of a man who had learned wisdom and patience from life, as Sir Daniel claimed for himself? Was it the clock of a man to trust your life to? He seemed to see a tyrant growing old and blind and fierce in a dark tower, a tyrant winding and winding again at his clock, peering from his windows, wishing time away until his enemy might fall alive into his hand, and be hoisted in an iron cage on his castle walls to satisfy the barbarous instinct for revenge.

No matter. He saw in his mind's eye too the deep clear water undulating over weed at the foot of the cliffs at Zikinzir, and he saw the wild Asiatic vine reaching out over the sea its tendrils which already clasped ruin and rock, and he saw the ice-wall of the Caucasus above the rim of forest – and his heart lifted, free of doubt. What cared he for stratagems and traps? What was danger and death to Captain Vinegar, compared to the poor half-life of a Tresham Pitcher as straitened by England's order as ever Roland Farr was straitened by death into his stained-glass window?

"Well, sir, do you go to Mingrelia for us?" asked Sir Daniel.

Pitcher had in his pocket the wrapped fragment of Mingrelian coal which he had intended showing Sir Daniel. This he now, in case of treachery, would withhold. He would show his treasure instead to the emissaries of Herr Novis, or of Ismail Bey, if those were the enemy hands into which he stepped ashore at Zikinzir. He would put down the hoarded stake on the last turn of the cards, and save his life.

"Well, sir," repeated Sir Daniel impatiently, "do you go out again?"

"To spread your gas-lamps and steam-trains to the ends of the earth? It ain't work I care about, I must own."

"You may forget any long purpose which don't please you, Captain, for you will have adventures enough along the way to keep you in spirits, I don't doubt. A man in your line should be content with short views. So," he said, rubbing his knuckles with a kind of eagerness inseparable from the idea of an unsprung trap, "so, Captain Vinegar, you will return to Mingrelia and finish the game, eh?"

APPENDIX A

from an incomplete m.s.
"Journal of Adventure"

Having terminated a sojourn of some few months in England, which, albeit brief as the clock measures time, was yet amply tedious in its innumerable irritations to weary me very thoroughly with the "nation of shopkeepers" which our brave old country is fast becoming – having terminated, as I say, such a *longueur* in my rolling-stone existence, behold me now, having thrown myself together with my wards into a railway carriage at the London Bridge Station, rattling down through Kent towards Folkestone, and the "dark broad seas" which promise adventure beyond the narrow confines of our shores. No longer am I condemned to "gnaw the nail of eagerness on the carpet of delay." Above my head are a pair of much-travelled valises: opposite to me sits my veiled charge, heiress to the Mingrelian throne, her enchanting daughter beside her: before the three of us lies a long and perilous journey to the heart of "the frosty Caucasus": truly, nothing is wanting to complete this latter-day picture which, *mutatis mutandis*, might have served to preface a romance of that "true old time" when "every morning brought a noble chance, and every chance brought out a noble knight."

It was with a happy satisfaction that I smoked my cigar (no Mingrelian lady objects to the perfume of *tumbaky*) and saw the Kent orchards whirled away behind me at railway speed. There had been a period in the last months when this trim county of little fields and shaws and hopyards had seemed likely to bound my horizon for evermore. But (besides a hearty contempt for any man who will lie all his life under a plum-tree in hopes that the ripe fruit will drop into his mouth) I understood now, looking out upon the Kent landscape, how much there had always been of reconciling myself to these Kent views and Kent hillocks and Kent copses which the snorting engine dashed me past. As railway pace scattered autumn's leaves and nuts from the hazels beside the track, so were my hopes and memories of that time, when I had seemed set fair to rusticate into a Kent squire, scattered abroad in the impetus of this new adventure, and gone into the past.

Instead there arose before my eyes that grim country which was now my destination. In place of Wealden knolls I saw ice-slopes loom above mist and forest, saw snow-plumes blow from rock-chimneys above, and heard the cataract mutter from the valley below. As the warrior bound for distant ordeals hears already, through the prattle of home scenes, that clash of arms which, as well as quickening the blood, makes the home scene as insipid to him as the nursery rocking-horse to a spirited boy, so did I feel the insipidity of England, with the awful grandeur of the Caucasus, and its tasks and ordeals, already in my eye.

What, then, was my task, the reader may ask? No less a one than to pacify a wilderness, gentle reader, and to prepare a warlike people for the onset of peace and trade.

This commission – this crusade, I had almost said – I had accepted from Sir D— F— whilst his guest at the Castle of R—, that Welsh Camelot he has caused to rise into towers beside the Western ocean. He had formed a commercial company with Herr N— for the purpose of trading across the Caucasus and the Caspian into Persia, at a time when it had been very generally hoped, and expected, that a vigorous prosecution of the war in the Crimea would break Russia's hold upon the Caucasus and pacify, on the Allies' behalf, the Mingrelian passes to the Caspian. But the High Command (anxious to toady the French rather than to satisfy their own countrymen, as is commonly the case with aristocrats) – the High Command had seen fit to break off the war just as we had warmed to the work, and the Caucasus remained as doubtful and as dubious a territory as it had been when I had quitted its shores in a cutter-ful of refugees almost a twelvemonth since.

Now, in Mingrelia there lies a pass, the Mamisson of 9282 feet, which, not being a glacier pass, is the route over the Caucasus best adapted to caravan trafic, and is, moreover, without a doubt the historic pass of Pliny's description in which were situate the iron-sheathed gates erected by Pompey to preserve the civilised Imperial world from savagedom and misrule beyond. These gates at the end of the world I proposed to open. Through them would be carried, from Mingrelia into Tartary, the civilising torch of trade. Thus it will readily be seen that in Mingrelia – in a pacified and treaty-fied Mingrelia – lies the key to the forward advance of our civilisation, and the general progress of mankind.

A fact well known to Sir D— F— was that I had under my protection the rightful heiress to the Mingrelian throne, this same veiled lady opposite to me in the railway carriage now, whose father, the late ruler, had been killed in an affray some eight months previous. In consequence, Sir D— would have made pretty nearly any terms with me to have undertaken his cause, and return with the Princess Mazi to her kingdom.

However, I was not minded to drive a hard bargain with the great contractor, for I fully shared his sentiments as to the benefits to be conferred upon the fractious Mingrelians by awakening them from barbarism and welding them into the comity of trading nations. I have ever held that the soldier and the missionary expend in vain their energies in contending with the obtuseness of the savage, until the first step towards his enlightenment has been made by commerce. The savage must first be taught to covet. He must be taught to want more than the mere necessities of food and drink; he must be made to want, for instance, fine clothing for himself, and showy furnishings for his rude hut, and a handful of beads for his woman: want is the *sine qua non*. Now, to supply his wants, and satisfy his covetousness, our savage will produce an article to barter; in short, he will become industrious, and industry is the first great certain stride towards that high ground of our own civilisation where the streets are lit with gas-lamps, and the peace is kept by constables, and shop-windows pander to every whim of John Bull's desires.

We had talked over the matter of Mingrelia, I remember, in the billiards' room of R— Castle, where my old comrade H— was knocking the ivories about a magnificent new table, whose slate was the product of Sir D—'s own quarries. Upon my questioning whether or no the Princess Mazi would consent to a return to her native heath, Sir D—

had struck the table with his fist (thereby much upsetting poor H—'s stroke) and had growled out with characteristic plainness of speech: "Consent? Be hanged to consent! – I should as soon ask of this here slate if it consented to having billiards played upon it, as ask of that female if she consents to perform what's required of her."

With those words ringing in my mind, I stole a glance now across the railway carriage at my charge. Veiled, sullen, brooding, she had not accompanied me entirely willingly, I own. It had been necessary to point out to her that she had scant alternative but to return to her duty, for, with the disappearance from the scene of T— P—, she had come pretty well to the bottom of her resources in England. Though she had claimed that she had been offered "protection" by one, Crabtree,* an infamous moneylender, he had of course abandoned her cause at the first intimation that I meant business. I could not help feeling a little sorry for the Princess. Europe had been a sad disappointment to her: or, rather, her misunderstanding from afar of herself at a European capital, had upset her ideas. It had been inconceivable to her, when first I had seen her in Mingrelia, that any city could outshine Piatigorsk, where her childhood had been passed as a hostage: then she had seen Constantinople, and had supposed that she had seen everything – had supposed, too, that by her conquest of Pera's half-bred society, she had conquered everywhere. London, though, had overwhelmed her utterly by its size and settled grandeur. At home she had talked big of her father's treaty with the English Queen (whom she had thought to be a mere *satrap* of the Sultan of Turkey); but a view even of the outside of the Buckingham Palace had shown her the absurdity of her ideas, and had more or less crushed her spirits. Nonetheless she had not been eager to return to Mingrelia.

If the advantages of Commerce were not altogether sufficiently compelling attractions to draw back its ruling princess to Mingrelia, I must own that I, too, would not have flung myself quite so eagerly into a railway train for the East had I felt no inducement save the prosperity of the Transcaspian Trading Company. No, hang it, the romance of the adventure was what appealed! – to unlock Pompey's *pylae caucasiae* – to see again the snowy cone of Kasbek above the forest – to hear the

---

* I here write his name in full, and defy him to deny his base part in the affair.

hoarse tumult of the cataract – to ride through the snowflakes of Gothic woods and lodge in stone castles amongst mail-coated warriors – these were the dread magnets compelling me out of England to try conclusions with the old tempter once more in the wide East.

Especially did the "hollow thunder" of the waterfall haunt my mind in dreams and waking. There is a certain cavern, veiled by the falling cataract, seemingly the very matrix of that wild mountain kingdom, towards which a siren's song had lured my thoughts from tame England. So charged was the air of this cavern with water-vapour, so mightily roared the falls which concealed its mouth, that it might have stood for that very grotto in which – "hidden in the deeps, sitting on the bases of the hills" – there dwelt the Lady who had wrought the brand Excalibur. And she, who had in old times shown me this cave at the heart of her kingdom, and who now sat across the railway carriage from me behind her veil – would she not recover her old wild gorgeous spirit amongst her native mountains, and become again what once she was, the chieftainess, the heroine of a romance riding at the head of her barbarous horsemen – the *princesse lointaine* whose prisoner I had once been?

During our railway journey she was nervous, unhappy, unsettled. Whilst I played any number of games of Beggar-my-neighbour with Shkara, the child with whom I was fast friends, the Princess neither joined in our fun nor spoke a word. At the stations she looked anxiously out, and once tried the door, which I had taken care to lock; I supposed that she was concerned for the old servant, Hannah, travelling with her portmanteaux in the second class: but, in light of what was to happen, I have no doubt that she was looking out for her accomplice even then.

I should perhaps have been suspicious, had I not been concerned myself (in the intervals of Beggar-my-neighbour) with one aspect of Sir D—'s commission to me. He had promoted a man named Snave, a kind of bullying navvy, quite out of his proper sphere to be chief contractor for any Caucasian railway works; and this creature was likely, I feared, to consider his appointment superior to mine. Sir D— had replied bluntly to my request for authority over Snave, as was natural enough for a gentleman over a mere labourer, saying he "employed no gentlemen" about his work. So be it, thought I: I should be obliged to try conclusions with this Snave, when sufficiently far from civilisation, as I had done once before on a Welsh moor long before, to discover which one of us was to command, and which obey.

* * *

It was blackest midnight when I was roused from slumber in the Folkestone hotel by the sharp pang of a claw affixed in my shoulder. Starting up as though I had fallen victim to the vampire, I made out, by the rushlight she carried, the wrinkled face of old Hannah clamped round by her nightcap and bent down close to my own.

"She's awa oot!" croaked out this beldame.

"Who's away?" Already, though, I had sprung from my couch and was throwing my travelling cloak over my night-clothes.

"Herself. There's a bolster in her bed and the bairn asleep."

Our rooms adjoined, and it was the work of a moment to confirm this intelligence – there slept Shkara beside a bolster representing her fond mother – whilst a moment more served to rouse the house and question the servants who came tumbling about us at my urgent jangling of bells and thumping upon doors. The ostler thought he had seen a growler in the street, a figure dart into it from the hotel, an order given – he thought.

"What order?" I shook him till his teeth rattled.

"Railway I b'lieve," stammered out he.

Pitching him from me, I was off like the wind, slippered as I was, my cloak flying out behind, hatless, nightshirt tucked above my knees, perhaps the queerest figure that ever ran through the Folkestone streets at midnight.

Fortunately it was not half-a-mile to the railroad station. I had dashed under its arch, and out upon its platform, before ticket clerk or porter well knew I was amongst them. Smoky flares guttered out a chancy light. I had espied two figures lurking at the platform's end, and was striding toward them, when round some near corner of the track there burst upon the scene the fierce black fantom of a steam-engine blasting forth its smoke shot through with sparks and dragging garish carriages behind it. On strode I through smoke and steam toward those two guilty figures, one ulstered and behatted, the other cloaked and bonnetted, who were even now pressing forward upon the slowing carriages in their anxiety to be aboard. With a jerk and rattle the train stopped, hissing out volumes of steam. The ulstered figure had wrenched open a carriage door when I was upon him. Off tumbled his hat, and I recognised the flushed dome and watery eyes – in which gleamed a caitiff terror – of Crabtree.

I had seized him, and my instinct was to strike him down. Yet what was he but the accomplice of infernal perfidy? Its instigator I could not strike. Nathless I had grasped her arm full tight, and was not like to let it go, no, not though the steam engine itself should attempt to drag her from her duty to her kingdom, to her child, and to myself. The Princess was too valuable a property to risk for the sake of revenging myself upon her creature. Up now came chattering and jabbering the railway officials with their demands to see my ticket. Before the knave Crabtree could squeak out his complaint – before the spitting hell-cat I had fast by her arm could utter an English word – I had turned upon these clerks and told them with a good deal of fierceness that the lady and I were seeing off a friend upon the London train.

Now, how it was that the craven Crabtree ever had <u>worked</u> himself up into the situation of running off with the Princess I do not know, though I will wager that it was she who imposed her will in the matter, and he who complied. I made out very certainly that there was much of relief in the way in which the base recreant now shrank himself into a railway carriage stuttering out "that he supposed they must give it up". No doubt he had reflected that such a poor creature as himself could form but a stepping-stone, to be used and spurned, by a woman of the Princess's dark and fervent purposes. "If looks could kill", his life would not have been worth a farthing's purchase under the gaze which the Mingrelian virago threw into the carriage after him. I contented myself with kicking his hat under the train before I "about-turned" my captive, and "quick-marched" her into the clouds of steam exhaled by the engine, which enveloped us from the importunities of the railway officials very much as those clouds sent by the gods of old used to enable a hero to escape his enemies on the plains of Troy.

I had returned the Princess to the bed in which her daughter still slept, and had locked the door upon her, and had returned to my own chamber, but I could not at once compose myself into the sleep from which Hannah had roused me.

The incident had upset my soldier's notion of what is owing in chivalrous behaviour towards the sex. Many years since, a child on a Scotch moor, I had interposed myself between a young female and the laird's sons, whom I had taken to be her oppressors and pursuers. But something in that ragged girl's look, as she had stood waiting to be caught rather than fleeing in the interval which my attack on her molesters had gained for her, had struck me with contrary and bewildering thoughts. Only now, in light of my midnight excursion to the Folkestone station, did that Scotch girl's ambiguous stance explain itself to me. I had not interposed between the laird's sons and their prey, but between the female and the gratification of her desires. So much I now understood, in light of the flares casting their beams upon the Princess's features at the Folkestone station. The female is not innocent, as I had supposed. My chivalry had been based upon a false premise, on that Scotch moor and ever after, until this.

Well, thought I with a grim smile as I lay down to repose myself on the eve of this fresh adventure – well, if the chivalric instinct had been until now my Achilles heel, perhaps in mending it opportunely I had armoured myself at all points at last. The Princess I would regard as no "fair lady" to whom chivalric duty was owing, but as a mere valuable property, like the coal in my valise, to be protected on account of her negotiability at journey's end. That was Sir D— F—'s idea of the matter, expressed so forcibly when he had struck his fist on his billiards' table slate, and that was the spirit in which I had rescued the female from Crabtree.

Yet with this practical nineteenth-century view of things I found I could not rest content. Ere Morpheus would claim me, my mind had run on to a further conclusion. A true knight must lief lay down his life in defence of a lady's honour, no matter if the lady have no shred of honour left her, and be unworthy of the least respect: yet it must be done, the sacrifice of life itself must if necessary be made, for it is in truth the knight's own name and honour, not at all that of the "fair lady" which is at stake in the event. So, my boyish instinct long ago on the Scotch moor had after all been a right one, to defend the virtue of the ragged maid be she never so wanton.

Such was my conclusion. And so I slept "the sleep of the just" at last, with the words of old Juvenal upon my lips:

Summum crede nefas animam praeferre pudori
Et propter vitam vivendi perdere causas.

[Believe me, there is no greater blasphemy than to prefer mere life to honour, and to give up the real point of living for the sake of staying alive.]

APPENDIX B

from *The Spectator*, November 11th, 1856
A SHAMEFUL INCIDENT

Intelligence has reached us of certain events in Mingreeliah which must throw a grave doubt upon the wisdom (some would say, the sanity) of the aristocratic cabal entrusted by this nation with, amongst too much else, the safe-keeping of British interests in the Caucasus after the late war. The melancholy fact is, that Captain Vinegar, the author and traveller, has been murdered by tribesmen, and that Mingreeliah, which had promised fair to become the model of what British trade and British engineering may achieve amongst the wild tribes, is plunged once more into barbarism under the Russian Bear.

Word of this tragedy was brought to the outside world by a Mr Snave, a contractor, who has lately been ousted from Allastchink, the Mingreelian capital, with a broken head as a result of the affray in which Captain Vinegar lost his life.

It seems that Snave and Vinegar, along with the Mingreelian Princess whom they purposed placing upon her father's throne, were proceeding through a tract of moorland when they were attacked by native horsemen intent (as they thought) upon seizing the Princess and her daughter for hostages, or worse. Vinegar rode to her rescue and was slain, sword in hand. Snave, who had heard Russian or German spoken by one of the horsemen, and was by no means certain that the attackers were not accomplices of the Princess rather than her assailants, lay low behind a rock, but was struck on the head by an impudent boy coming on him from behind. Regaining consciousness after an interval, Snave asserts that he buried Vinegar where he fell, as befits so gallant and chivalrous an officer, and dragged himself down the mountain to Allastchink.

Such is the melancholy event: let us now observe how it has been improved upon by interested parties. We understand that Herr Novis, the Vienna banker, has felt obliged, as a result of so violent an episode, to safeguard his commercial interests in the area (we explain for the benefit of readers with no map at hand that the Mamisson Pass leads through the Caucasus to Persia's richest marts) by drafting into Mingreeliah a strong contingent of Russian Cossacks to support the perfidious Princess upon her puppet-throne.

And what of British interests? Is the aristocratic cabal aforesaid so slavishly devoted to forwarding the interest of their Austrian and Russian cousins, at the expense of the mere British middle-class, that no protest is to be made at this shameless jobbery? Where is the contingent of British redcoats to ensure safe passage to British goods through the Mamisson Pass? Is it to surrender at once to a Vienna banker and a rabble of Cossacks that so many thousand brave Englishmen laid down their lives in the Crimea?

If it be truly impossible to secure the independance and freedom of the Mingreelians under British protection, as the Ministry pretends, then should we not have been told so before a great English contractor expended his treasure, and a gallant English officer his blood, in a noble attempt to further civilisation and our national interest in that barbarous region? We await, without much hope, a satisfactory reply.